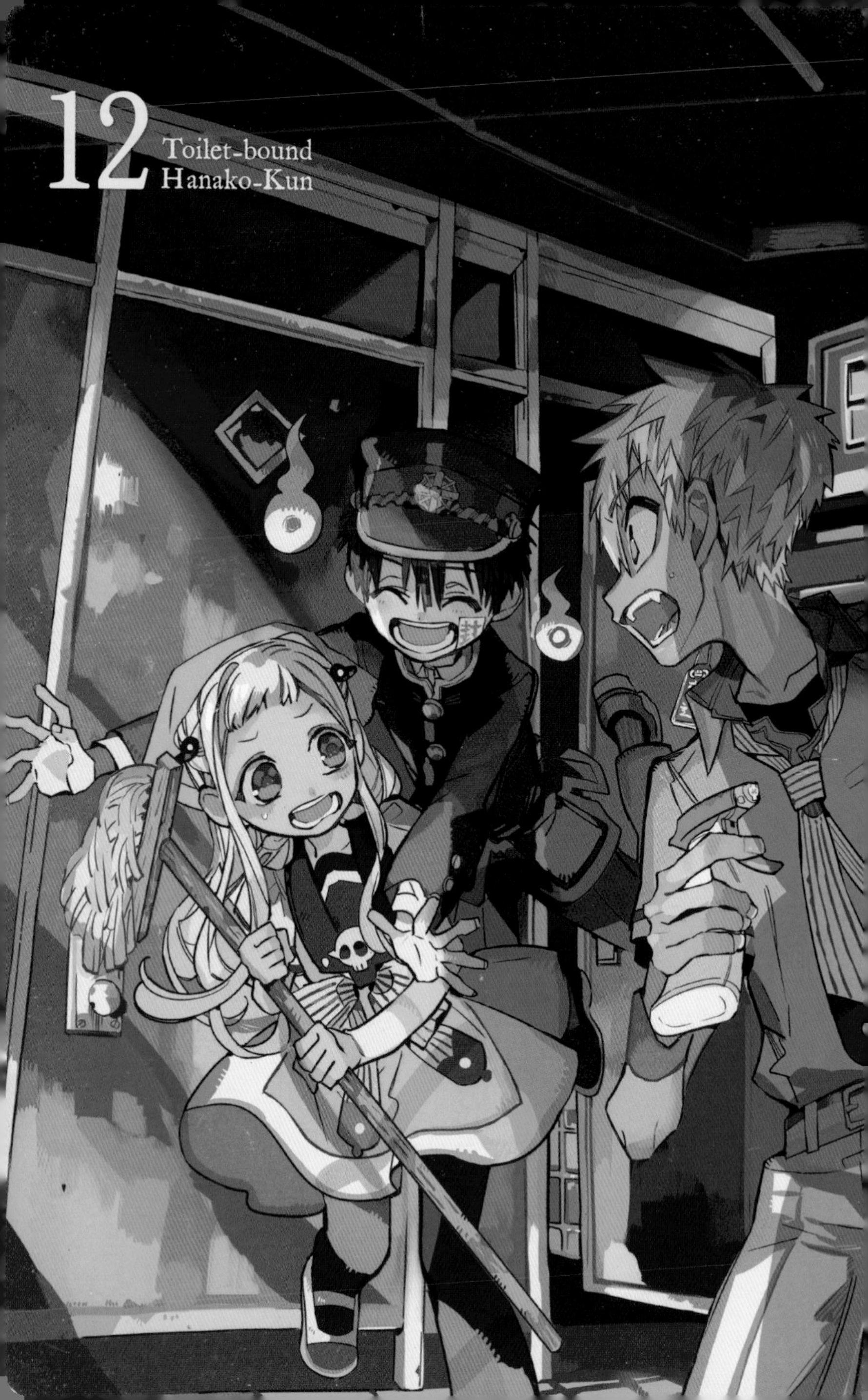
12
Toilet-bound
Hanako-Kun

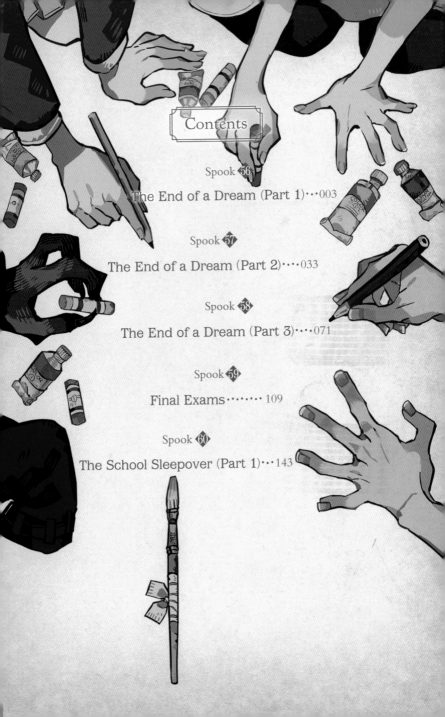

Contents

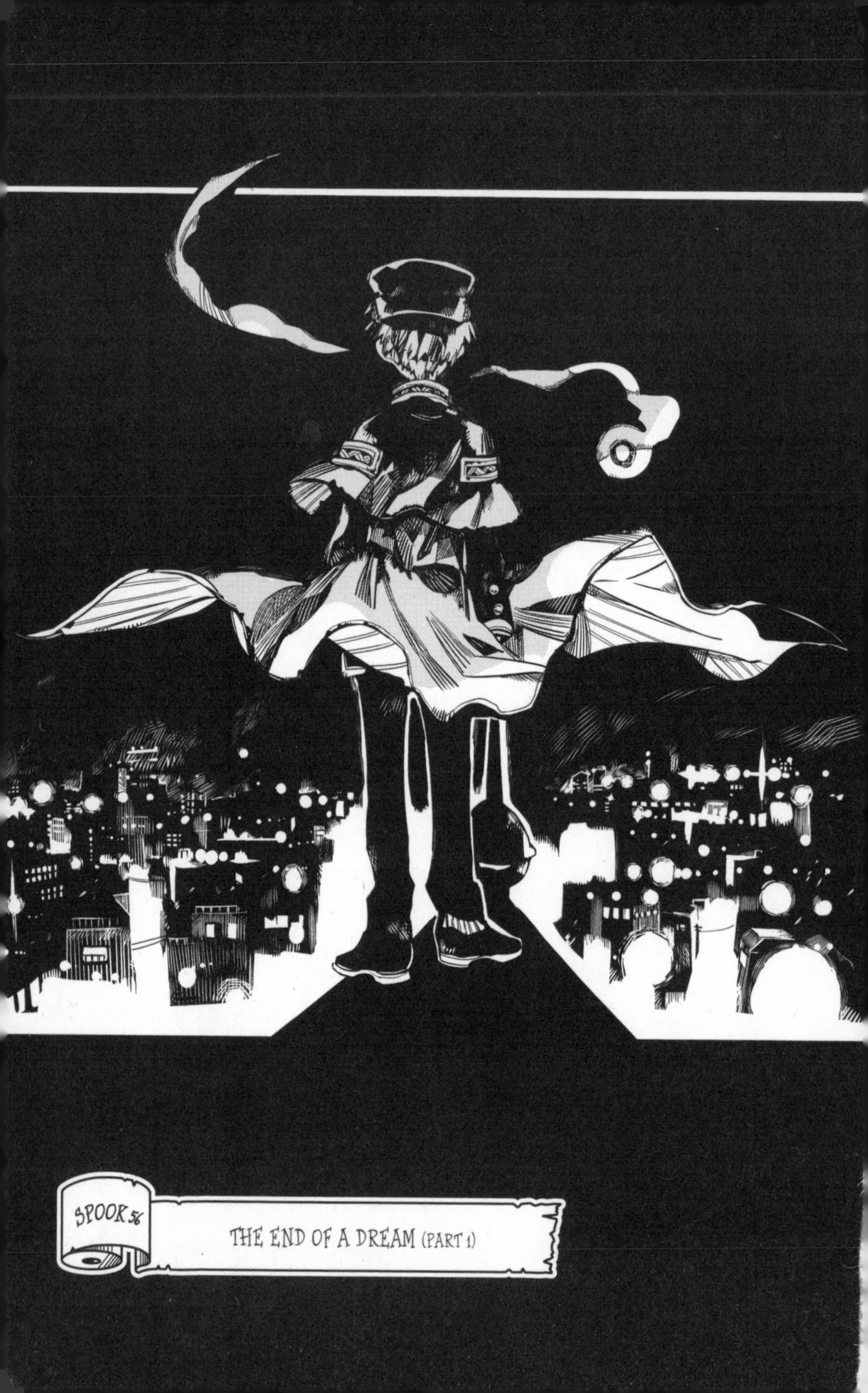
SPOOK 56
THE END OF A DREAM (PART 1)

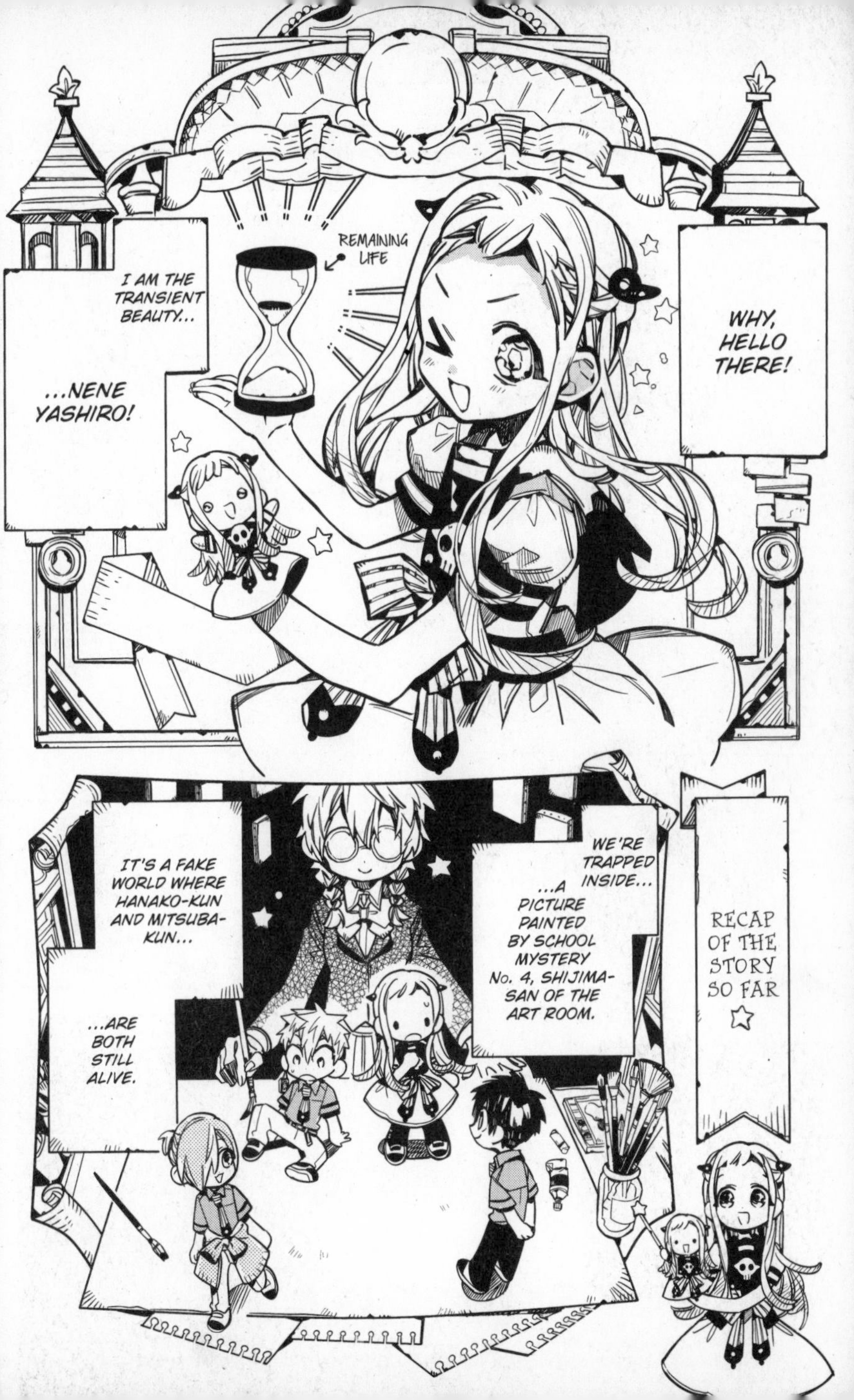
WHY, HELLO THERE!
REMAINING LIFE
I AM THE TRANSIENT BEAUTY...
...NENE YASHIRO!
RECAP OF THE STORY SO FAR ☆
WE'RE TRAPPED INSIDE...
...A PICTURE PAINTED BY SCHOOL MYSTERY No. 4, SHIJIMA-SAN OF THE ART ROOM.
IT'S A FAKE WORLD WHERE HANAKO-KUN AND MITSUBA-KUN...
...ARE BOTH STILL ALIVE.

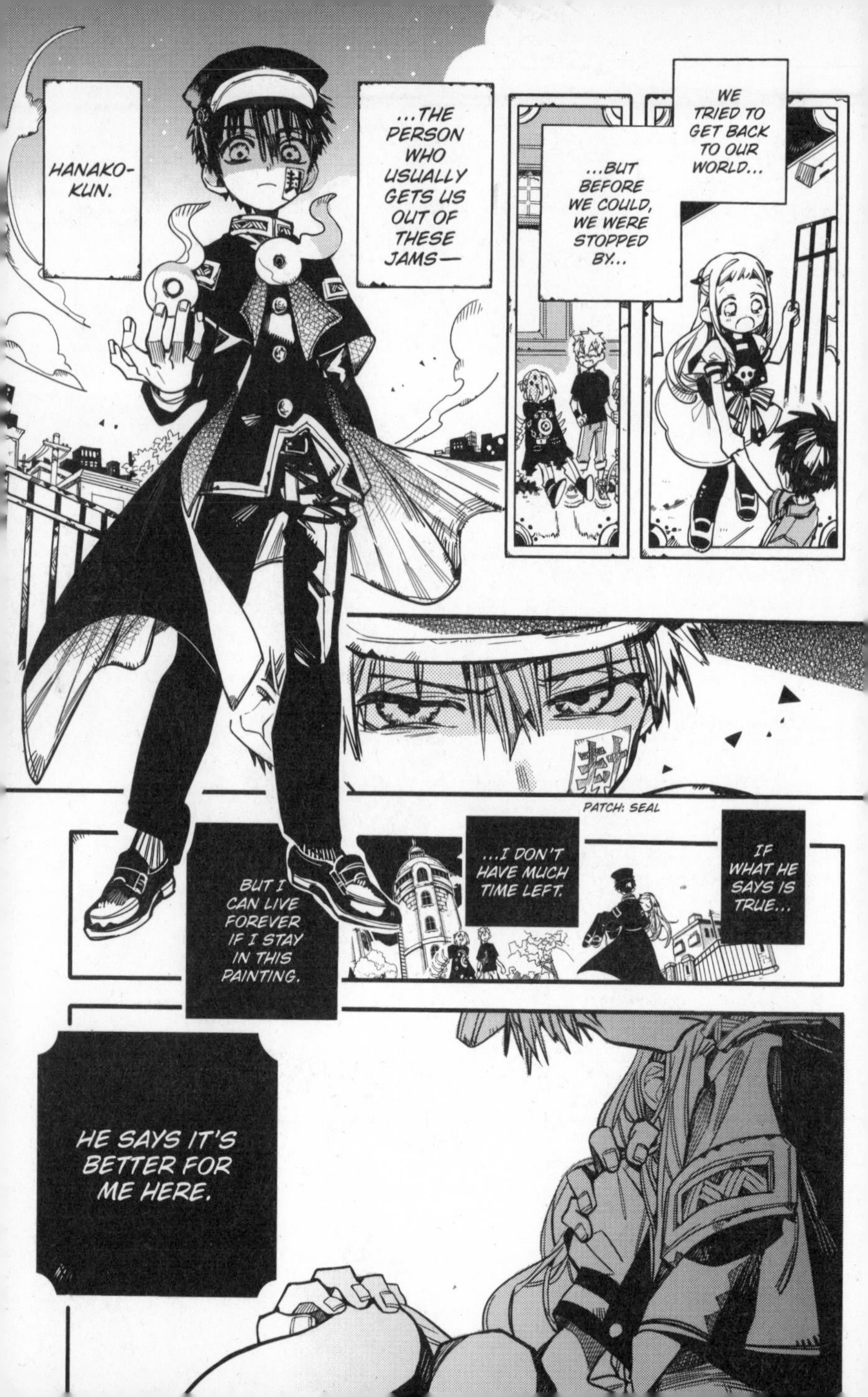

WE TRIED TO GET BACK TO OUR WORLD...
...BUT BEFORE WE COULD, WE WERE STOPPED BY...
...THE PERSON WHO USUALLY GETS US OUT OF THESE JAMS—
HANAKO-KUN.
PATCH: SEAL
IF WHAT HE SAYS IS TRUE...
...I DON'T HAVE MUCH TIME LEFT.
BUT I CAN LIVE FOREVER IF I STAY IN THIS PAINTING.
HE SAYS IT'S BETTER FOR ME HERE.

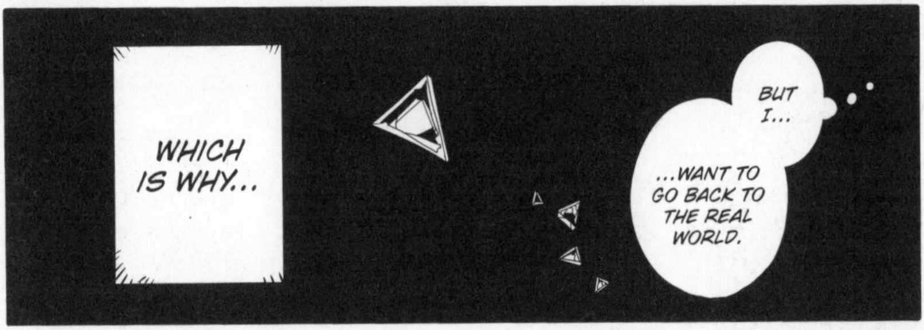
BUT I... ...WANT TO GO BACK TO THE REAL WORLD.
WHICH IS WHY...

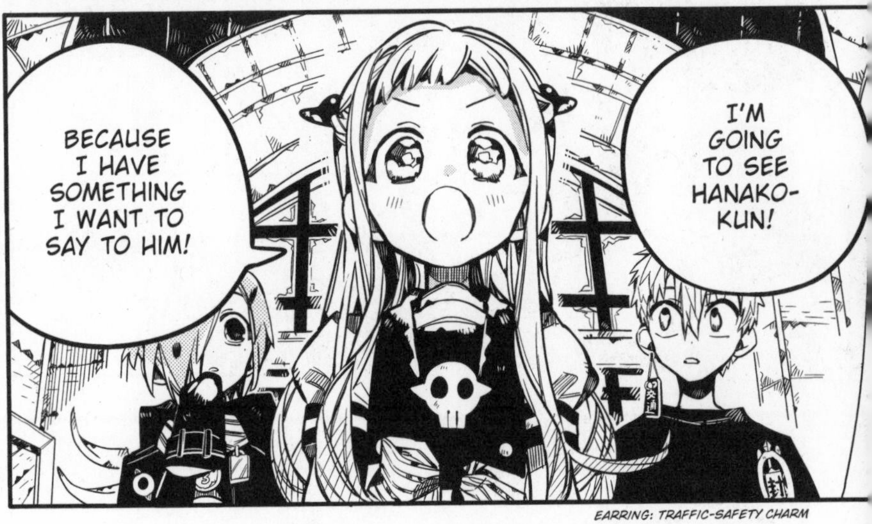
I'M GOING TO SEE HANAKO-KUN!
BECAUSE I HAVE SOMETHING I WANT TO SAY TO HIM!

EARRING: TRAFFIC-SAFETY CHARM

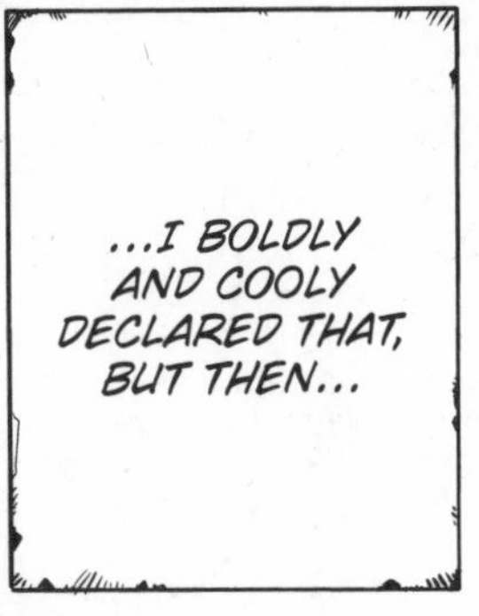
...I BOLDLY AND COOLY DECLARED THAT, BUT THEN...

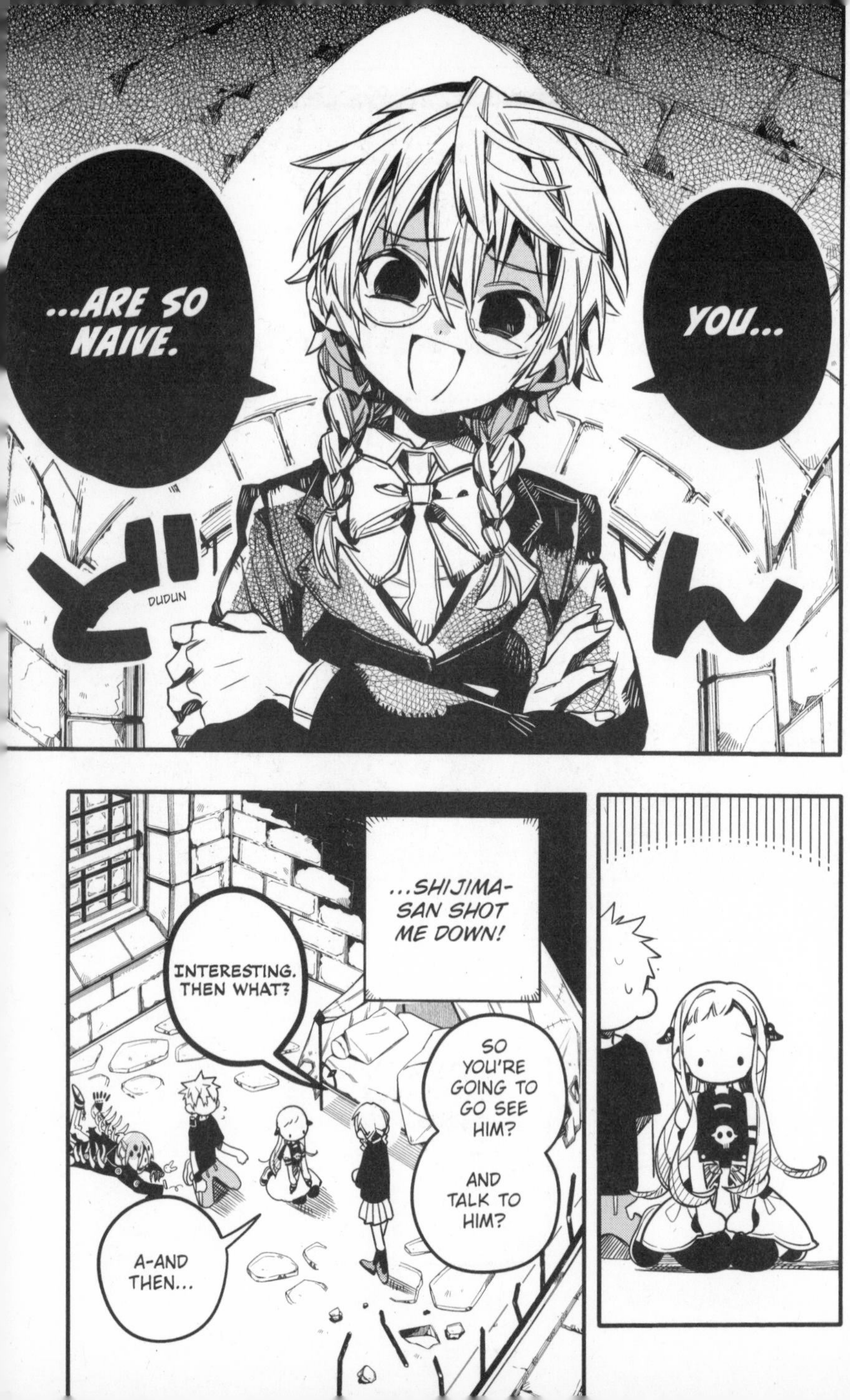
YOU...
...ARE SO NAIVE.
どん
DUDUN
...SHIJIMA-SAN SHOT ME DOWN!
INTERESTING. THEN WHAT?
SO YOU'RE GOING TO GO SEE HIM?
AND TALK TO HIM?
A-AND THEN...

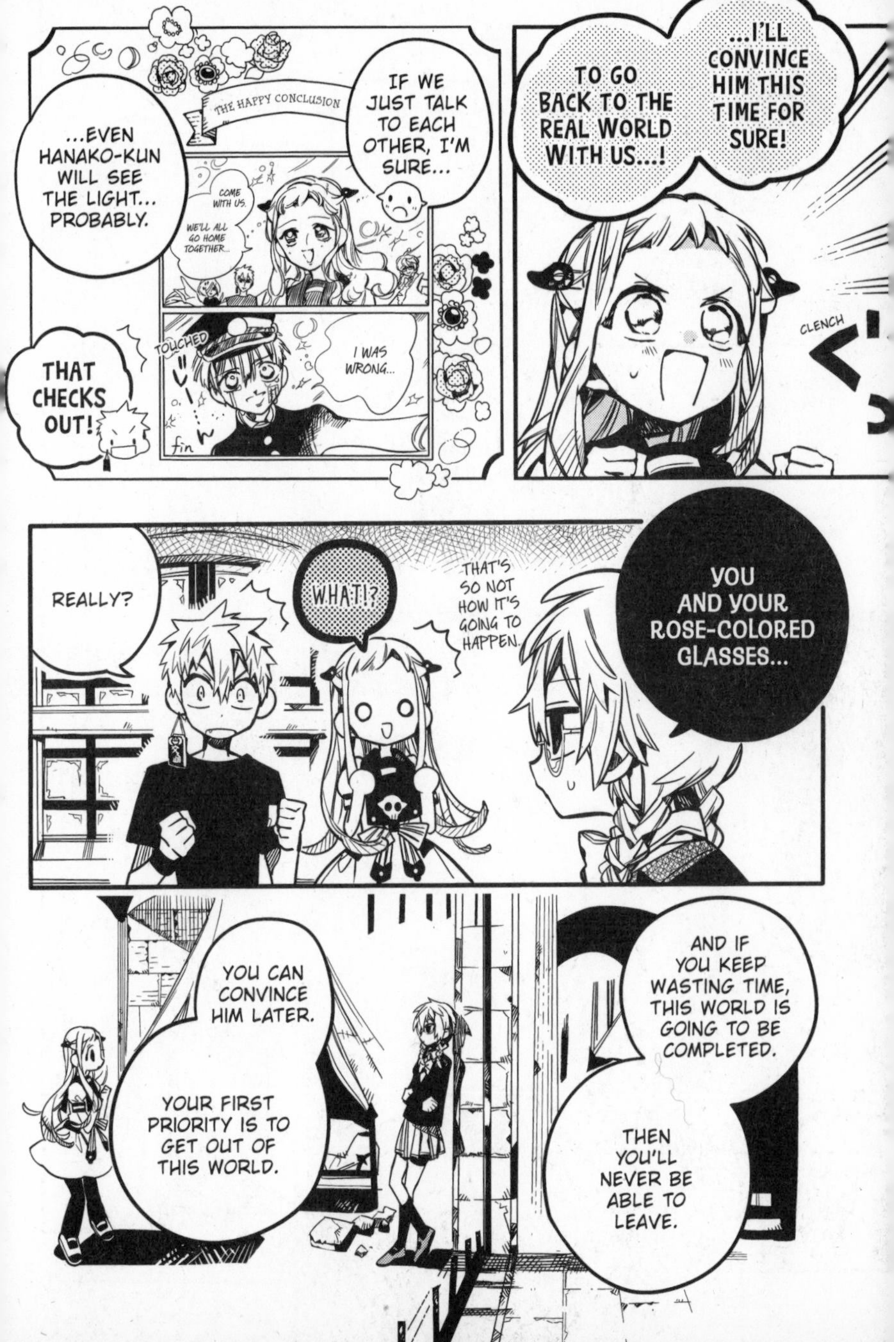
...I'LL CONVINCE HIM THIS TIME FOR SURE!
TO GO BACK TO THE REAL WORLD WITH US...!
CLENCH
IF WE JUST TALK TO EACH OTHER, I'M SURE...
...EVEN HANAKO-KUN WILL SEE THE LIGHT... PROBABLY.
THE HAPPY CONCLUSION
COME WITH US.
WE'LL ALL GO HOME TOGETHER...
I WAS WRONG...
TOUCHED
fin
THAT CHECKS OUT!
YOU AND YOUR ROSE-COLORED GLASSES...
THAT'S SO NOT HOW IT'S GOING TO HAPPEN.
WHAT!?
REALLY?
AND IF YOU KEEP WASTING TIME, THIS WORLD IS GOING TO BE COMPLETED.
THEN YOU'LL NEVER BE ABLE TO LEAVE.
YOU CAN CONVINCE HIM LATER.
YOUR FIRST PRIORITY IS TO GET OUT OF THIS WORLD.

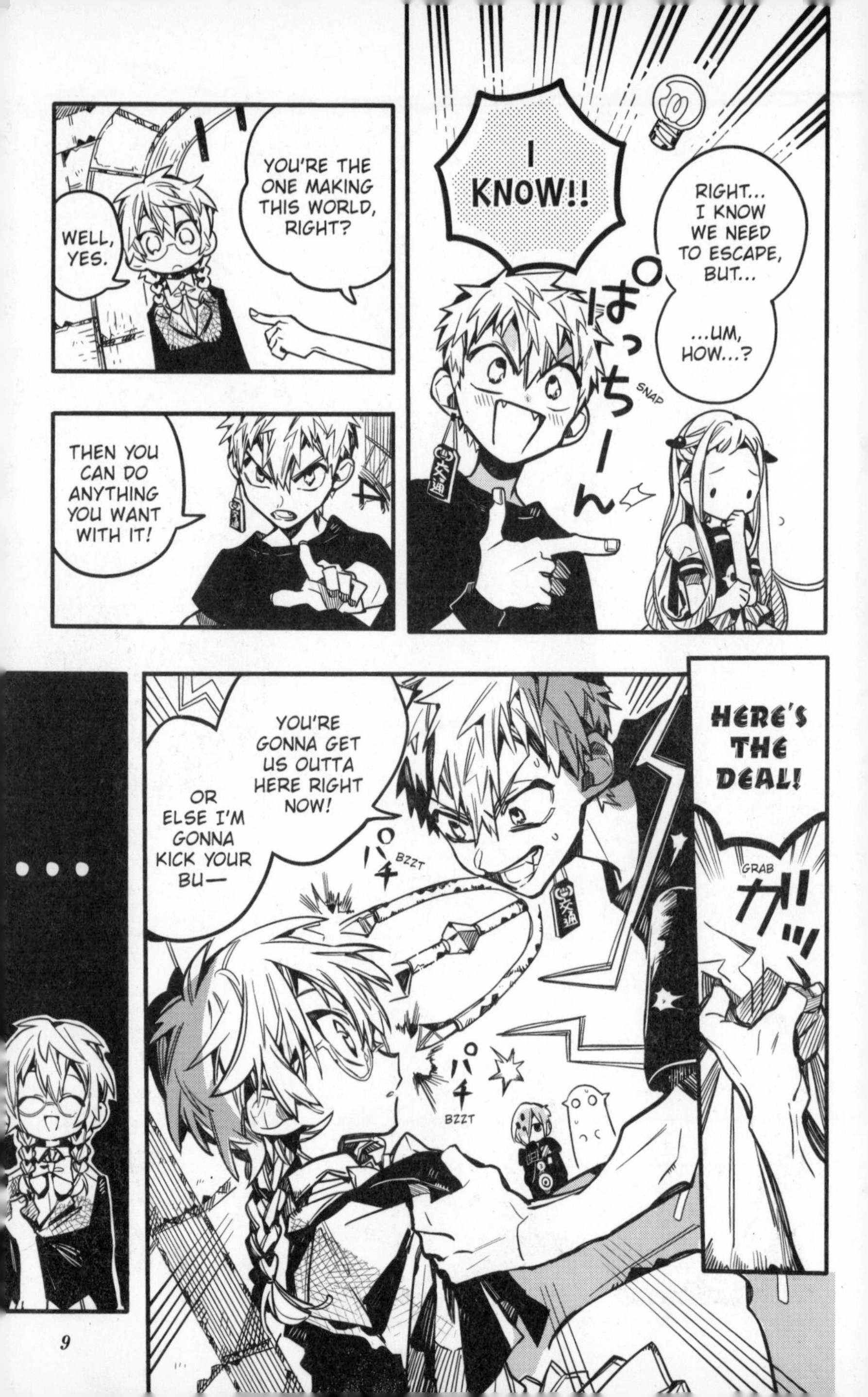
RIGHT... I KNOW WE NEED TO ESCAPE, BUT...
...UM, HOW...?
I KNOW!!
ぱっちーん
SNAP
YOU'RE THE ONE MAKING THIS WORLD, RIGHT?
WELL, YES.
THEN YOU CAN DO ANYTHING YOU WANT WITH IT!
HERE'S THE DEAL!
ガッ
GRAB
YOU'RE GONNA GET US OUTTA HERE RIGHT NOW!
OR ELSE I'M GONNA KICK YOUR BU—
パチ
BZZT
パチ
BZZT
• • •

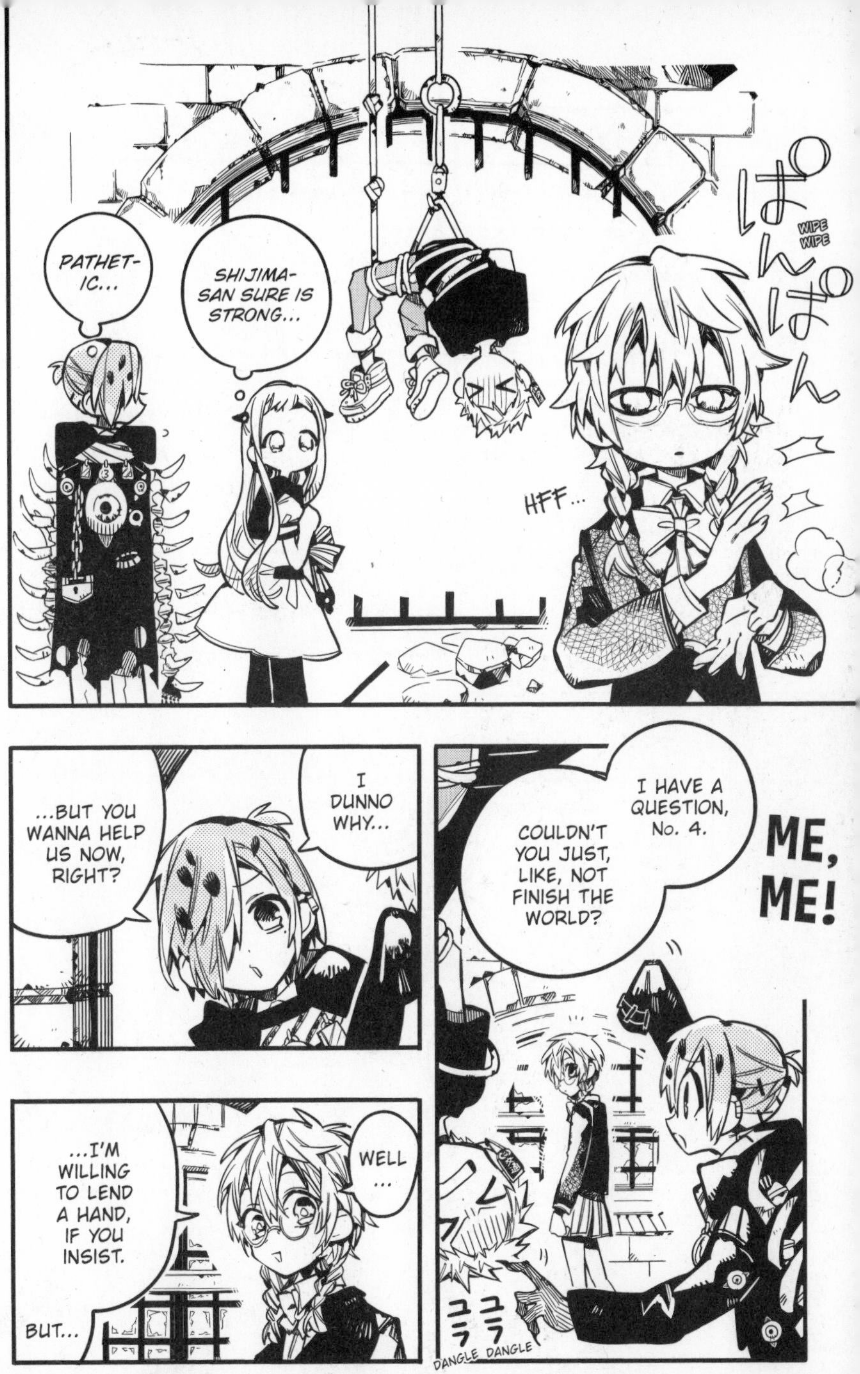
ぱんぱん
WIPE WIPE
SHIJIMA-SAN SURE IS STRONG...
PATHETIC...
HFF...
ME, ME!
I HAVE A QUESTION, No. 4.
COULDN'T YOU JUST, LIKE, NOT FINISH THE WORLD?
ユラユラ
DANGLE DANGLE
I DUNNO WHY...
...BUT YOU WANNA HELP US NOW, RIGHT?
WELL...
...I'M WILLING TO LEND A HAND, IF YOU INSIST.
BUT...

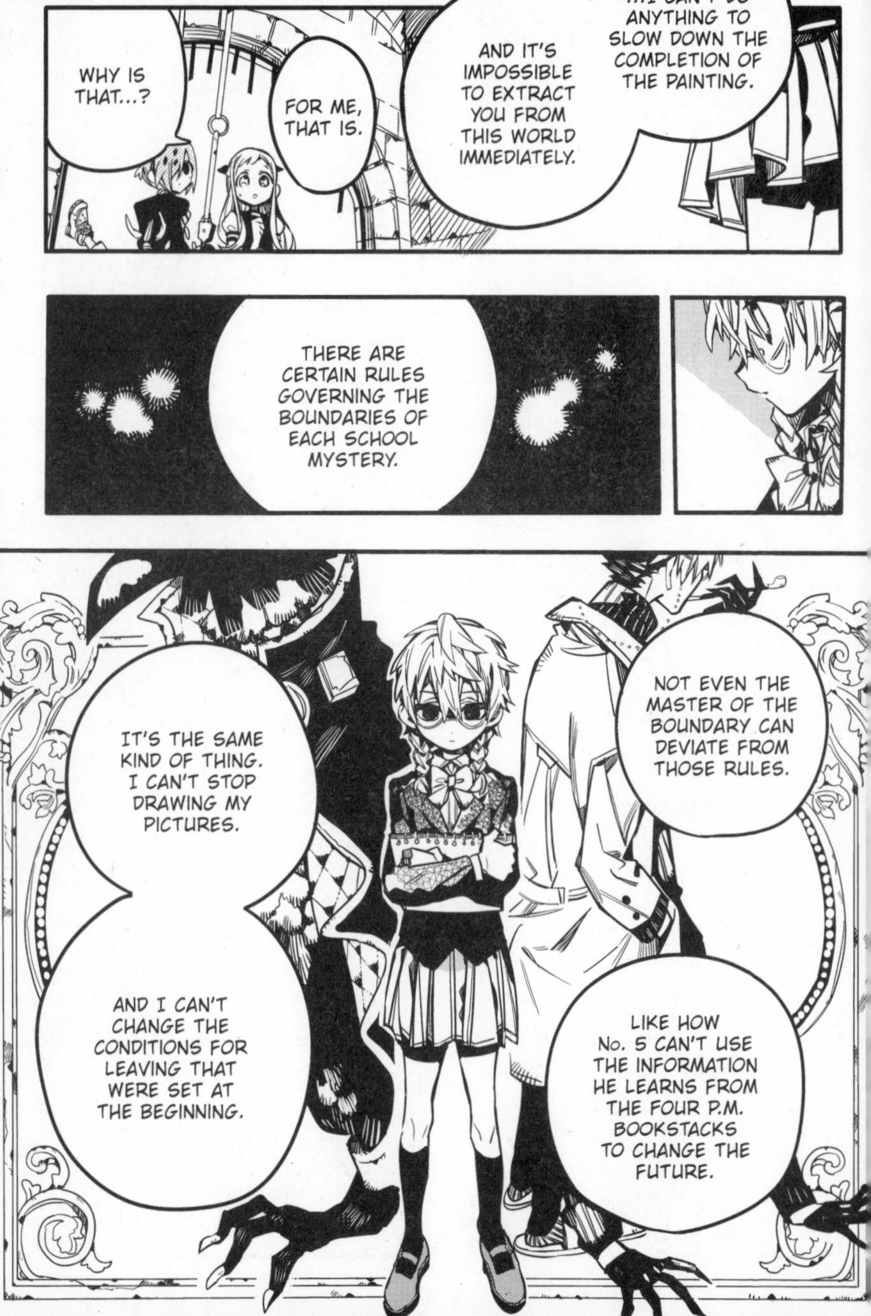
...I CAN'T DO ANYTHING TO SLOW DOWN THE COMPLETION OF THE PAINTING.
AND IT'S IMPOSSIBLE TO EXTRACT YOU FROM THIS WORLD IMMEDIATELY.
FOR ME, THAT IS.
WHY IS THAT...?
THERE ARE CERTAIN RULES GOVERNING THE BOUNDARIES OF EACH SCHOOL MYSTERY.
NOT EVEN THE MASTER OF THE BOUNDARY CAN DEVIATE FROM THOSE RULES.
LIKE HOW No. 5 CAN'T USE THE INFORMATION HE LEARNS FROM THE FOUR P.M. BOOKSTACKS TO CHANGE THE FUTURE.
IT'S THE SAME KIND OF THING. I CAN'T STOP DRAWING MY PICTURES.
AND I CAN'T CHANGE THE CONDITIONS FOR LEAVING THAT WERE SET AT THE BEGINNING.

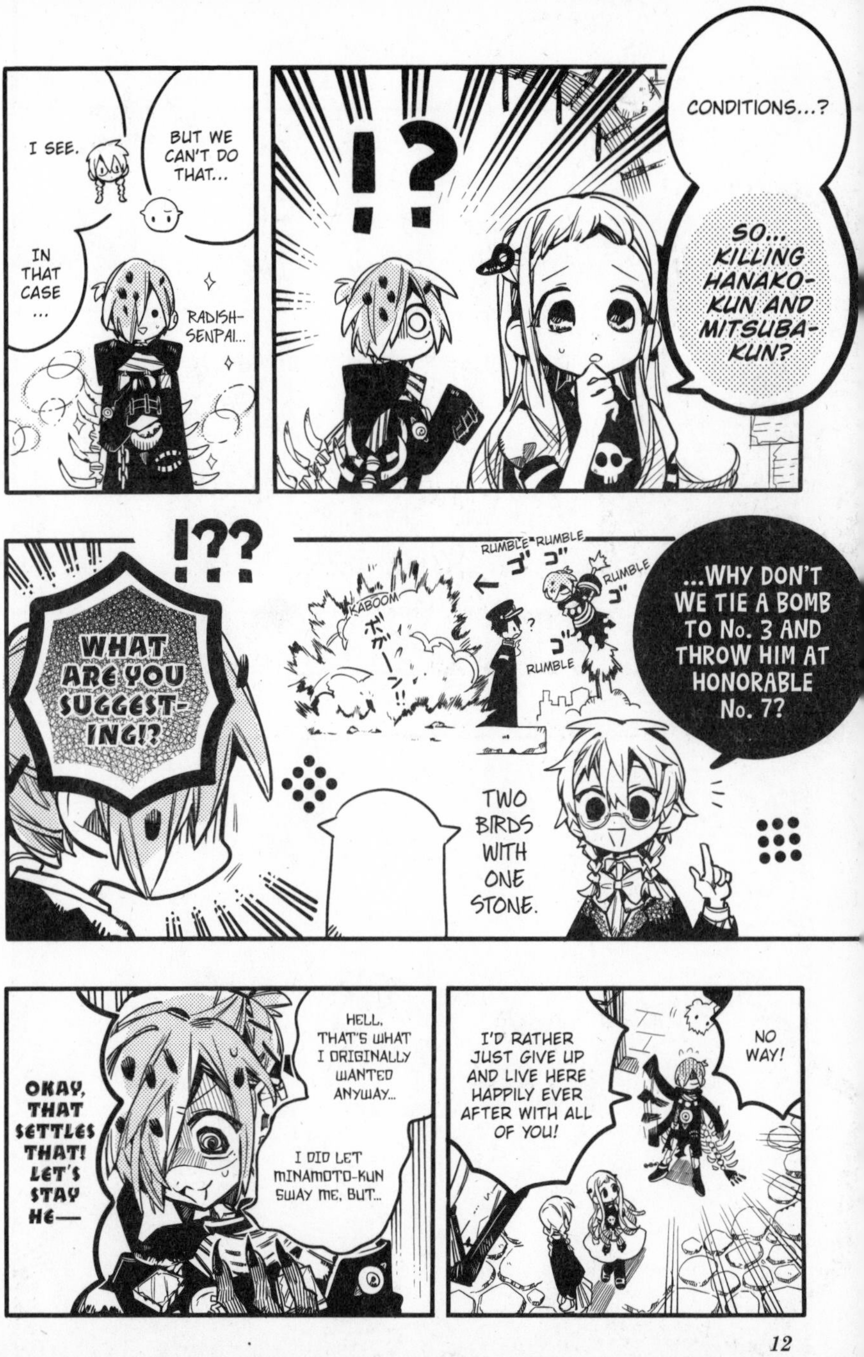
CONDITIONS...?
SO... KILLING HANAKO-KUN AND MITSUBA-KUN?
!?
BUT WE CAN'T DO THAT...
I SEE.
IN THAT CASE...
RADISH-SENPAI...
...WHY DON'T WE TIE A BOMB TO No. 3 AND THROW HIM AT HONORABLE No. 7?
RUMBLE RUMBLE
RUMBLE
RUMBLE
KABOOM
TWO BIRDS WITH ONE STONE.
!??
WHAT ARE YOU SUGGEST-ING!?
NO WAY!
I'D RATHER JUST GIVE UP AND LIVE HERE HAPPILY EVER AFTER WITH ALL OF YOU!
HELL, THAT'S WHAT I ORIGINALLY WANTED ANYWAY...
I DID LET MINAMOTO-KUN SWAY ME, BUT...
OKAY, THAT SETTLES THAT! LET'S STAY HE—

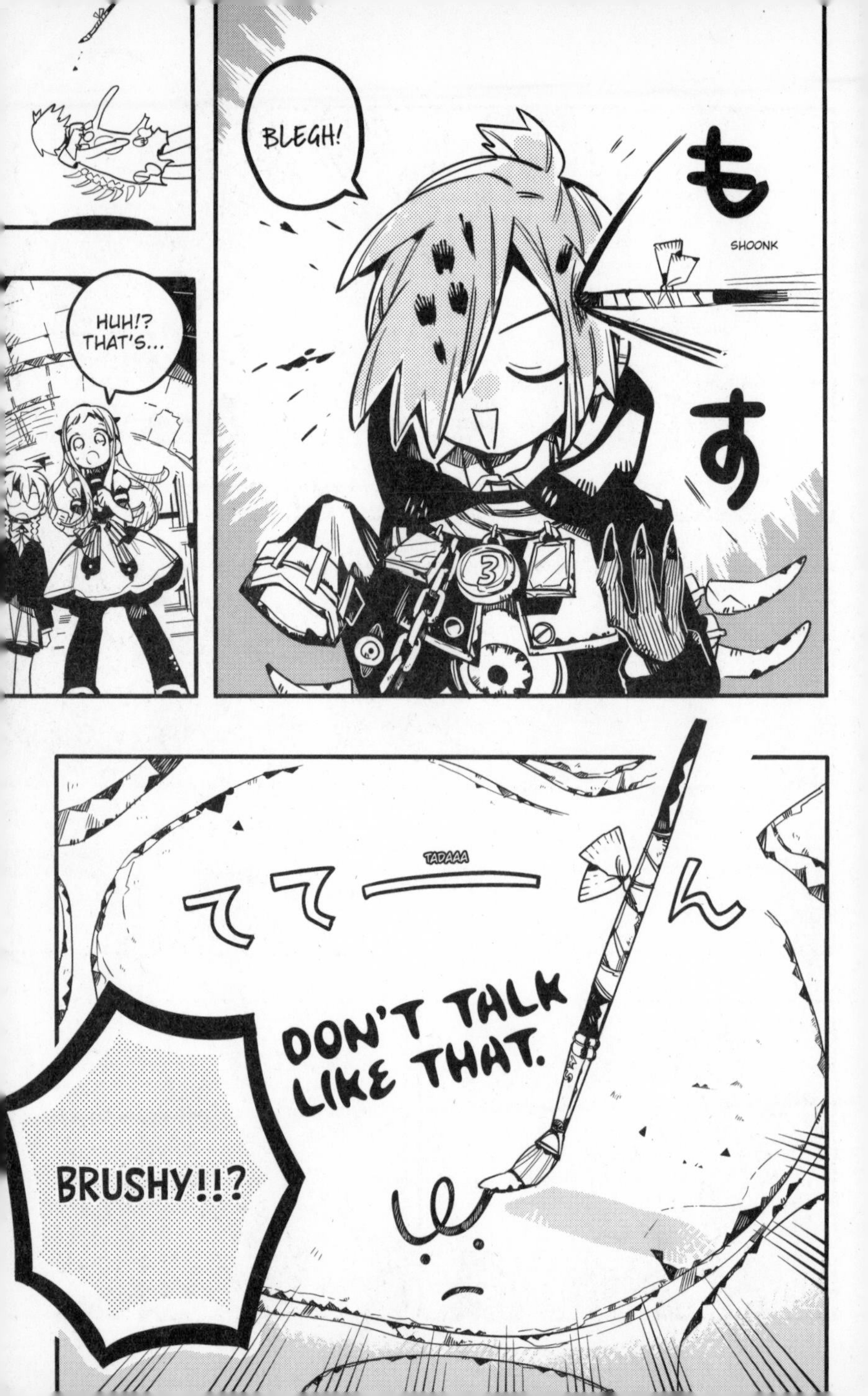
BLEGH!
も
SHOONK
す
HUH!? THAT'S...
てて——ん
TADAAA
DON'T TALK LIKE THAT.
BRUSHY!!?

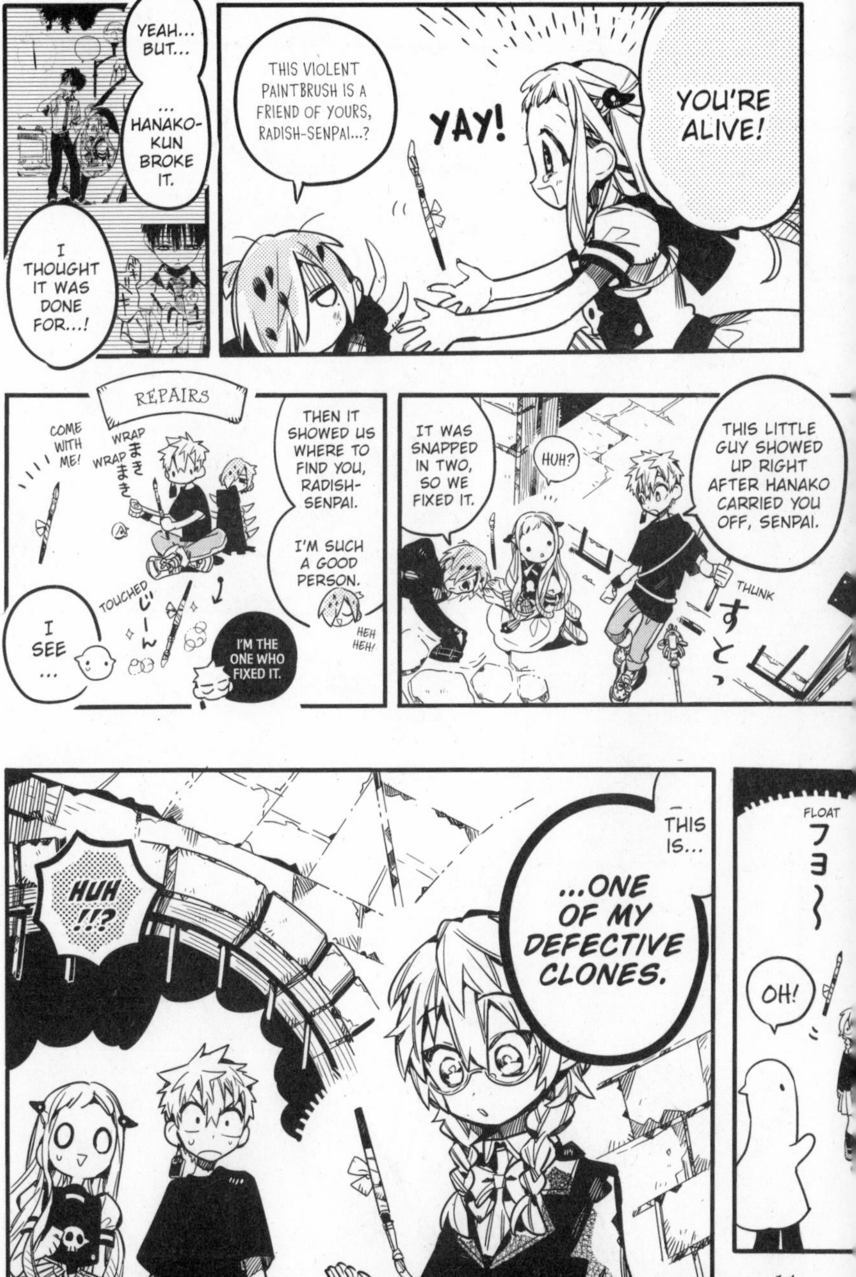
YOU'RE ALIVE!
YAY!
THIS VIOLENT PAINTBRUSH IS A FRIEND OF YOURS, RADISH-SENPAI...?
YEAH... BUT...
...HANAKO-KUN BROKE IT.
I THOUGHT IT WAS DONE FOR...!
THIS LITTLE GUY SHOWED UP RIGHT AFTER HANAKO CARRIED YOU OFF, SENPAI.
THUNK すとっ
HUH?
IT WAS SNAPPED IN TWO, SO WE FIXED IT.
REPAIRS
THEN IT SHOWED US WHERE TO FIND YOU, RADISH-SENPAI.
I'M SUCH A GOOD PERSON.
HEH HEH!
WRAP WRAP まきまき
COME WITH ME!
TOUCHED じーん
I'M THE ONE WHO FIXED IT.
I SEE...
FLOAT フヨ〜
OH!
THIS IS...
...ONE OF MY DEFECTIVE CLONES.
HUH!!?

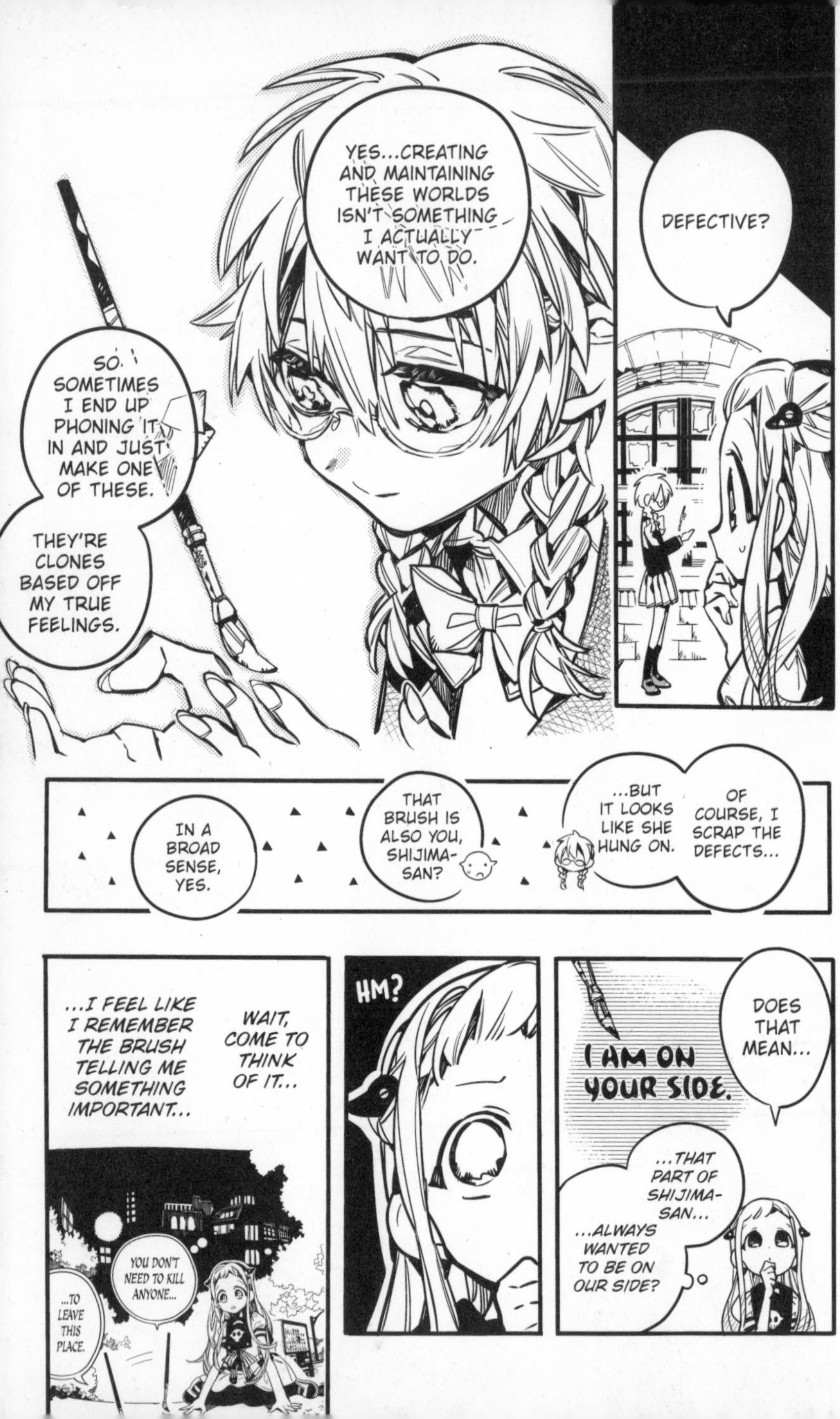
DEFECTIVE?
YES...CREATING AND MAINTAINING THESE WORLDS ISN'T SOMETHING I ACTUALLY WANT TO DO.
SO. SOMETIMES I END UP PHONING IT IN AND JUST MAKE ONE OF THESE.
THEY'RE CLONES BASED OFF MY TRUE FEELINGS.
OF COURSE, I SCRAP THE DEFECTS...
...BUT IT LOOKS LIKE SHE HUNG ON.
THAT BRUSH IS ALSO YOU, SHIJIMA-SAN?
IN A BROAD SENSE, YES.
DOES THAT MEAN...
I AM ON YOUR SIDE.
...THAT PART OF SHIJIMA-SAN...
...ALWAYS WANTED TO BE ON OUR SIDE?
HM?
WAIT, COME TO THINK OF IT...
...I FEEL LIKE I REMEMBER THE BRUSH TELLING ME SOMETHING IMPORTANT...
YOU DON'T NEED TO KILL ANYONE...
...TO LEAVE THIS PLACE.

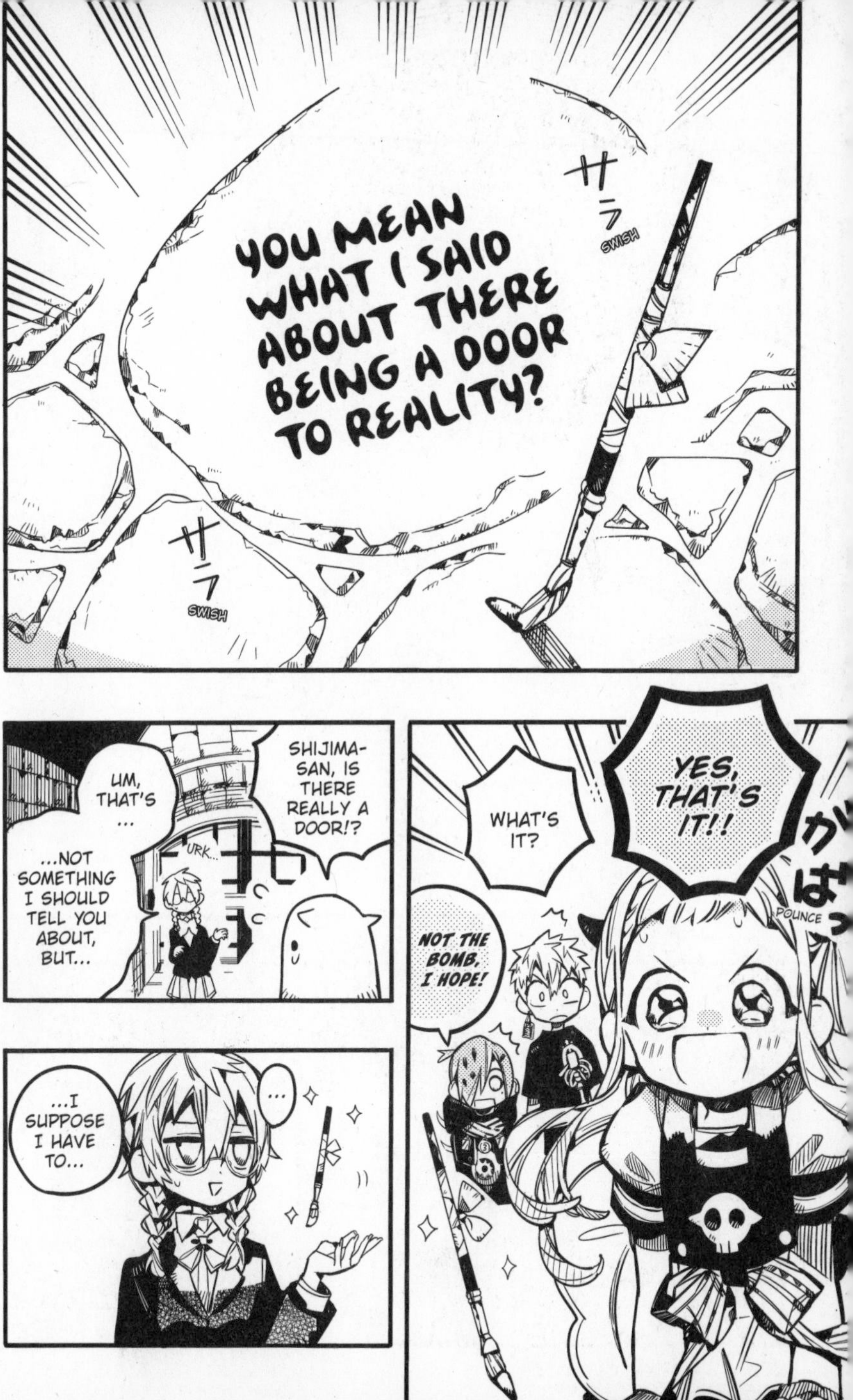
サラ
SWISH
YOU MEAN WHAT I SAID ABOUT THERE BEING A DOOR TO REALITY?
サラ
SWISH
YES, THAT'S IT!!
がばっ
POUNCE
WHAT'S IT?
NOT THE BOMB, I HOPE!
SHIJIMA-SAN, IS THERE REALLY A DOOR!?
UM, THAT'S ...
URK...
...NOT SOMETHING I SHOULD TELL YOU ABOUT, BUT...
...
...I SUPPOSE I HAVE TO...

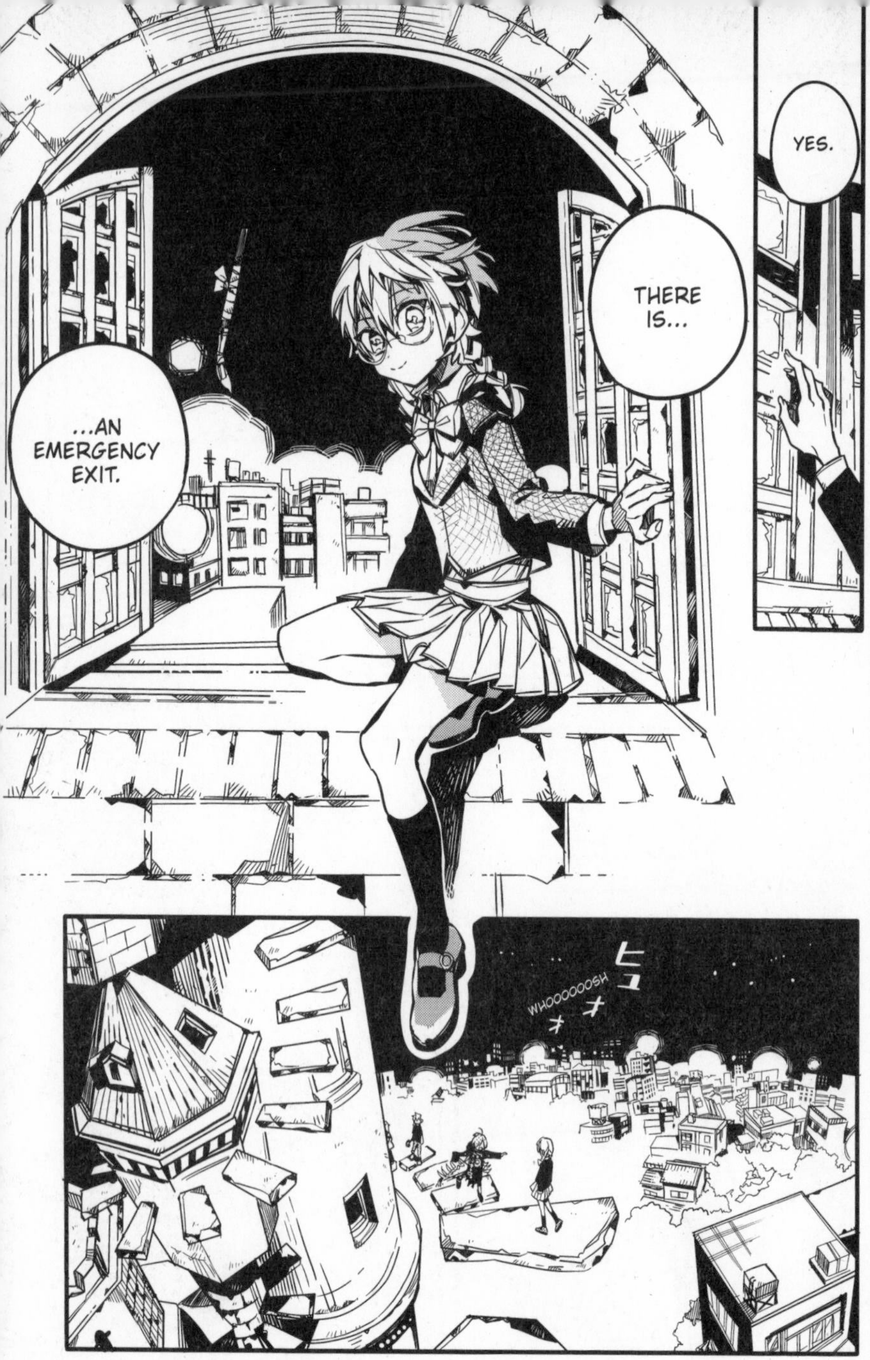
YES.
THERE IS...
...AN EMERGENCY EXIT.
ヒュオオ
WHOOOOOOSH

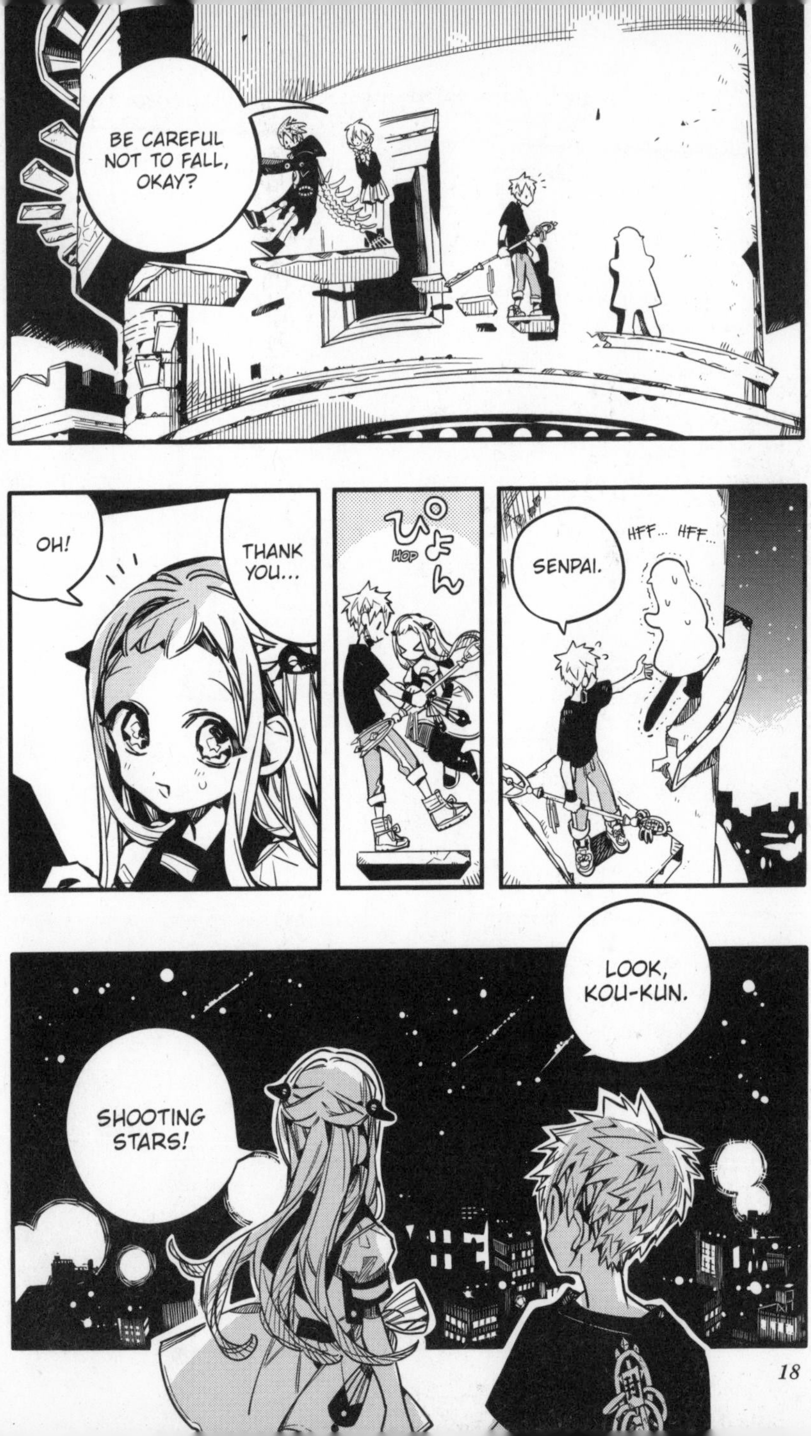
BE CAREFUL NOT TO FALL, OKAY?
HFF... HFF...
SENPAI.
ぴょん
HOP
THANK YOU...
OH!
LOOK, KOU-KUN.
SHOOTING STARS!

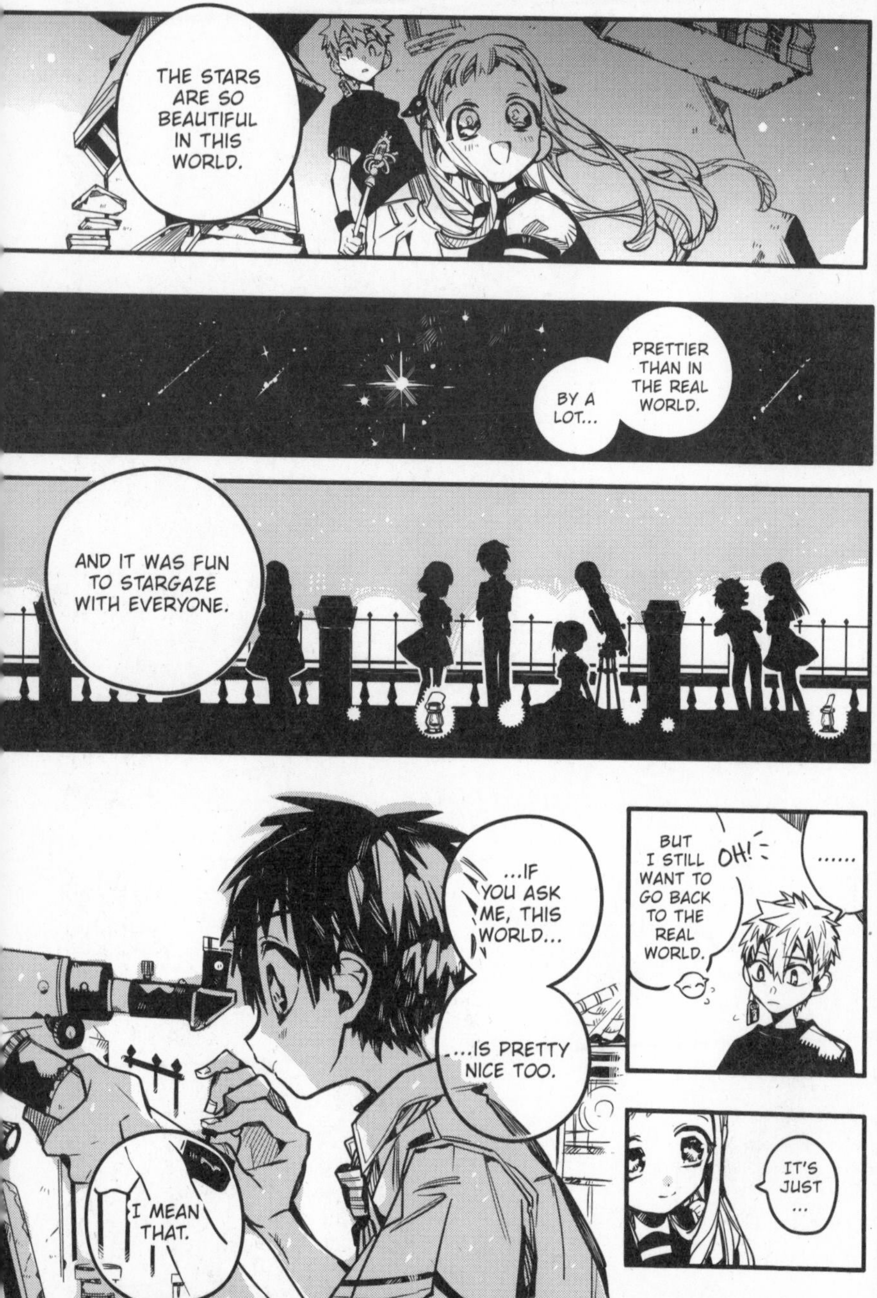
THE STARS ARE SO BEAUTIFUL IN THIS WORLD.
PRETTIER THAN IN THE REAL WORLD.
BY A LOT...
AND IT WAS FUN TO STARGAZE WITH EVERYONE.
......
OH!
BUT I STILL WANT TO GO BACK TO THE REAL WORLD.
IT'S JUST ...
...IF YOU ASK ME, THIS WORLD...
...IS PRETTY NICE TOO.
I MEAN THAT.

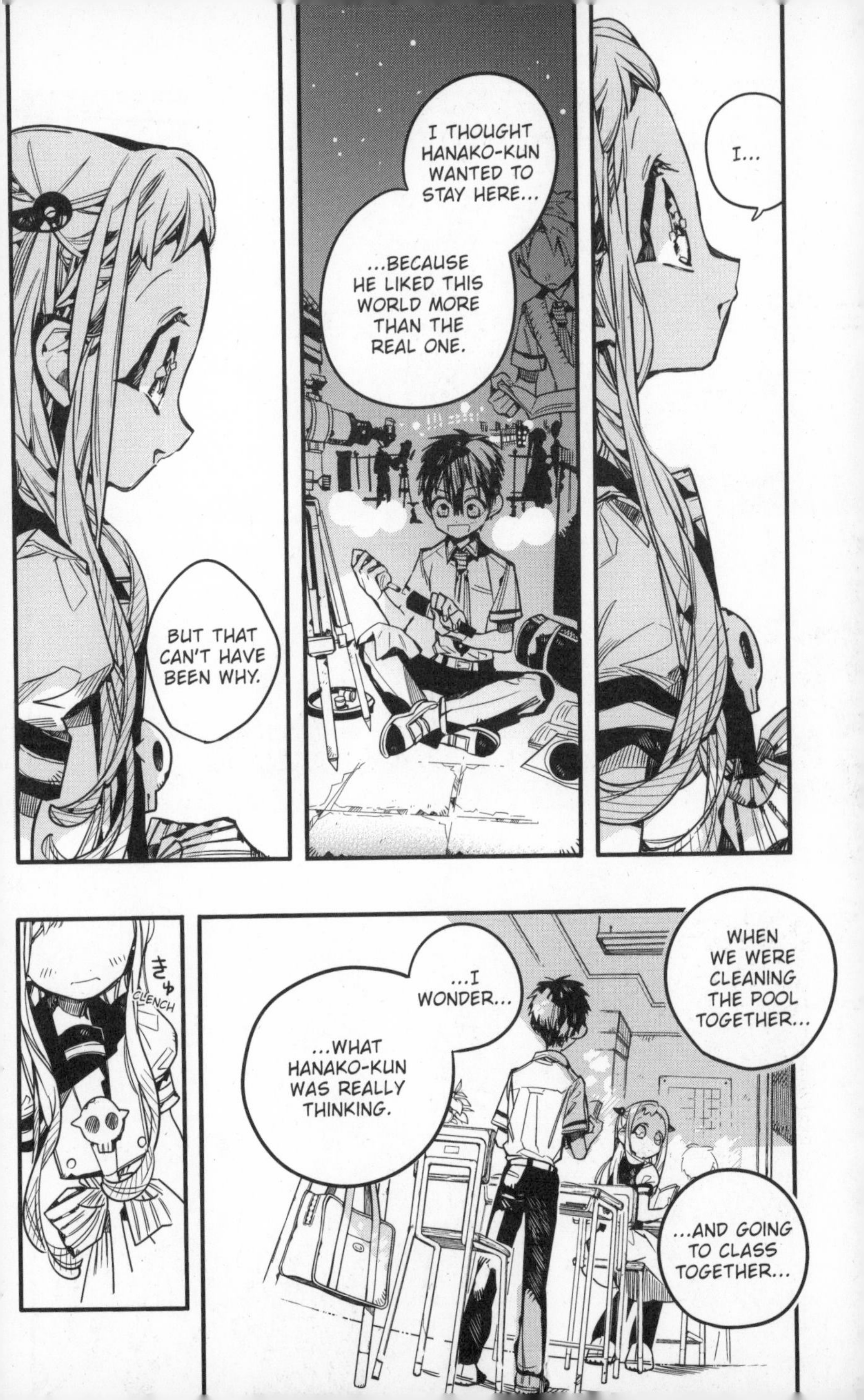
I...
I THOUGHT HANAKO-KUN WANTED TO STAY HERE...
...BECAUSE HE LIKED THIS WORLD MORE THAN THE REAL ONE.
BUT THAT CAN'T HAVE BEEN WHY.
WHEN WE WERE CLEANING THE POOL TOGETHER...
...AND GOING TO CLASS TOGETHER...
...I WONDER...
...WHAT HANAKO-KUN WAS REALLY THINKING.
きゅ
CLENCH

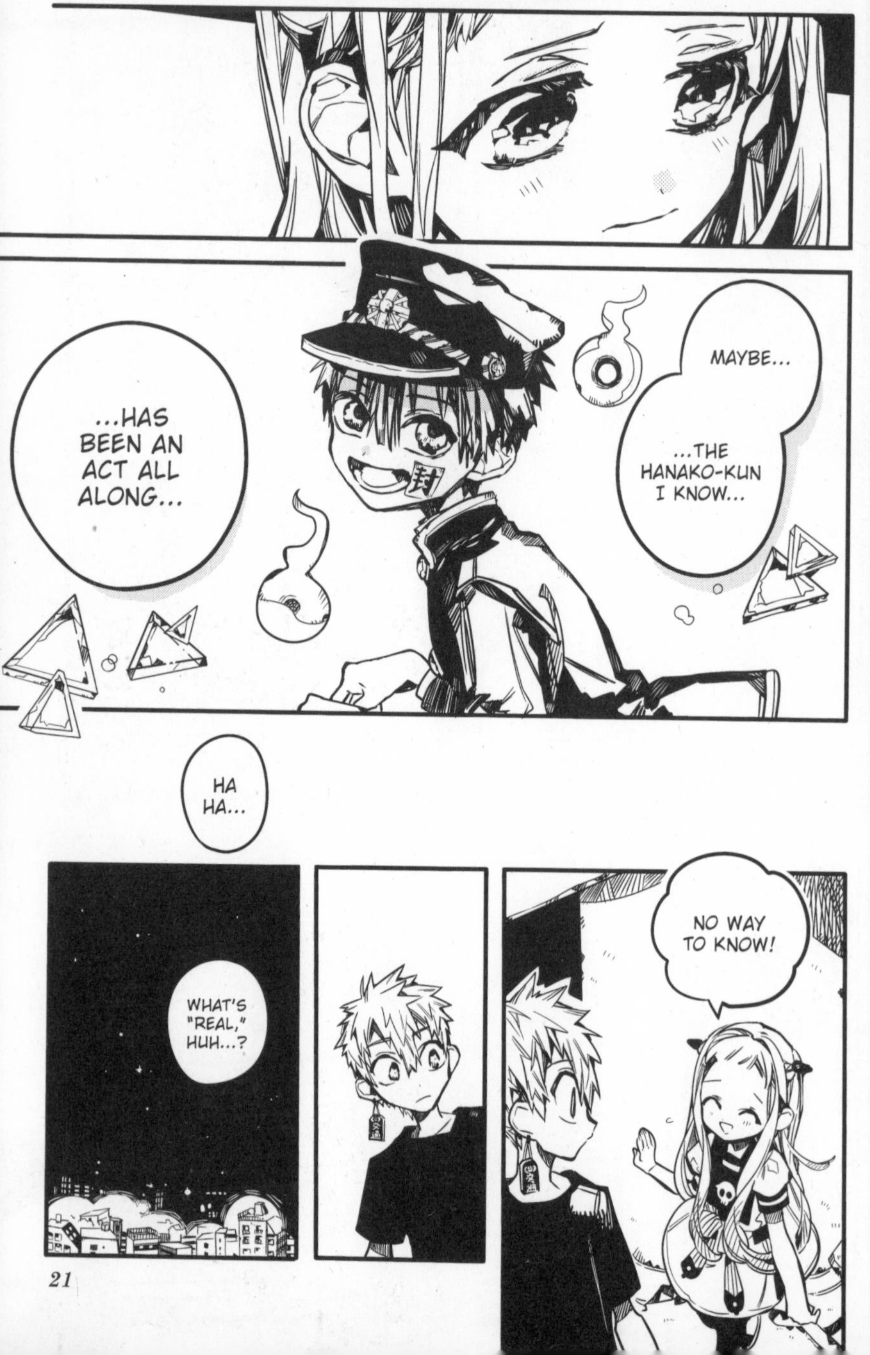
MAYBE...
...THE HANAKO-KUN I KNOW...
...HAS BEEN AN ACT ALL ALONG...
HA HA...
NO WAY TO KNOW!
WHAT'S "REAL," HUH...?

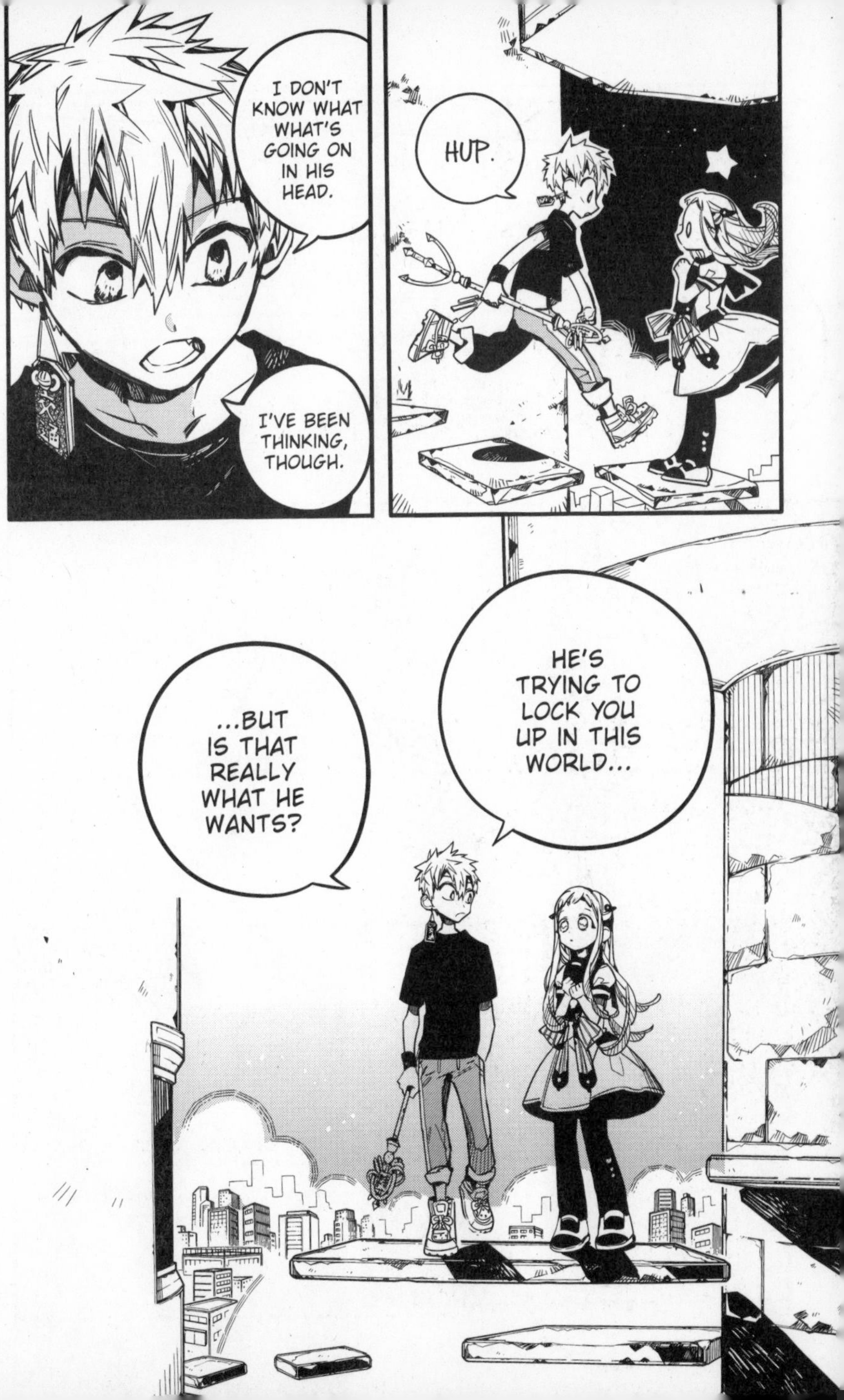
HUP.
I DON'T KNOW WHAT WHAT'S GOING ON IN HIS HEAD.
I'VE BEEN THINKING, THOUGH.
HE'S TRYING TO LOCK YOU UP IN THIS WORLD...
...BUT IS THAT REALLY WHAT HE WANTS?

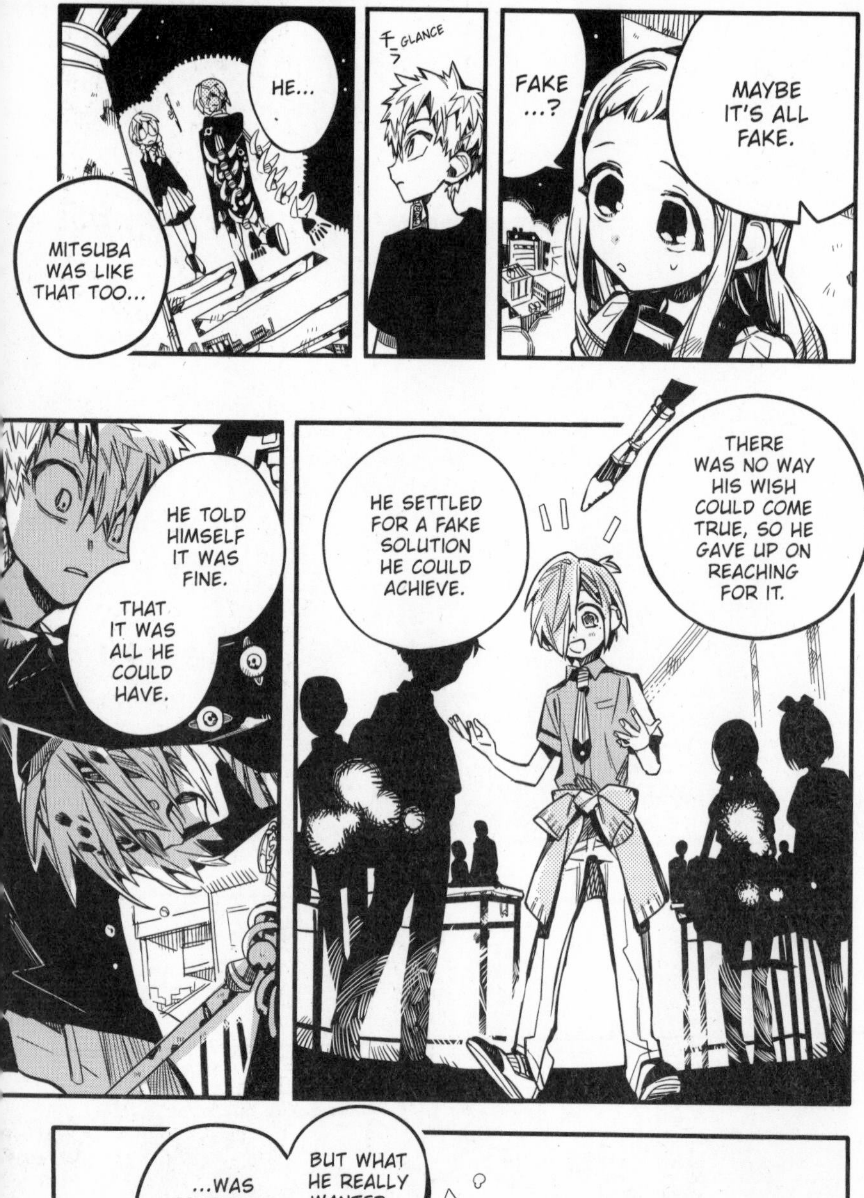
MAYBE IT'S ALL FAKE.
FAKE ...?
GLANCE
HE...
MITSUBA WAS LIKE THAT TOO...
THERE WAS NO WAY HIS WISH COULD COME TRUE, SO HE GAVE UP ON REACHING FOR IT.
HE SETTLED FOR A FAKE SOLUTION HE COULD ACHIEVE.
HE TOLD HIMSELF IT WAS FINE.
THAT IT WAS ALL HE COULD HAVE.
BUT WHAT HE REALLY WANTED...
...WAS SOMETHING ELSE ENTIRELY.

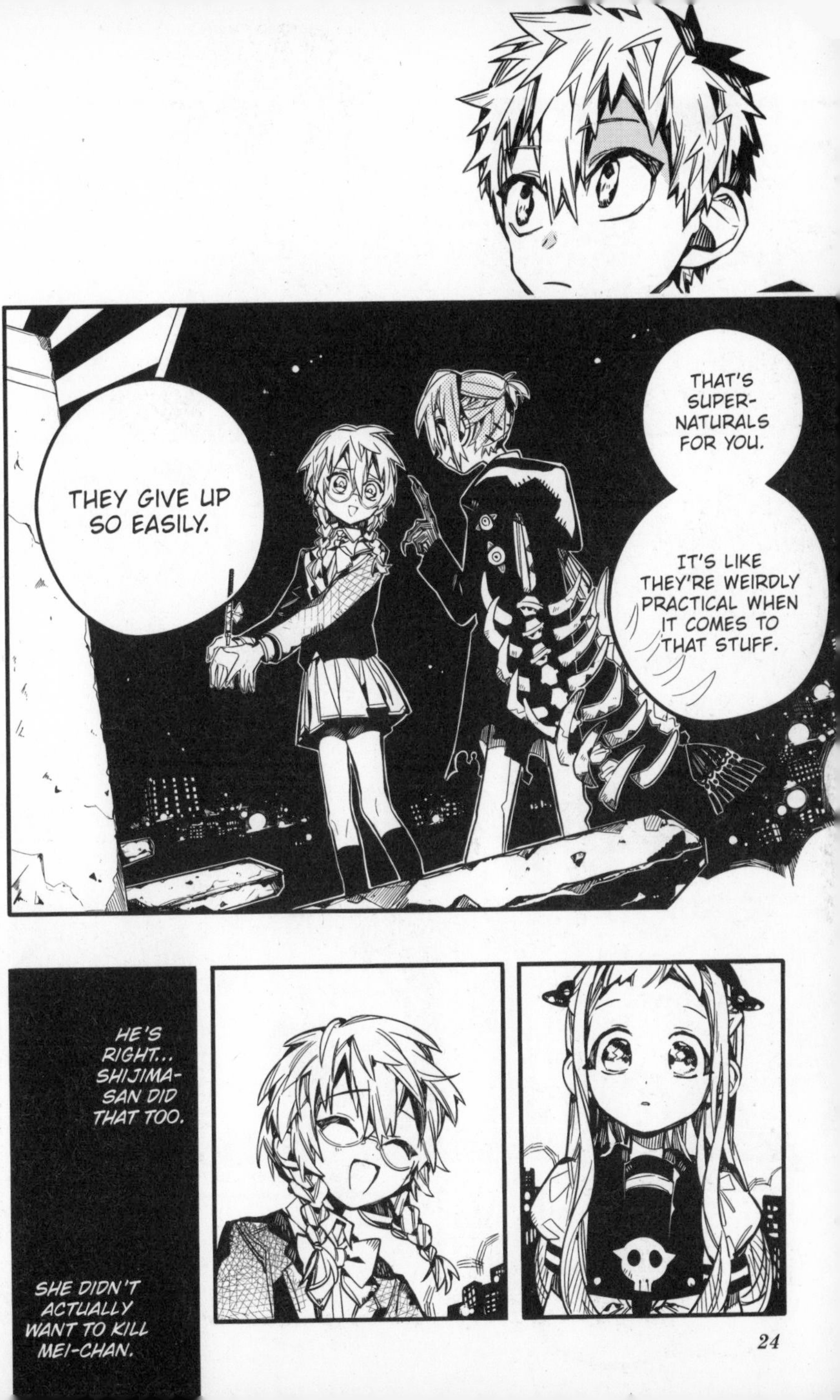
THAT'S SUPER-NATURALS FOR YOU.
IT'S LIKE THEY'RE WEIRDLY PRACTICAL WHEN IT COMES TO THAT STUFF.
THEY GIVE UP SO EASILY.
HE'S RIGHT... SHIJIMA-SAN DID THAT TOO.
SHE DIDN'T ACTUALLY WANT TO KILL MEI-CHAN.

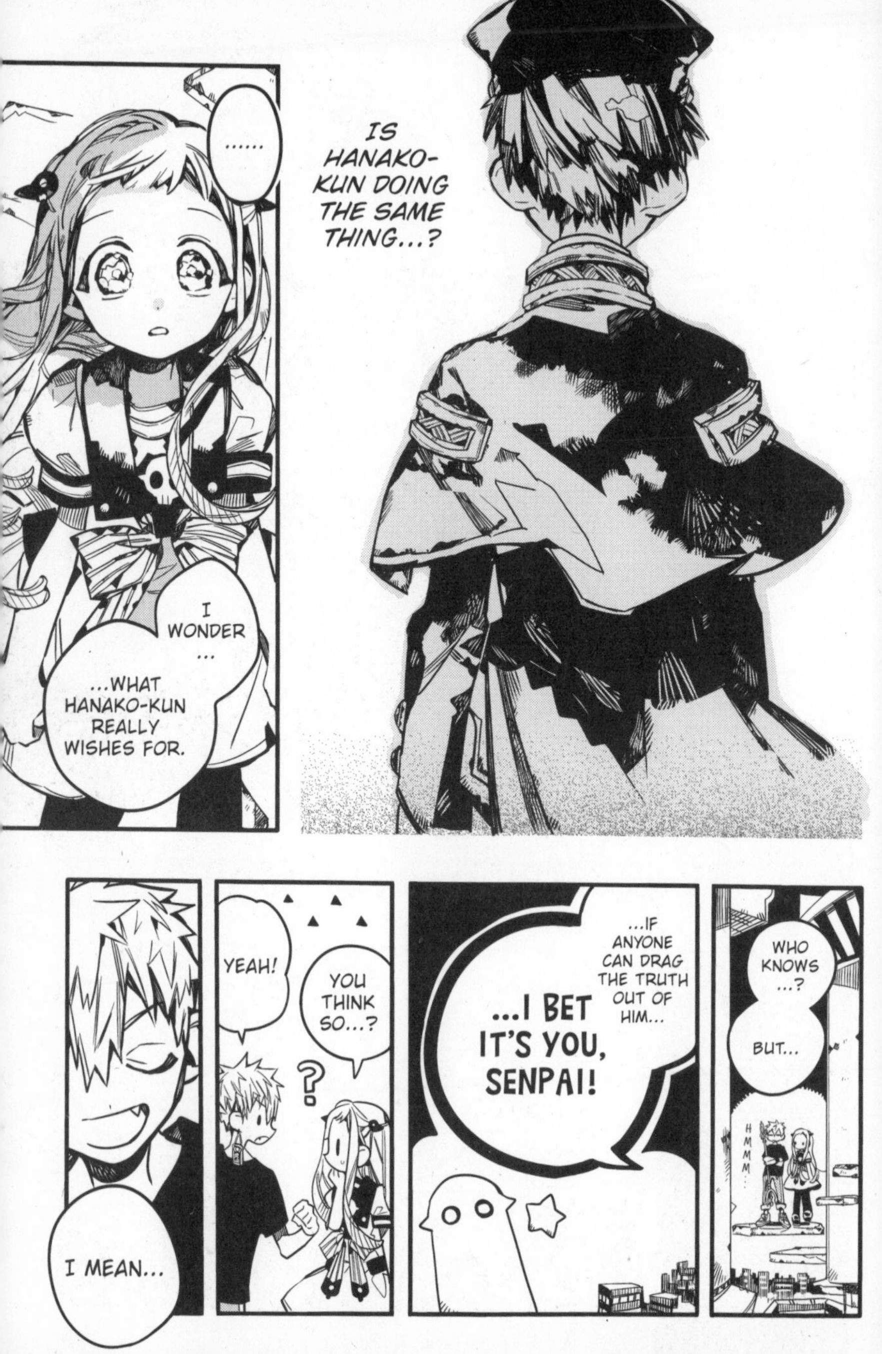
IS HANAKO-KUN DOING THE SAME THING...?
......
I WONDER ...
...WHAT HANAKO-KUN REALLY WISHES FOR.
WHO KNOWS ...?
BUT...
HMMM...
...IF ANYONE CAN DRAG THE TRUTH OUT OF HIM...
...I BET IT'S YOU, SENPAI!
YOU THINK SO...?
YEAH!
I MEAN...

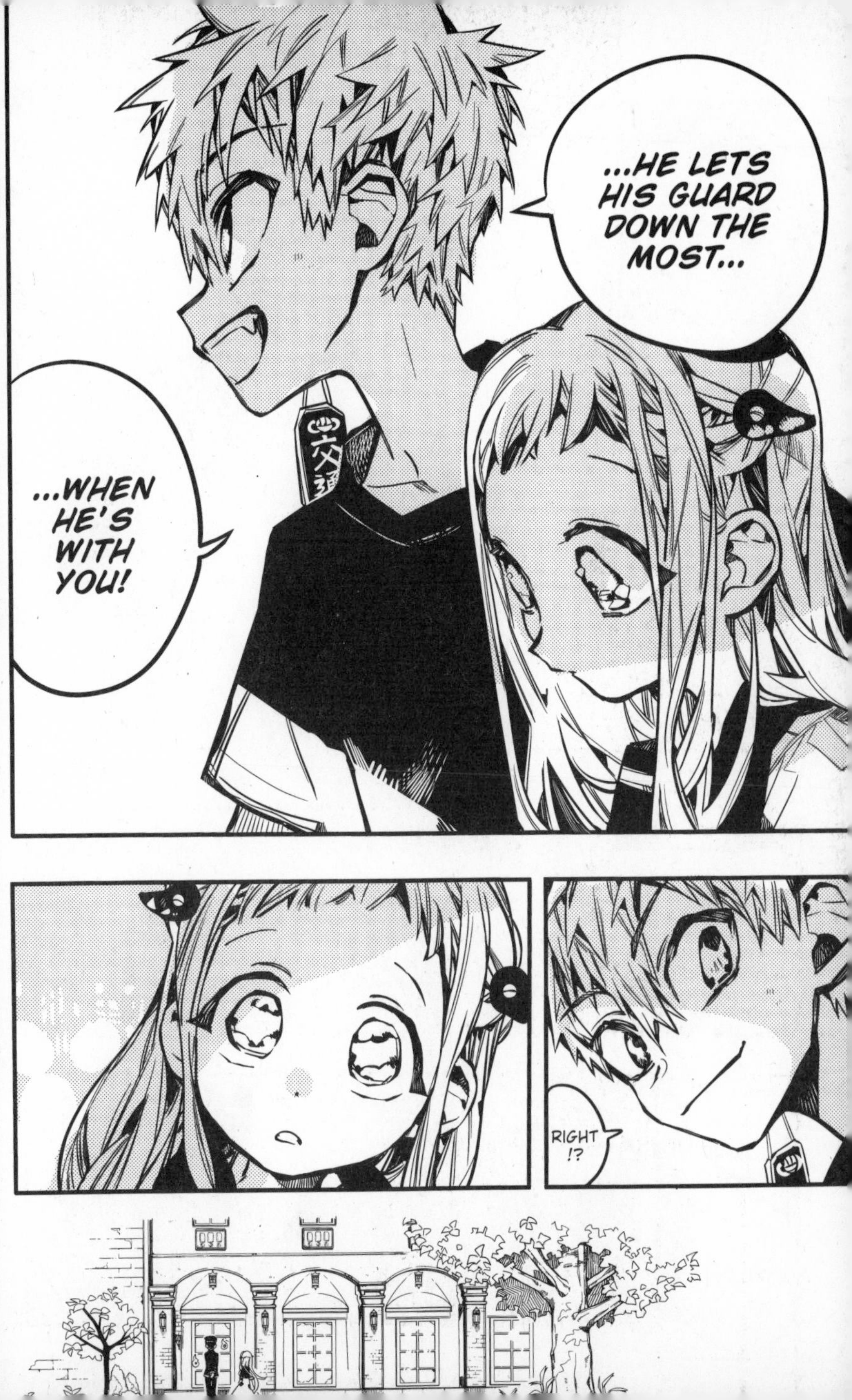
...HE LETS HIS GUARD DOWN THE MOST...
...WHEN HE'S WITH YOU!
RIGHT !?

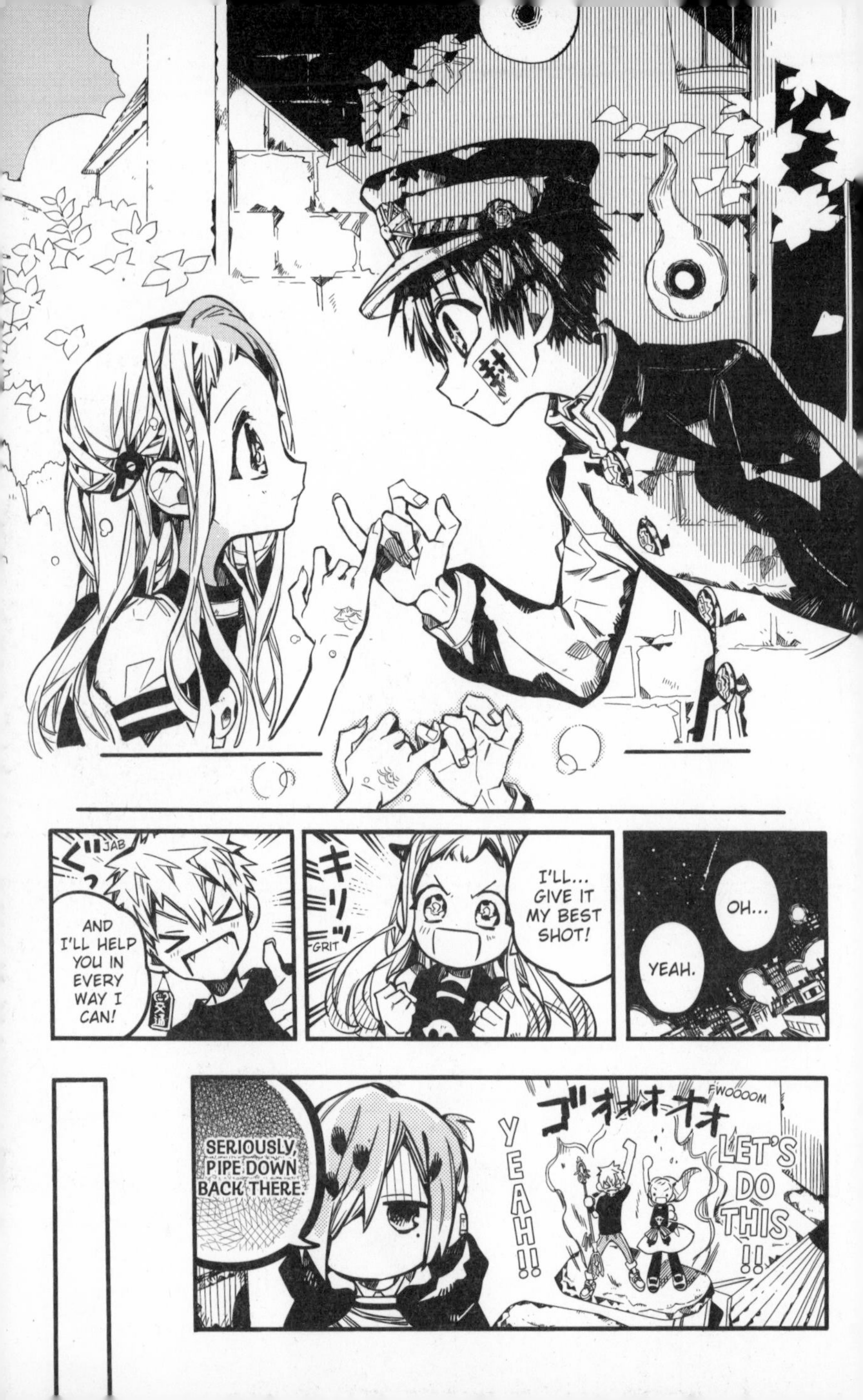
OH...
YEAH.
キリッ
GRIT
I'LL... GIVE IT MY BEST SHOT!
ぐっ
JAB
AND I'LL HELP YOU IN EVERY WAY I CAN!
ゴオオオオオ
FWOOOOM
LET'S DO THIS!!
YEAH!!
SERIOUSLY, PIPE DOWN BACK THERE.

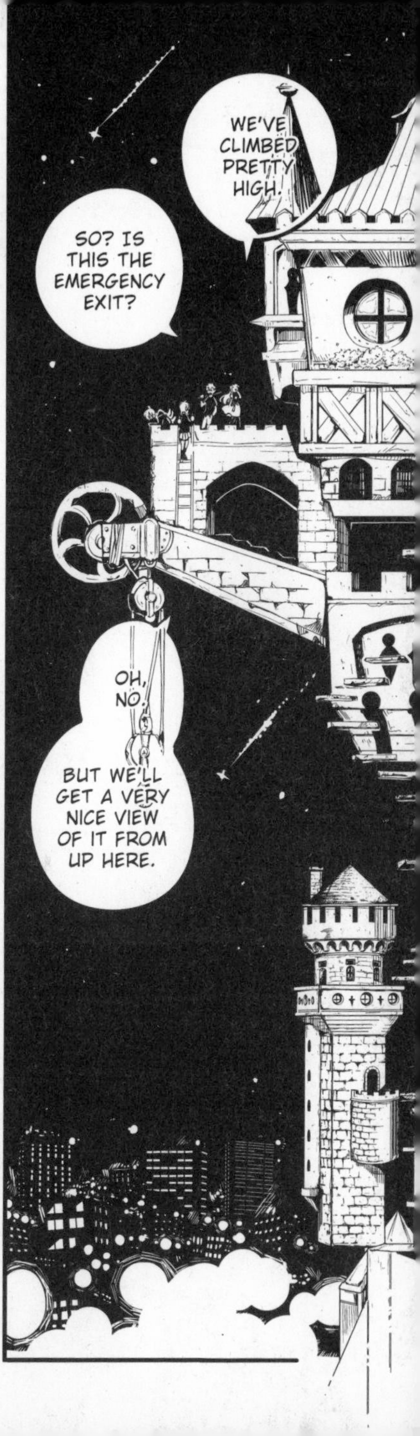
WE'VE CLIMBED PRETTY HIGH.
SO? IS THIS THE EMERGENCY EXIT?
OH, NO.
BUT WE'LL GET A VERY NICE VIEW OF IT FROM UP HERE.

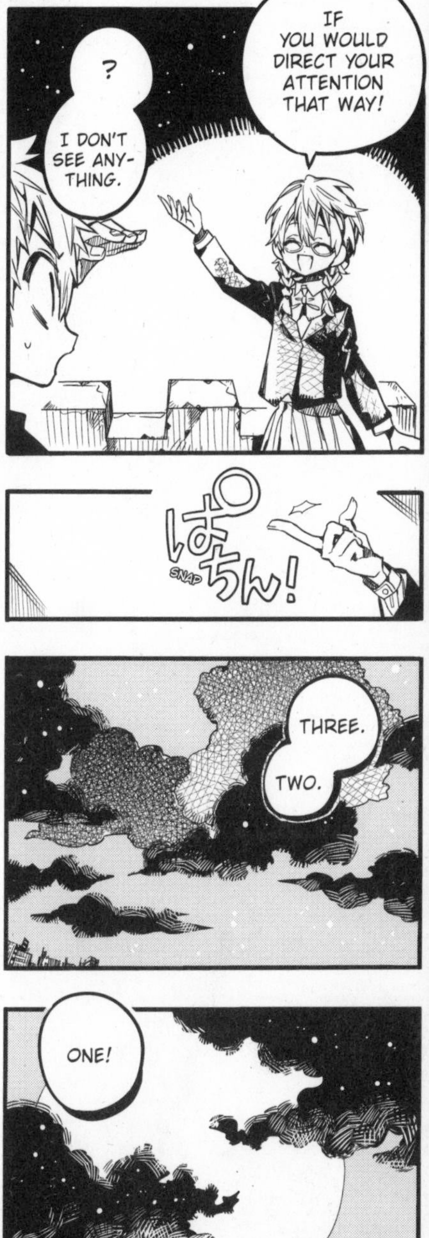
IF YOU WOULD DIRECT YOUR ATTENTION THAT WAY!
?
I DON'T SEE ANY-THING.
ぱちん!
SNAP
THREE.
TWO.
ONE!

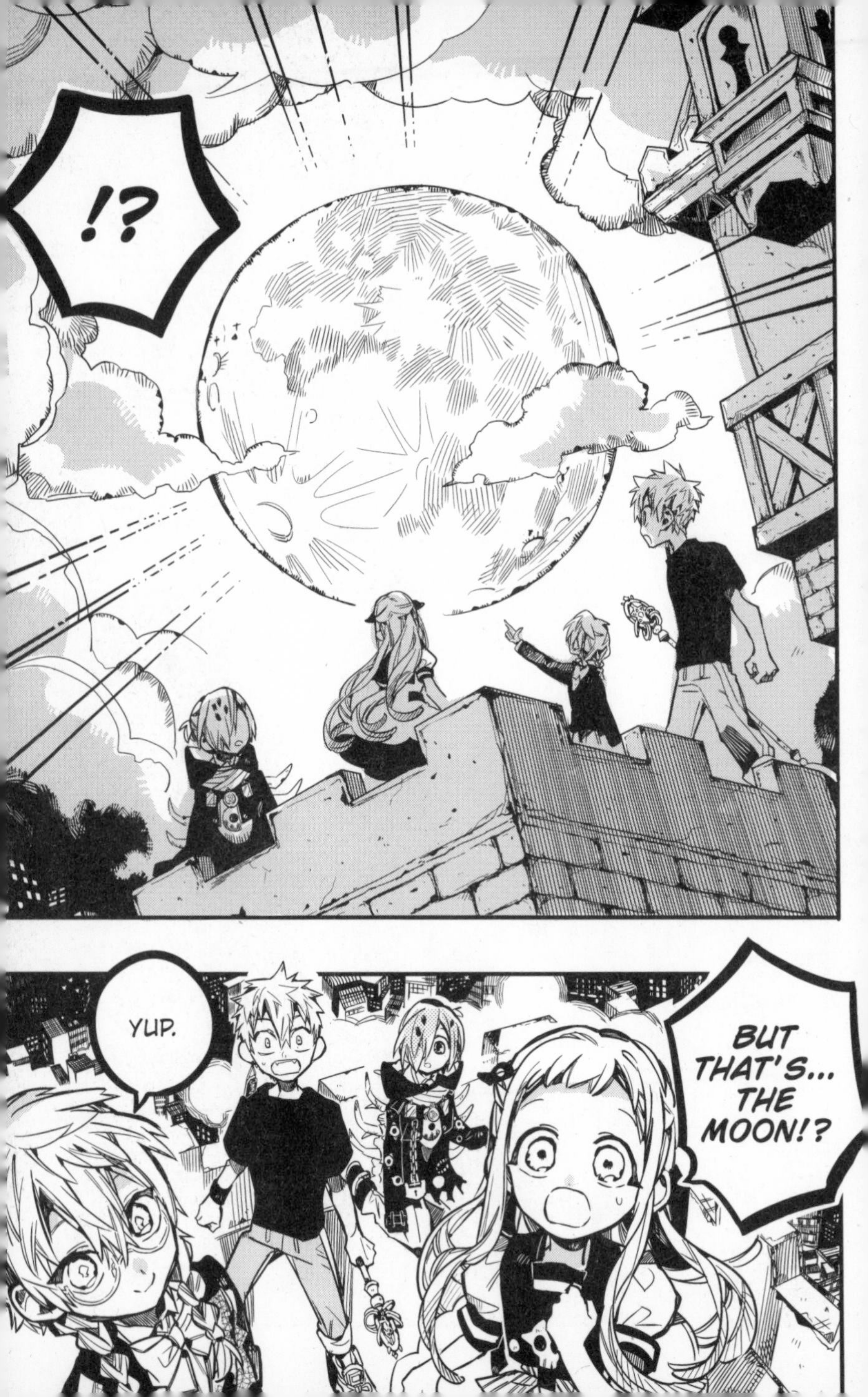
!?
BUT THAT'S... THE MOON!?
YUP.

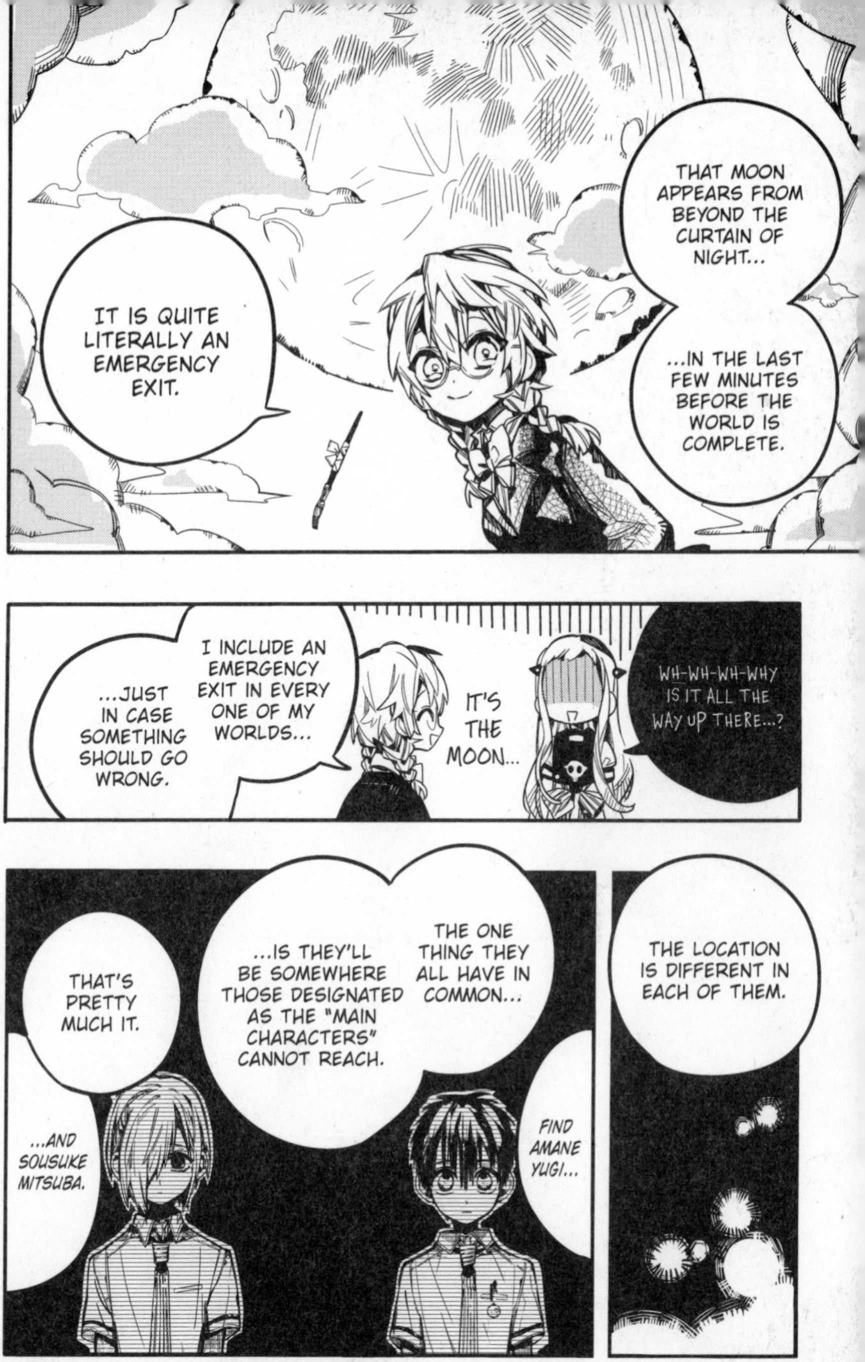
THAT MOON APPEARS FROM BEYOND THE CURTAIN OF NIGHT...
...IN THE LAST FEW MINUTES BEFORE THE WORLD IS COMPLETE.
IT IS QUITE LITERALLY AN EMERGENCY EXIT.
WH-WH-WH-WHY IS IT ALL THE WAY UP THERE...?
IT'S THE MOON...
I INCLUDE AN EMERGENCY EXIT IN EVERY ONE OF MY WORLDS...
...JUST IN CASE SOMETHING SHOULD GO WRONG.
THE LOCATION IS DIFFERENT IN EACH OF THEM.
THE ONE THING THEY ALL HAVE IN COMMON...
...IS THEY'LL BE SOMEWHERE THOSE DESIGNATED AS THE "MAIN CHARACTERS" CANNOT REACH.
FIND AMANE YUGI...
...AND SOUSUKE MITSUBA.
THAT'S PRETTY MUCH IT.

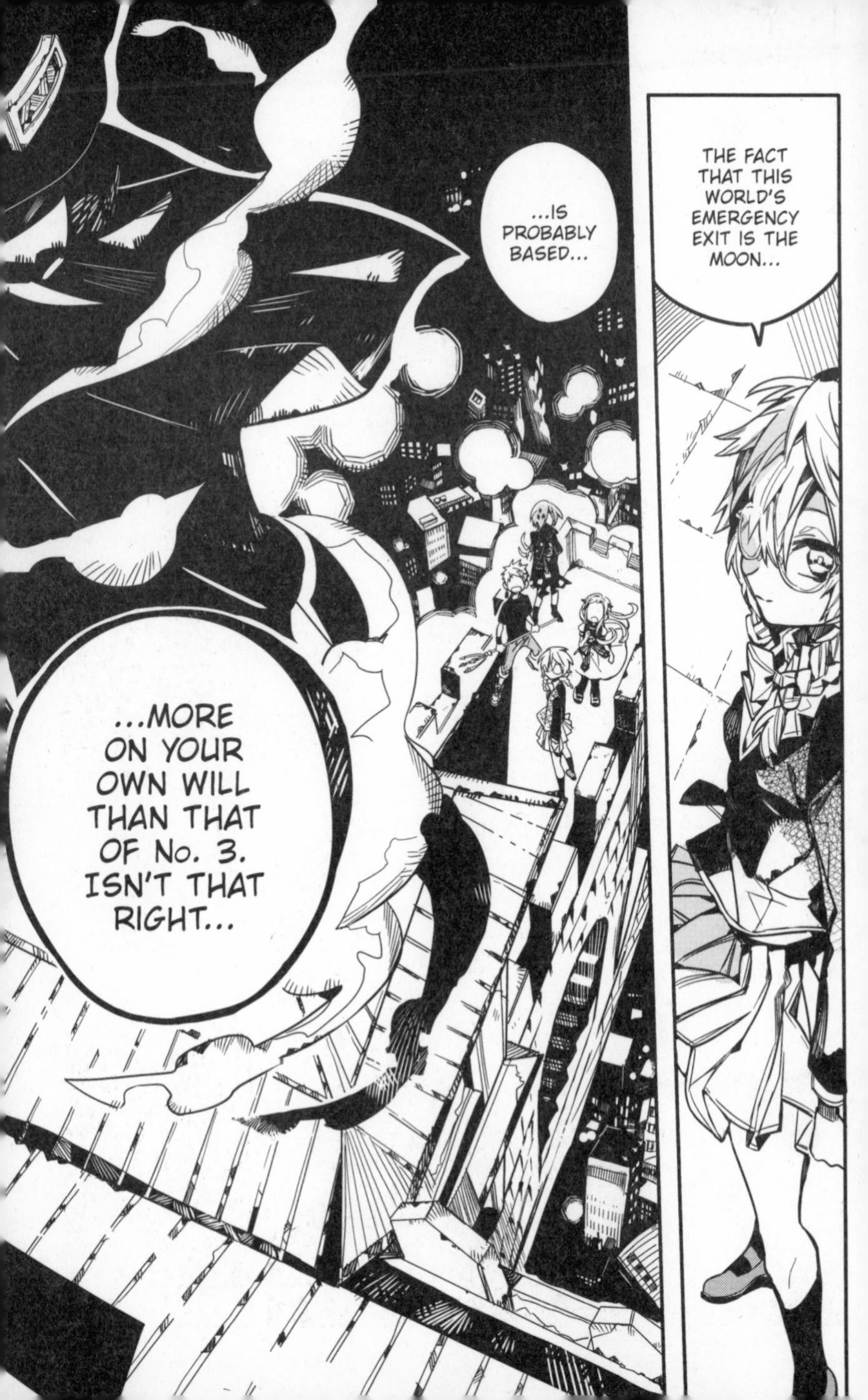
THE FACT THAT THIS WORLD'S EMERGENCY EXIT IS THE MOON...
...IS PROBABLY BASED...
...MORE ON YOUR OWN WILL THAN THAT OF No. 3. ISN'T THAT RIGHT...

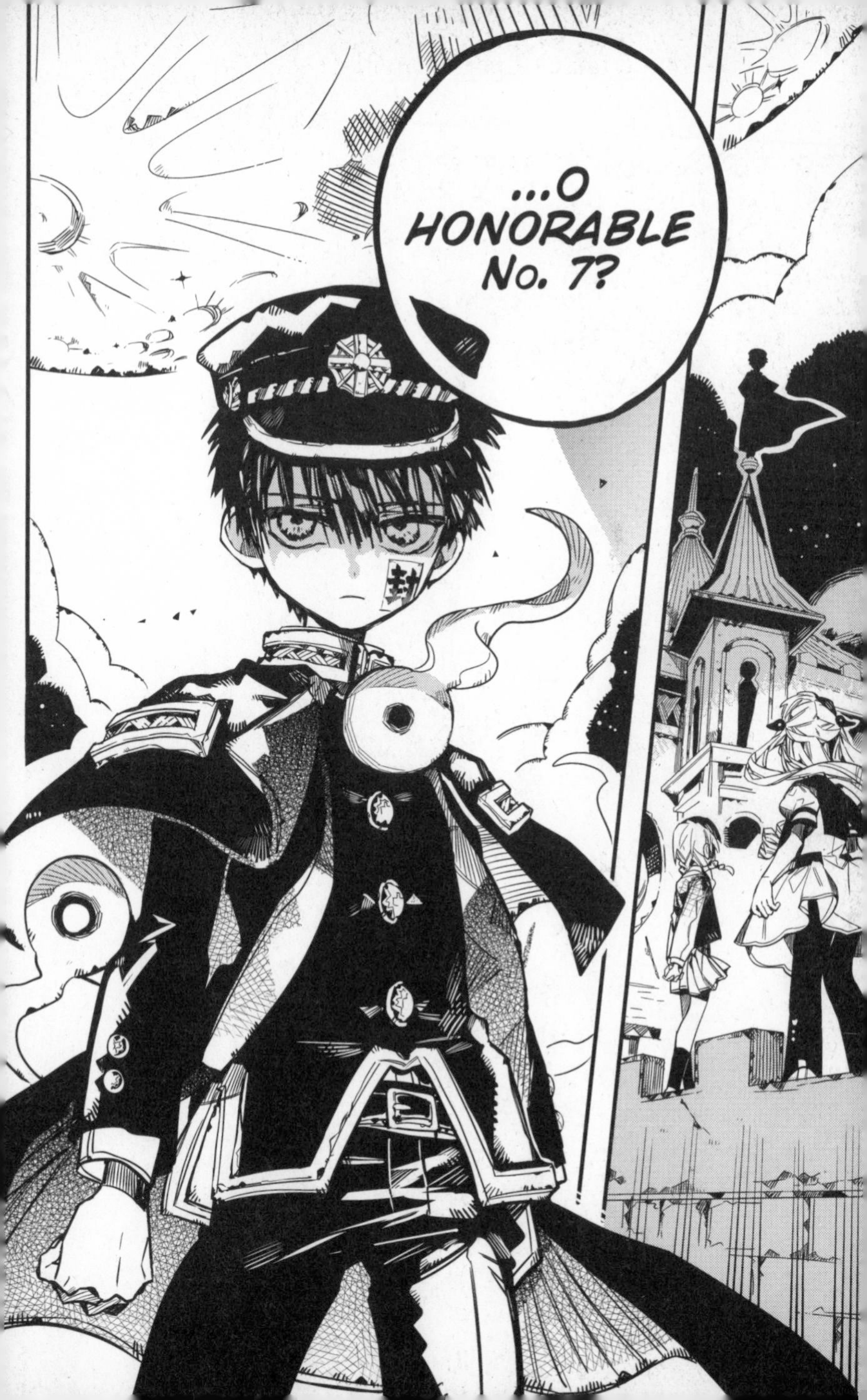
...O HONORABLE No. 7?

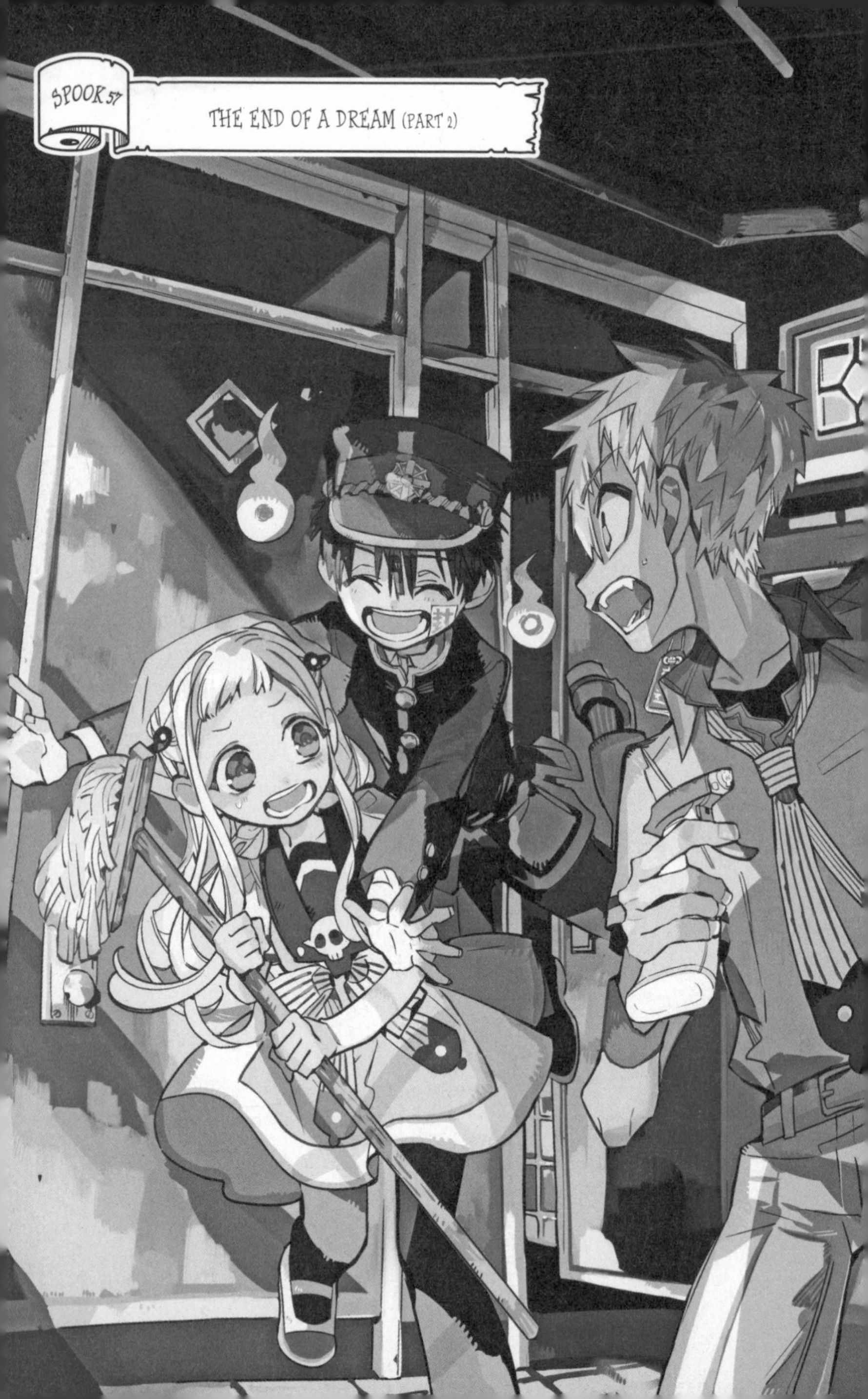
SPOOK 57
THE END OF A DREAM (PART 2)

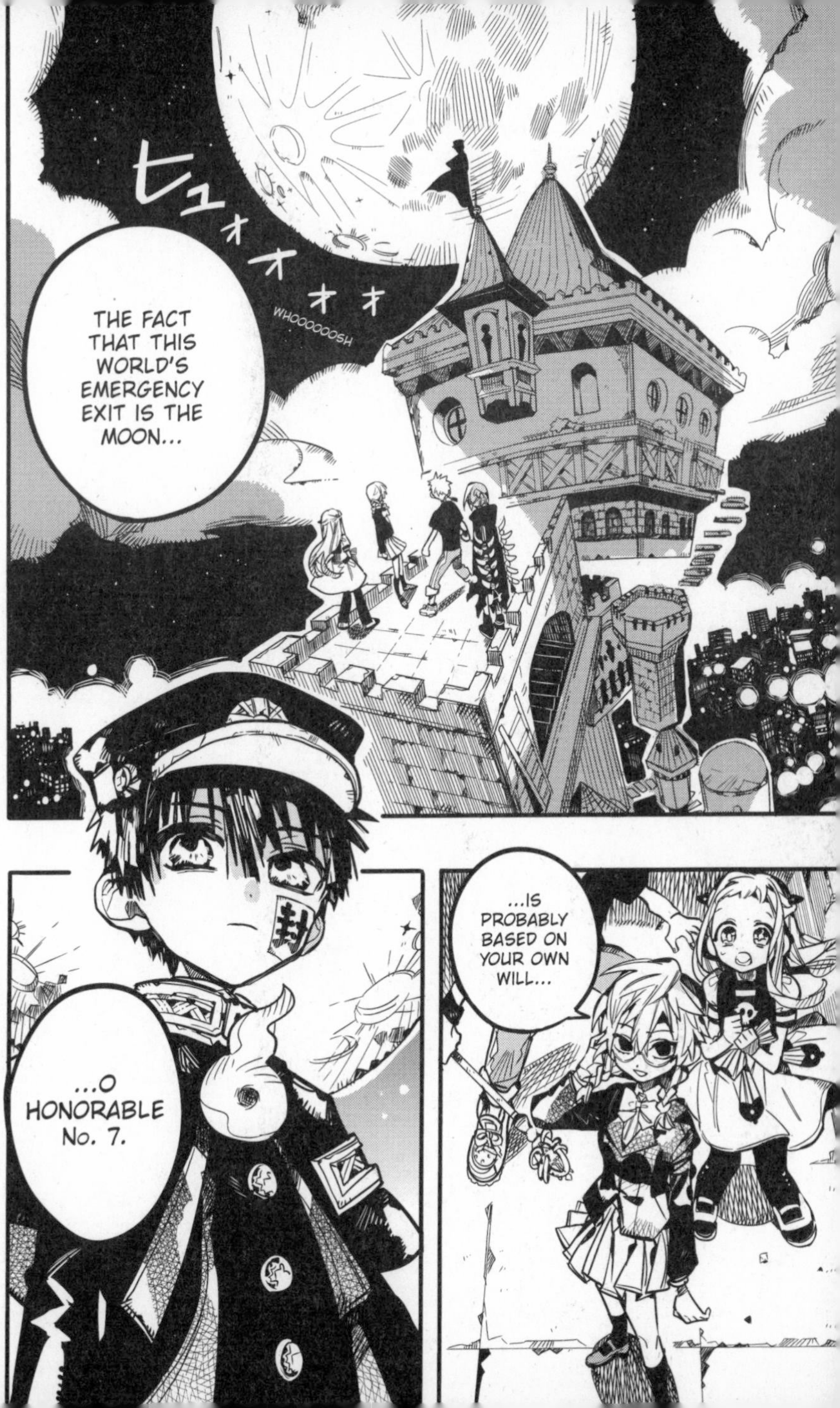
ヒュオオオオ
WHOOOOOOSH
THE FACT THAT THIS WORLD'S EMERGENCY EXIT IS THE MOON...
...IS PROBABLY BASED ON YOUR OWN WILL...
...O HONORABLE No. 7.

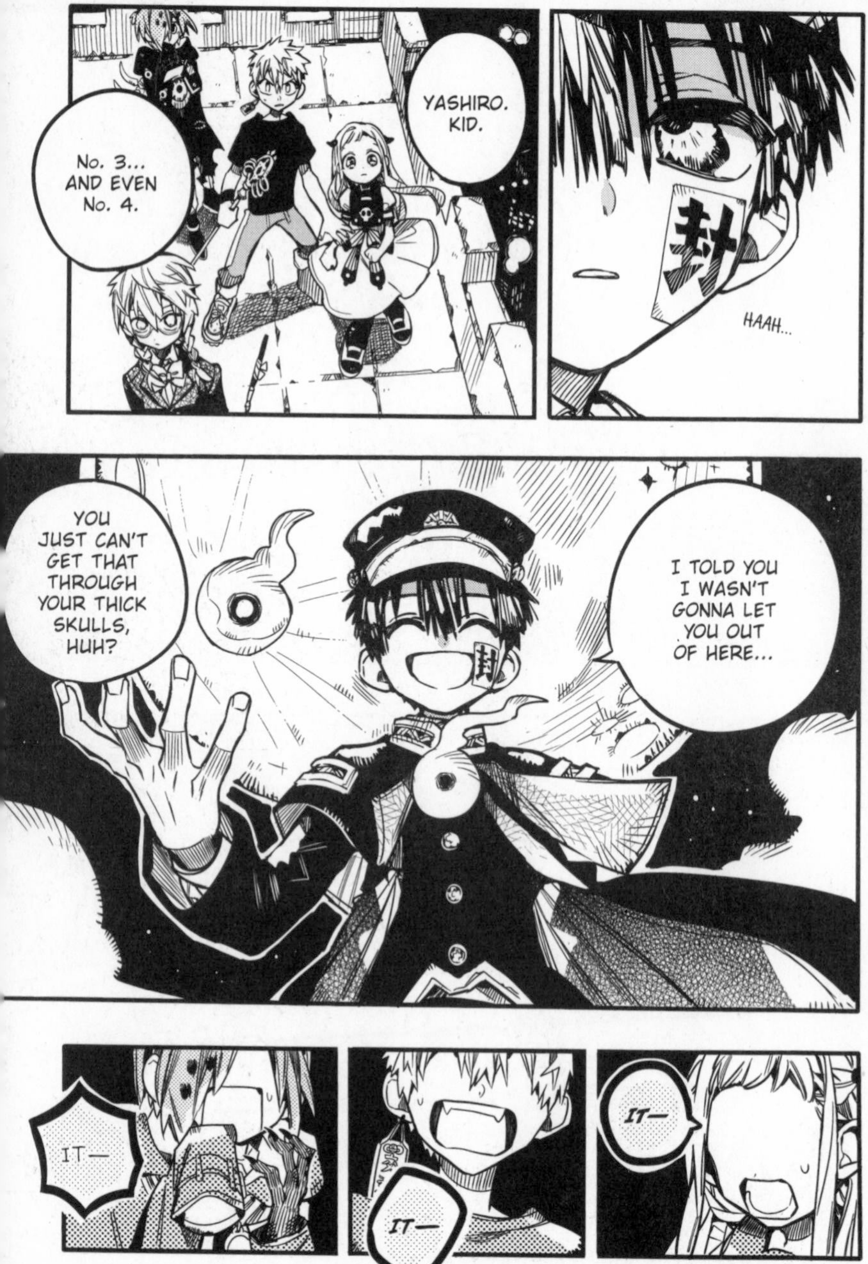
HAAH...
YASHIRO. KID.
No. 3... AND EVEN No. 4.
I TOLD YOU I WASN'T GONNA LET YOU OUT OF HERE...
YOU JUST CAN'T GET THAT THROUGH YOUR THICK SKULLS, HUH?
IT—
IT—
IT—

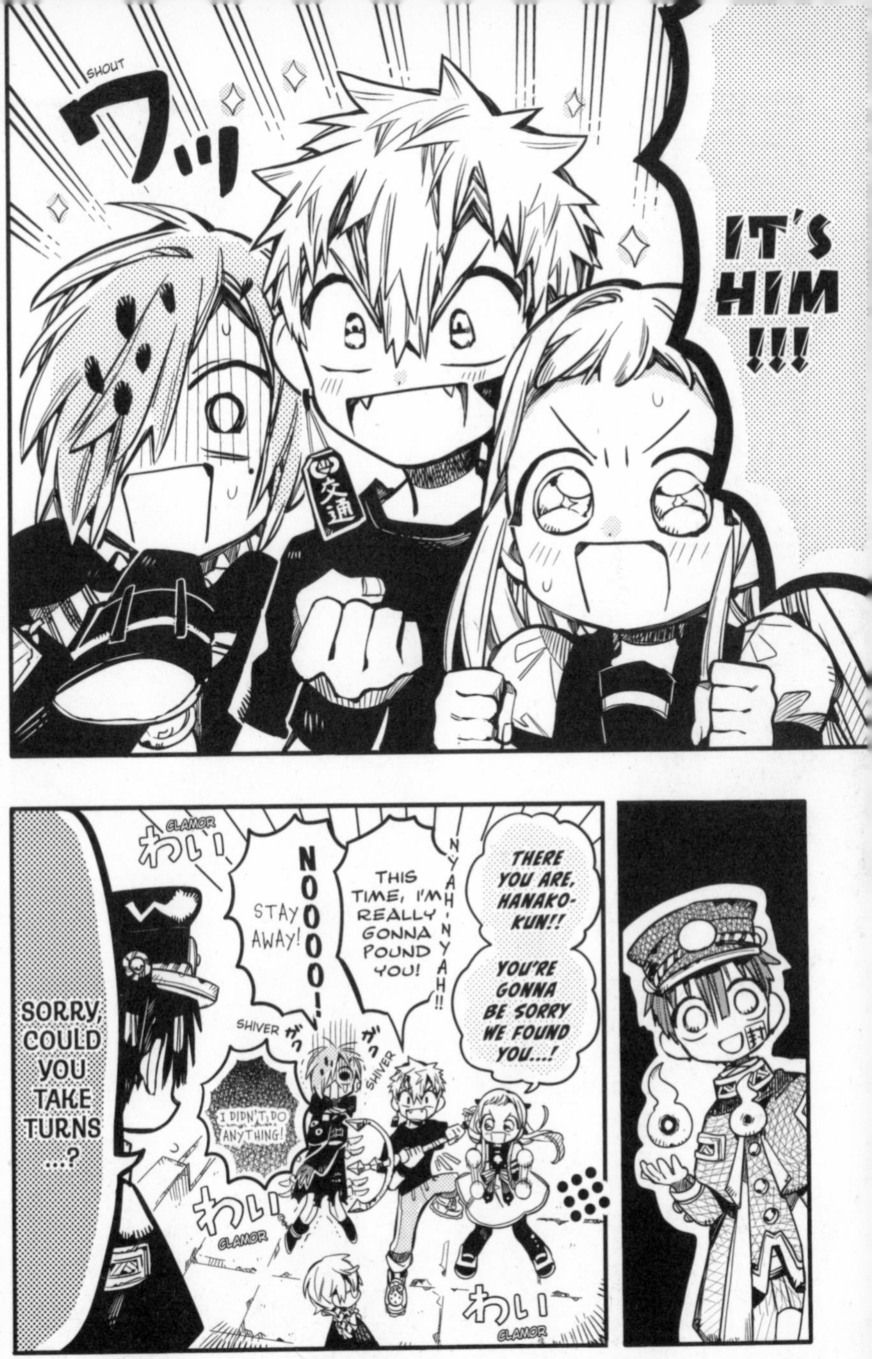
IT'S HIM!!!
ワッ
SHOUT
THERE YOU ARE, HANAKO-KUN!!
YOU'RE GONNA BE SORRY WE FOUND YOU...!
NYAH-NYAH!!
THIS TIME, I'M REALLY GONNA POUND YOU!
NOOOOO!
STAY AWAY!
わい
CLAMOR
ガク
SHIVER
ガク
SHIVER
I DIDN'T DO ANYTHING!
わい
CLAMOR
わい
CLAMOR
SORRY, COULD YOU TAKE TURNS ...?

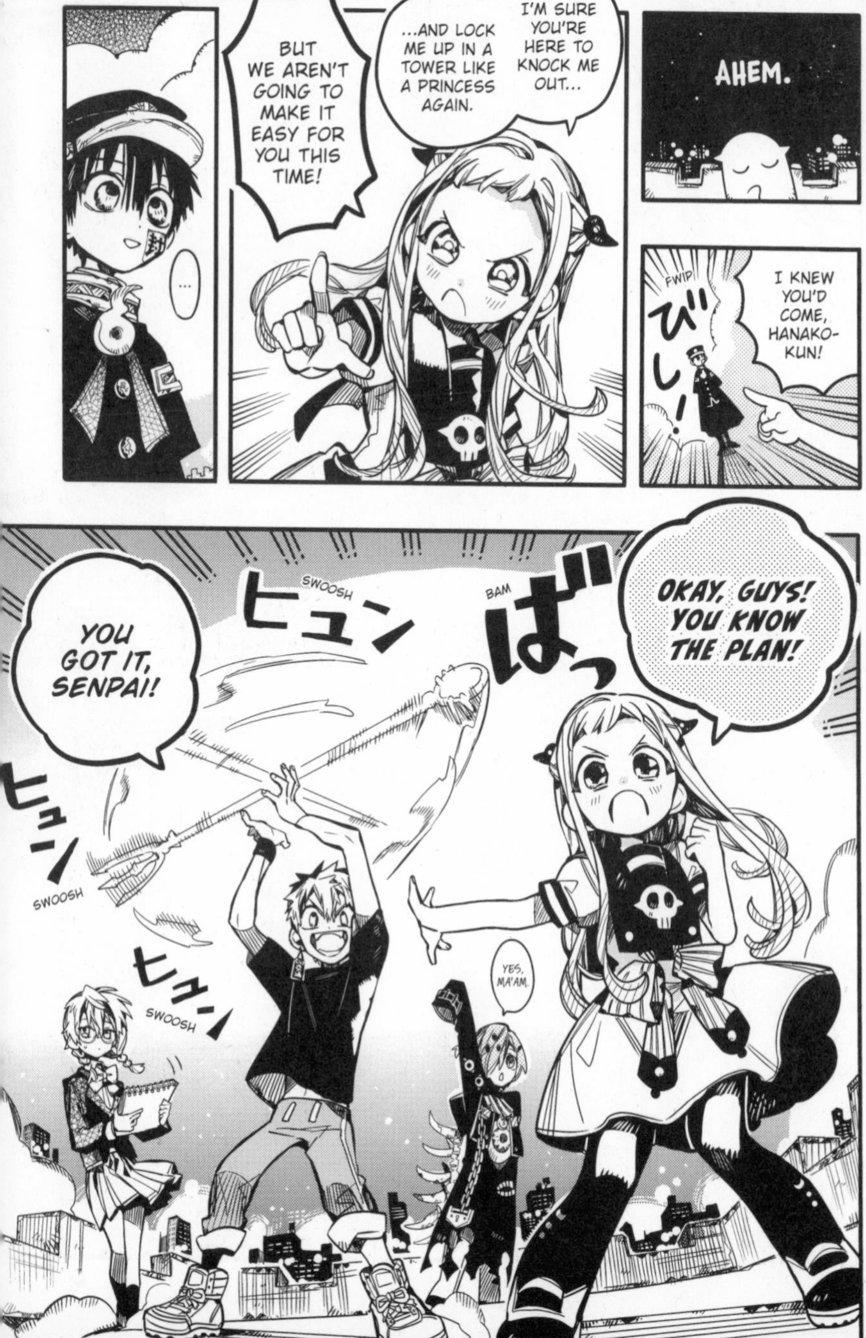
AHEM.
FWIP
びし!
I KNEW YOU'D COME, HANAKO-KUN!
I'M SURE YOU'RE HERE TO KNOCK ME OUT...
...AND LOCK ME UP IN A TOWER LIKE A PRINCESS AGAIN.
BUT WE AREN'T GOING TO MAKE IT EASY FOR YOU THIS TIME!
...
OKAY, GUYS! YOU KNOW THE PLAN!
BAM
ばっ
SWOOSH
ヒュン
YOU GOT IT, SENPAI!
ヒュン
SWOOSH
YES, MA'AM.
ヒュン
SWOOSH

バチ
BZZT
バチ
BZZT
バチ
BZZT
HERE I COME, HANAKO!
BURST
CRACKLE
パチッ
!

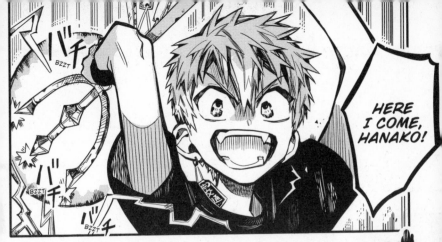

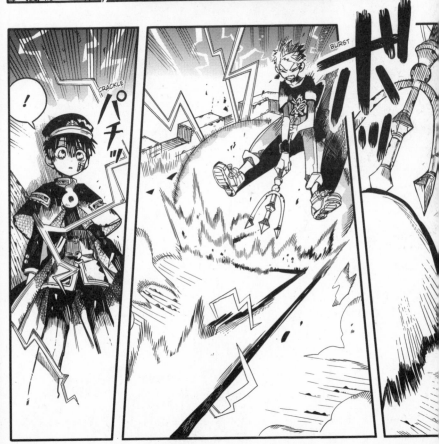

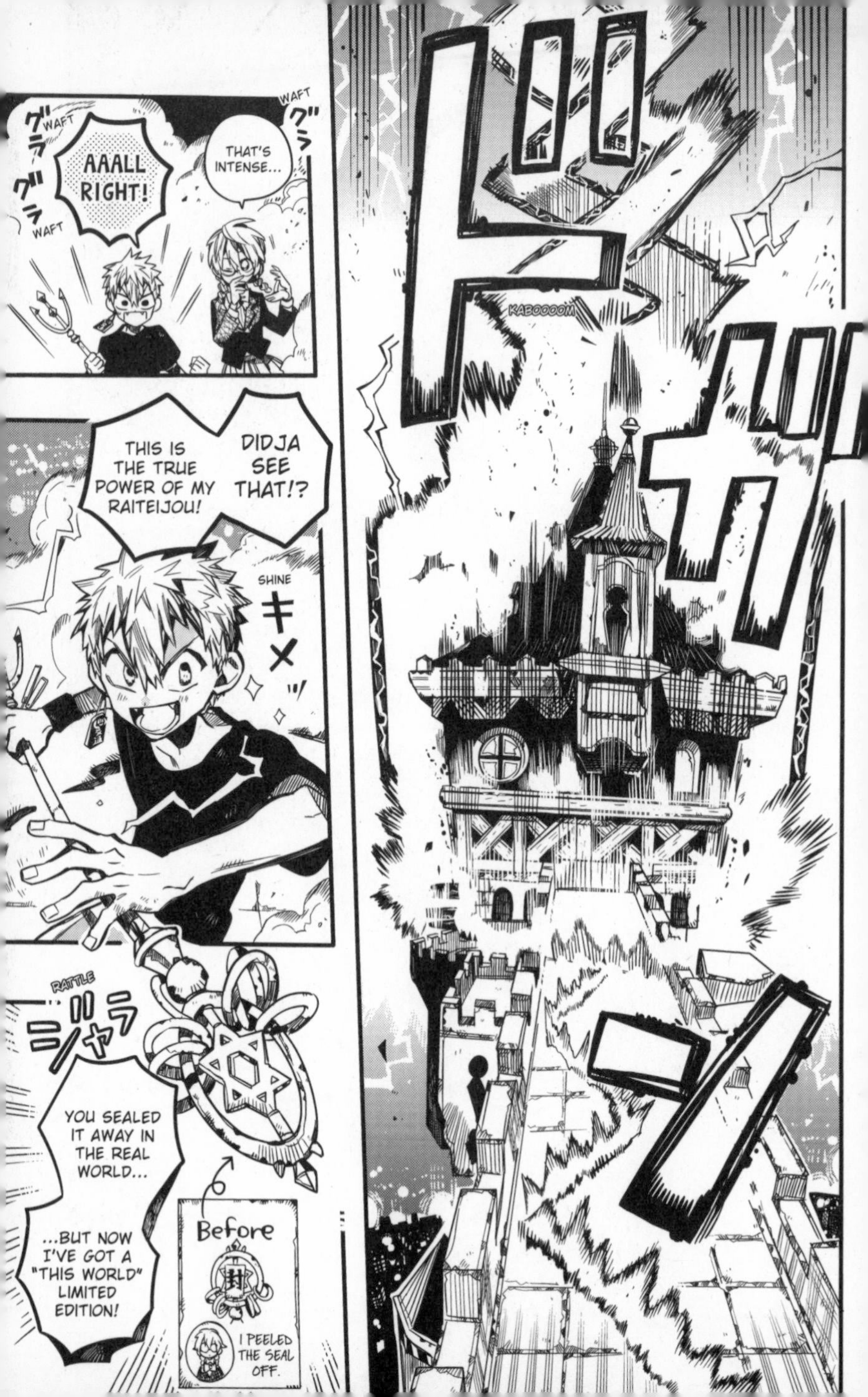
KABOOOOM
WAFT
グラ
THAT'S INTENSE...
グラグラ
WAFT
AAALL RIGHT!
WAFT
DIDJA SEE THAT!?
THIS IS THE TRUE POWER OF MY RAITEIJOU!
SHINE
キメッ
RATTLE
ジャラ
YOU SEALED IT AWAY IN THE REAL WORLD...
...BUT NOW I'VE GOT A "THIS WORLD" LIMITED EDITION!
Before
封
I PEELED THE SEAL OFF.

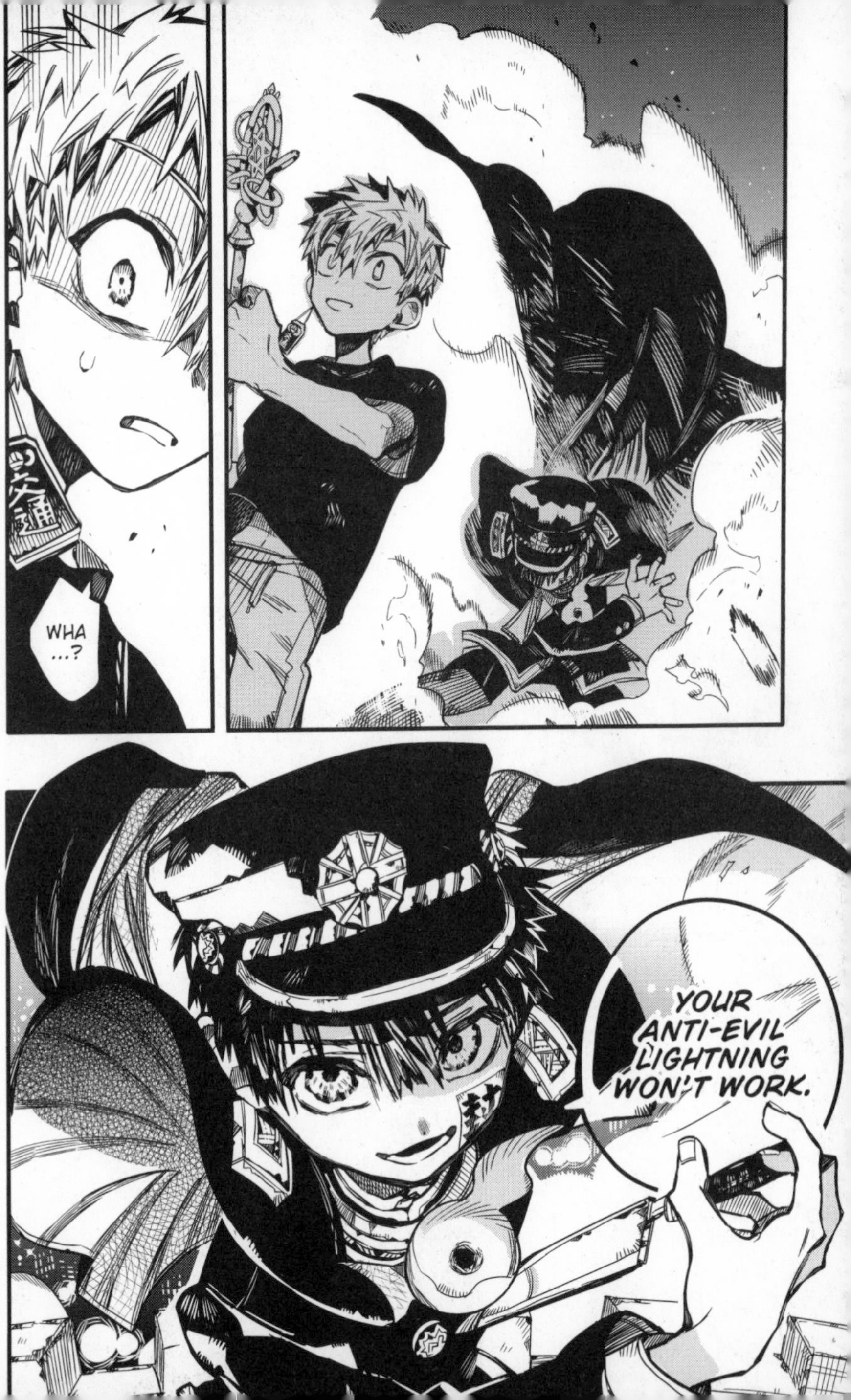
WHA ...?
YOUR ANTI-EVIL LIGHTNING WON'T WORK.

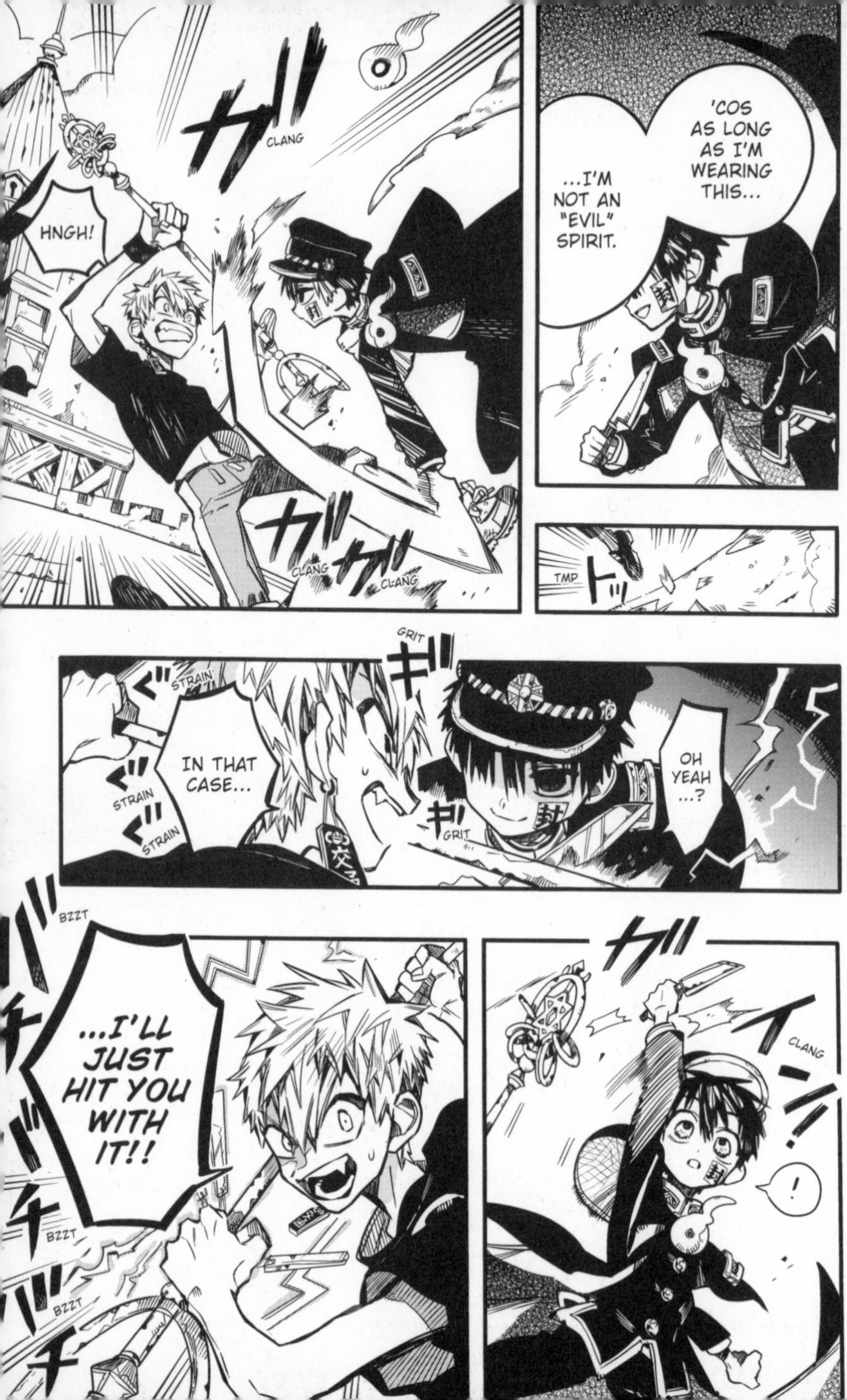
'COS AS LONG AS I'M WEARING THIS...
...I'M NOT AN "EVIL" SPIRIT.
TMP
CLANG
HNGH!
CLANG
CLANG
GRIT
OH YEAH ...?
GRIT
STRAIN
IN THAT CASE...
STRAIN
STRAIN
CLANG
!
BZZT
...I'LL JUST HIT YOU WITH IT!!
BZZT
BZZT

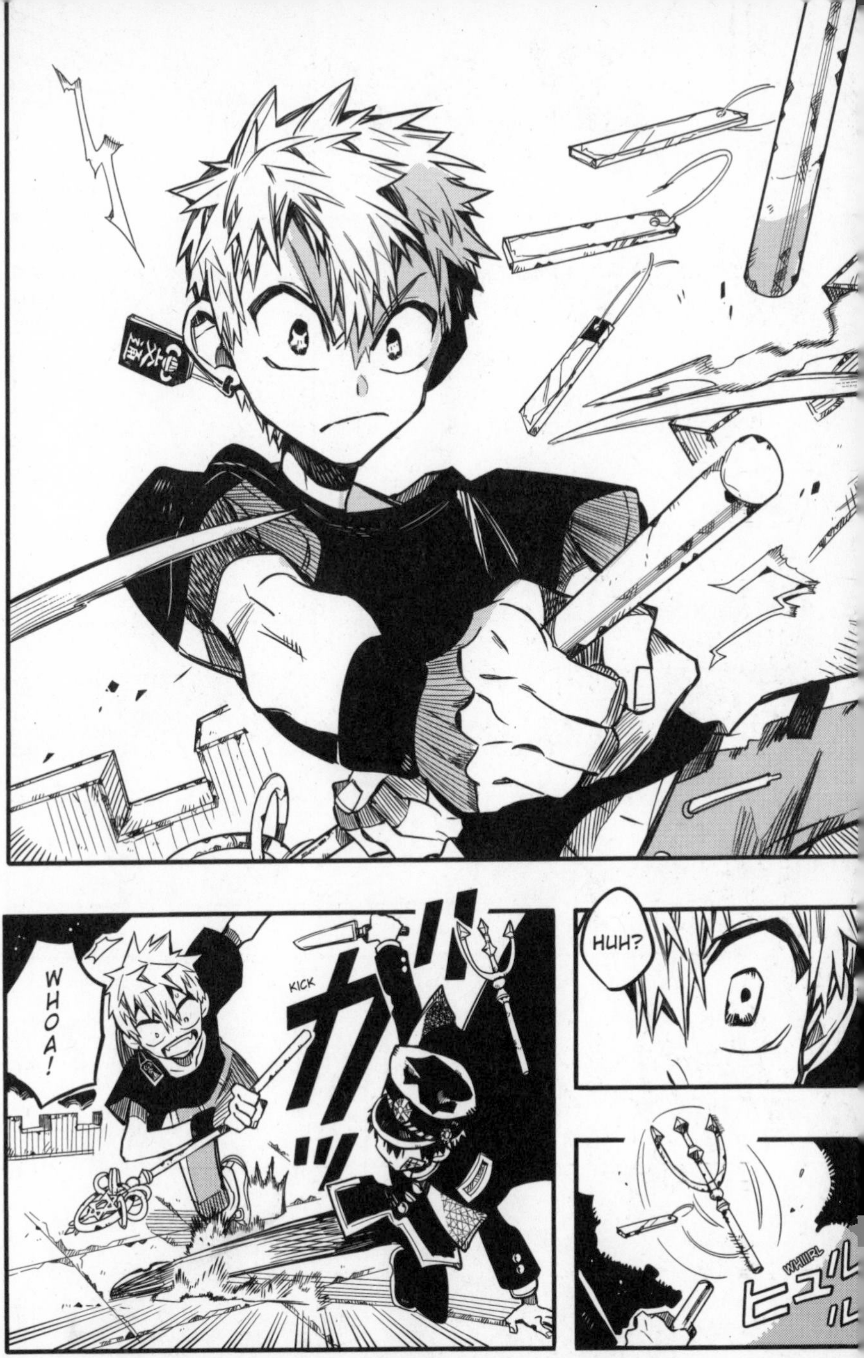
HUH?
WHIRL
ヒュルル
KICK
カッ
WHOA!

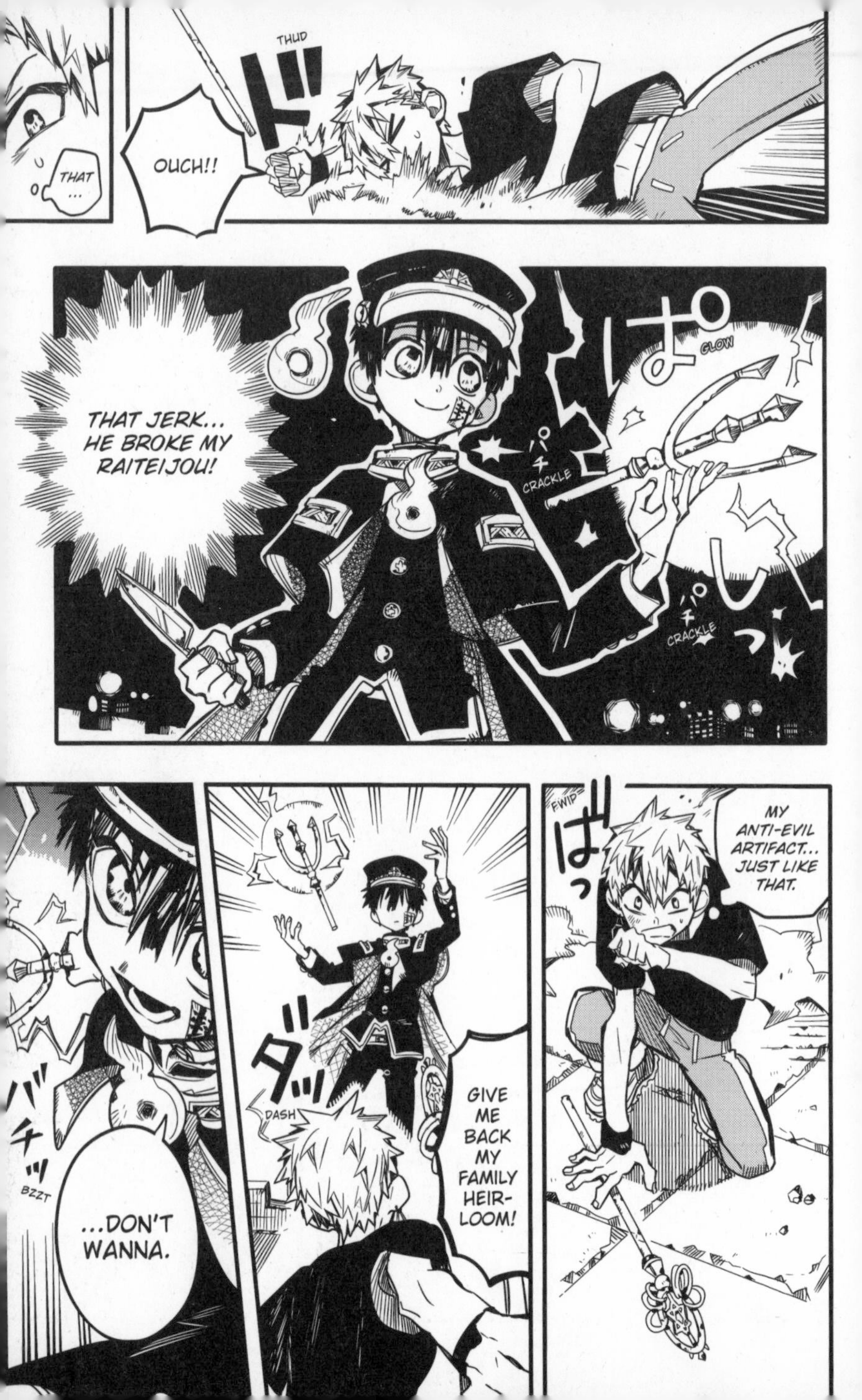
ド
THUD
OUCH!!
THAT ...
THAT JERK... HE BROKE MY RAITEIJOU!
ぱしっ
GLOW
パチ
CRACKLE
パチ
CRACKLE
ばっ
FWIP
MY ANTI-EVIL ARTIFACT... JUST LIKE THAT.
GIVE ME BACK MY FAMILY HEIR-LOOM!
ダッ
DASH
バチッ
BZZT
...DON'T WANNA.

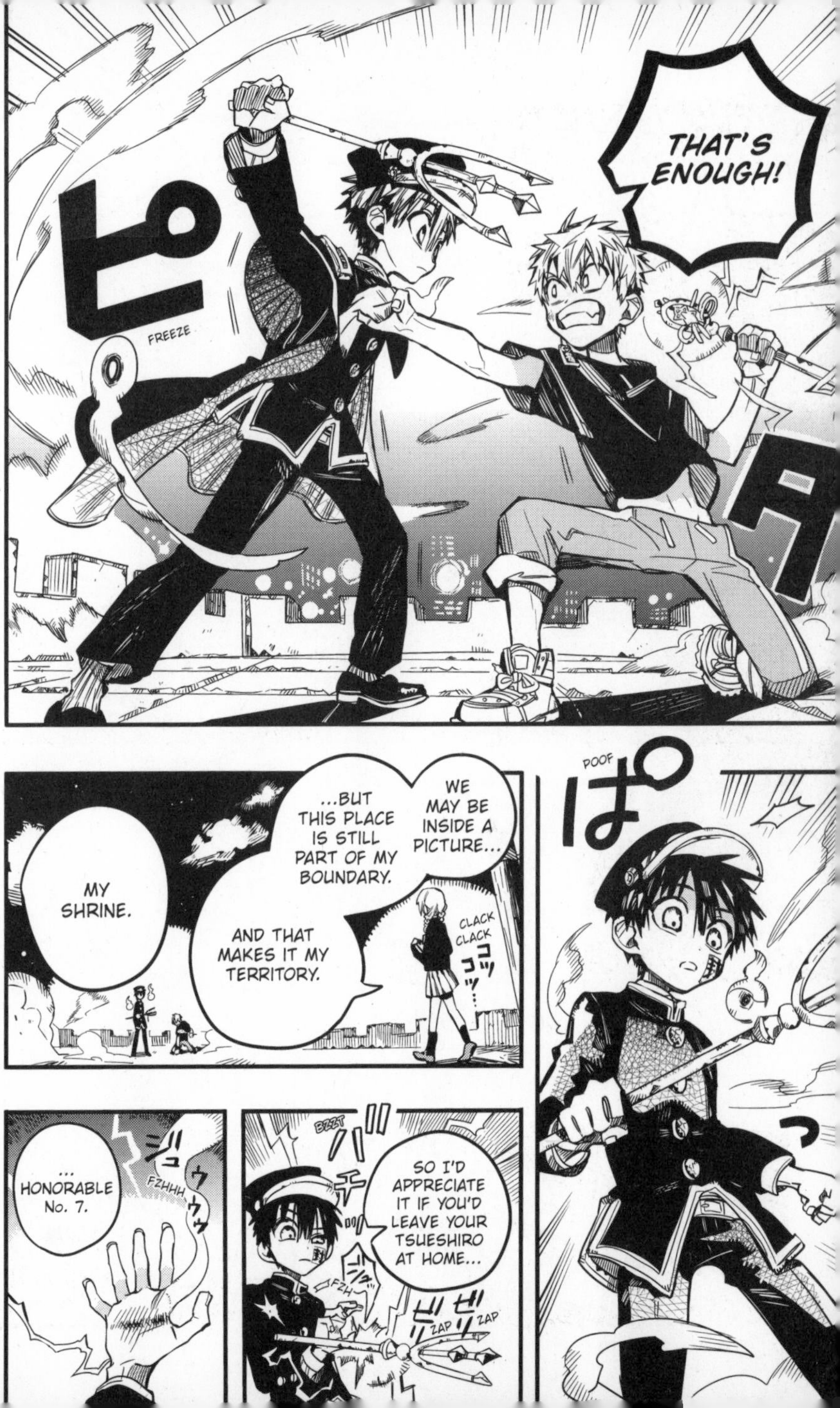
THAT'S ENOUGH!
ピ
FREEZE
タ
ぱ
POOF
っ
WE MAY BE INSIDE A PICTURE...
...BUT THIS PLACE IS STILL PART OF MY BOUNDARY.
CLACK CLACK
コツコツ…
AND THAT MAKES IT MY TERRITORY.
MY SHRINE.
BZZT
バチ
SO I'D APPRECIATE IT IF YOU'D LEAVE YOUR TSUESHIRO AT HOME...
FZH
ZAP ZAP
...HONORABLE No. 7.
FZHHH

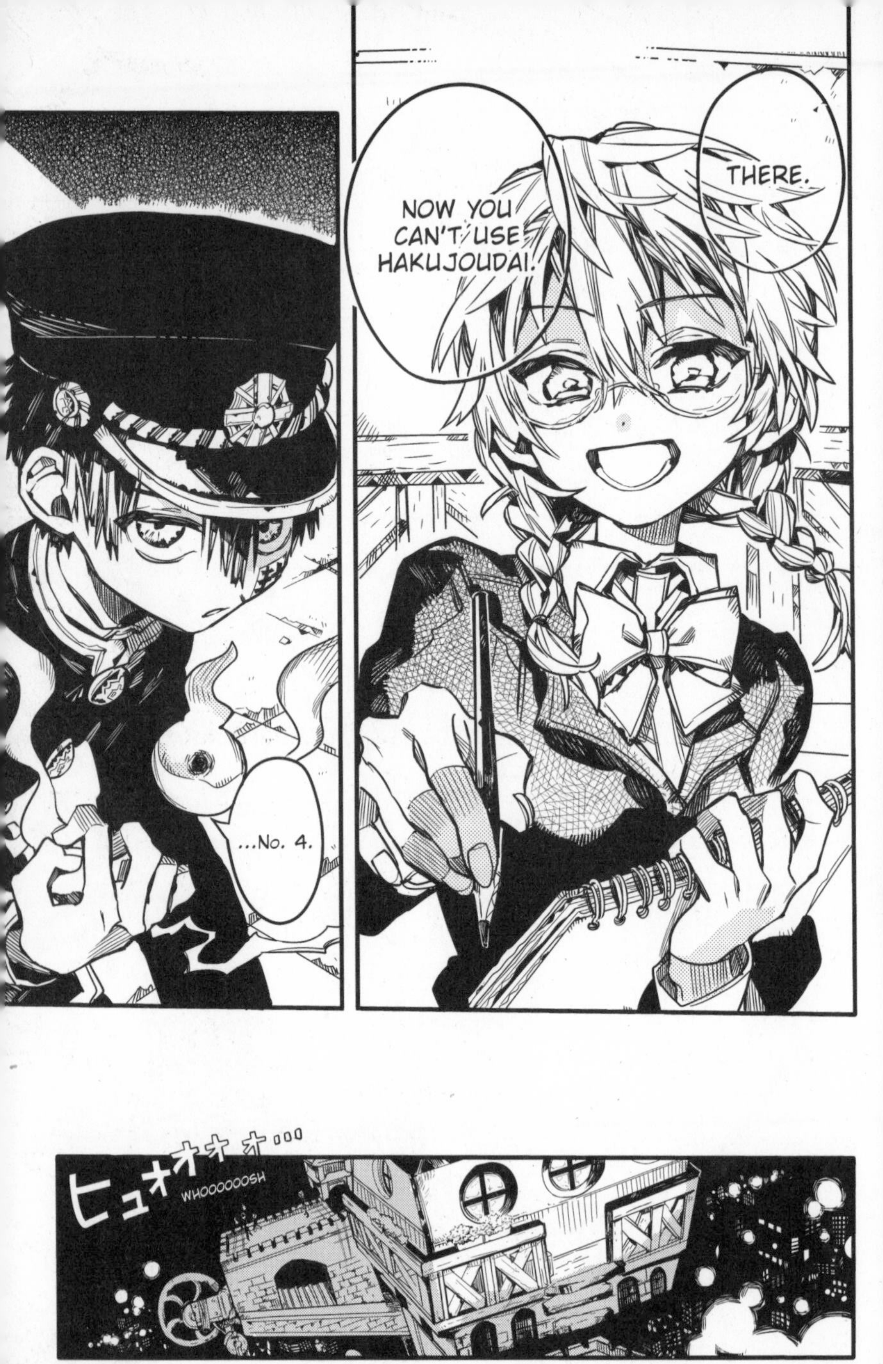
THERE.
NOW YOU CAN'T USE HAKUJOUDAI.
...No. 4.
ヒュオオオオ…
WHOOOOOOSH

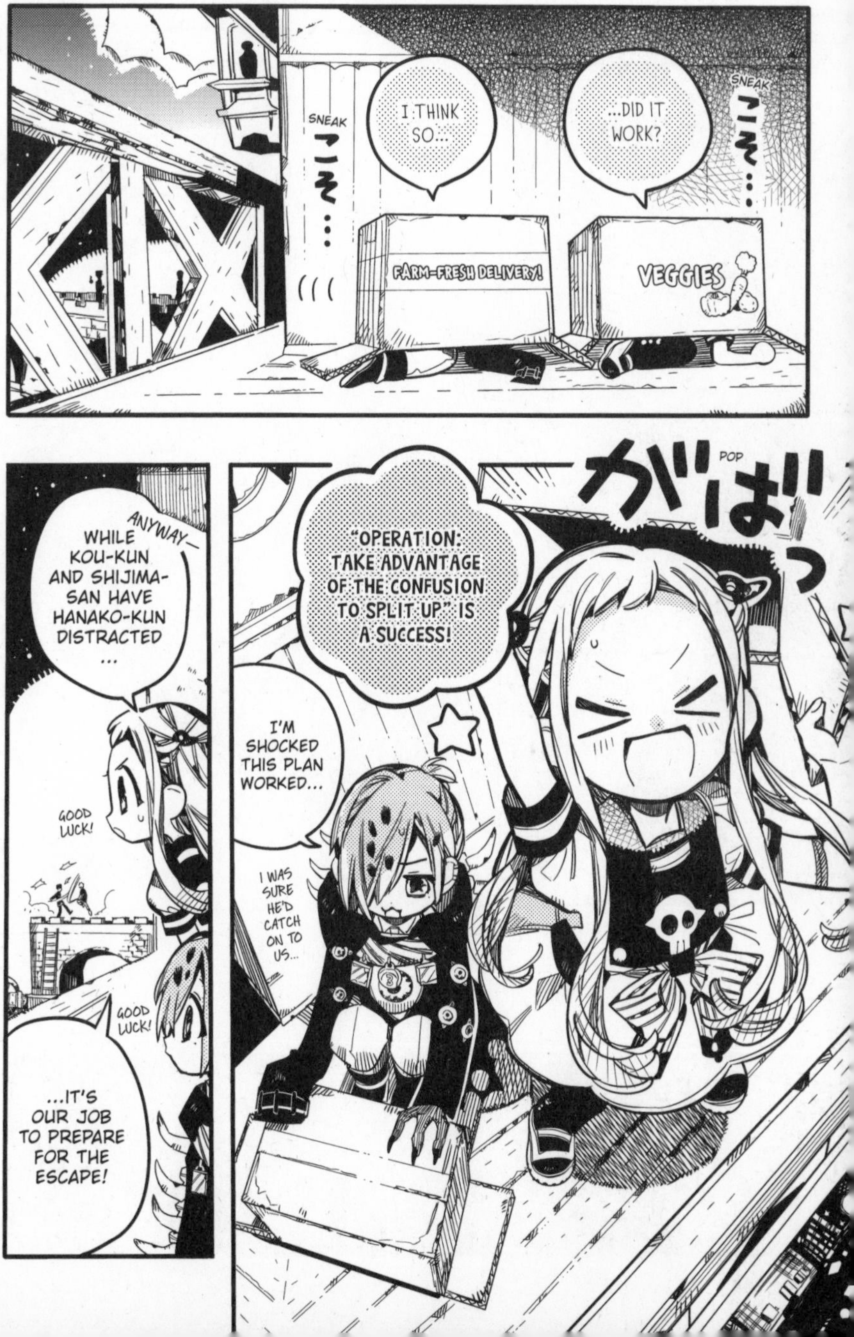
SNEAK
こそ…
...DID IT WORK?
I THINK SO...
SNEAK
こそ…
VEGGIES
FARM-FRESH DELIVERY!
POP
がばっ
"OPERATION: TAKE ADVANTAGE OF THE CONFUSION TO SPLIT UP" IS A SUCCESS!
I'M SHOCKED THIS PLAN WORKED...
I WAS SURE HE'D CATCH ON TO US...
ANYWAY— WHILE KOU-KUN AND SHIJIMA-SAN HAVE HANAKO-KUN DISTRACTED...
GOOD LUCK!
GOOD LUCK!
...IT'S OUR JOB TO PREPARE FOR THE ESCAPE!

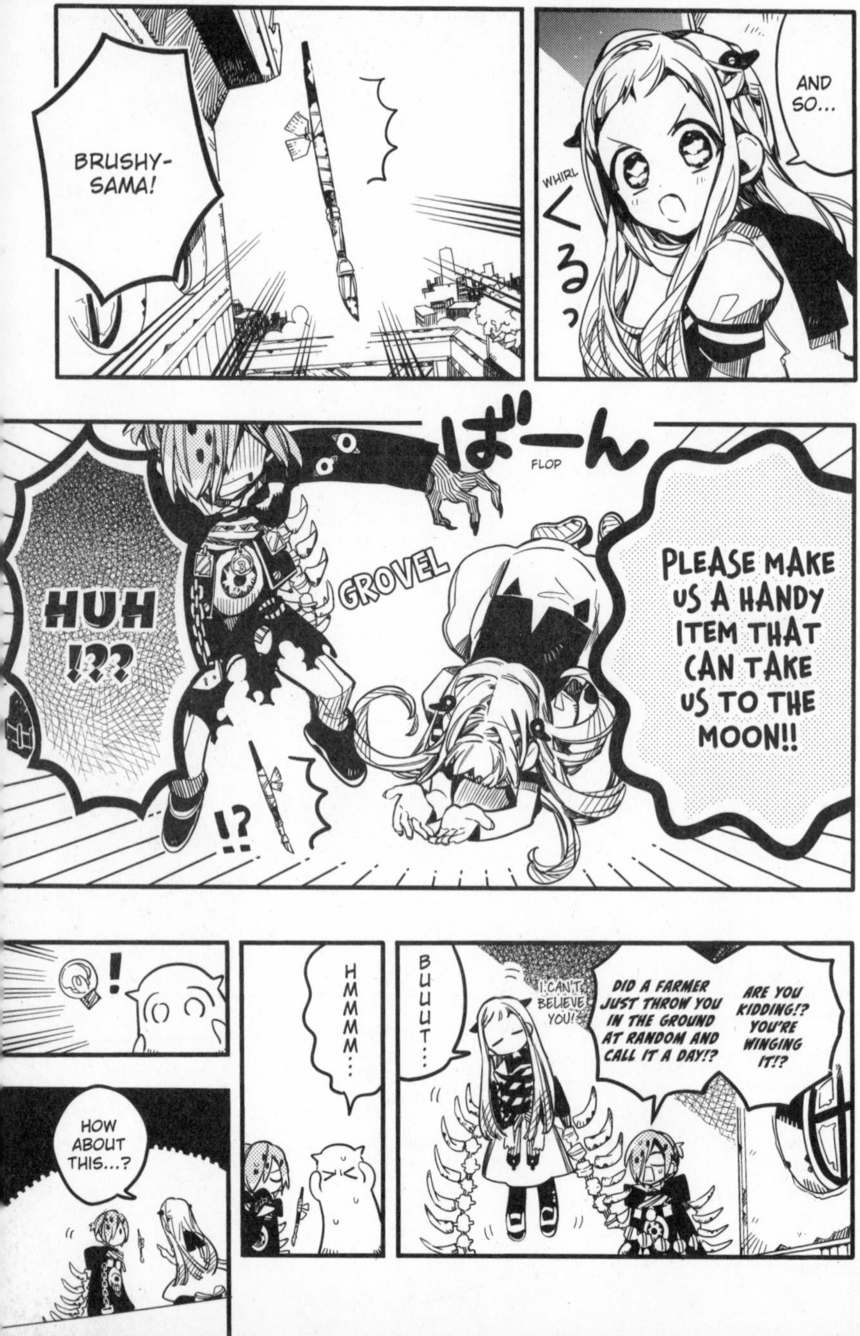
AND SO...
WHIRL
くるっ
BRUSHY-SAMA!
ばーん
FLOP
PLEASE MAKE US A HANDY ITEM THAT CAN TAKE US TO THE MOON!!
GROVEL
HUH!??
!?
ARE YOU KIDDING!? YOU'RE WINGING IT!?
DID A FARMER JUST THROW YOU IN THE GROUND AT RANDOM AND CALL IT A DAY!?
I CAN'T BELIEVE YOU!
BUUUT...
HMMMM...
!
HOW ABOUT THIS...?

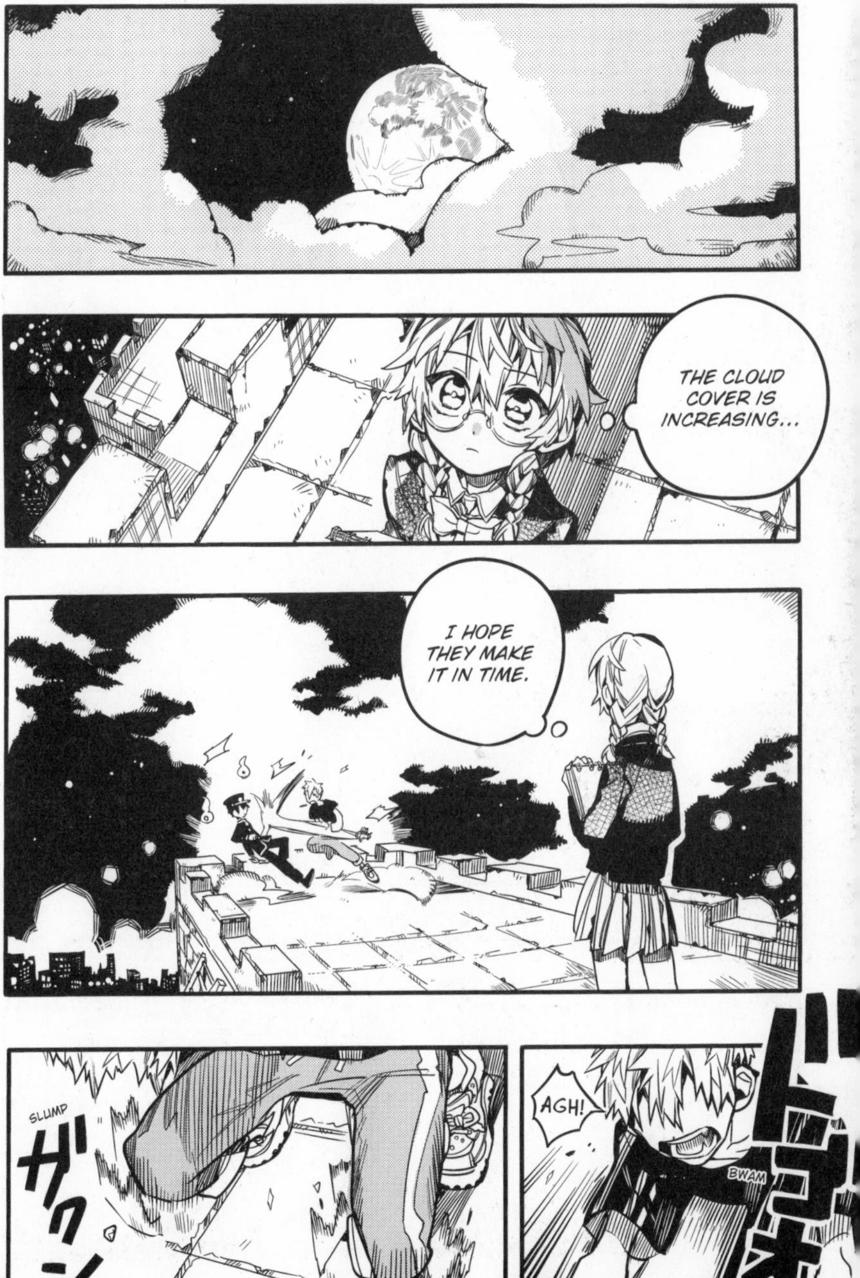
THE CLOUD COVER IS INCREASING...
I HOPE THEY MAKE IT IN TIME.
AGH!
BWAM
SLUMP
ガクン

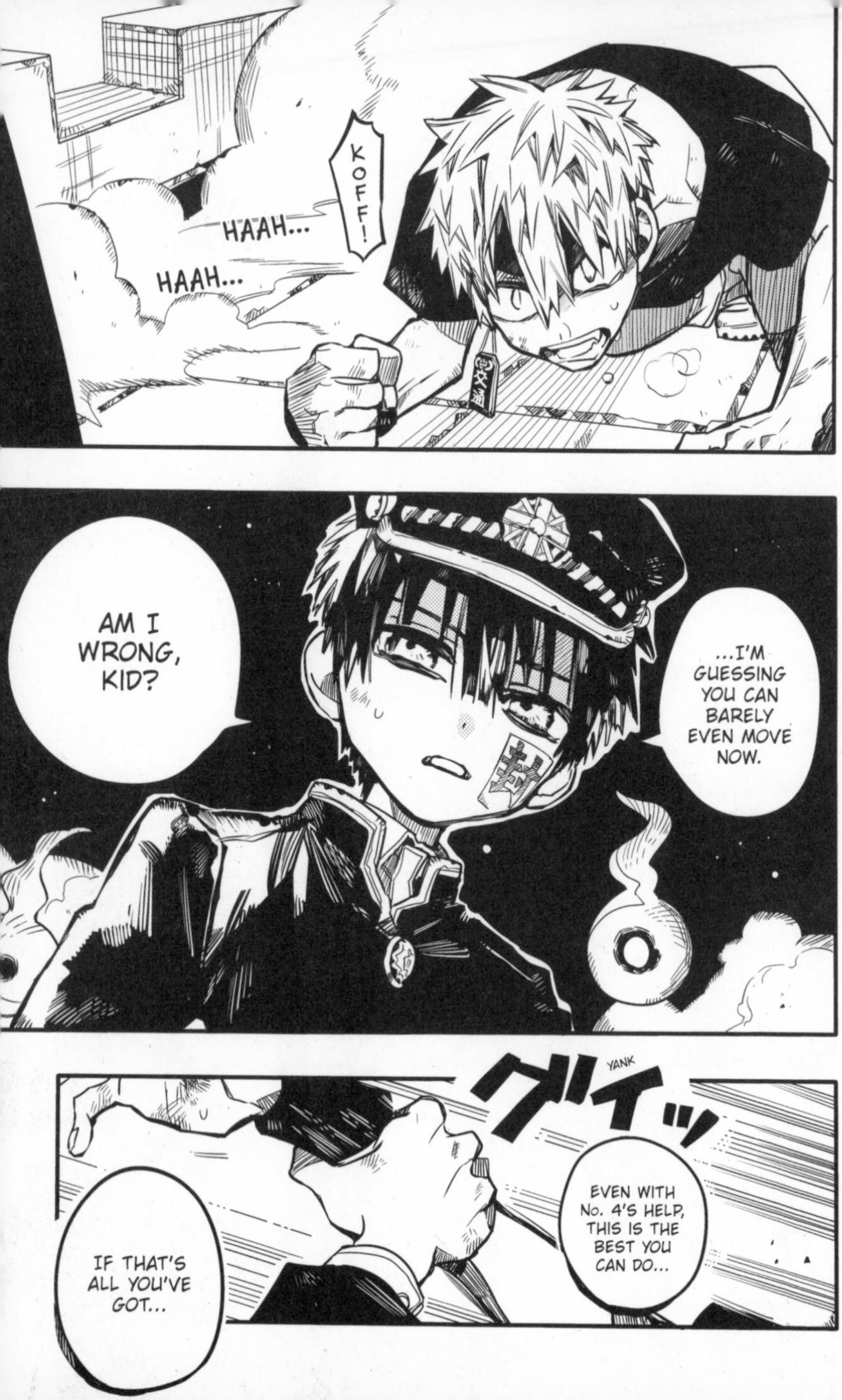
KOFF!
HAAH...
HAAH...
...I'M GUESSING YOU CAN BARELY EVEN MOVE NOW.
AM I WRONG, KID?
グイッ
YANK
EVEN WITH No. 4'S HELP, THIS IS THE BEST YOU CAN DO...
IF THAT'S ALL YOU'VE GOT...

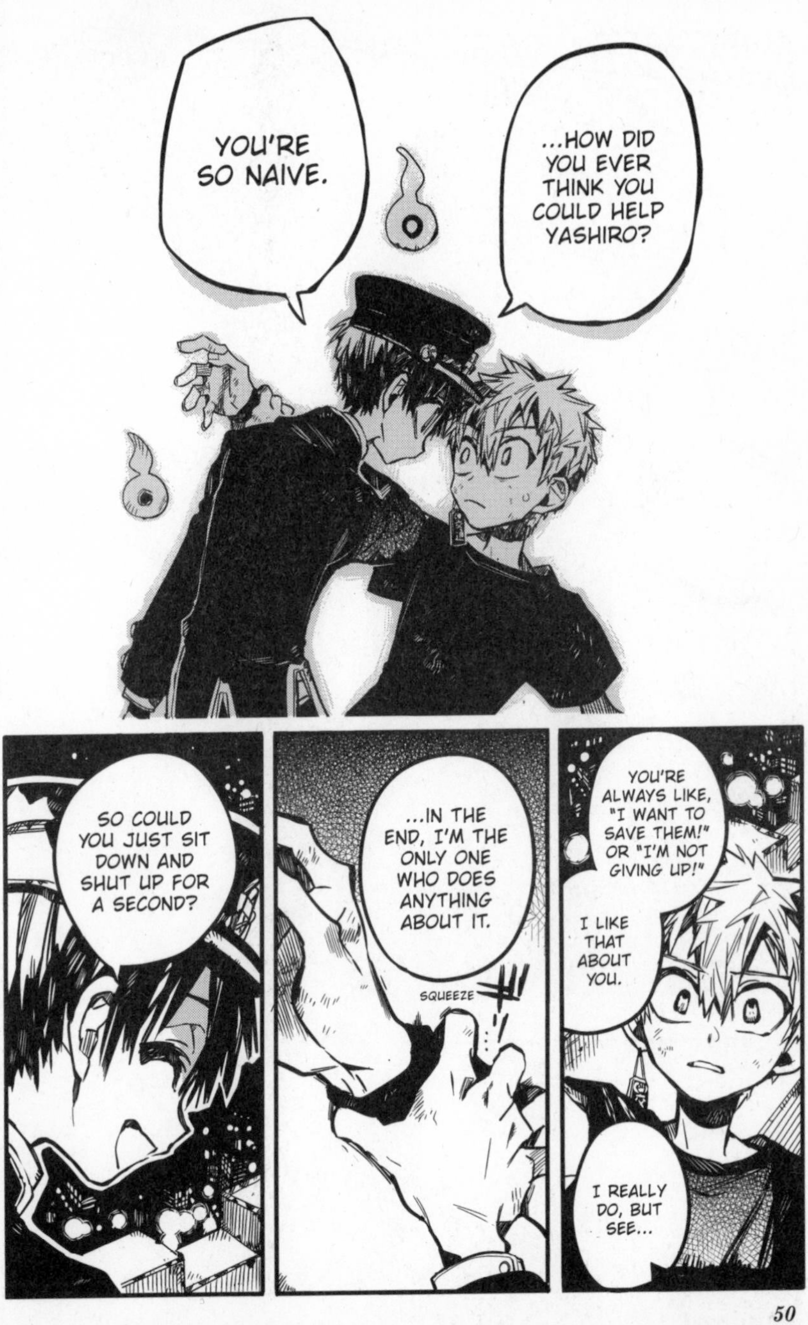
...HOW DID YOU EVER THINK YOU COULD HELP YASHIRO?
YOU'RE SO NAIVE.
YOU'RE ALWAYS LIKE, "I WANT TO SAVE THEM!" OR "I'M NOT GIVING UP!"
I LIKE THAT ABOUT YOU.
I REALLY DO, BUT SEE...
...IN THE END, I'M THE ONLY ONE WHO DOES ANYTHING ABOUT IT.
SQUEEZE
SO COULD YOU JUST SIT DOWN AND SHUT UP FOR A SECOND?

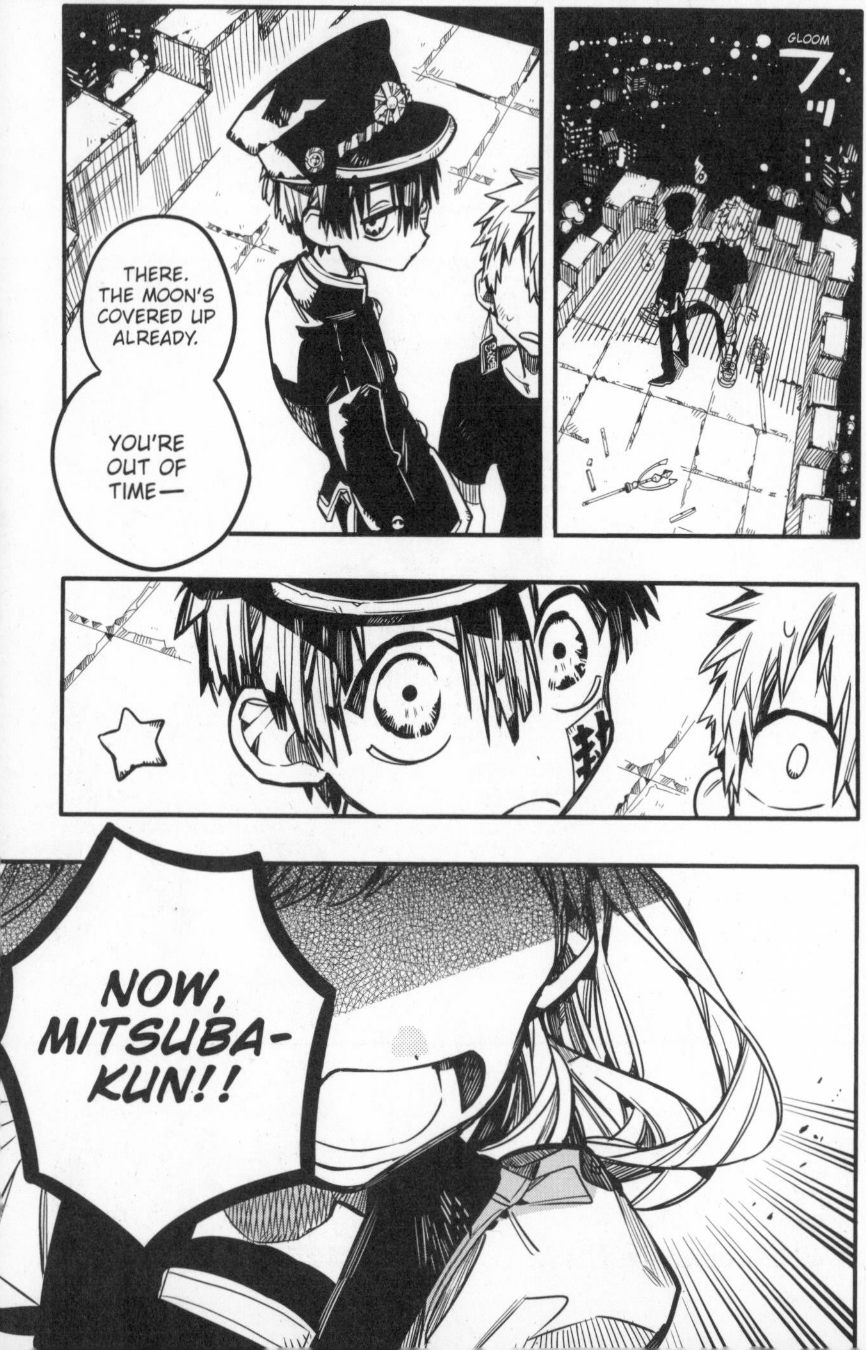
GLOOM
THERE. THE MOON'S COVERED UP ALREADY.
YOU'RE OUT OF TIME—
NOW, MITSUBA-KUN!!

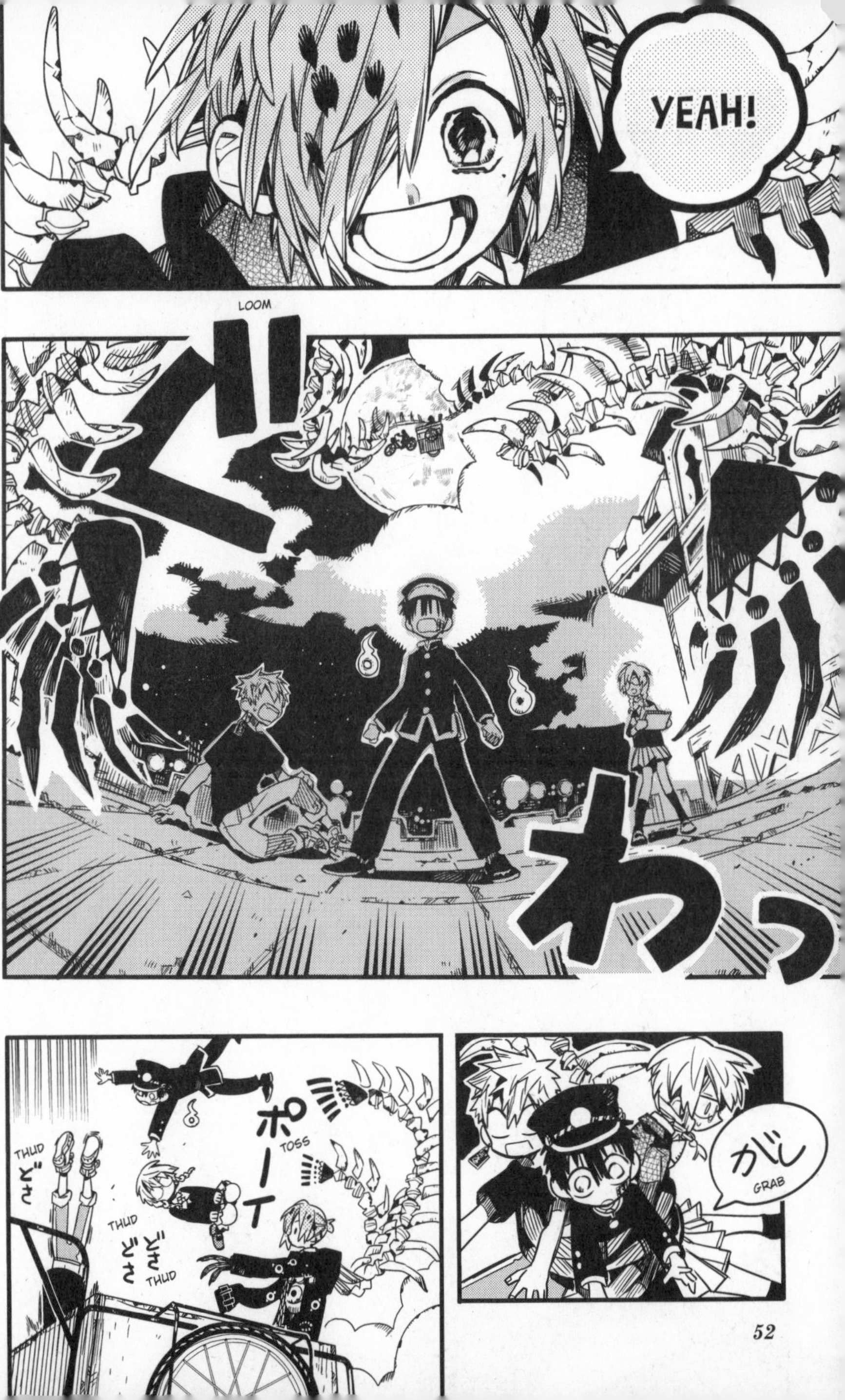
YEAH!
LOOM
わっ
がし
GRAB
ポーイ
TOSS
THUD
どさ
THUD
どさ
どさ
THUD

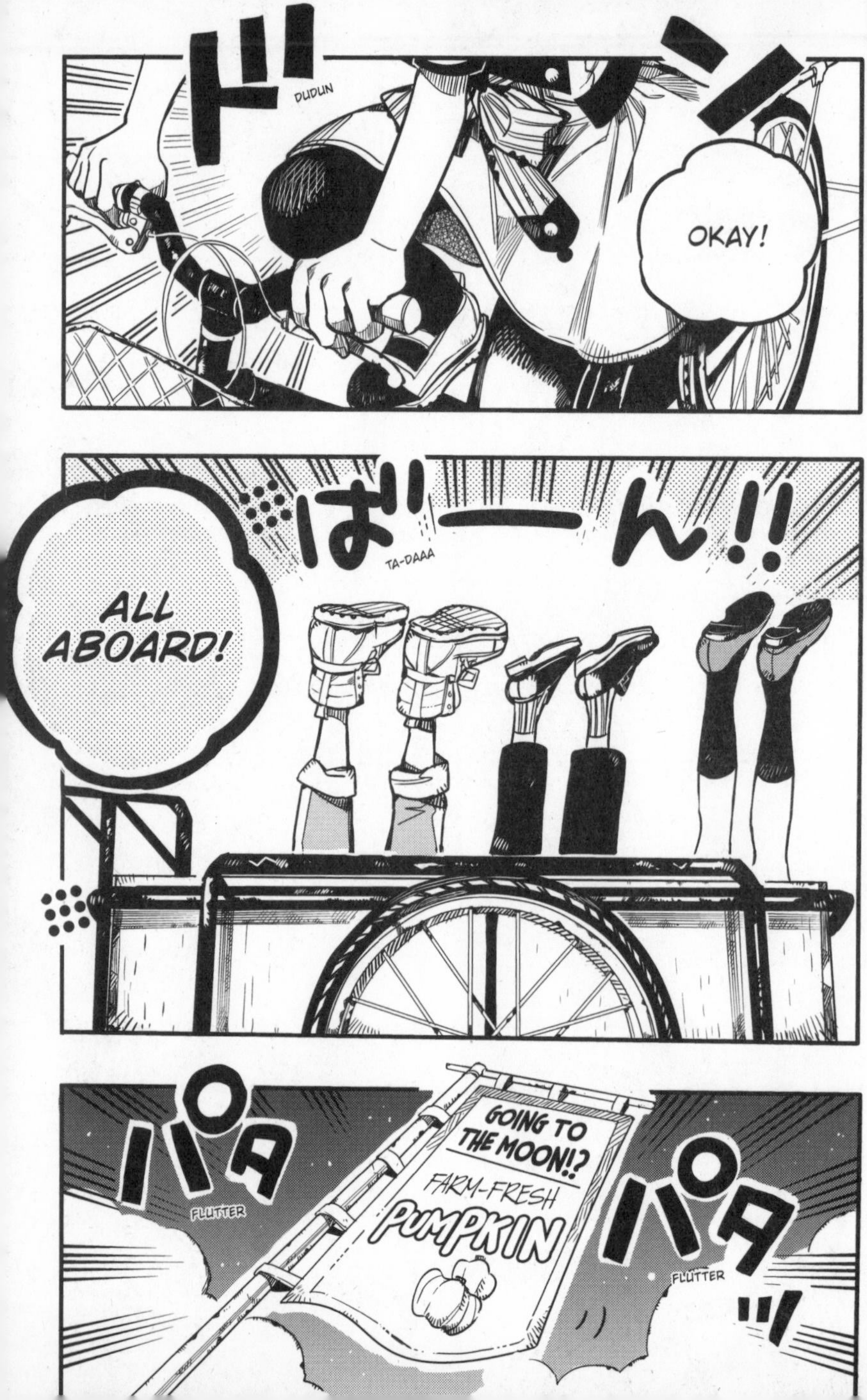
ドン
DUDUN
OKAY!
ばーん!!
TA-DAAA
ALL ABOARD!
GOING TO THE MOON!?
FARM-FRESH PUMPKIN
パタ
FLUTTER
パタッ
FLUTTER

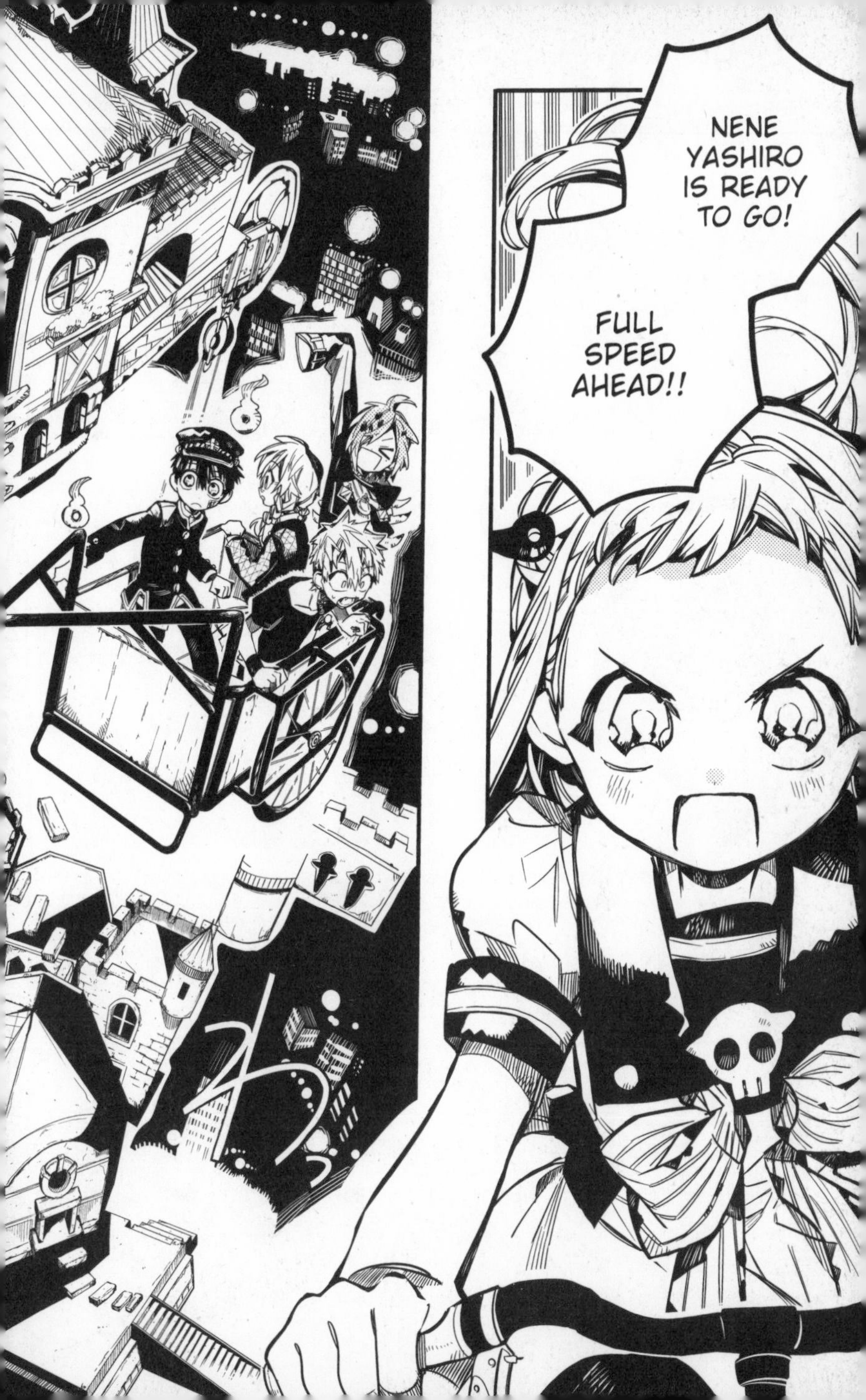
NENE YASHIRO IS READY TO GO!
FULL SPEED AHEAD!!

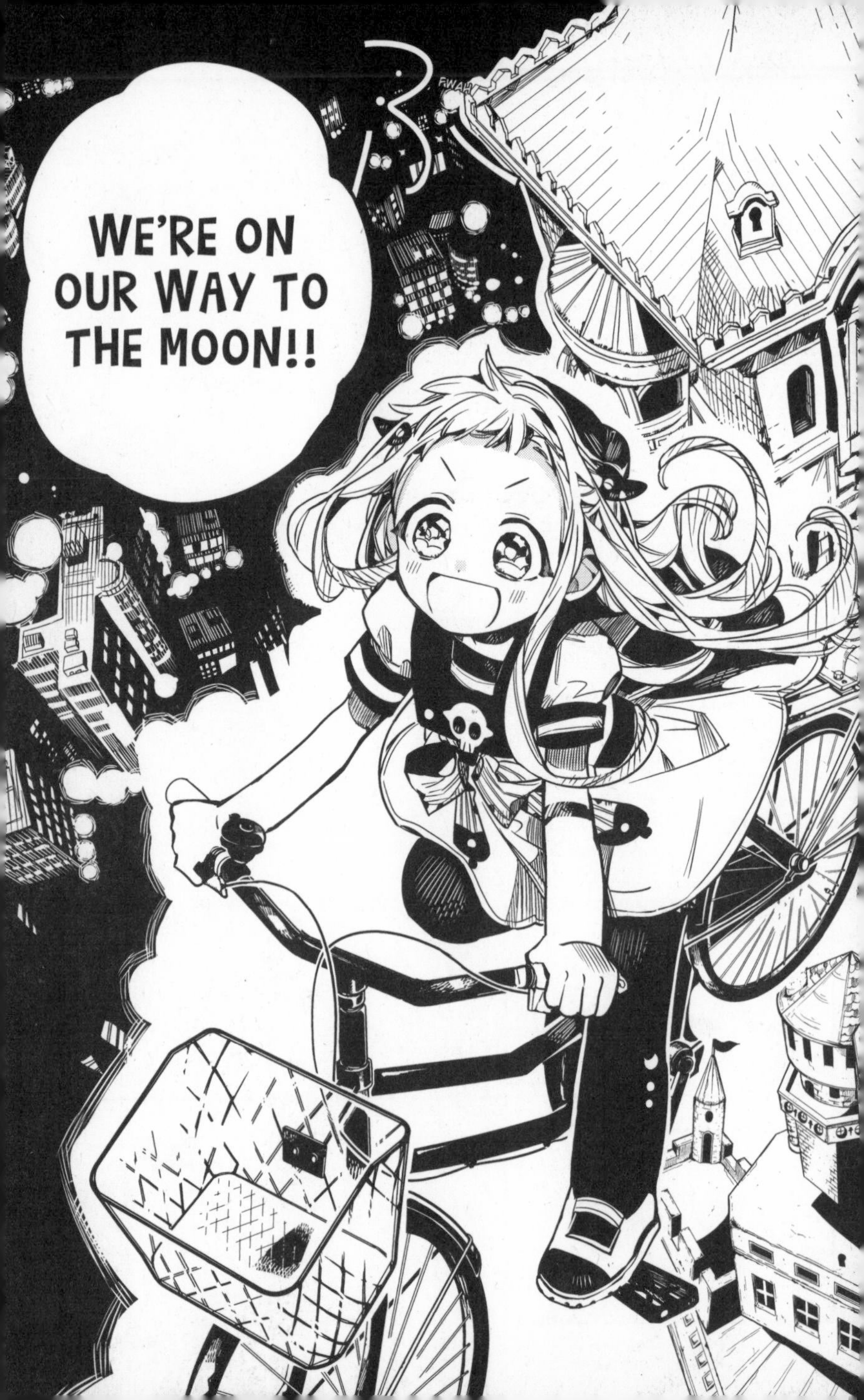
WE'RE ON OUR WAY TO THE MOON!!
FWAH

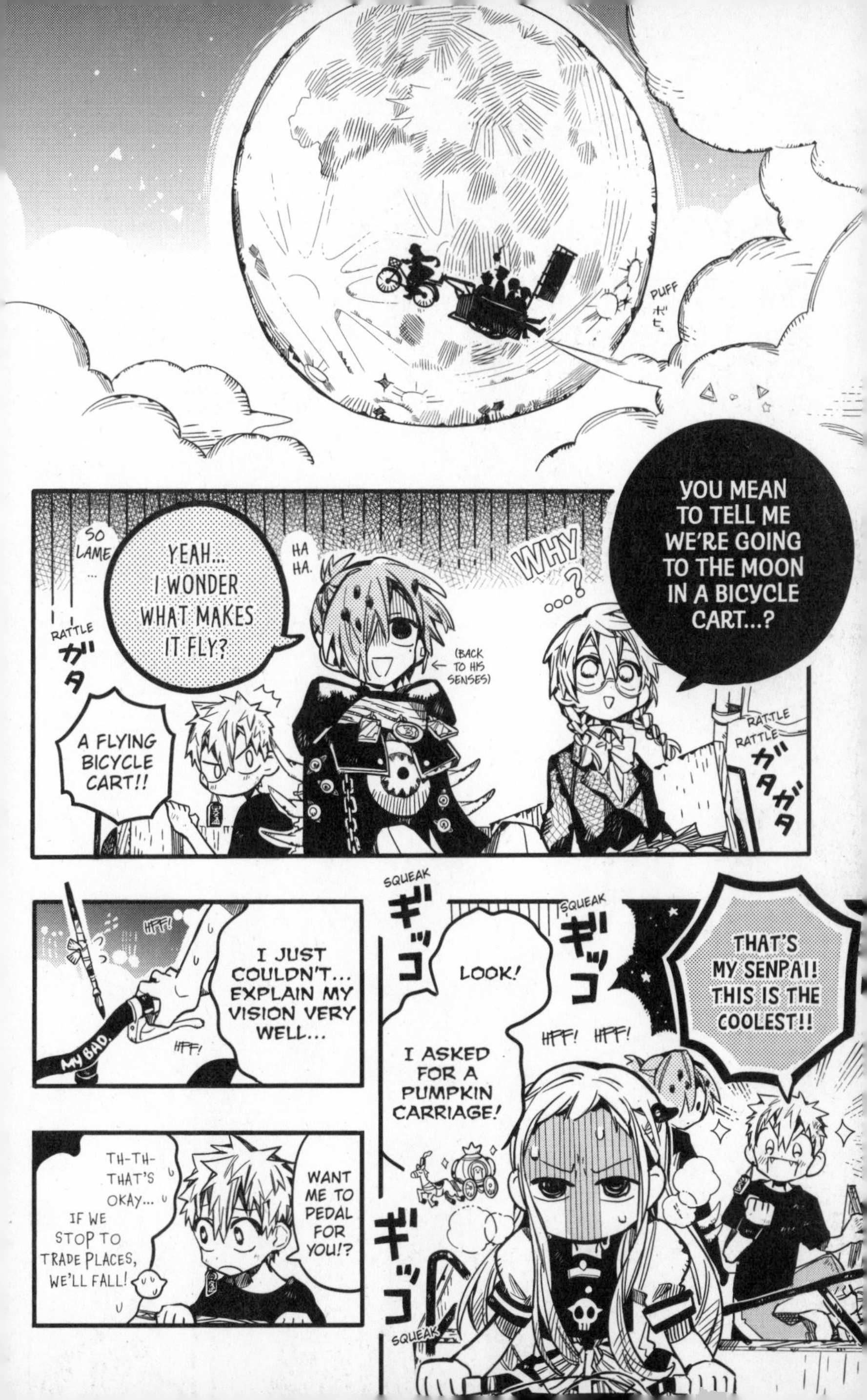
PUFF
ボヒュ
YOU MEAN TO TELL ME WE'RE GOING TO THE MOON IN A BICYCLE CART...?
WHY...?
RATTLE RATTLE
ガタガタ
(BACK TO HIS SENSES)
HA HA.
YEAH... I WONDER WHAT MAKES IT FLY?
SO LAME...
RATTLE
ガタ
A FLYING BICYCLE CART!!
THAT'S MY SENPAI! THIS IS THE COOLEST!!
SQUEAK
ギッコ
SQUEAK
ギッコ
LOOK!
HFF! HFF!
I ASKED FOR A PUMPKIN CARRIAGE!
ギッコ
SQUEAK
I JUST COULDN'T... EXPLAIN MY VISION VERY WELL...
HFF!
HFF!
MY BAD.
WANT ME TO PEDAL FOR YOU!?
TH-TH-THAT'S OKAY... IF WE STOP TO TRADE PLACES, WE'LL FALL!

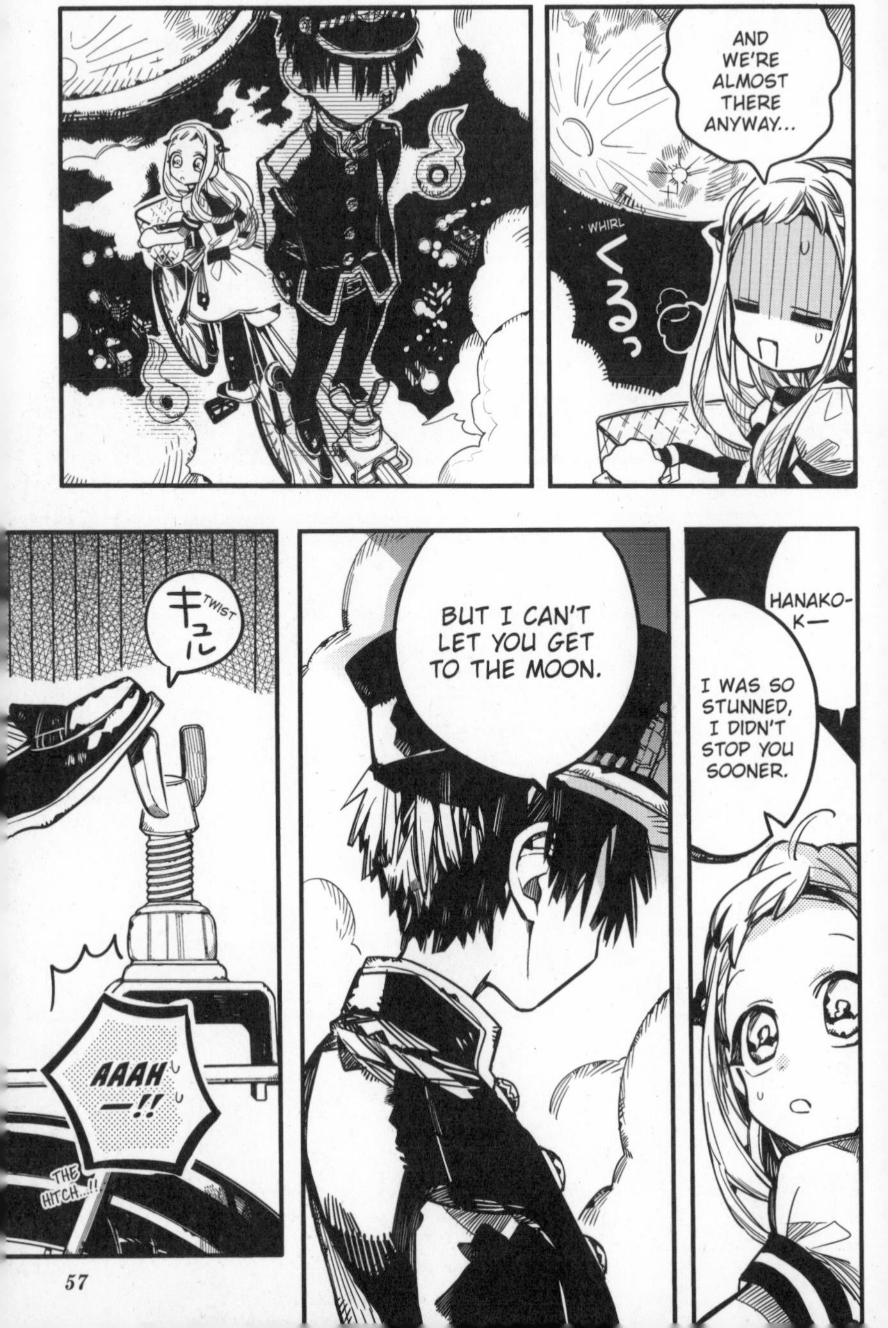
AND WE'RE ALMOST THERE ANYWAY...
WHIRL
くるっ
HANAKO-K—
I WAS SO STUNNED, I DIDN'T STOP YOU SOONER.
BUT I CAN'T LET YOU GET TO THE MOON.
キュル
TWIST
AAAH—!!
THE HITCH...!!

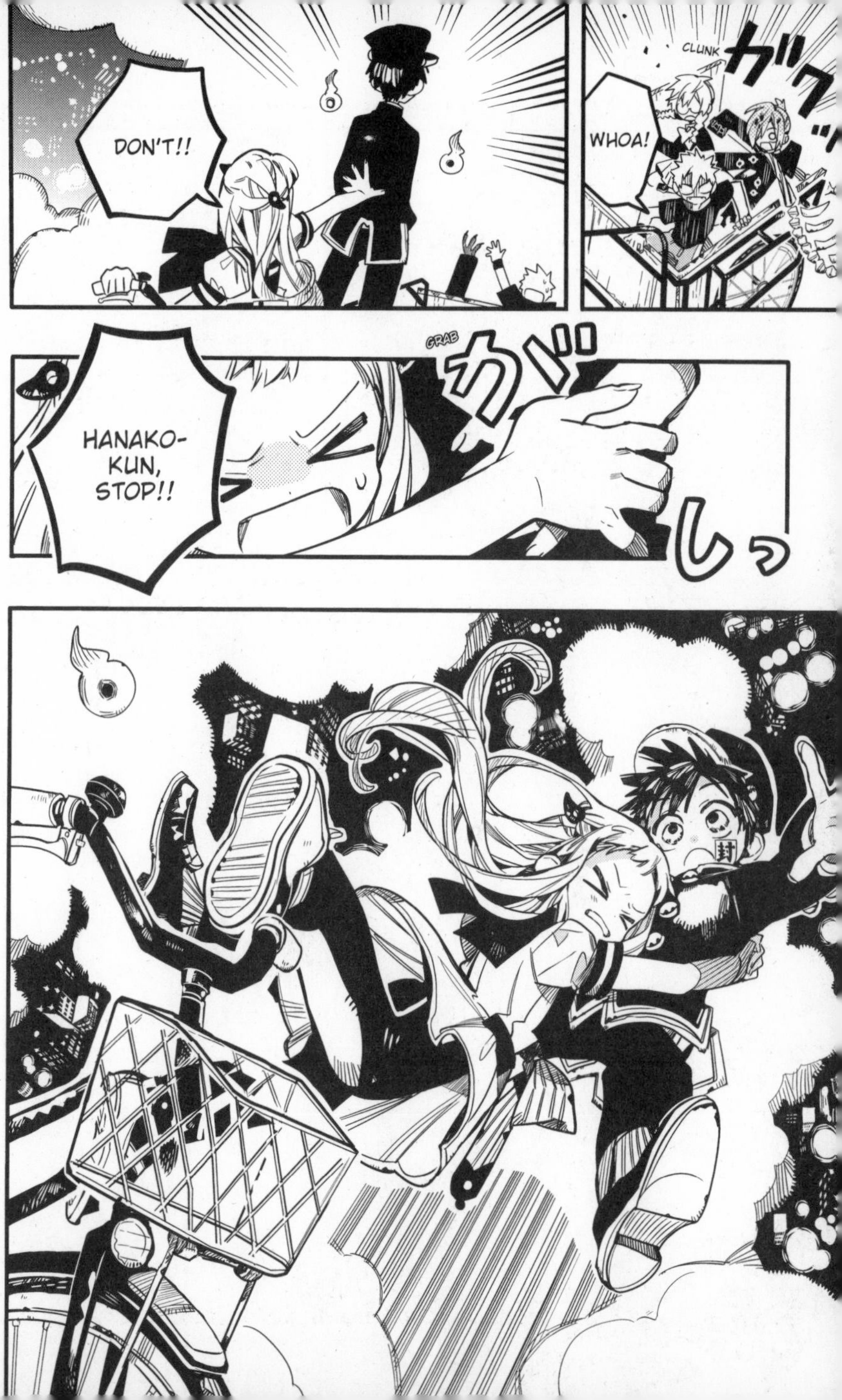
CLUNK
ガクッ
WHOA!
DON'T!!
GRAB
がしっ
HANAKO-KUN, STOP!!

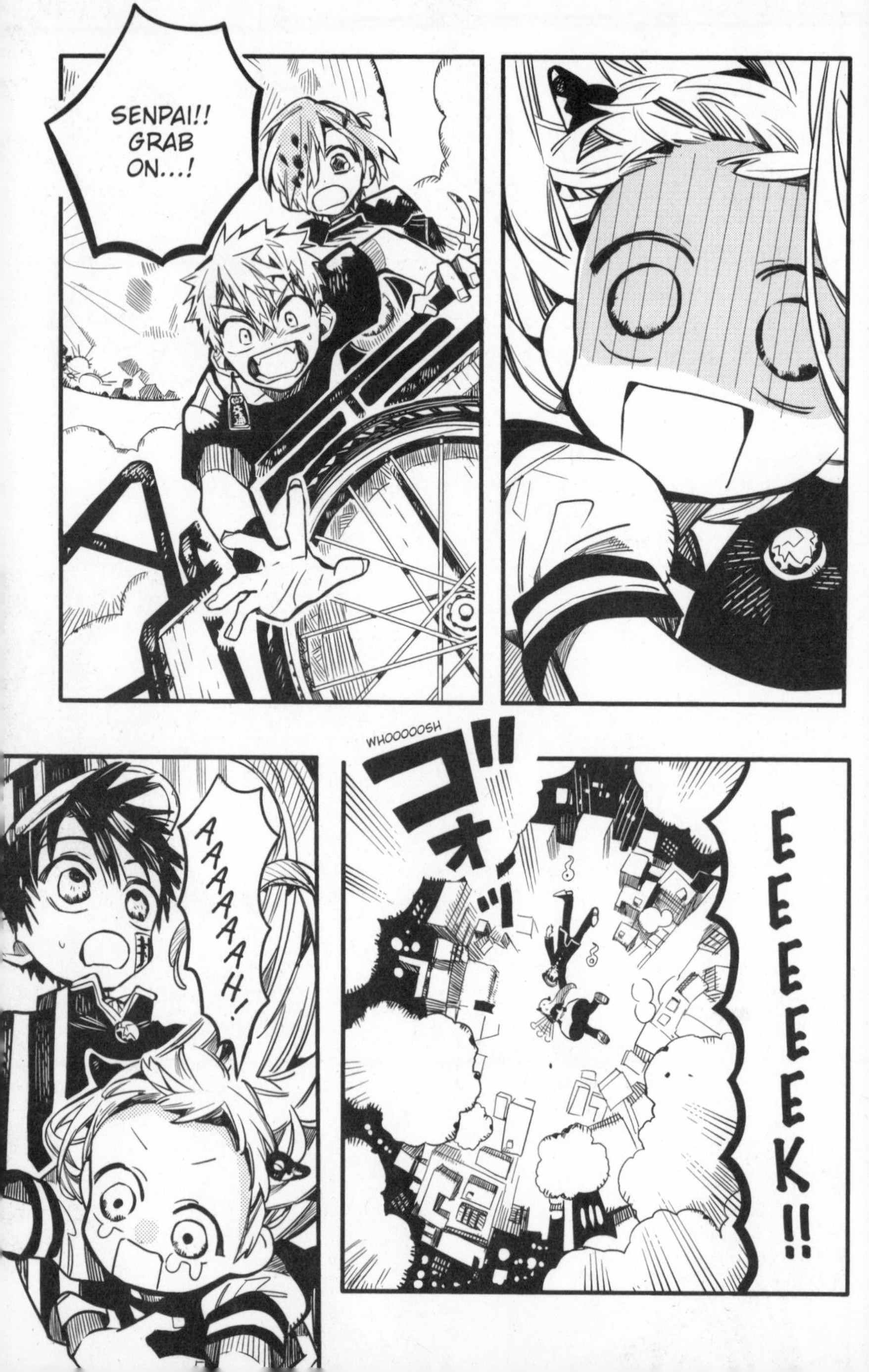
SENPAI!! GRAB ON...!
WHOOOOOSH
EEEEEEK!!
AAAAAAAH!

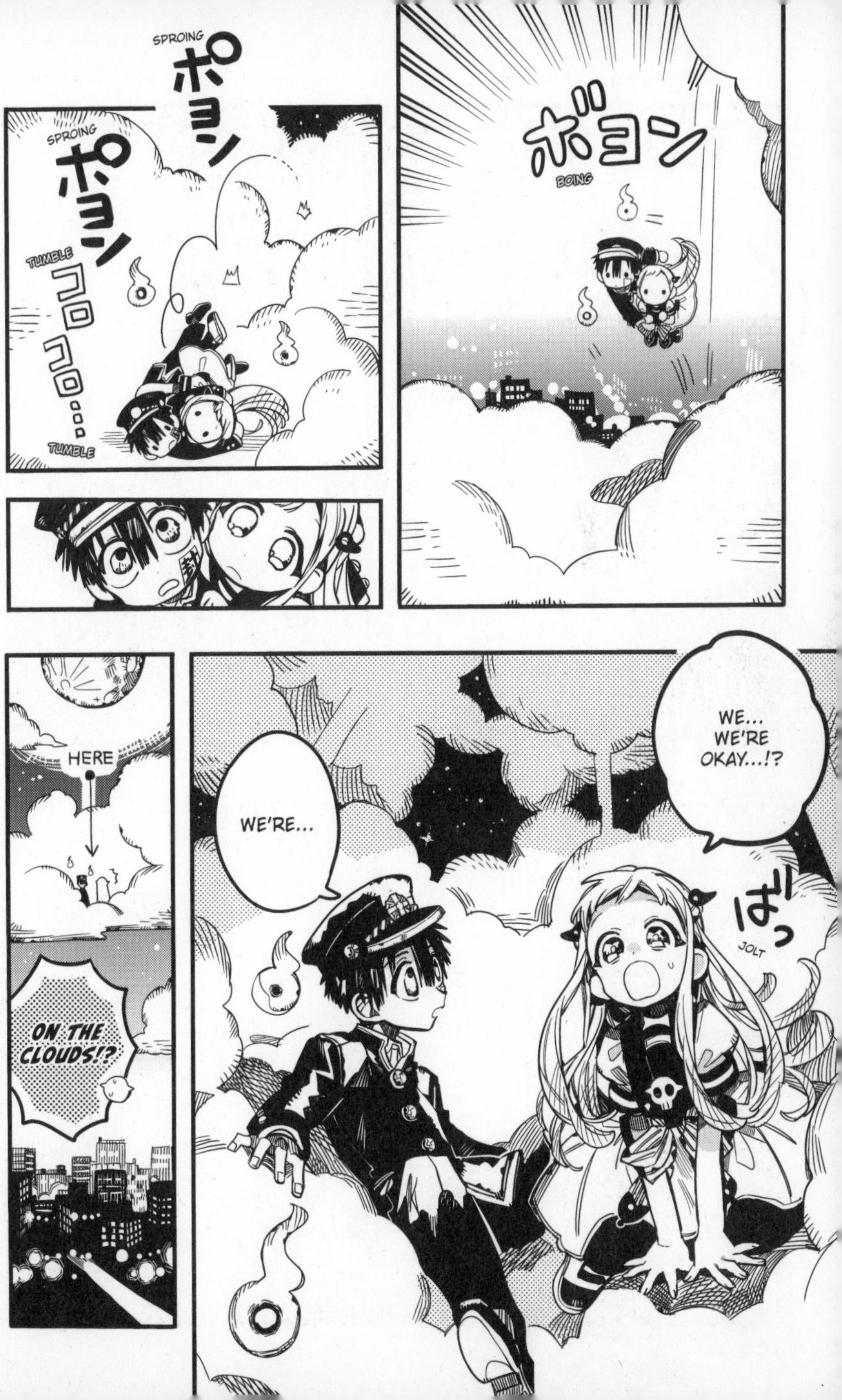
ボヨン
BOING
ポヨン
SPROING
ポヨン
SPROING
コロコロ…
TUMBLE
TUMBLE
WE... WE'RE OKAY...!?
ばっ
JOLT
WE'RE...
HERE
ON THE CLOUDS!?

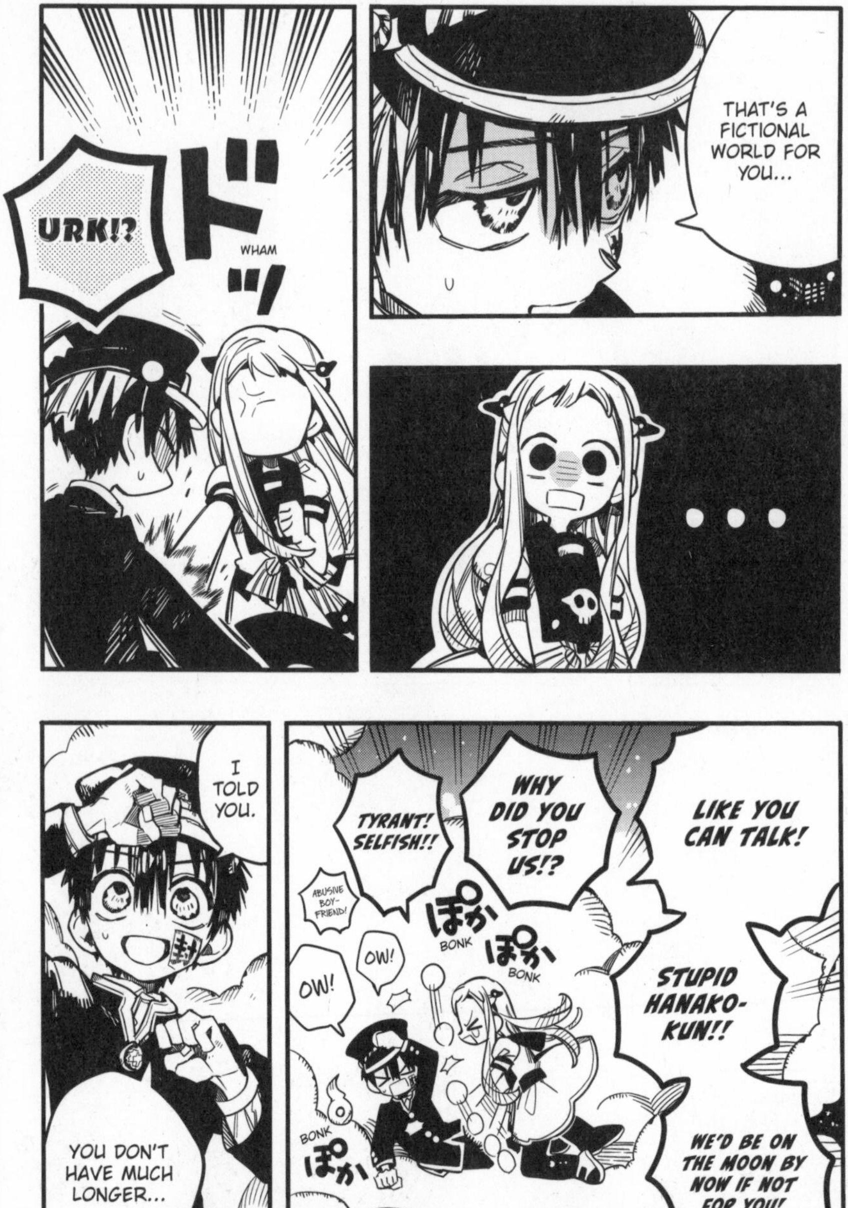
THAT'S A FICTIONAL WORLD FOR YOU...
...
URK!?
ドッ
WHAM
LIKE YOU CAN TALK!
WHY DID YOU STOP US!?
TYRANT! SELFISH!!
STUPID HANAKO-KUN!!
ABUSIVE BOY-FRIEND!
ぽか
BONK
ぽか
BONK
OW!
OW!
WE'D BE ON THE MOON BY NOW IF NOT FOR YOU!
BONK
ぽか
I TOLD YOU.
YOU DON'T HAVE MUCH LONGER...

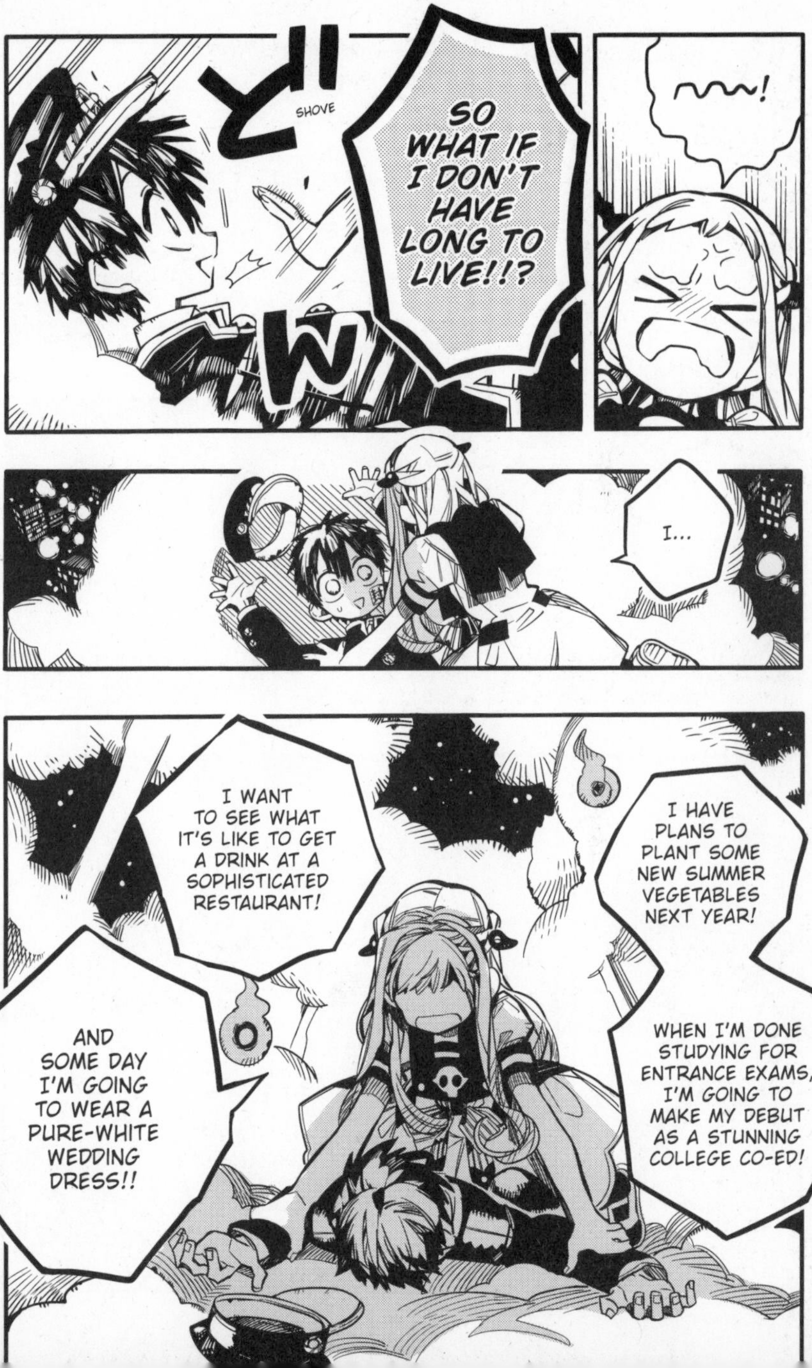
SHOVE
SO WHAT IF I DON'T HAVE LONG TO LIVE!!?
I...
I HAVE PLANS TO PLANT SOME NEW SUMMER VEGETABLES NEXT YEAR!
I WANT TO SEE WHAT IT'S LIKE TO GET A DRINK AT A SOPHISTICATED RESTAURANT!
WHEN I'M DONE STUDYING FOR ENTRANCE EXAMS, I'M GOING TO MAKE MY DEBUT AS A STUNNING COLLEGE CO-ED!
AND SOME DAY I'M GOING TO WEAR A PURE-WHITE WEDDING DRESS!!

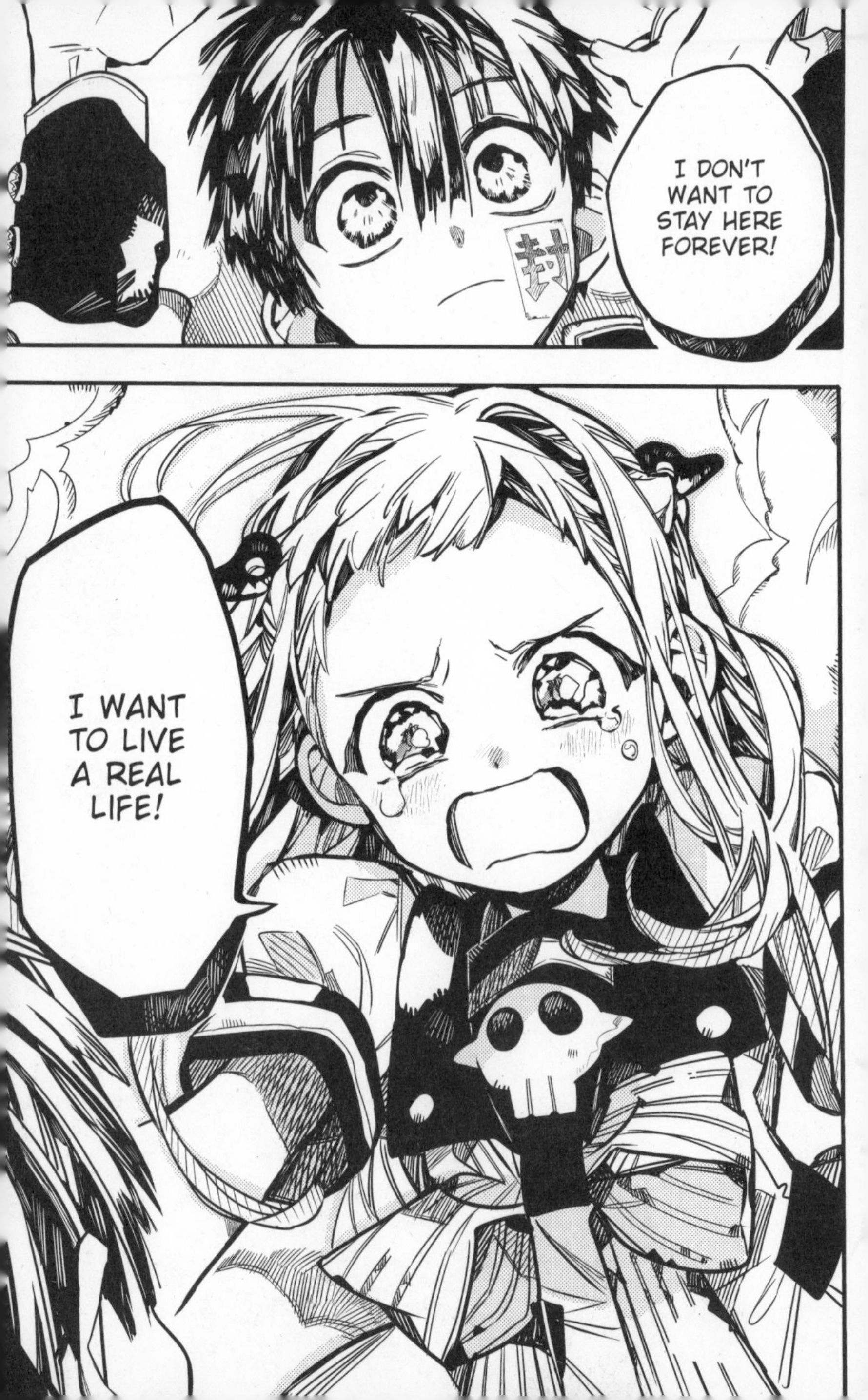
I DON'T WANT TO STAY HERE FOREVER!
I WANT TO LIVE A REAL LIFE!

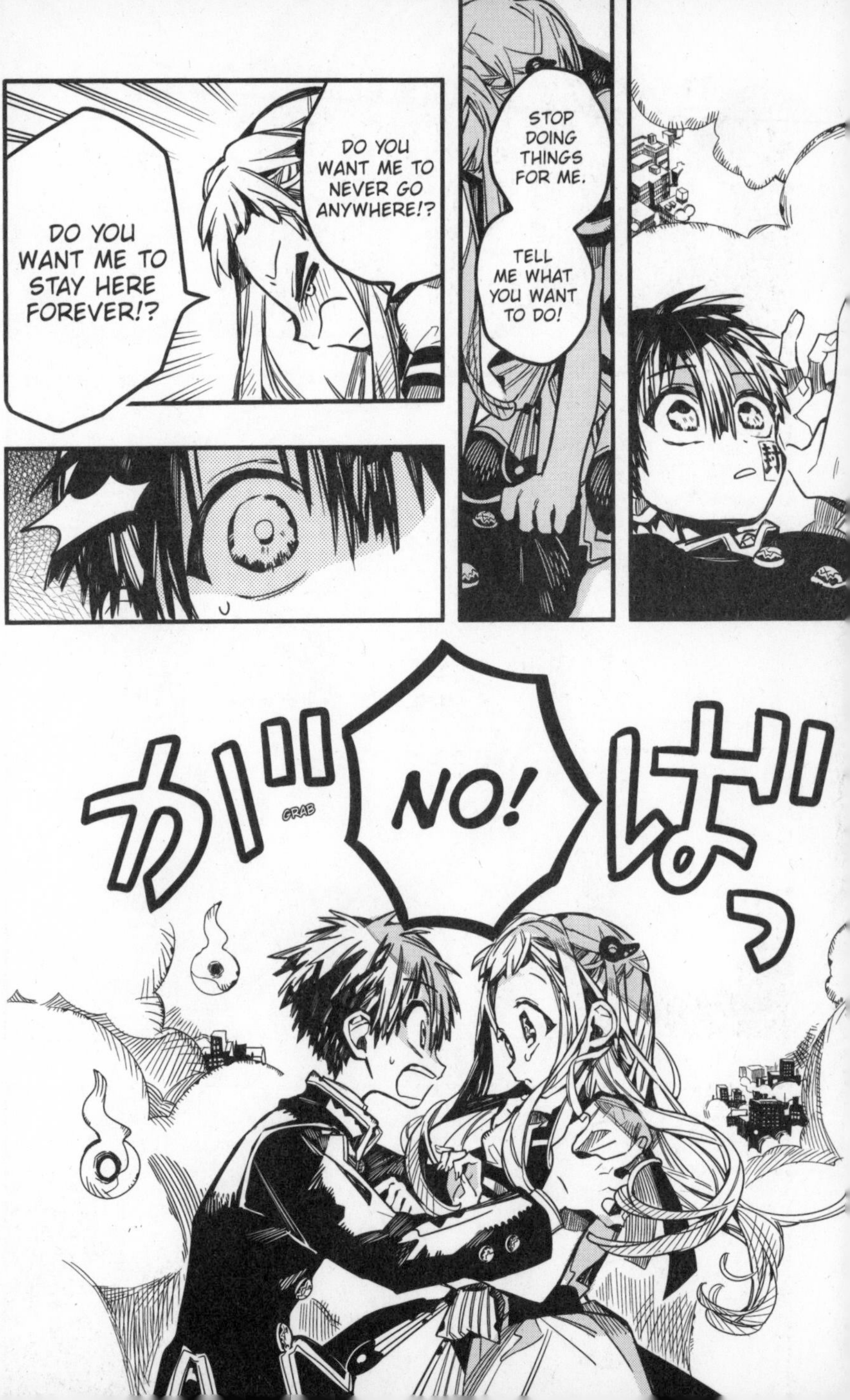
STOP DOING THINGS FOR ME.
TELL ME WHAT YOU WANT TO DO!
DO YOU WANT ME TO NEVER GO ANYWHERE!?
DO YOU WANT ME TO STAY HERE FOREVER!?
がばっ
GRAB
NO!

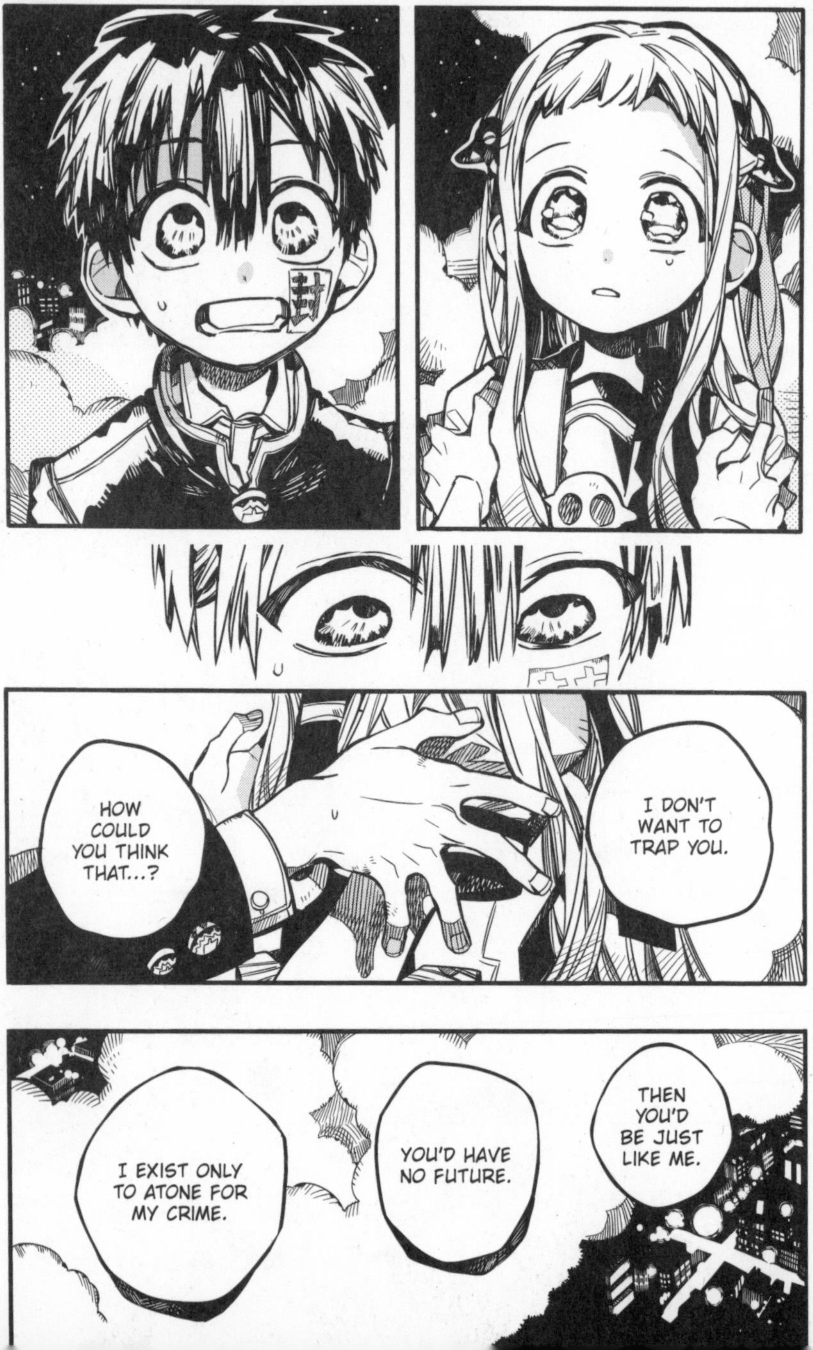
I DON'T WANT TO TRAP YOU.
HOW COULD YOU THINK THAT...?
THEN YOU'D BE JUST LIKE ME.
YOU'D HAVE NO FUTURE.
I EXIST ONLY TO ATONE FOR MY CRIME.

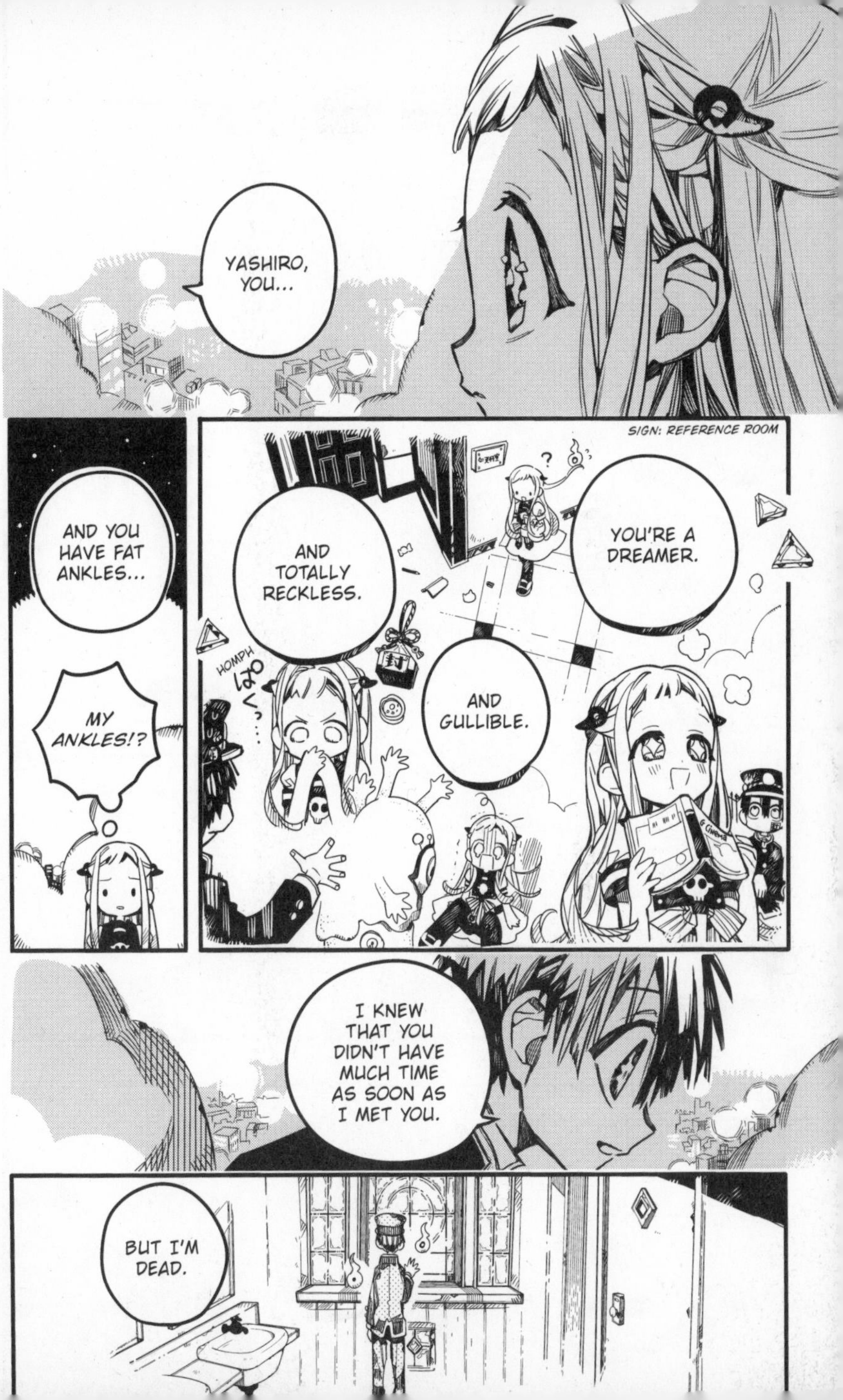
YASHIRO, YOU...
SIGN: REFERENCE ROOM
YOU'RE A DREAMER.
AND TOTALLY RECKLESS.
AND GULLIBLE.
HOMPH
AND YOU HAVE FAT ANKLES...
MY ANKLES!?
I KNEW THAT YOU DIDN'T HAVE MUCH TIME AS SOON AS I MET YOU.
BUT I'M DEAD.

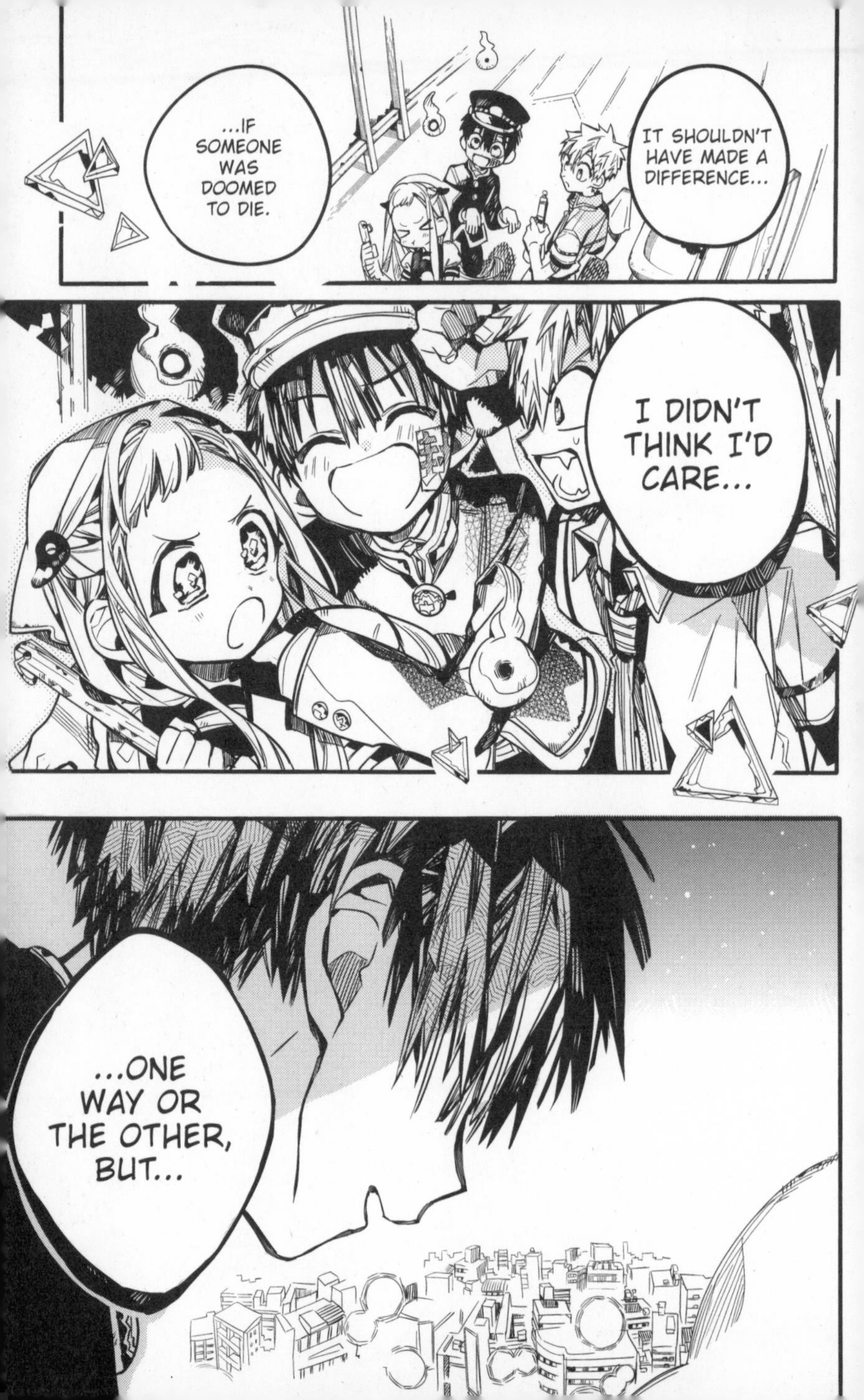
IT SHOULDN'T HAVE MADE A DIFFERENCE...
...IF SOMEONE WAS DOOMED TO DIE.
I DIDN'T THINK I'D CARE...
...ONE WAY OR THE OTHER, BUT...

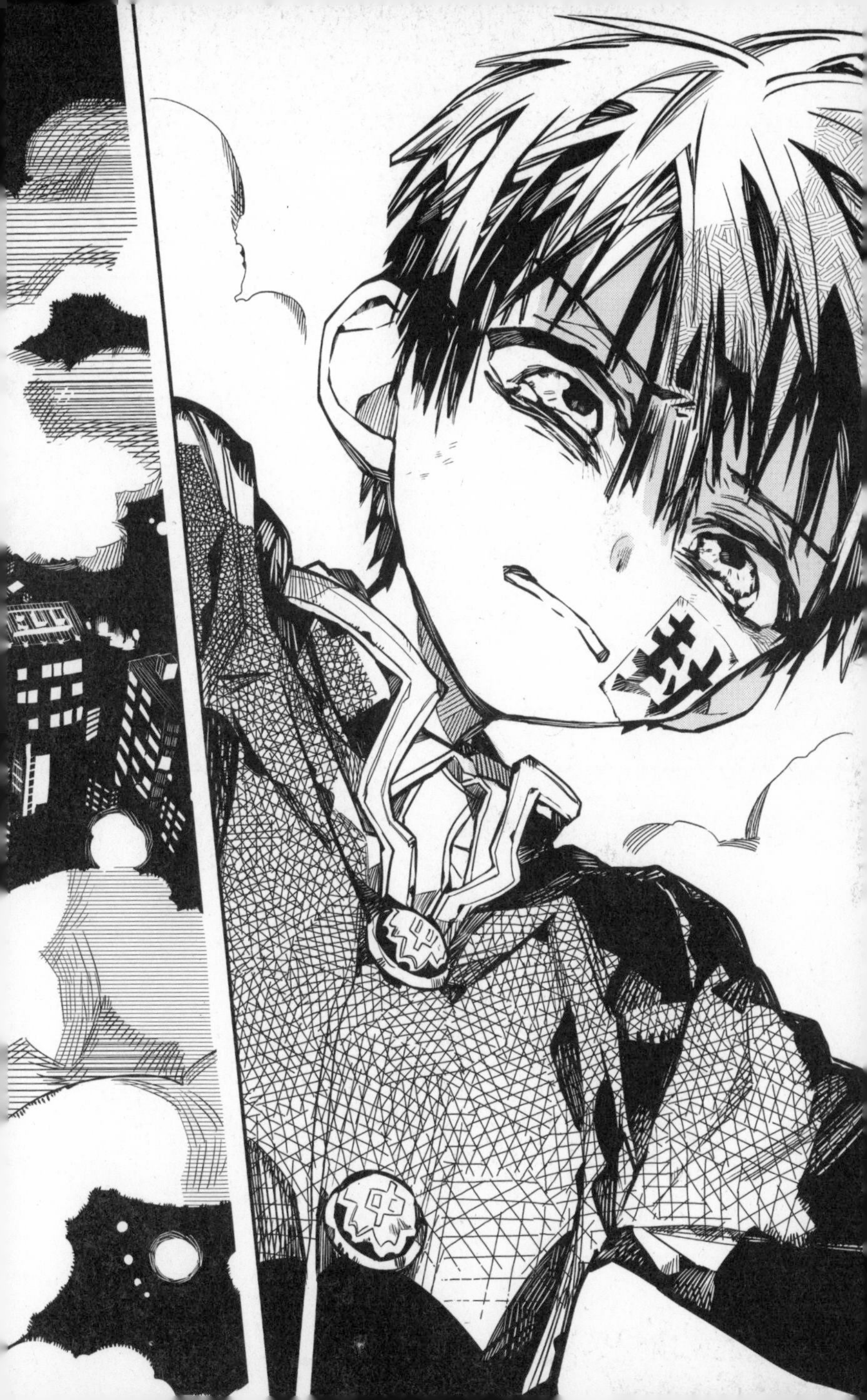

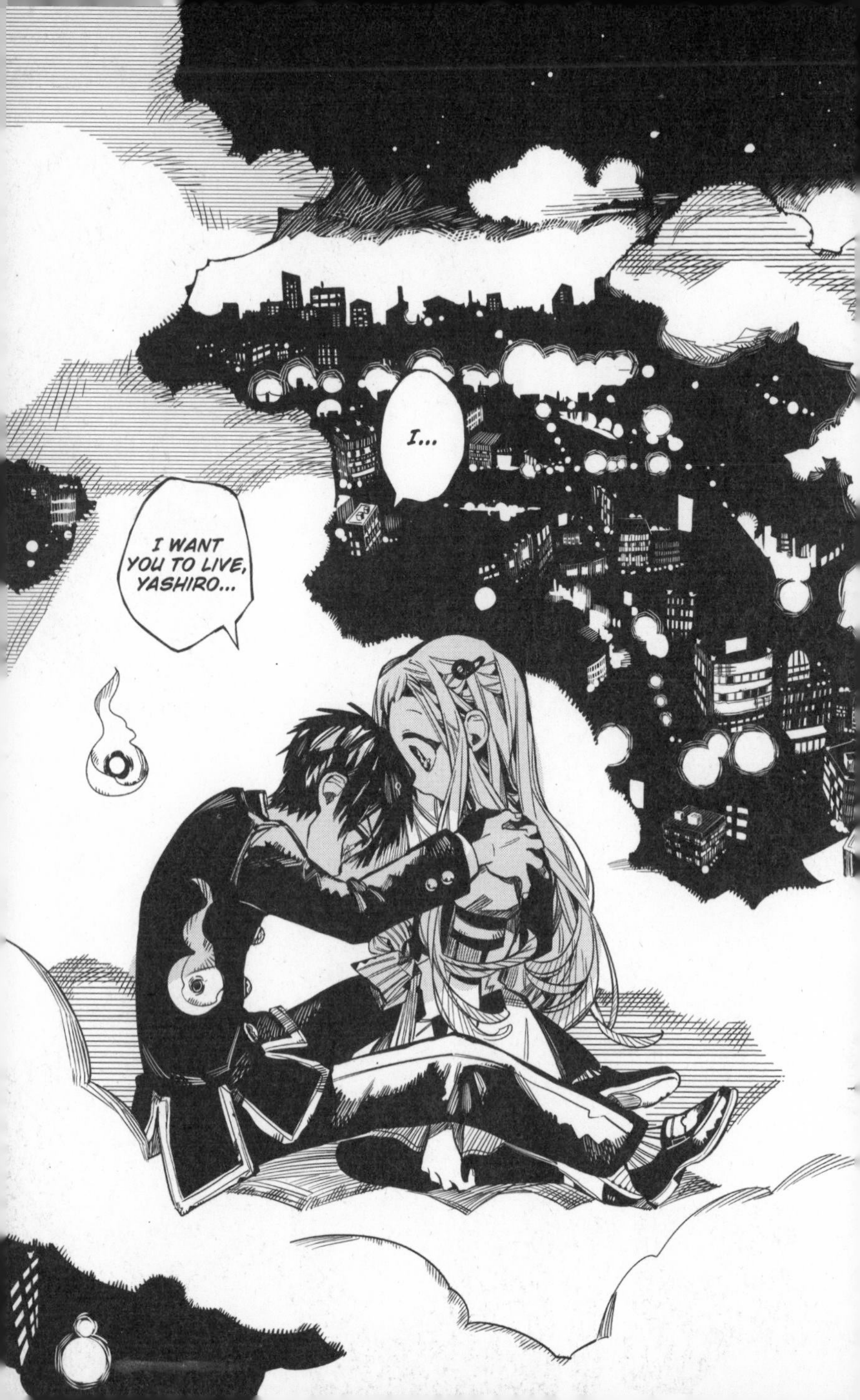
I...
I WANT YOU TO LIVE, YASHIRO...

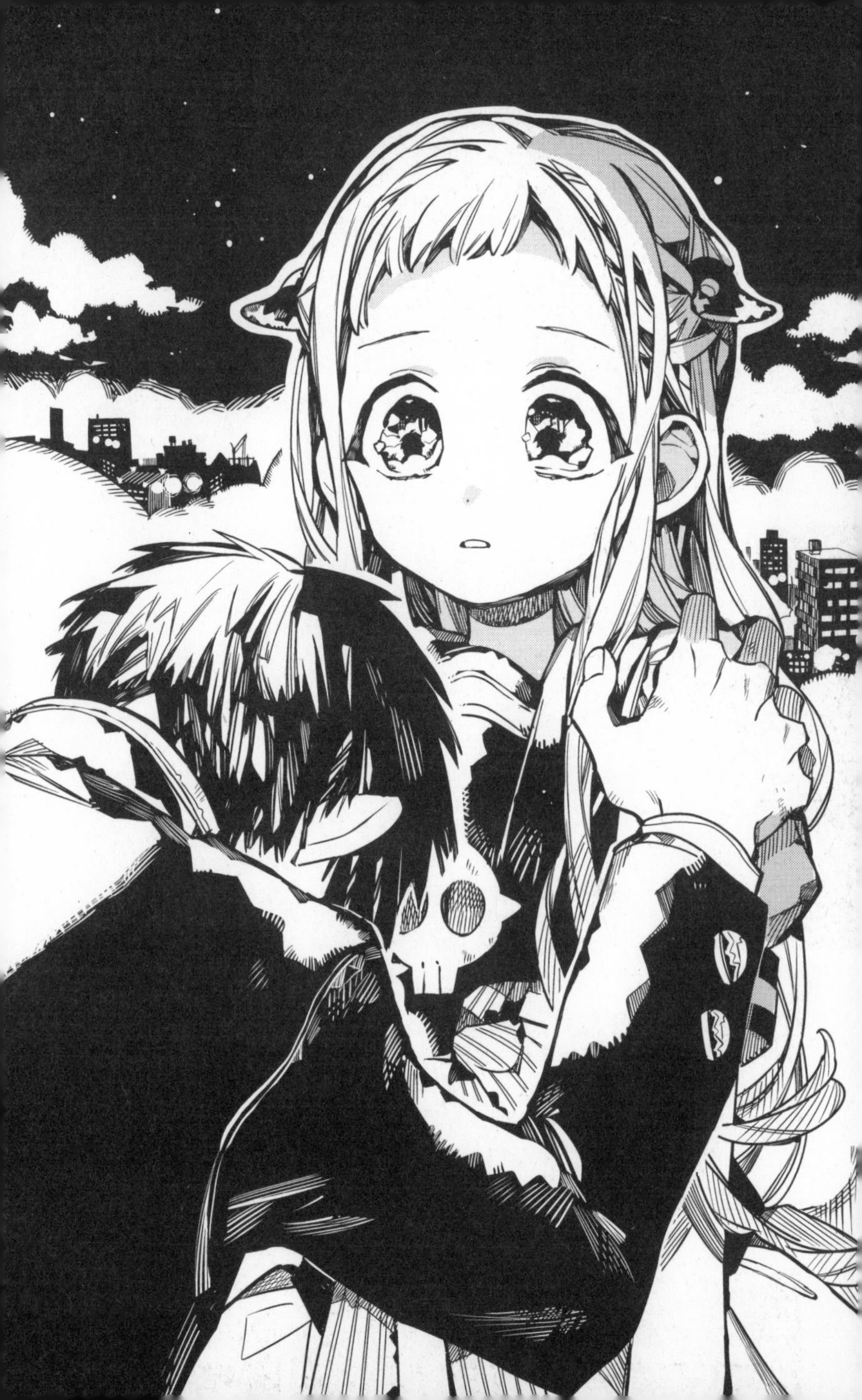

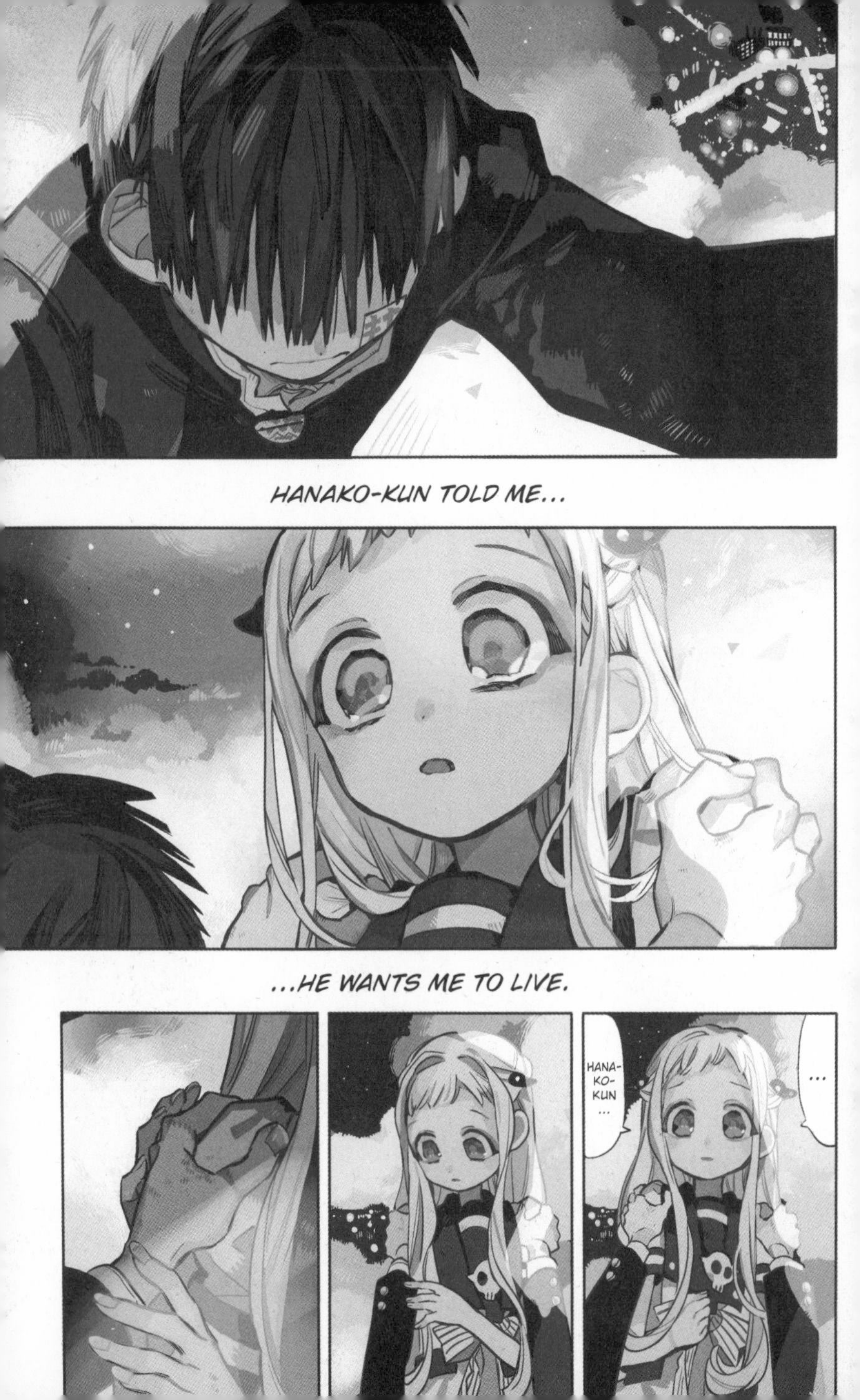
HANAKO-KUN TOLD ME...
...HE WANTS ME TO LIVE.
...
HANA-KO-KUN...

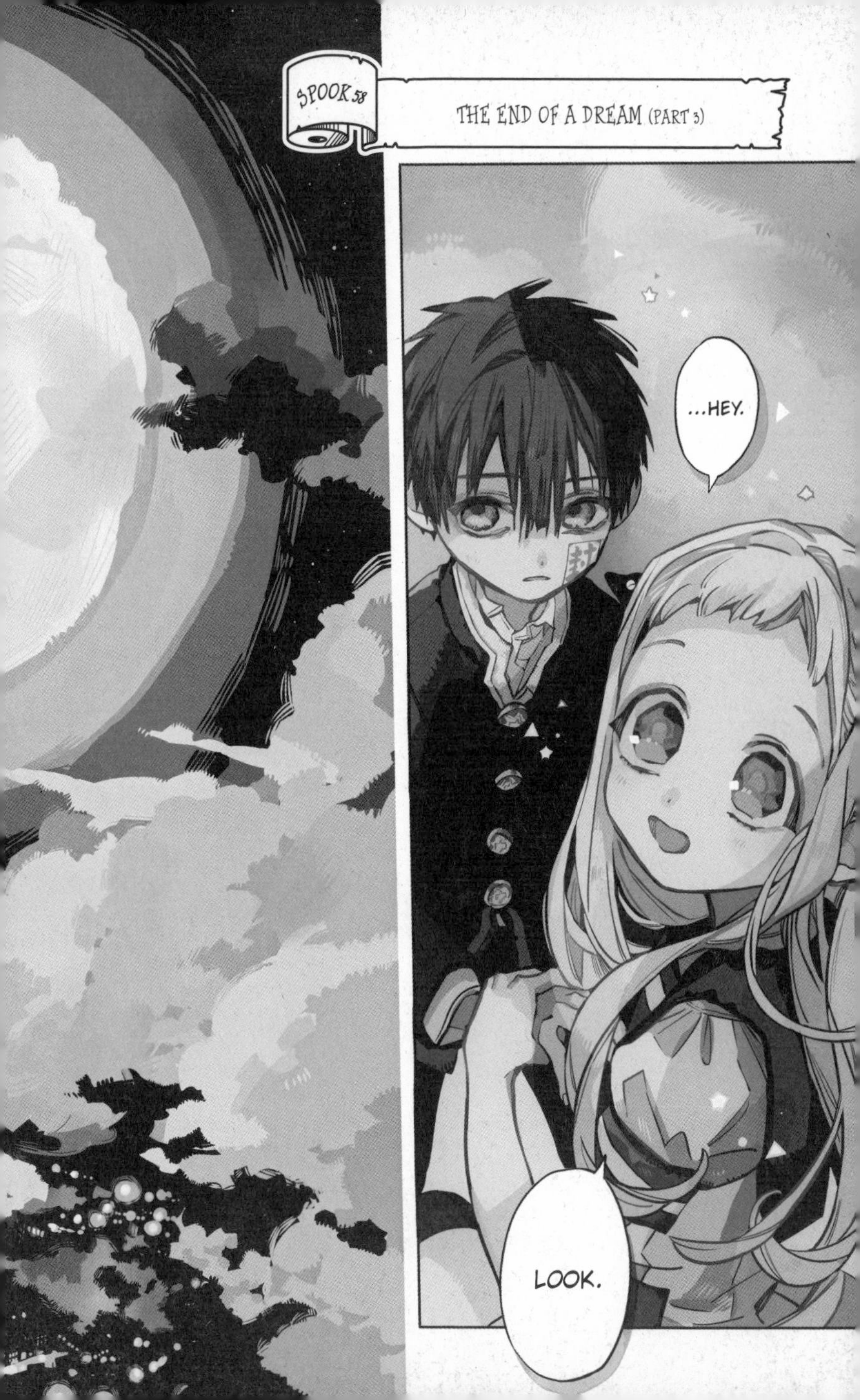
SPOOK 58
THE END OF A DREAM (PART 3)
...HEY.
LOOK.

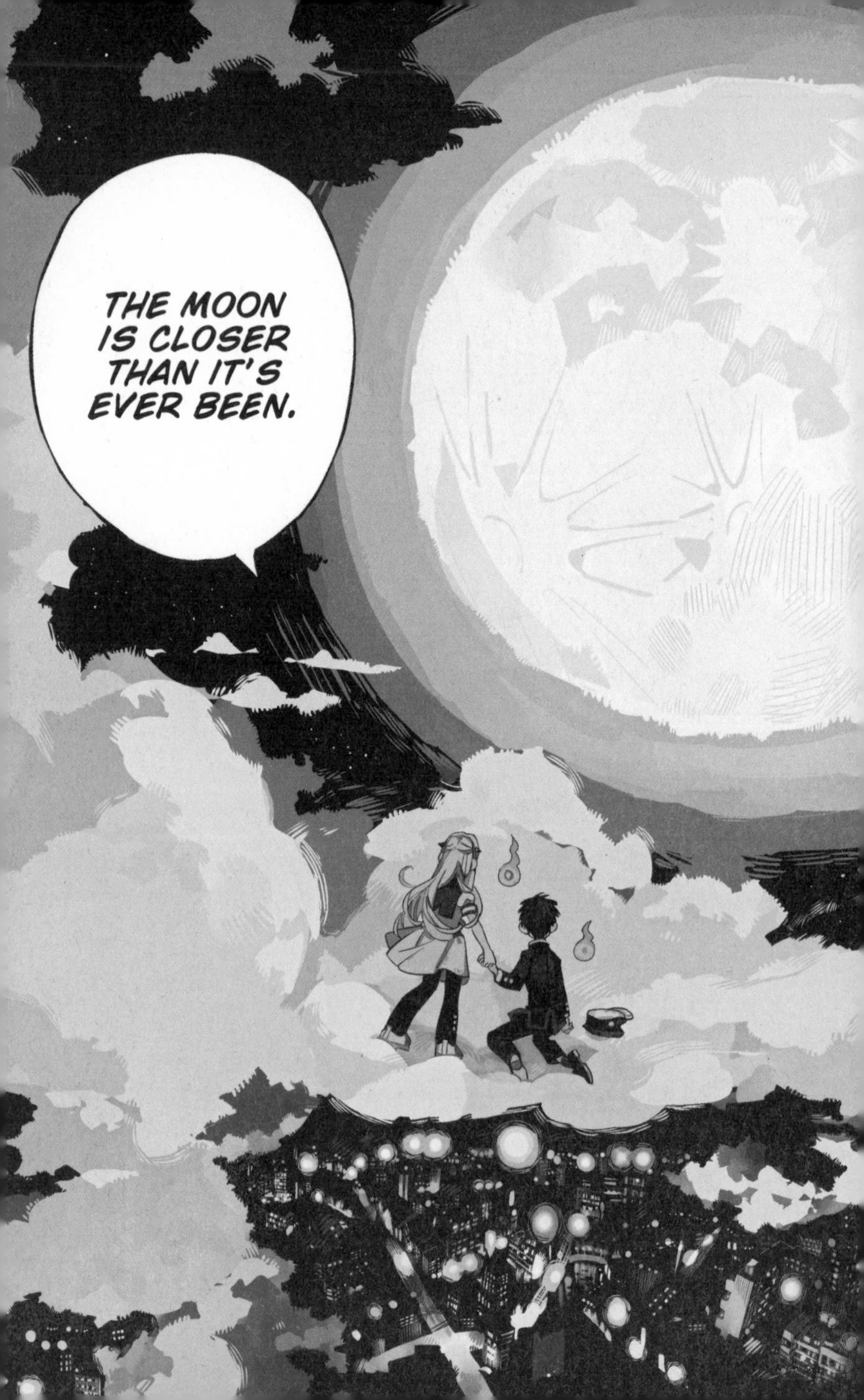
THE MOON IS CLOSER THAN IT'S EVER BEEN.

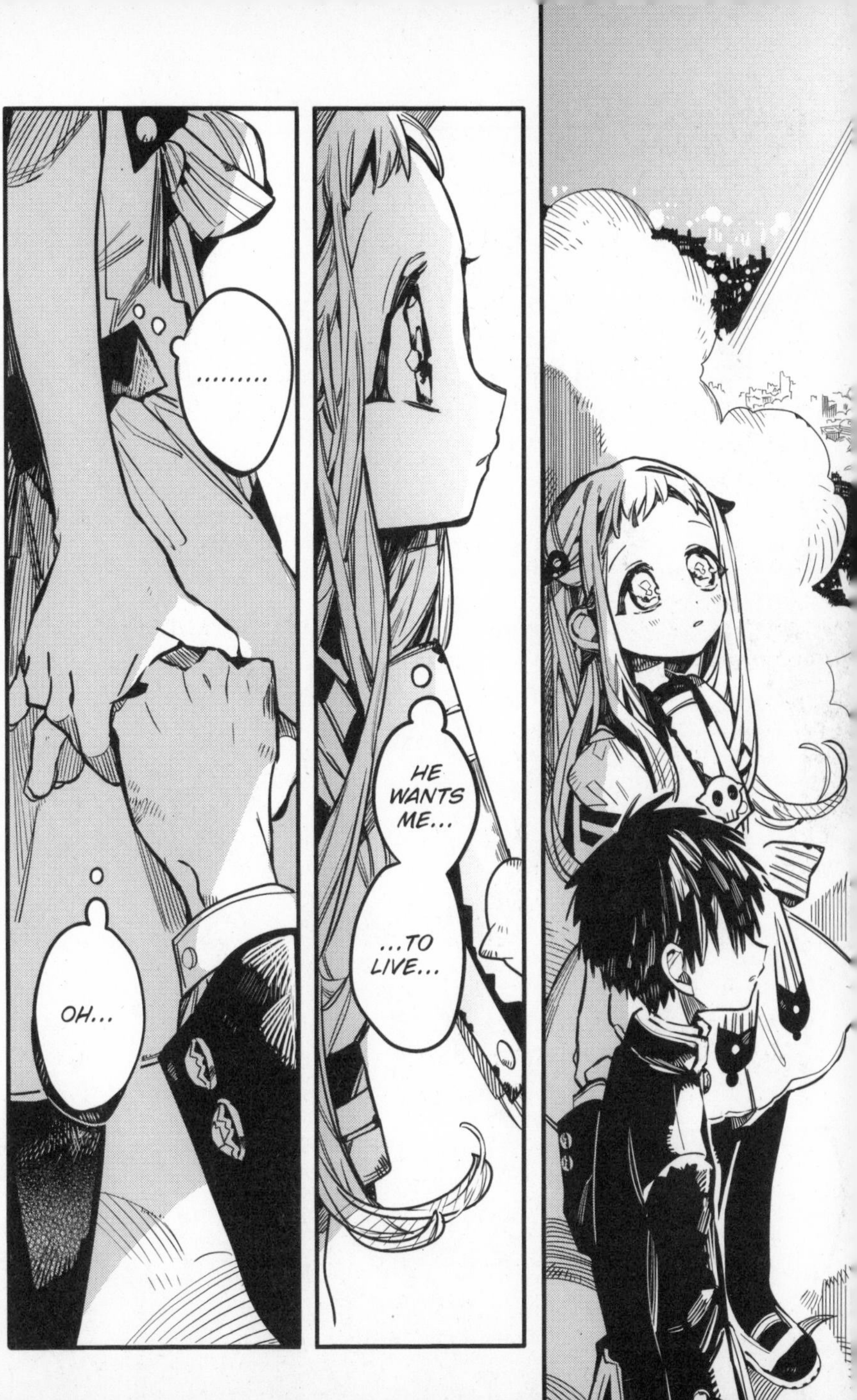
HE WANTS ME...
...TO LIVE...
....
OH...

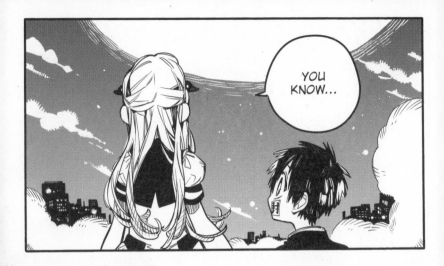

YOU KNOW...

...TSUCHI-GOMORI-SENSEI ONCE TOLD ME...

...THAT THE FIRST TIME SOMEONE WENT TO THE MOON...

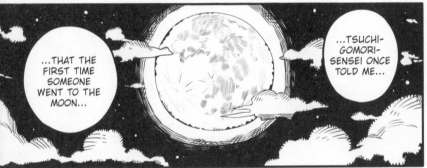

...EVERY-ONE...

...STARTED TO THINK THAT NOTHING WAS IMPOSSIBLE.

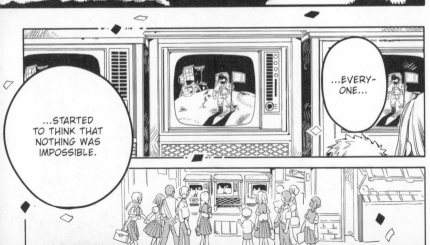

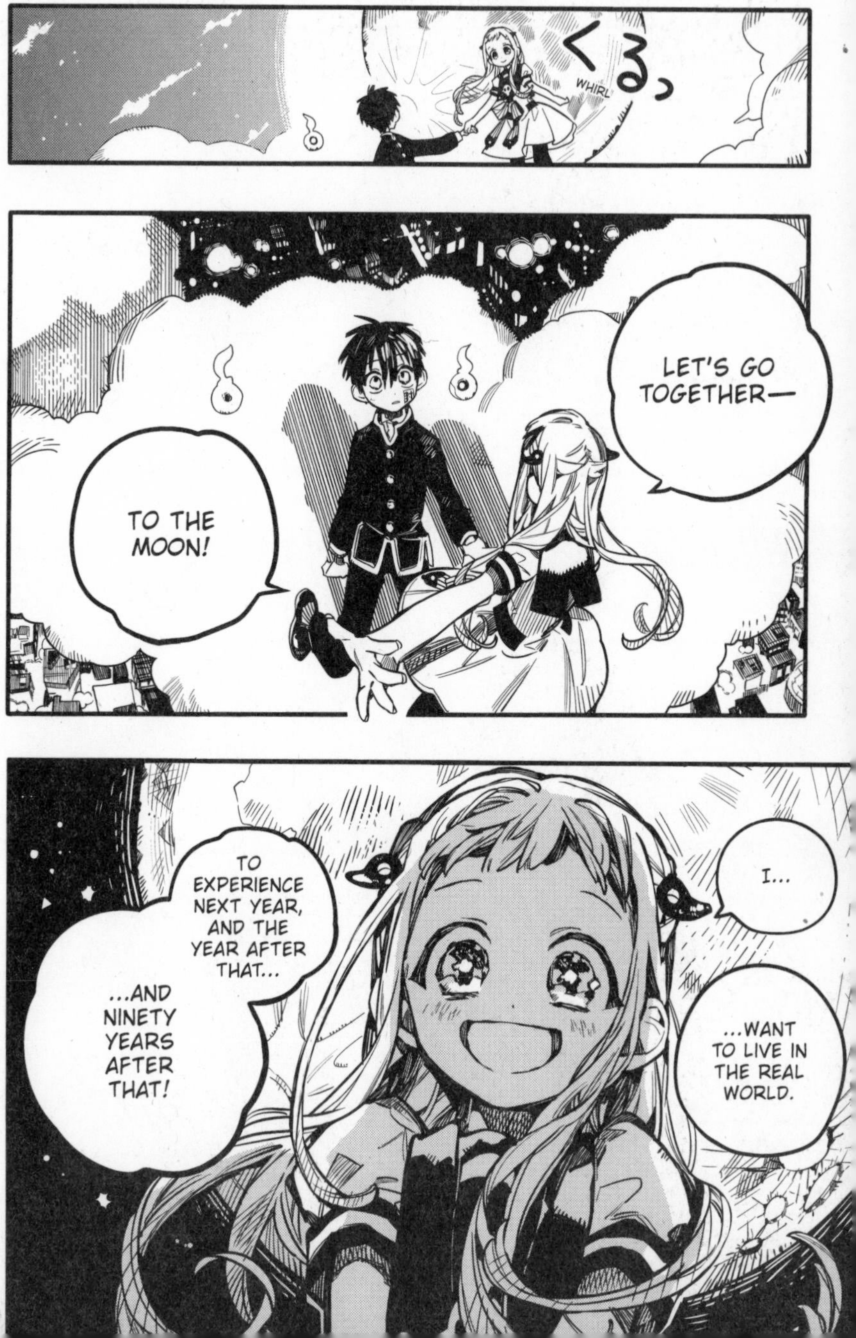
くるっ
WHIRL
LET'S GO TOGETHER—
TO THE MOON!
I...
...WANT TO LIVE IN THE REAL WORLD.
TO EXPERIENCE NEXT YEAR, AND THE YEAR AFTER THAT...
...AND NINETY YEARS AFTER THAT!

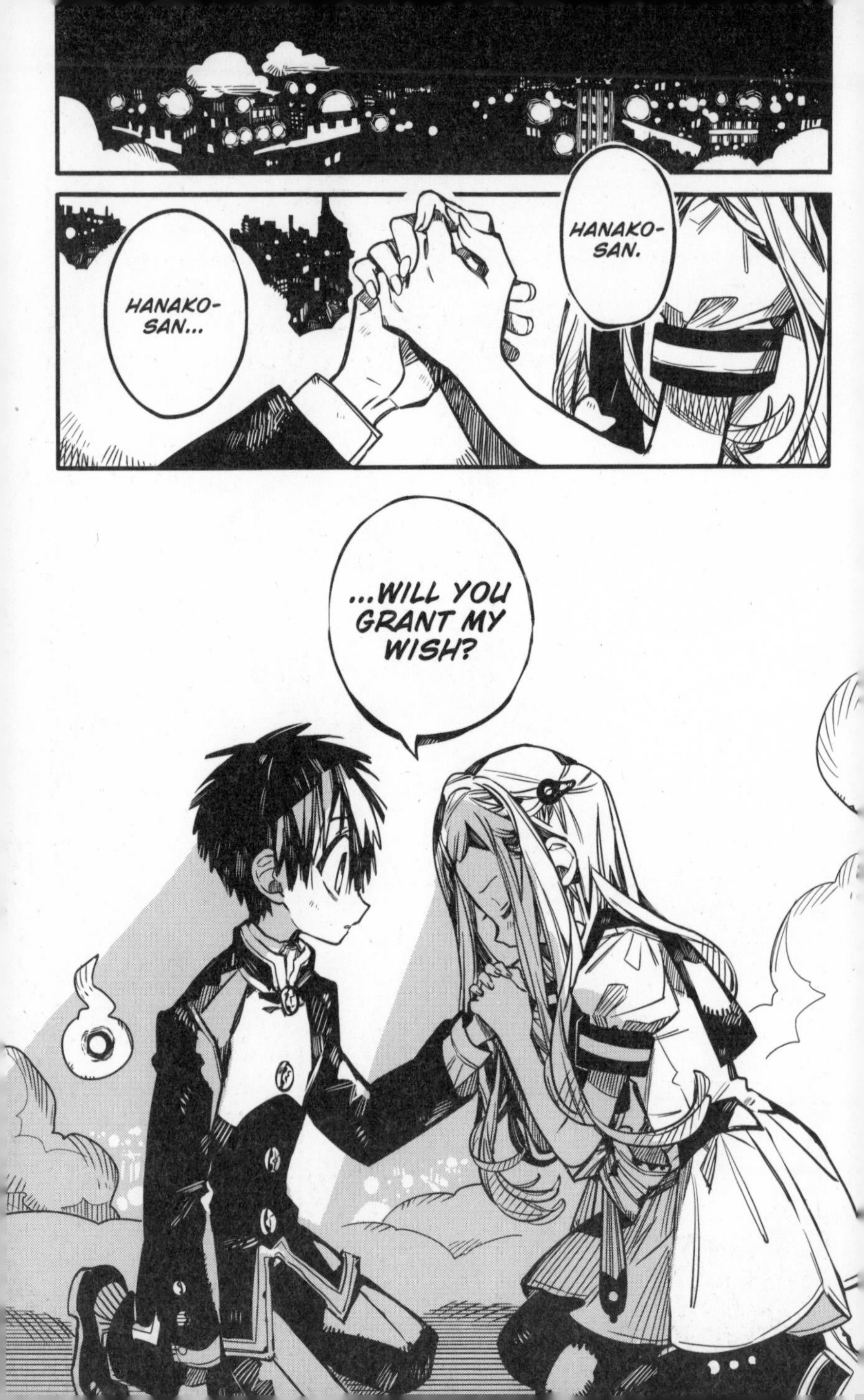
HANAKO-SAN.
HANAKO-SAN...
...WILL YOU GRANT MY WISH?

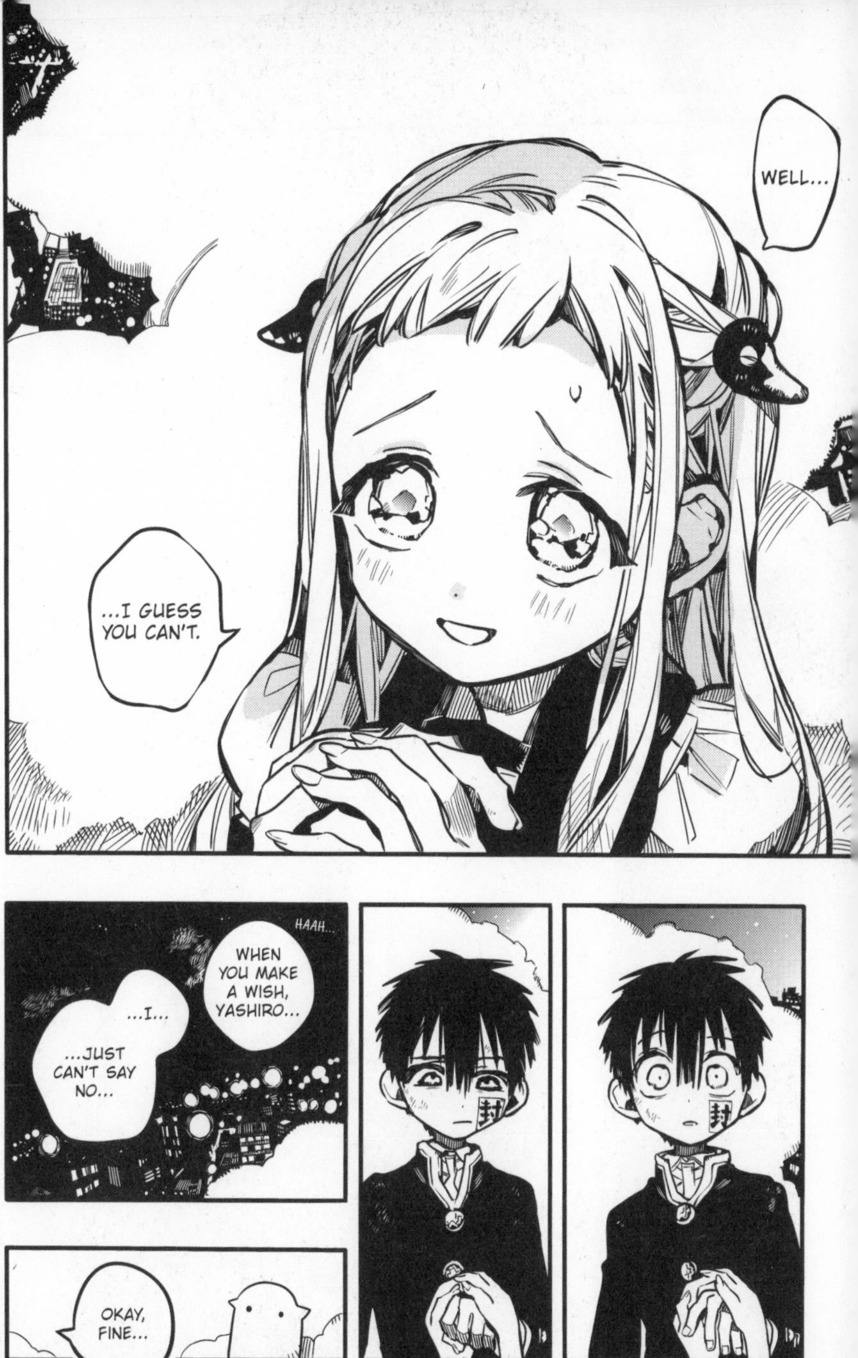
WELL...
...I GUESS YOU CAN'T.
HAAH...
WHEN YOU MAKE A WISH, YASHIRO...
...I...
...JUST CAN'T SAY NO...
OKAY, FINE...

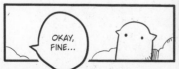

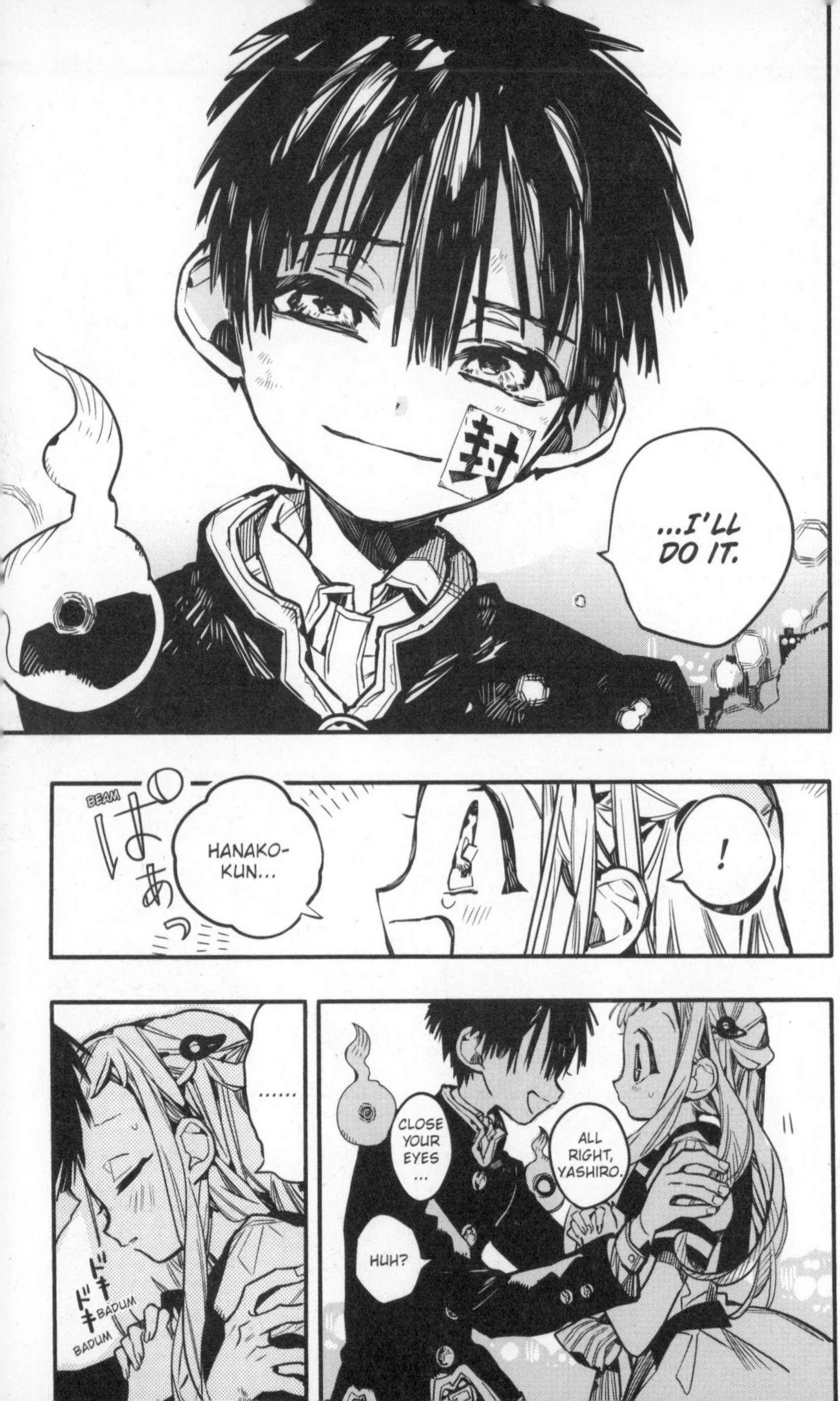
...I'LL DO IT.
!
HANAKO-KUN...
ぱあっ
BEAM
ALL RIGHT, YASHIRO.
CLOSE YOUR EYES ...
HUH?
......
ドキドキ
BADUM BADUM

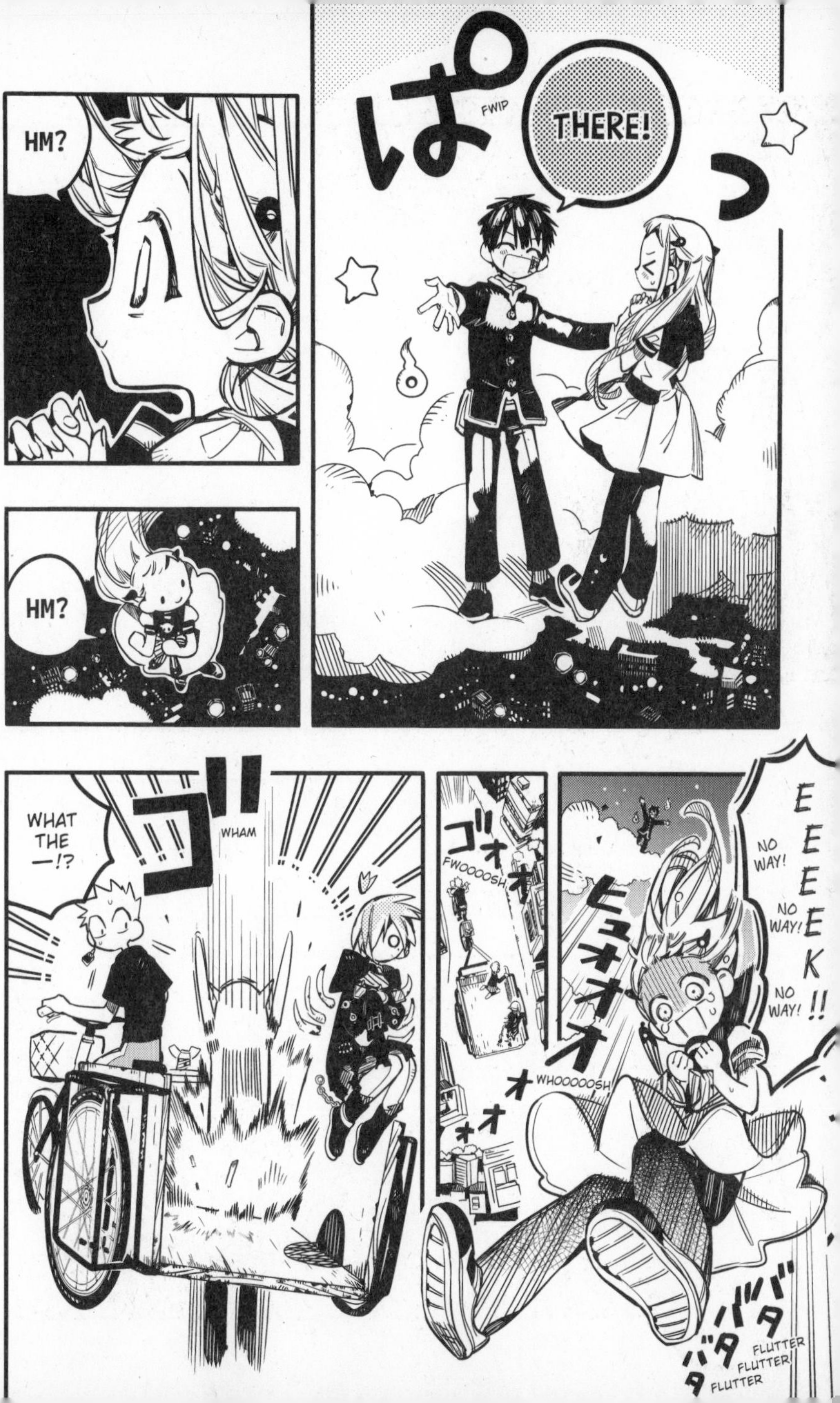
ぱっ
FWIP
THERE!
HM?
HM?
EEEEEK!!
NO WAY!
NO WAY!
NO WAY!
バタバタバタ
FLUTTER
FLUTTER
FLUTTER
ヒュオオオオオオ
WHOOOOOSH
ゴォオオ
FWOOOOSH
ゴッ
WHAM
WHAT THE—!?

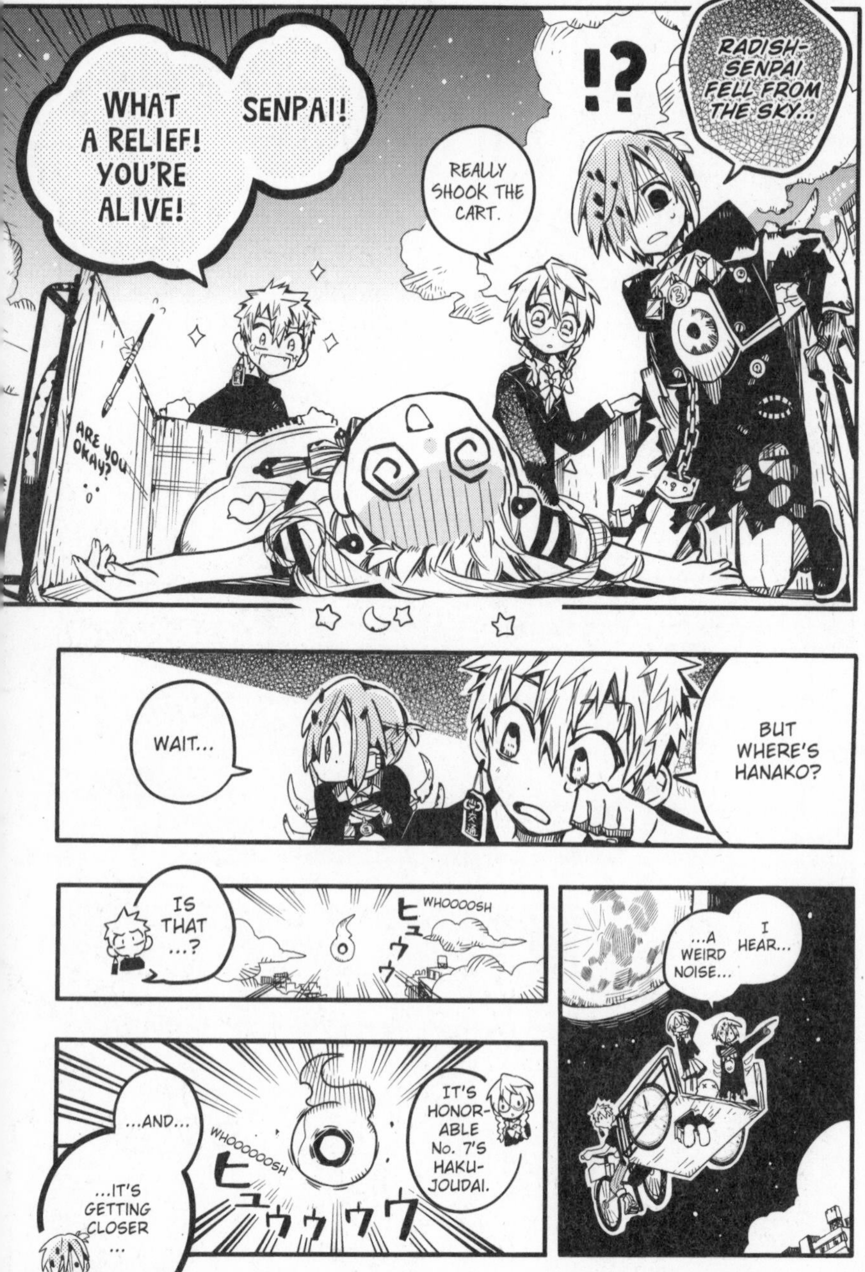
RADISH-SENPAI FELL FROM THE SKY...
!?
REALLY SHOOK THE CART.
SENPAI!
WHAT A RELIEF! YOU'RE ALIVE!
ARE YOU OKAY?
BUT WHERE'S HANAKO?
WAIT...
I HEAR...
...A WEIRD NOISE...
ヒュウウ
WHOOOOSH
IS THAT ...?
IT'S HONORABLE No. 7'S HAKUJOUDAI.
ヒュゥゥウウ
WHOOOOOOSH
...AND...
...IT'S GETTING CLOSER ...

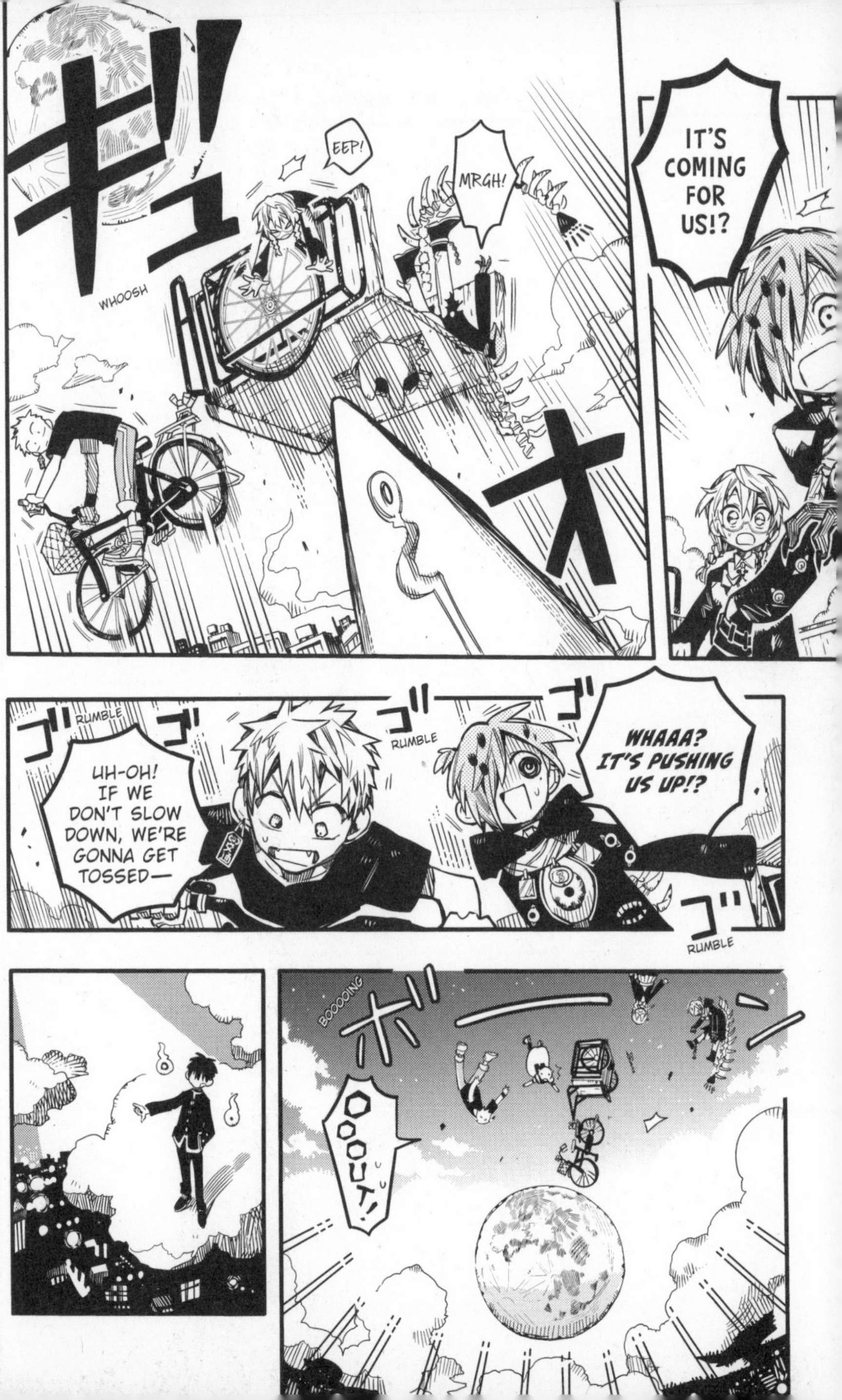

IT'S COMING FOR US!?
EEP!
MRGH!
WHOOSH
WHAAA? IT'S PUSHING US UP!?
RUMBLE
RUMBLE
RUMBLE
UH-OH! IF WE DON'T SLOW DOWN, WE'RE GONNA GET TOSSED—
RUMBLE
BOOOOING
OOOOUT!

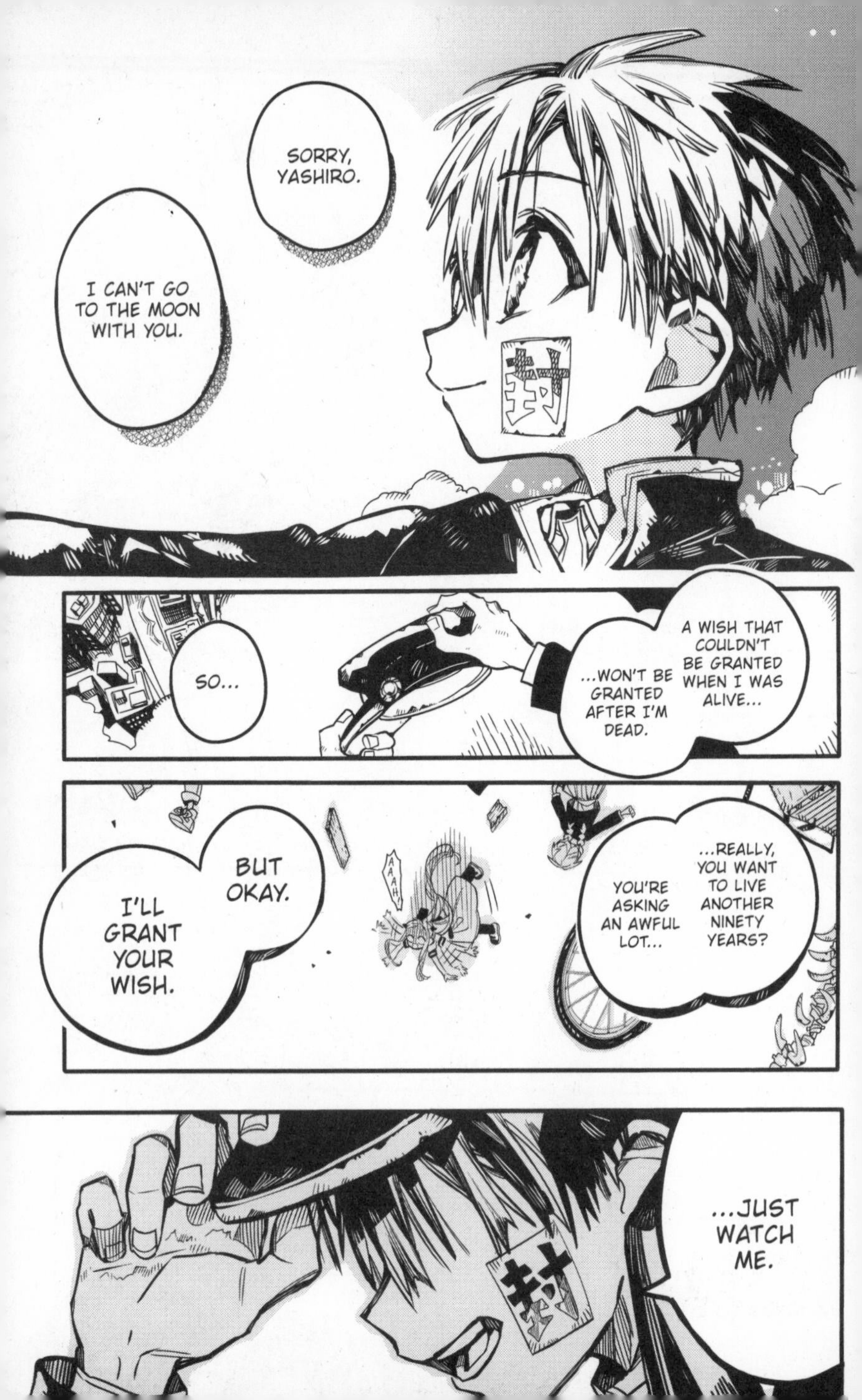
SORRY, YASHIRO.
I CAN'T GO TO THE MOON WITH YOU.
A WISH THAT COULDN'T BE GRANTED WHEN I WAS ALIVE...
...WON'T BE GRANTED AFTER I'M DEAD.
SO...
...REALLY, YOU WANT TO LIVE ANOTHER NINETY YEARS?
YOU'RE ASKING AN AWFUL LOT...
BUT OKAY.
I'LL GRANT YOUR WISH.
...JUST WATCH ME.

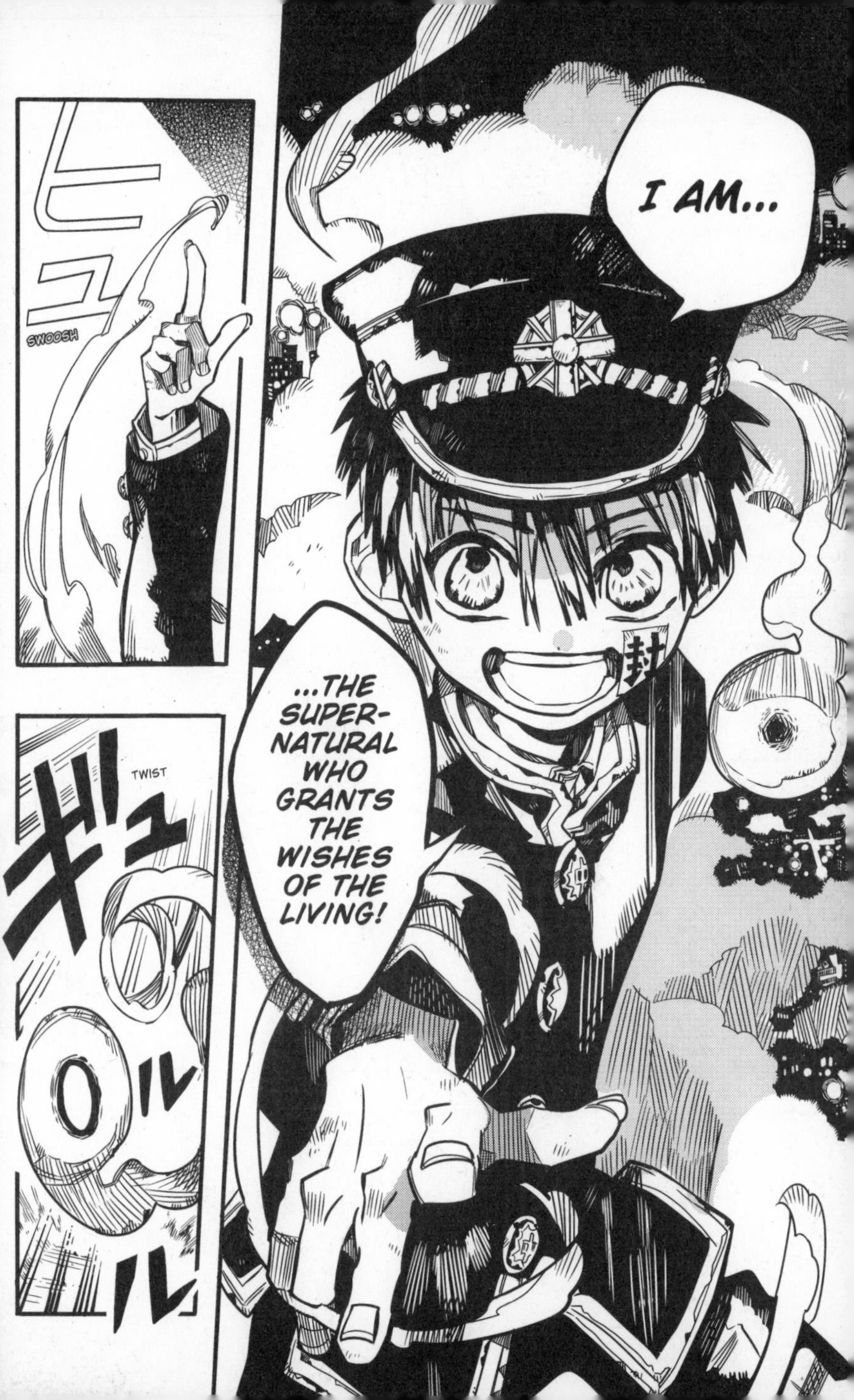
I AM...
...THE SUPER-NATURAL WHO GRANTS THE WISHES OF THE LIVING!
ヒュ
SWOOSH
ギュルル
TWIST

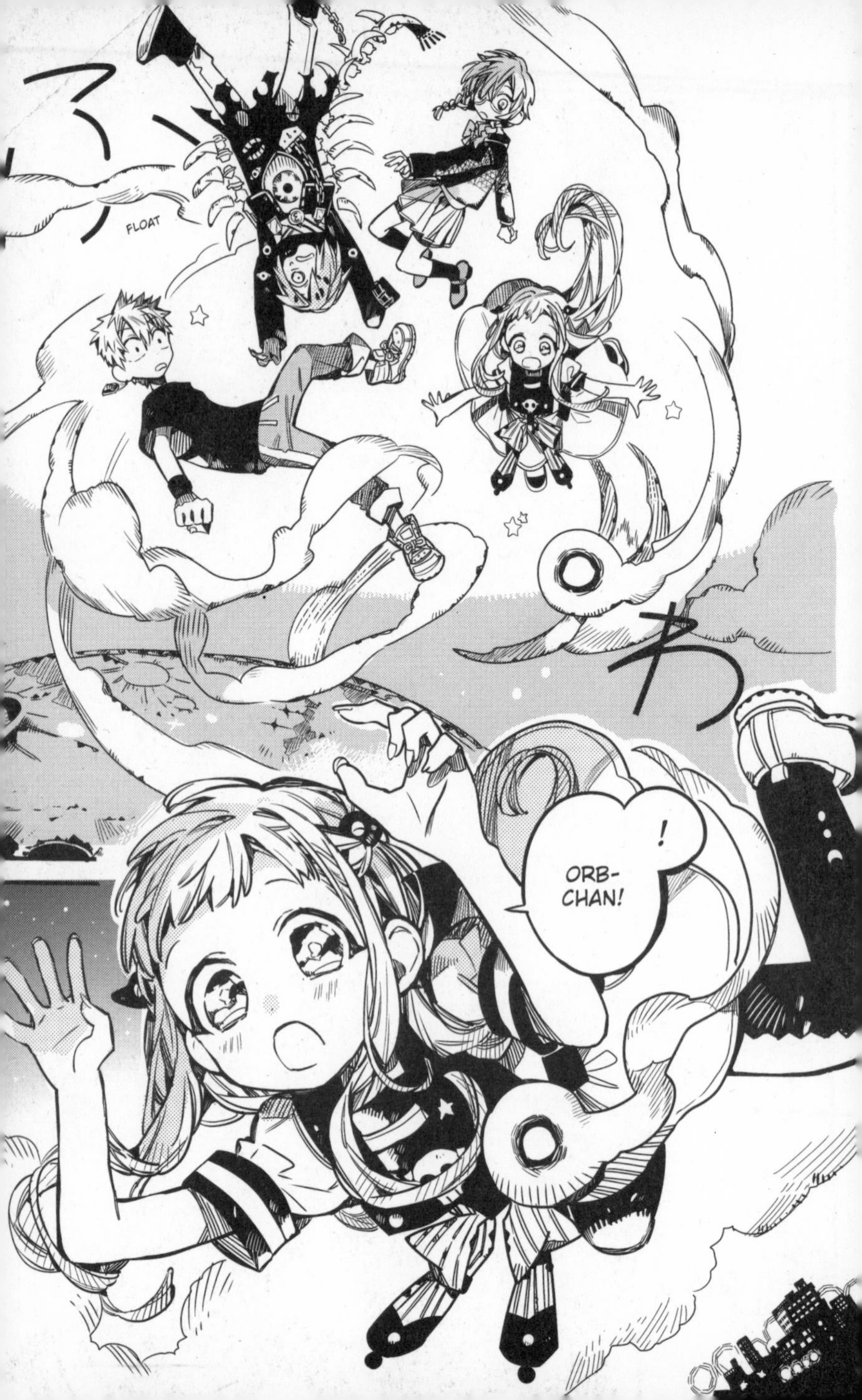
FLOAT
!
ORB-CHAN!

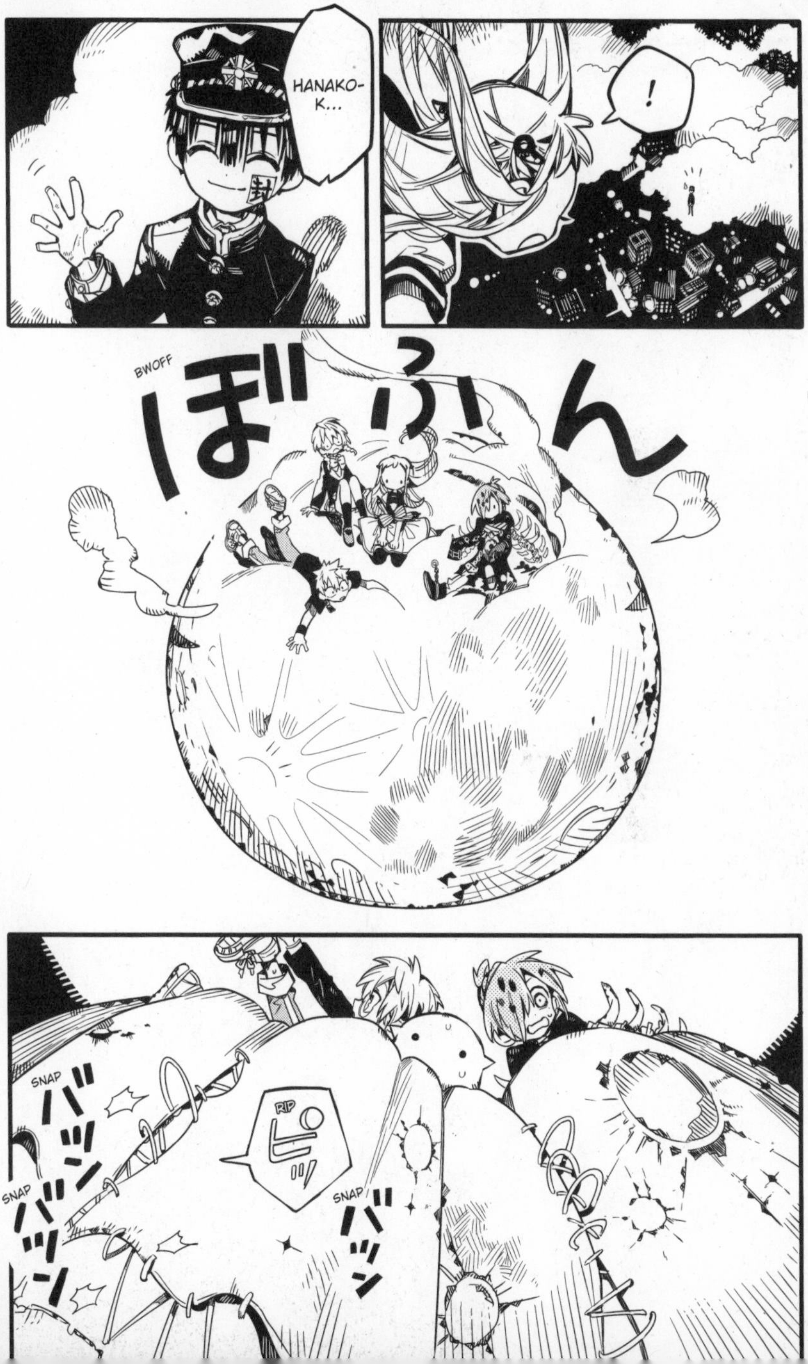
!
HANAKO-K...
BWOFF
ぼふん
RIP
ビリッ
SNAP
バッツン
SNAP
バッツン
SNAP
バッツン

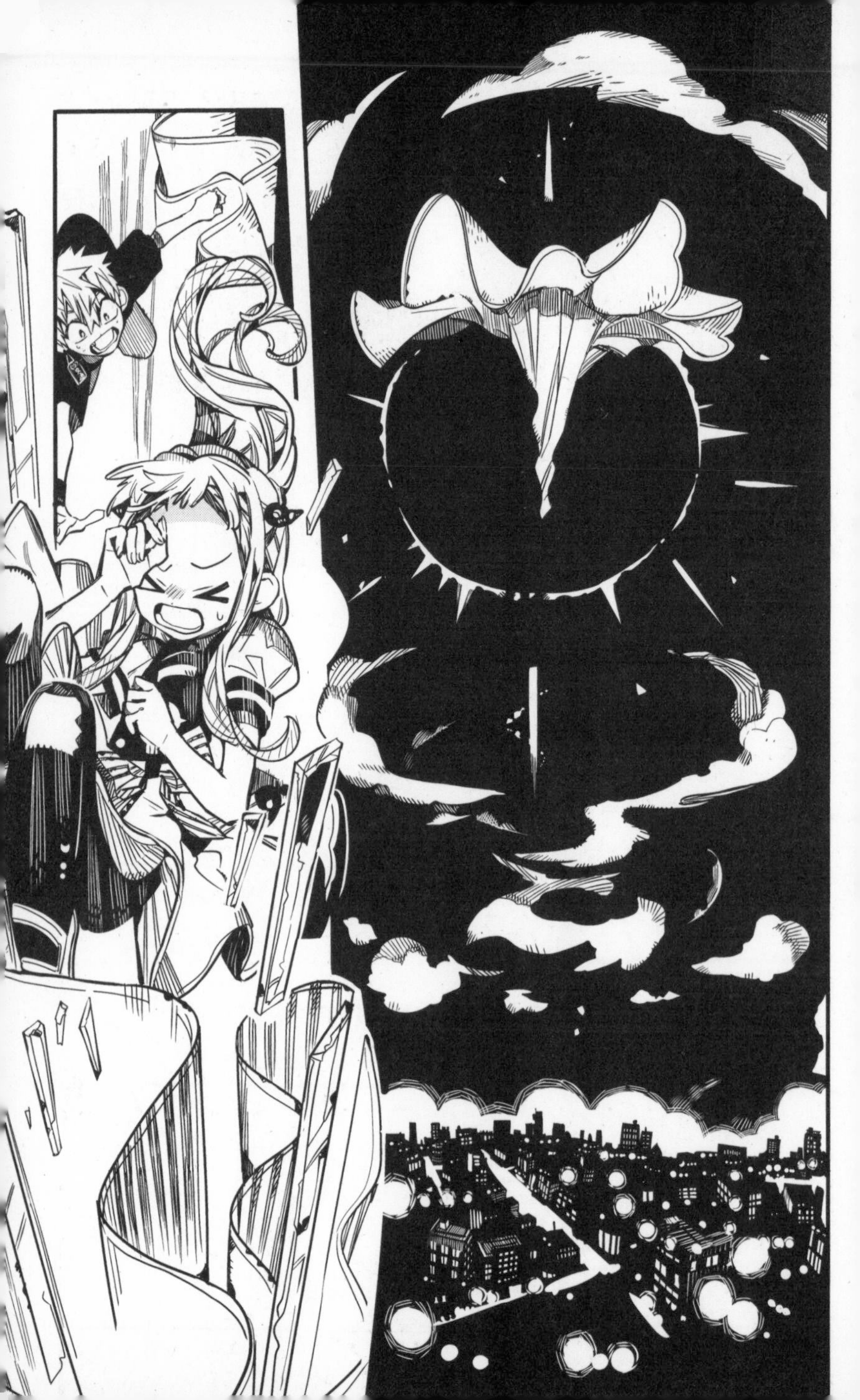

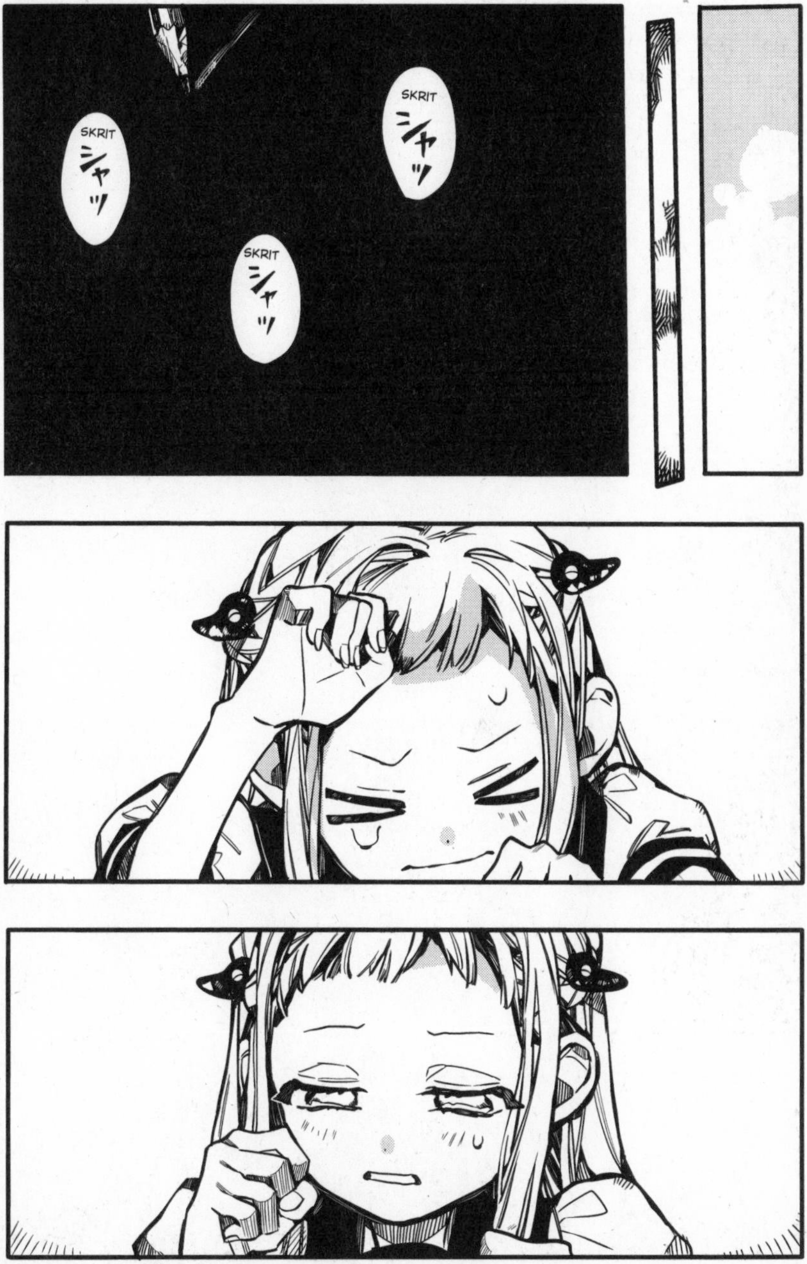
SKRIT シャッ
SKRIT シャッ
SKRIT シャッ

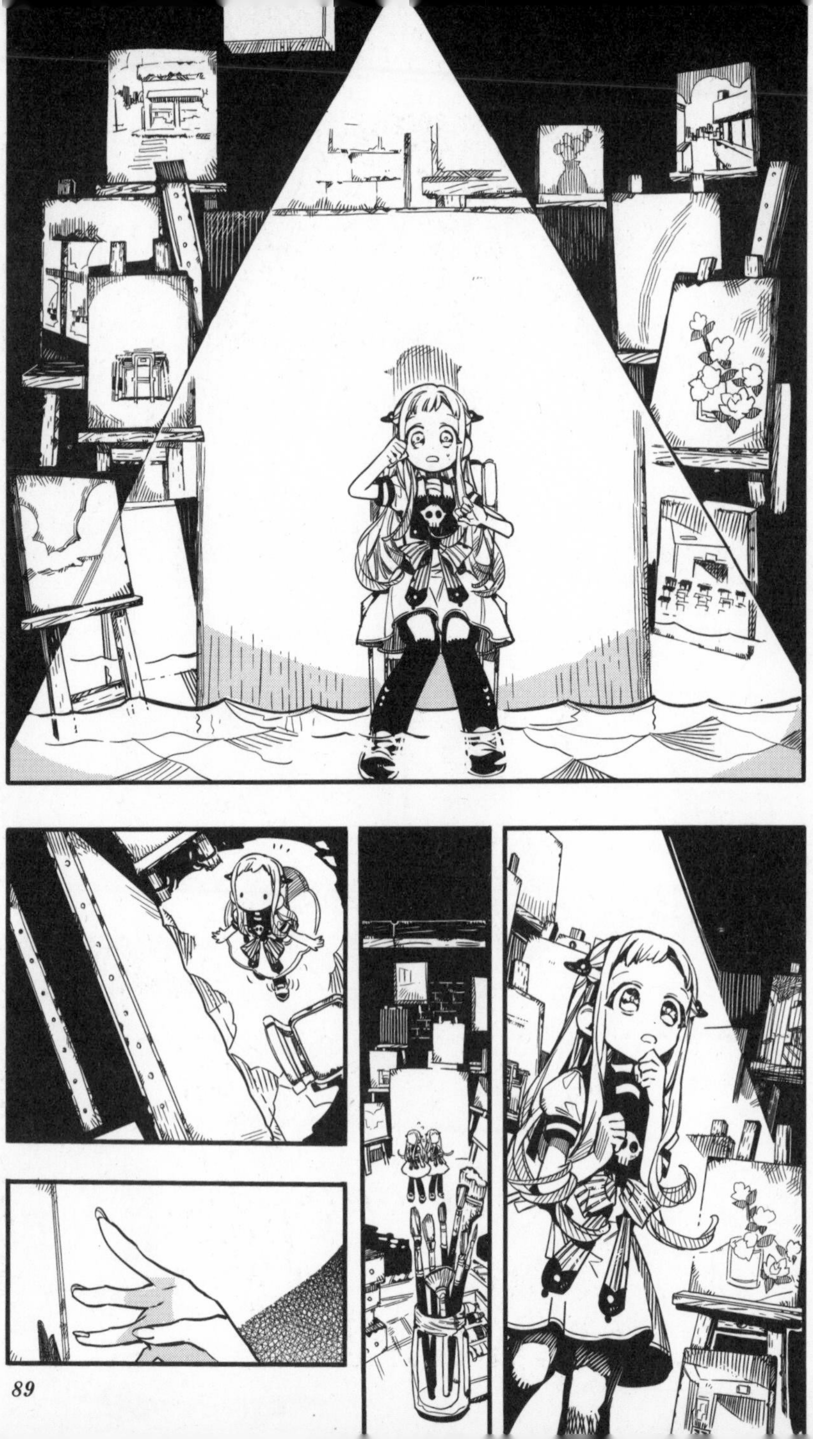

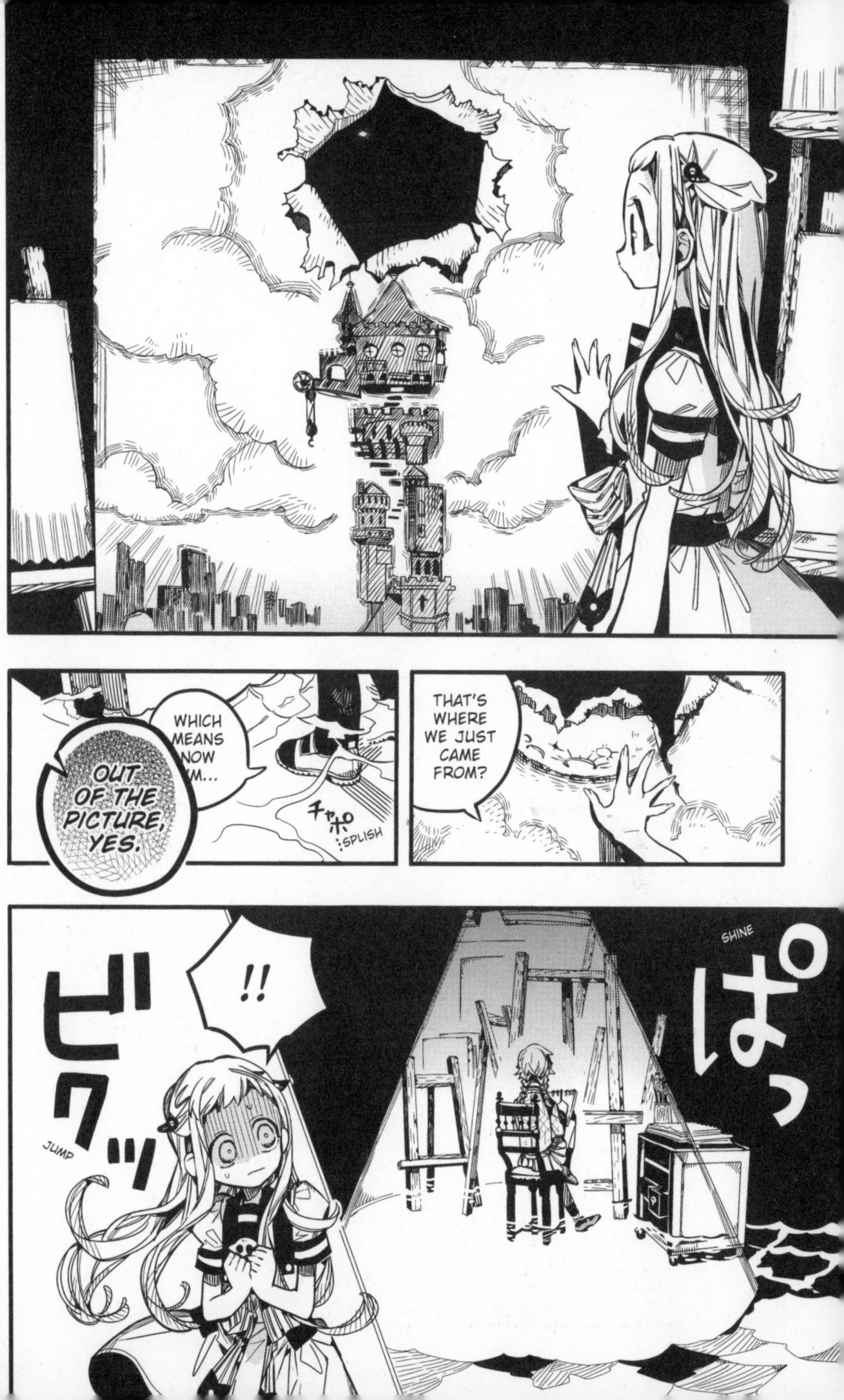
THAT'S WHERE WE JUST CAME FROM?
WHICH MEANS NOW I'M...
チャポ
SPLISH
OUT OF THE PICTURE, YES.
ぱっ
SHINE
!!
ビクッ
JUMP

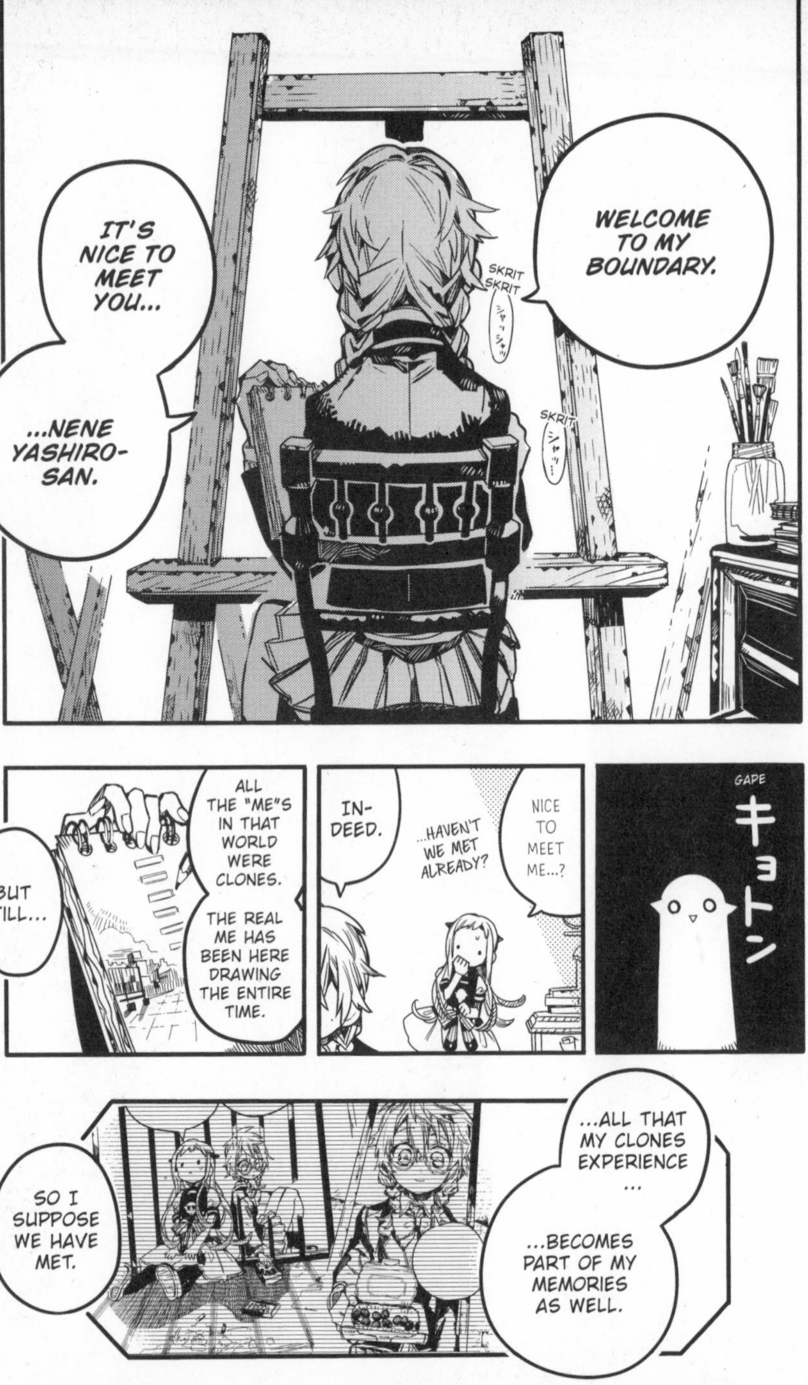
WELCOME TO MY BOUNDARY.
SKRIT SKRIT
シャッシャッ
SKRIT
シャッ…
IT'S NICE TO MEET YOU...
...NENE YASHIRO-SAN.
GAPE
キョトン
NICE TO MEET ME...?
...HAVEN'T WE MET ALREADY?
IN-DEED.
ALL THE "ME"S IN THAT WORLD WERE CLONES.
THE REAL ME HAS BEEN HERE DRAWING THE ENTIRE TIME.
BUT STILL...
...ALL THAT MY CLONES EXPERIENCE ...
...BECOMES PART OF MY MEMORIES AS WELL.
SO I SUPPOSE WE HAVE MET.

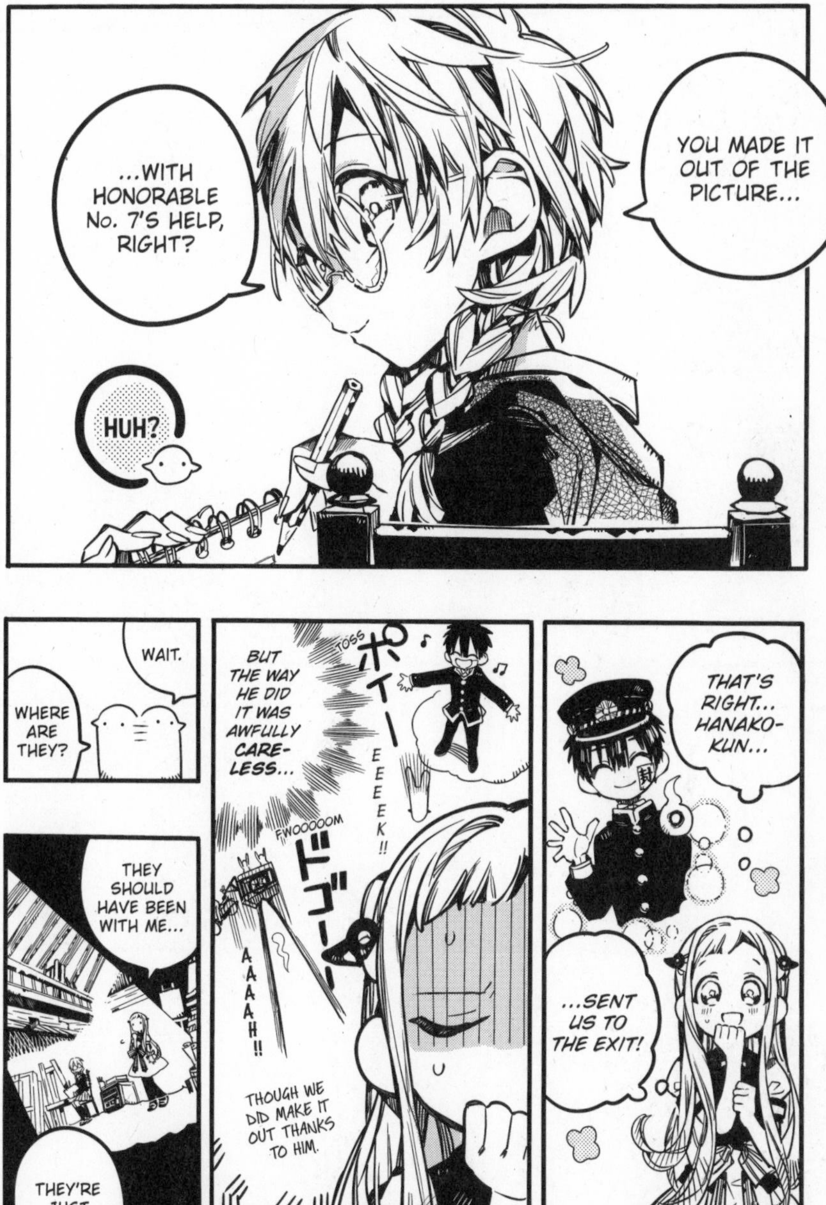
YOU MADE IT OUT OF THE PICTURE...
...WITH HONORABLE No. 7'S HELP, RIGHT?
HUH?
THAT'S RIGHT... HANAKO-KUN...
...SENT US TO THE EXIT!
TOSS
ポイー
BUT THE WAY HE DID IT WAS AWFULLY CARE-LESS...
EEEEK!!
FWOOOOOM
ドゴーー
AAAAAH!!
THOUGH WE DID MAKE IT OUT THANKS TO HIM.
WAIT.
WHERE ARE THEY?
THEY SHOULD HAVE BEEN WITH ME...
THEY'RE JUST FINE.

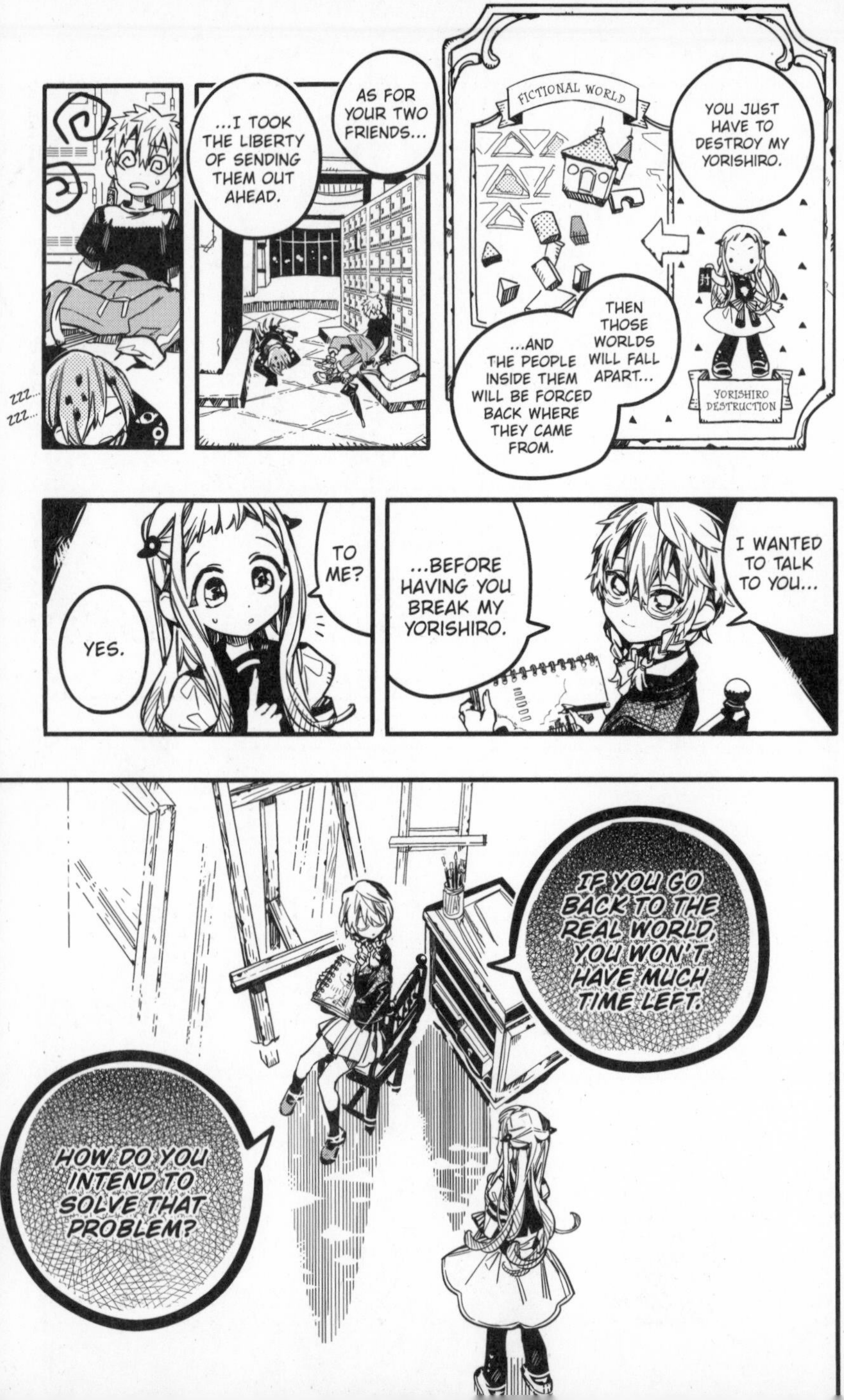
YOU JUST HAVE TO DESTROY MY YORISHIRO.
FICTIONAL WORLD
YORISHIRO DESTRUCTION
THEN THOSE WORLDS WILL FALL APART...
...AND THE PEOPLE INSIDE THEM WILL BE FORCED BACK WHERE THEY CAME FROM.
AS FOR YOUR TWO FRIENDS...
...I TOOK THE LIBERTY OF SENDING THEM OUT AHEAD.
ZZZ...
ZZZ...
I WANTED TO TALK TO YOU...
...BEFORE HAVING YOU BREAK MY YORISHIRO.
TO ME?
YES.
IF YOU GO BACK TO THE REAL WORLD, YOU WON'T HAVE MUCH TIME LEFT.
HOW DO YOU INTEND TO SOLVE THAT PROBLEM?

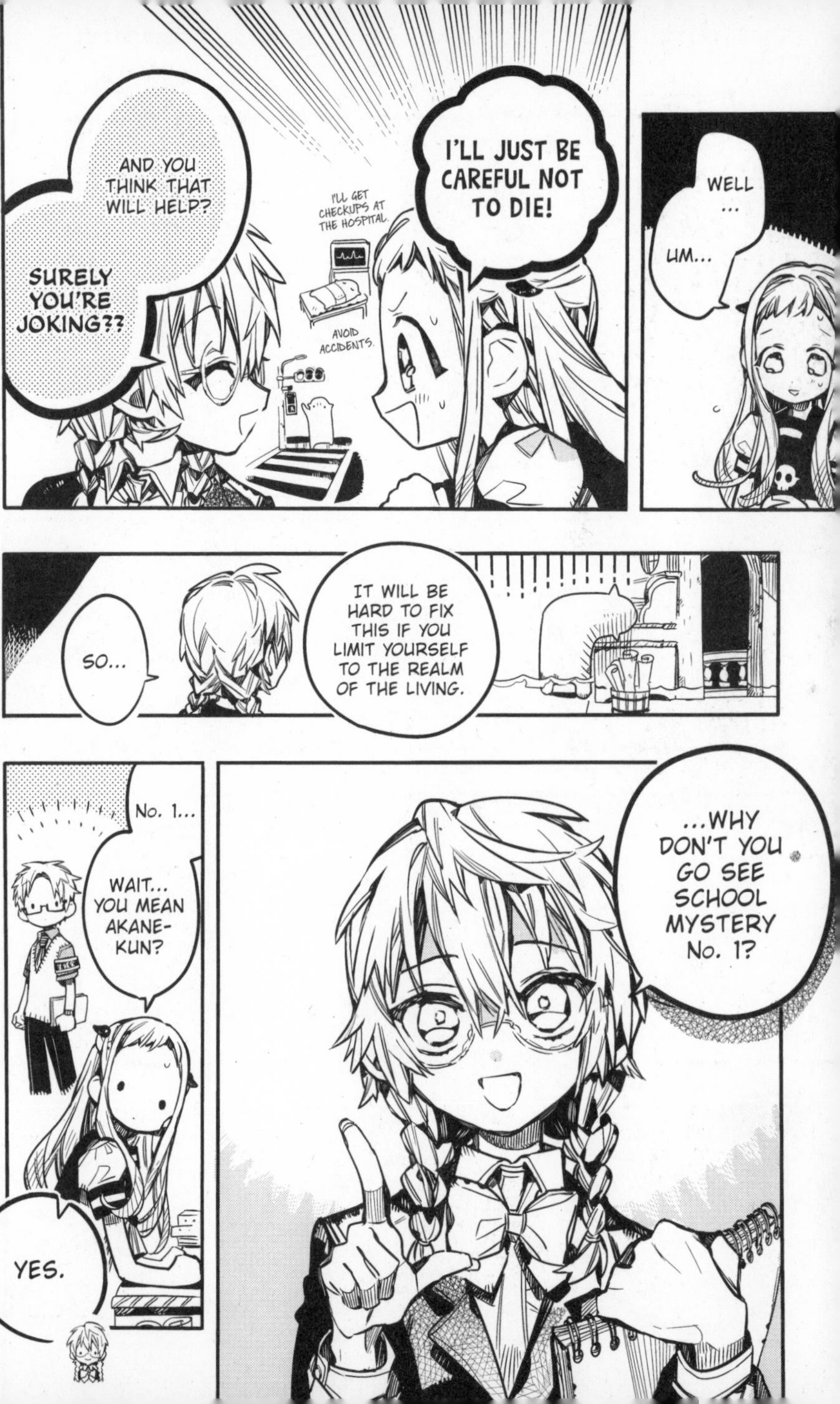
WELL ...
UM...
I'LL JUST BE CAREFUL NOT TO DIE!
I'LL GET CHECKUPS AT THE HOSPITAL.
AVOID ACCIDENTS.
AND YOU THINK THAT WILL HELP?
SURELY YOU'RE JOKING??
IT WILL BE HARD TO FIX THIS IF YOU LIMIT YOURSELF TO THE REALM OF THE LIVING.
SO...
...WHY DON'T YOU GO SEE SCHOOL MYSTERY No. 1?
No. 1...
WAIT... YOU MEAN AKANE-KUN?
YES.

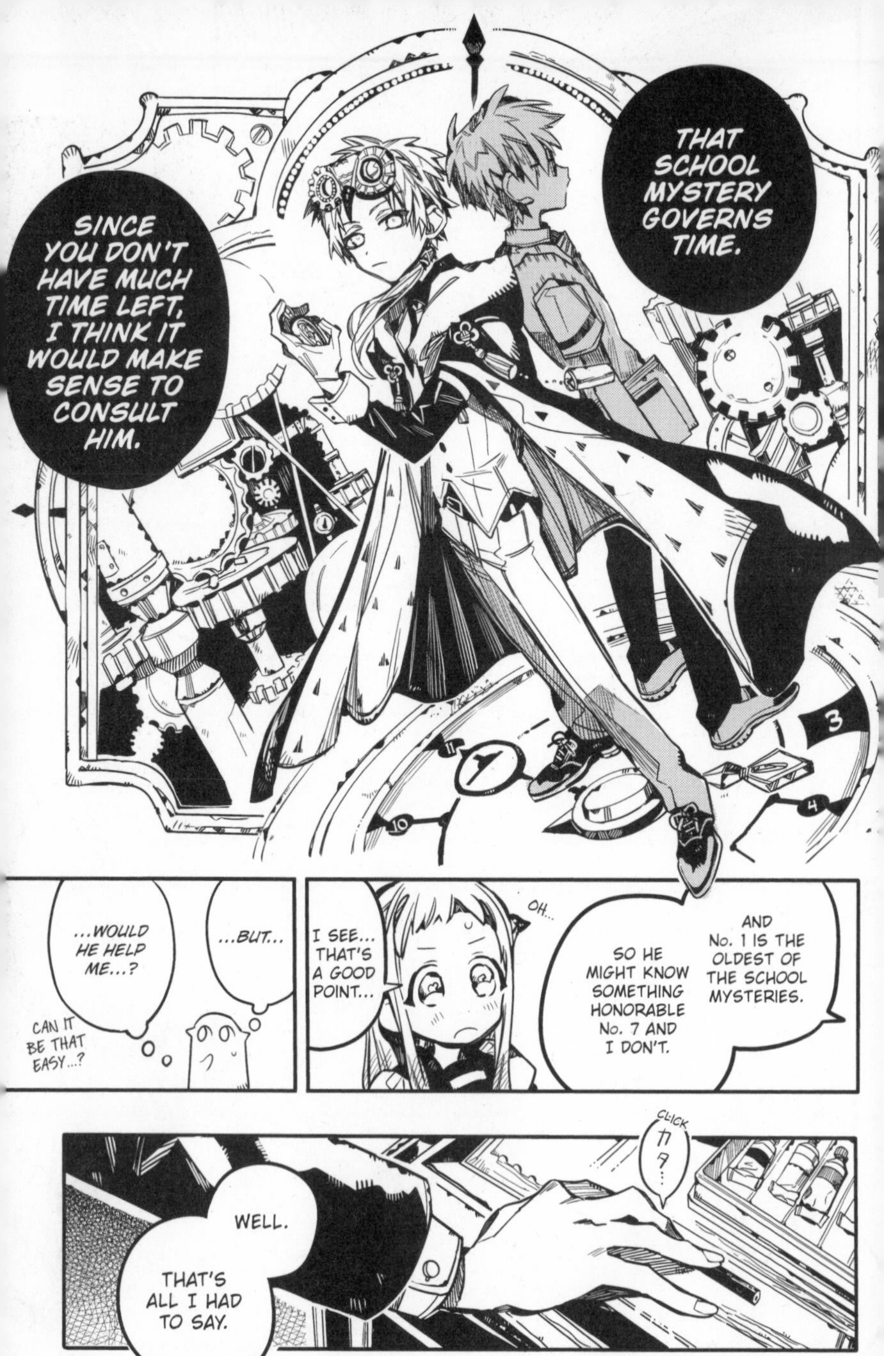

THAT SCHOOL MYSTERY GOVERNS TIME.
SINCE YOU DON'T HAVE MUCH TIME LEFT, I THINK IT WOULD MAKE SENSE TO CONSULT HIM.
AND No. 1 IS THE OLDEST OF THE SCHOOL MYSTERIES.
OH...
SO HE MIGHT KNOW SOMETHING HONORABLE No. 7 AND I DON'T.
I SEE... THAT'S A GOOD POINT...
...BUT...
...WOULD HE HELP ME...?
CAN IT BE THAT EASY...?
CLICK
カタ...
WELL.
THAT'S ALL I HAD TO SAY.

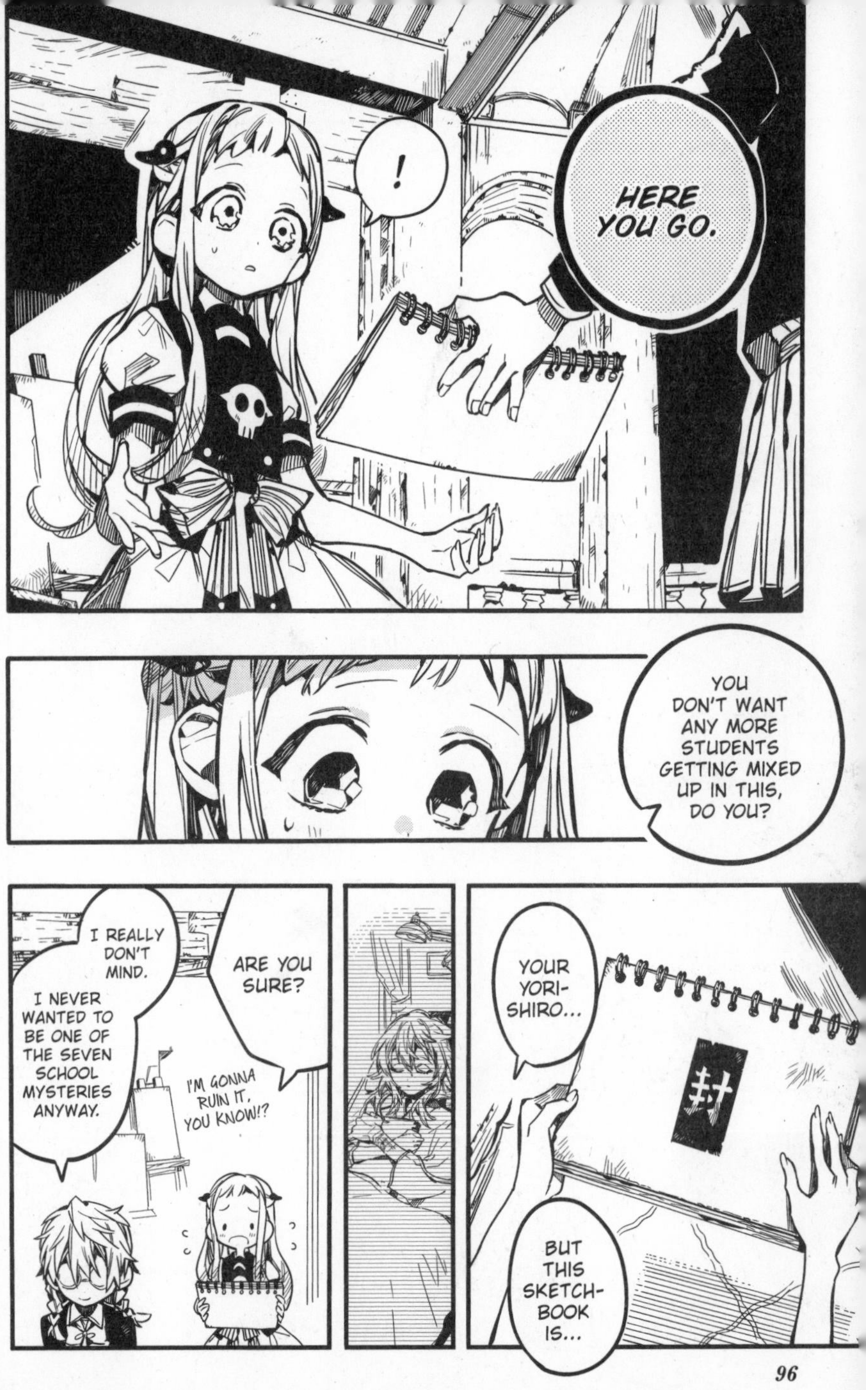
HERE YOU GO.
!
YOU DON'T WANT ANY MORE STUDENTS GETTING MIXED UP IN THIS, DO YOU?
YOUR YORI-SHIRO...
BUT THIS SKETCH-BOOK IS...
封
ARE YOU SURE?
I REALLY DON'T MIND.
I NEVER WANTED TO BE ONE OF THE SEVEN SCHOOL MYSTERIES ANYWAY.
I'M GONNA RUIN IT, YOU KNOW!?

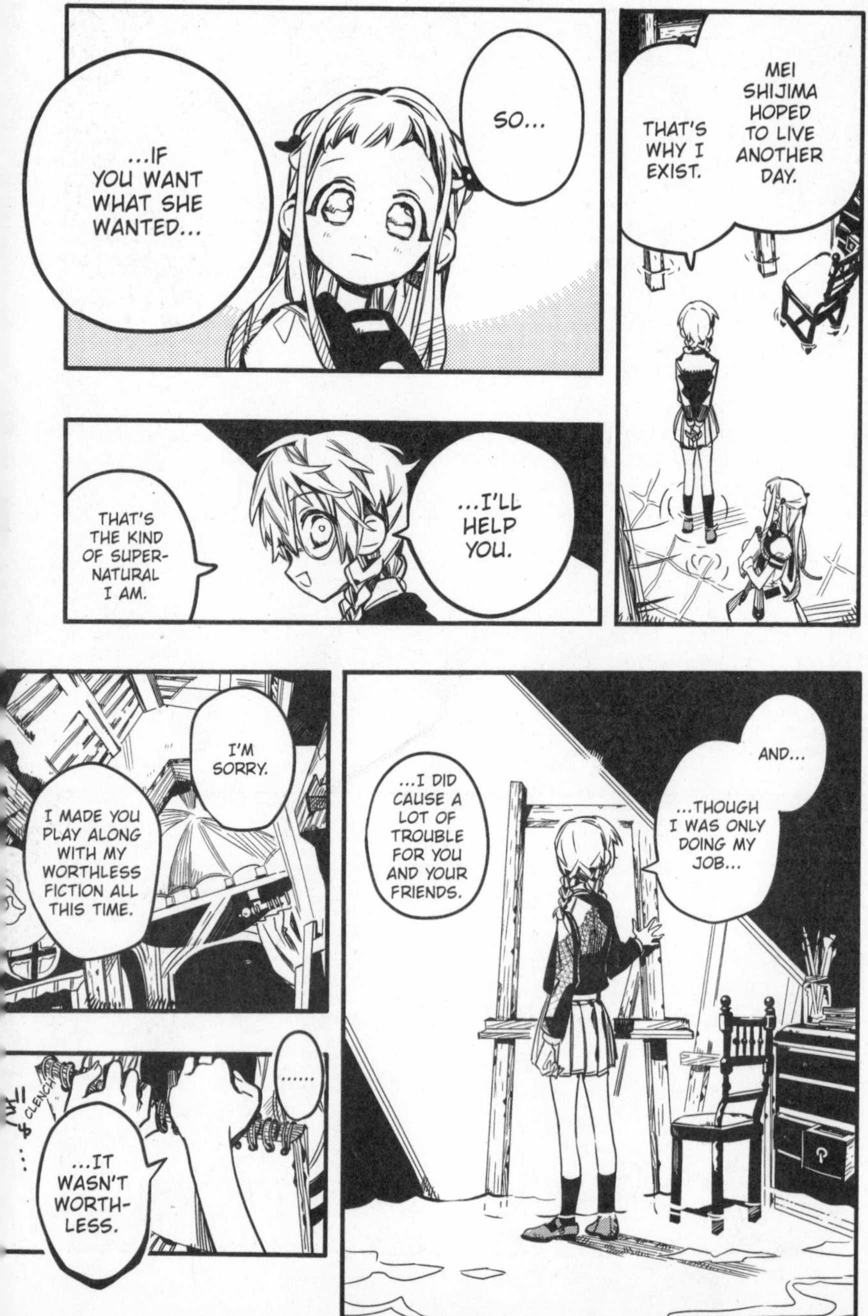
MEI SHIJIMA HOPED TO LIVE ANOTHER DAY.
THAT'S WHY I EXIST.
SO...
...IF YOU WANT WHAT SHE WANTED...
...I'LL HELP YOU.
THAT'S THE KIND OF SUPER-NATURAL I AM.
AND...
...THOUGH I WAS ONLY DOING MY JOB...
...I DID CAUSE A LOT OF TROUBLE FOR YOU AND YOUR FRIENDS.
I'M SORRY.
I MADE YOU PLAY ALONG WITH MY WORTHLESS FICTION ALL THIS TIME.
......
CLENCH
...IT WASN'T WORTH-LESS.

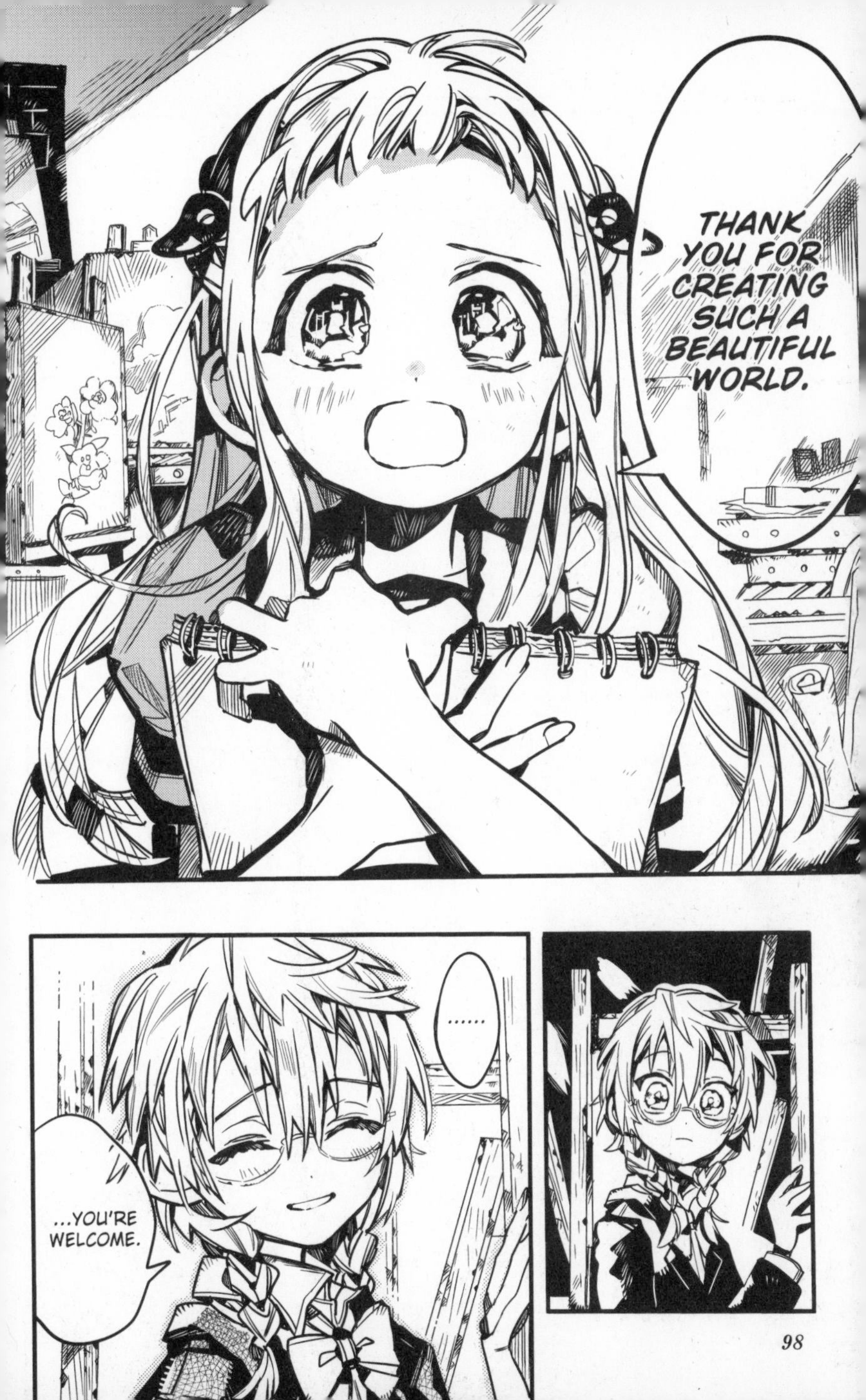
THANK YOU FOR CREATING SUCH A BEAUTIFUL WORLD.
......
...YOU'RE WELCOME.

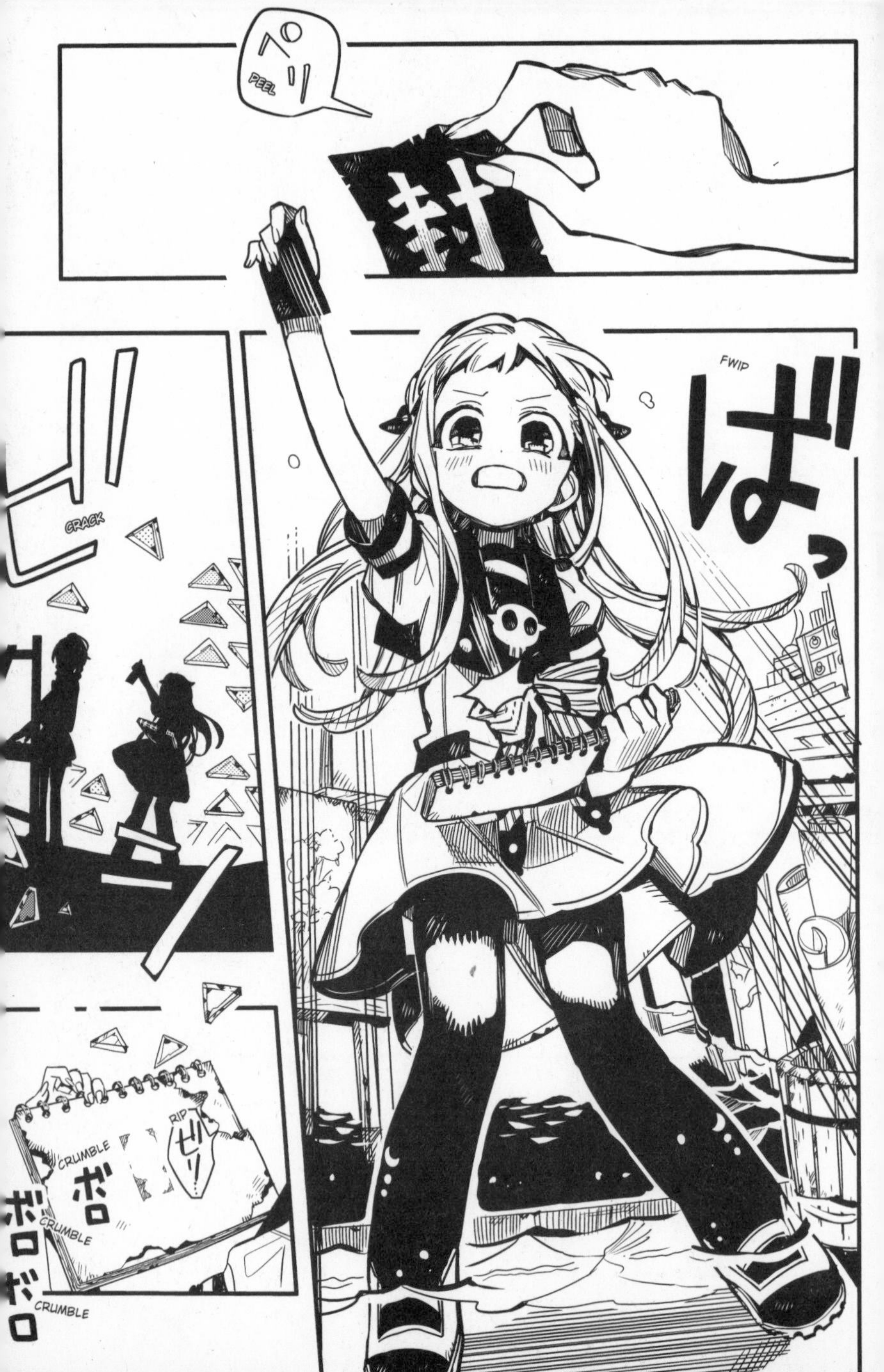

ペリ
PEEL
ばっ
FWIP
CRACK
ビリ
RIP
ボロ
CRUMBLE
CRUMBLE
ボロボロ
CRUMBLE

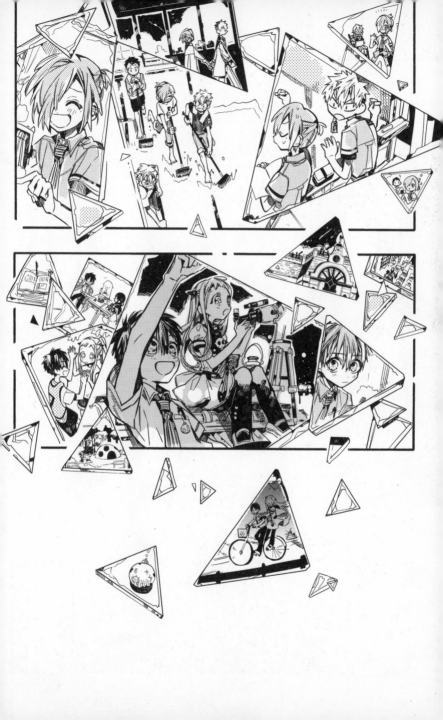

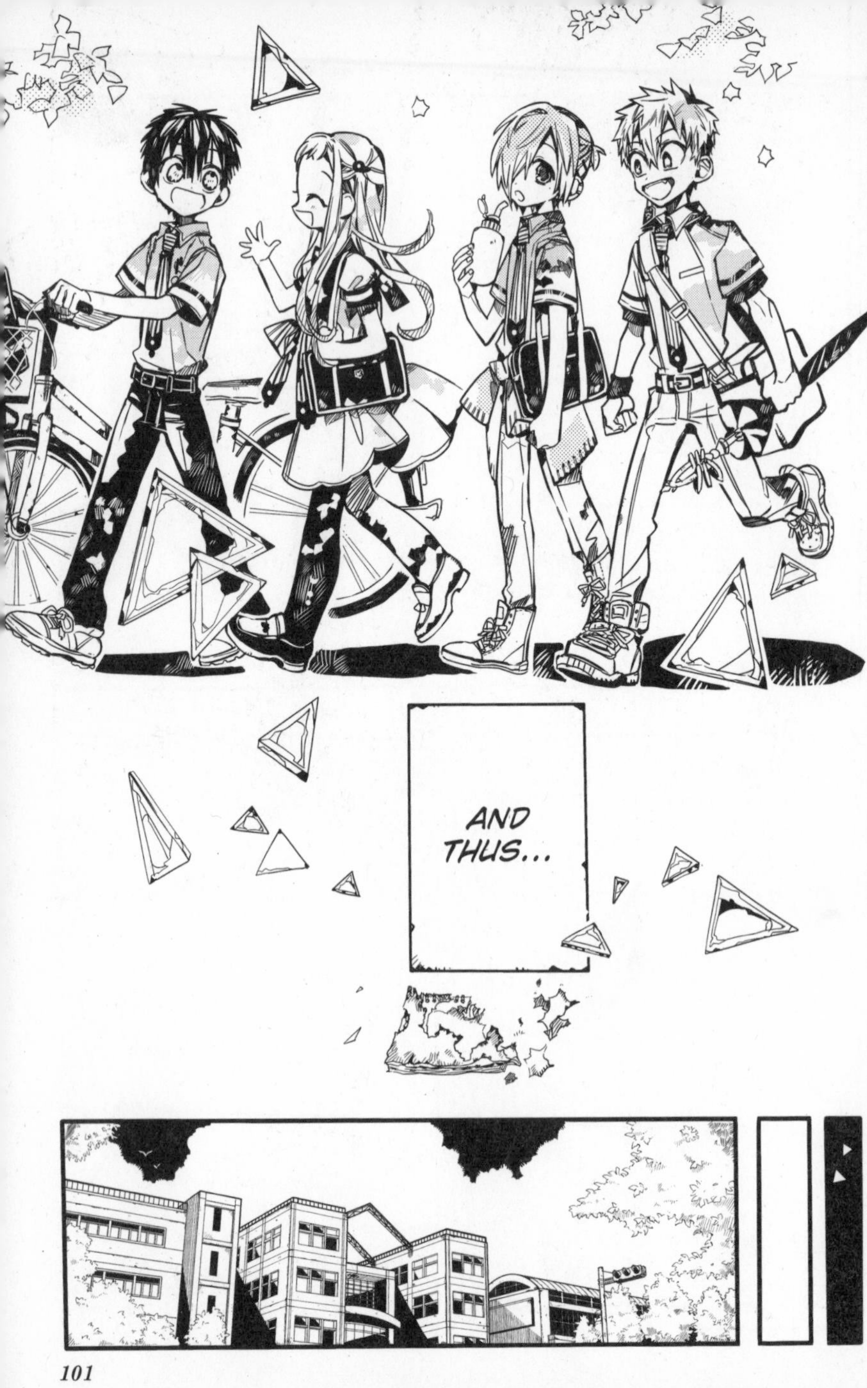
AND THUS...

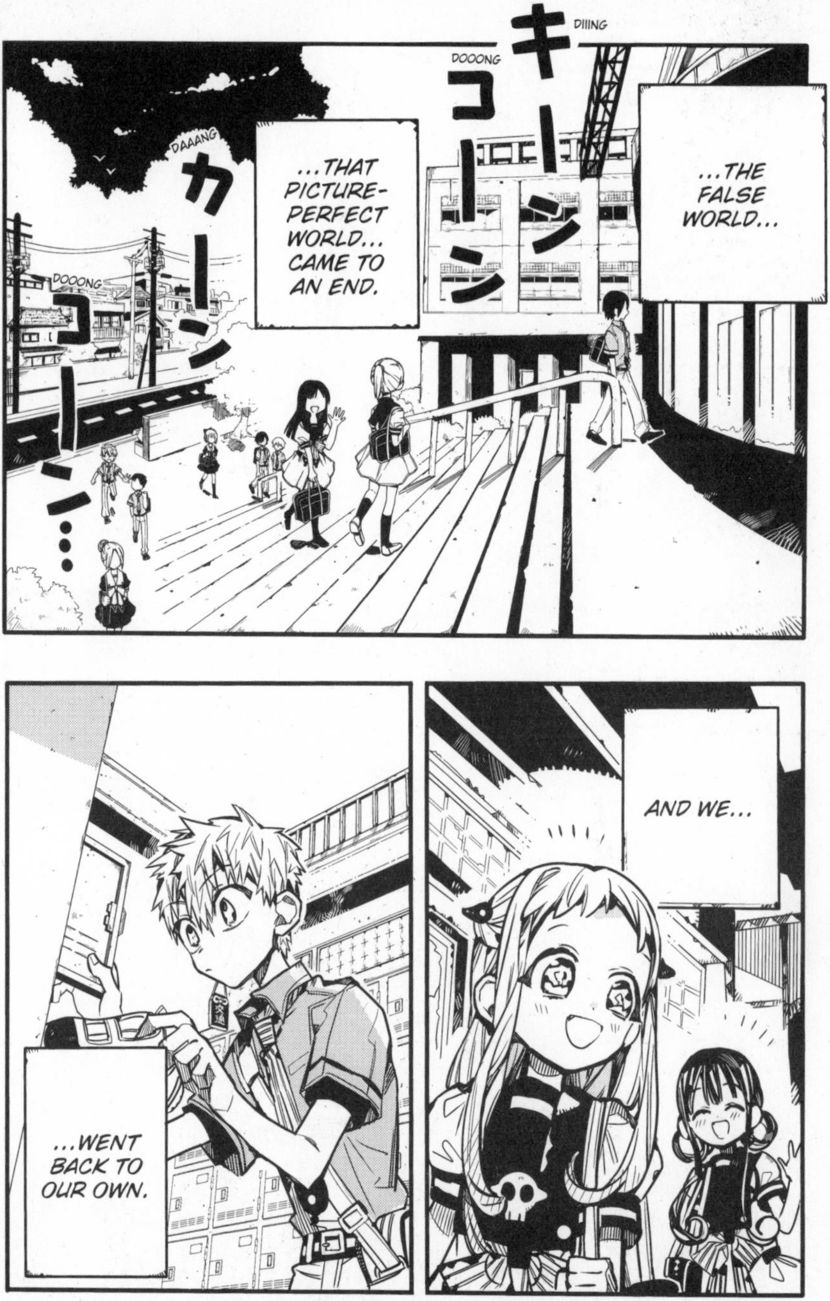
DIIING
DOOONG
...THE FALSE WORLD...
...THAT PICTURE-PERFECT WORLD... CAME TO AN END.
DAAANG
DOOONG
AND WE...
...WENT BACK TO OUR OWN.

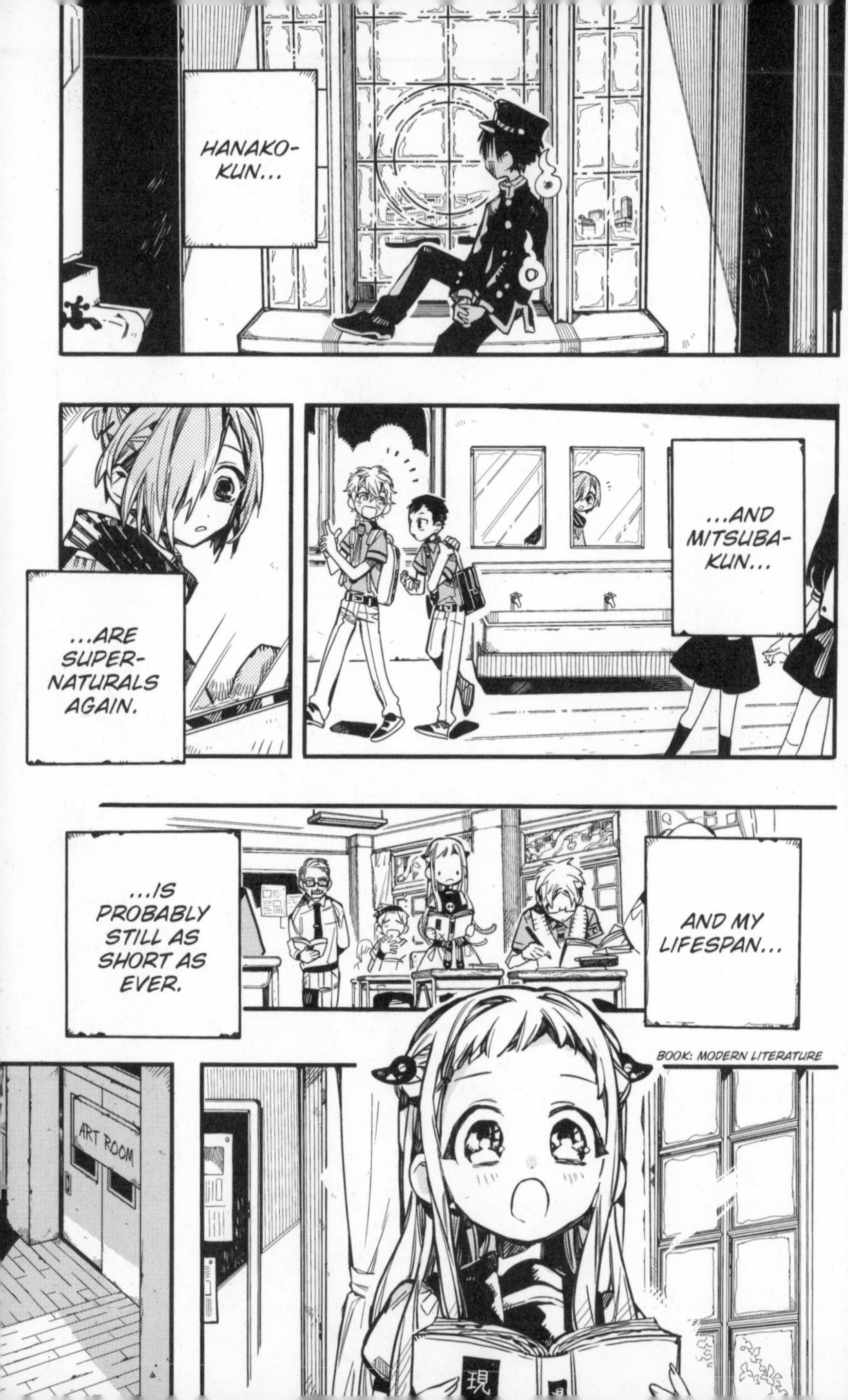
HANAKO-KUN...
...AND MITSUBA-KUN...
...ARE SUPER-NATURALS AGAIN.
AND MY LIFESPAN...
...IS PROBABLY STILL AS SHORT AS EVER.
BOOK: MODERN LITERATURE
ART ROOM

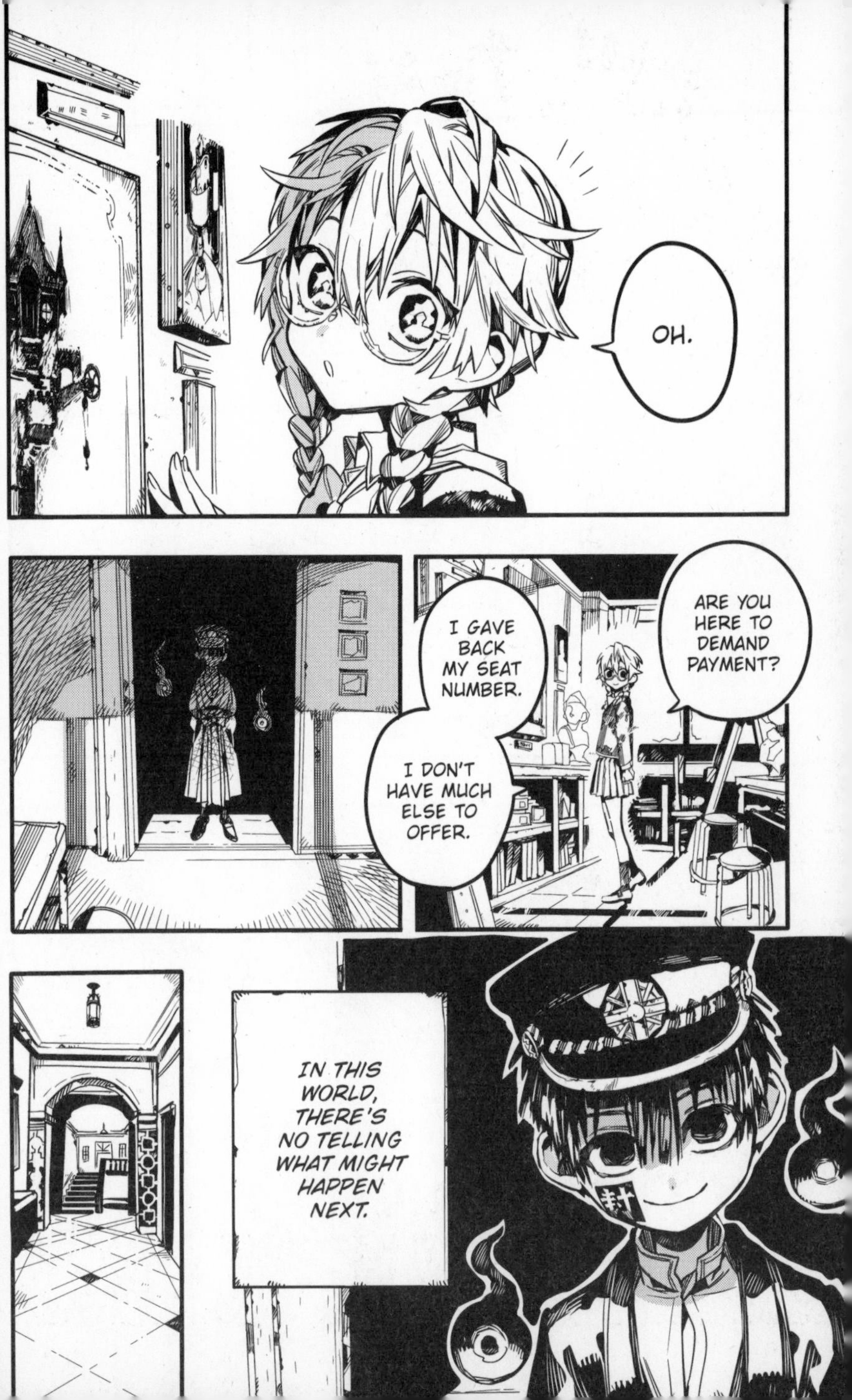
OH.
ARE YOU HERE TO DEMAND PAYMENT?
I GAVE BACK MY SEAT NUMBER.
I DON'T HAVE MUCH ELSE TO OFFER.
IN THIS WORLD, THERE'S NO TELLING WHAT MIGHT HAPPEN NEXT.

だだだ
TMP TMP TMP
たたた
TEP TEP TEP
ばったり…
BUMP
AH!
OH!
HEH HEH HEH...
ひょこ
POP
HAAANAKO-KUN!
HANAKO!

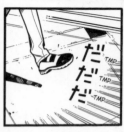

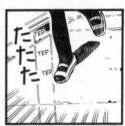

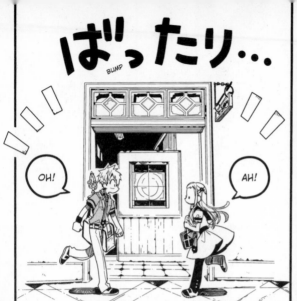

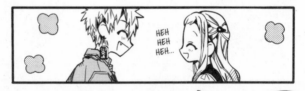

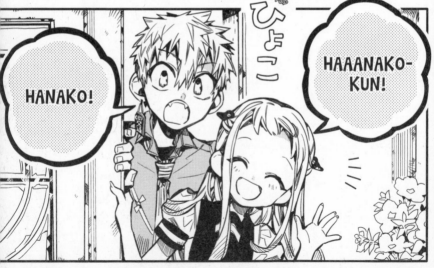

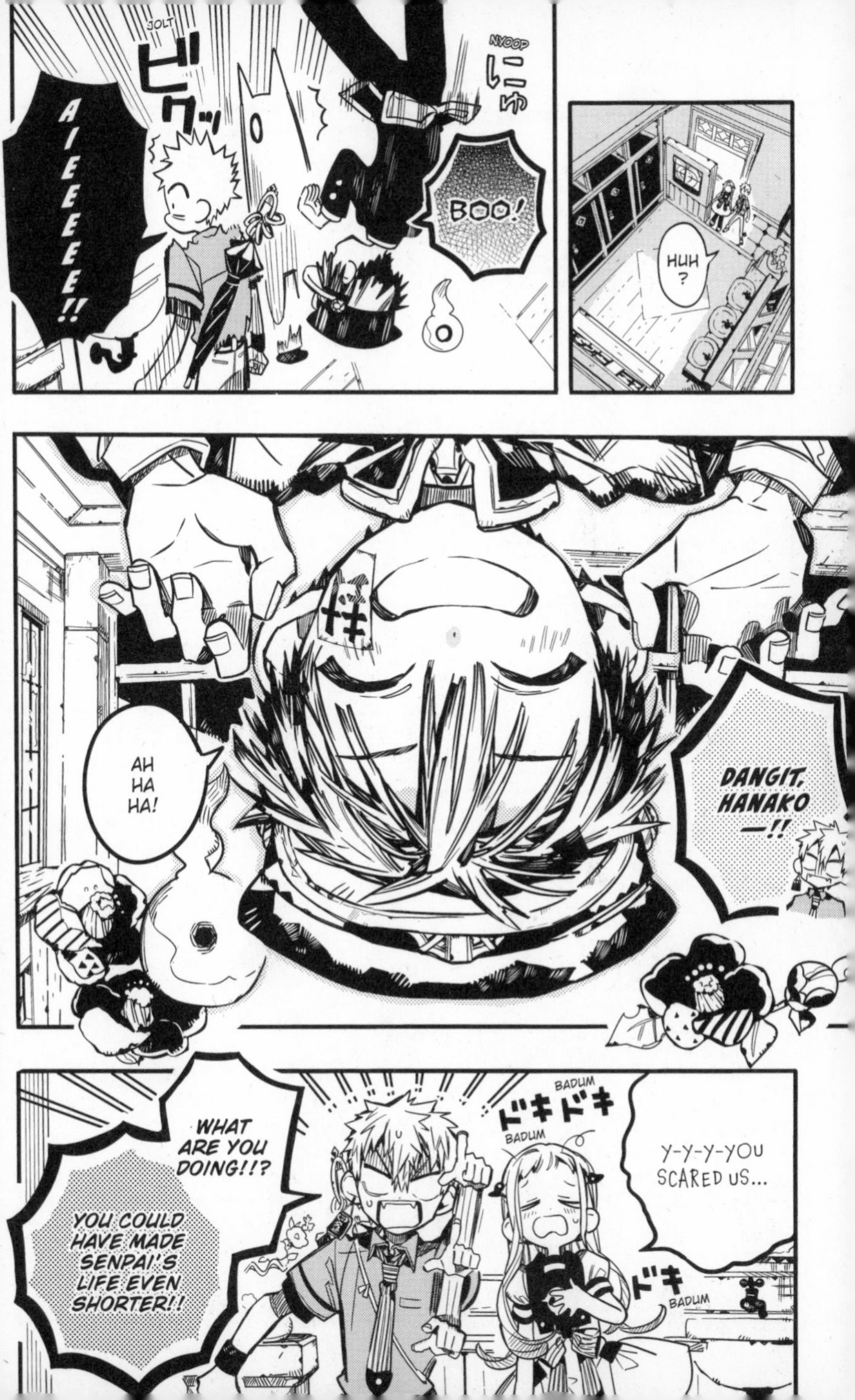
HUH?
NYOOP
にゅ
BOO!
JOLT
ビクッ
AIEEEEEE!!
DANGIT, HANAKO—!!
AH HA HA!
Y-Y-Y-YOU SCARED US...
BADUM
ドキドキ
BADUM
ドキ
BADUM
WHAT ARE YOU DOING!!?
YOU COULD HAVE MADE SENPAI'S LIFE EVEN SHORTER!!

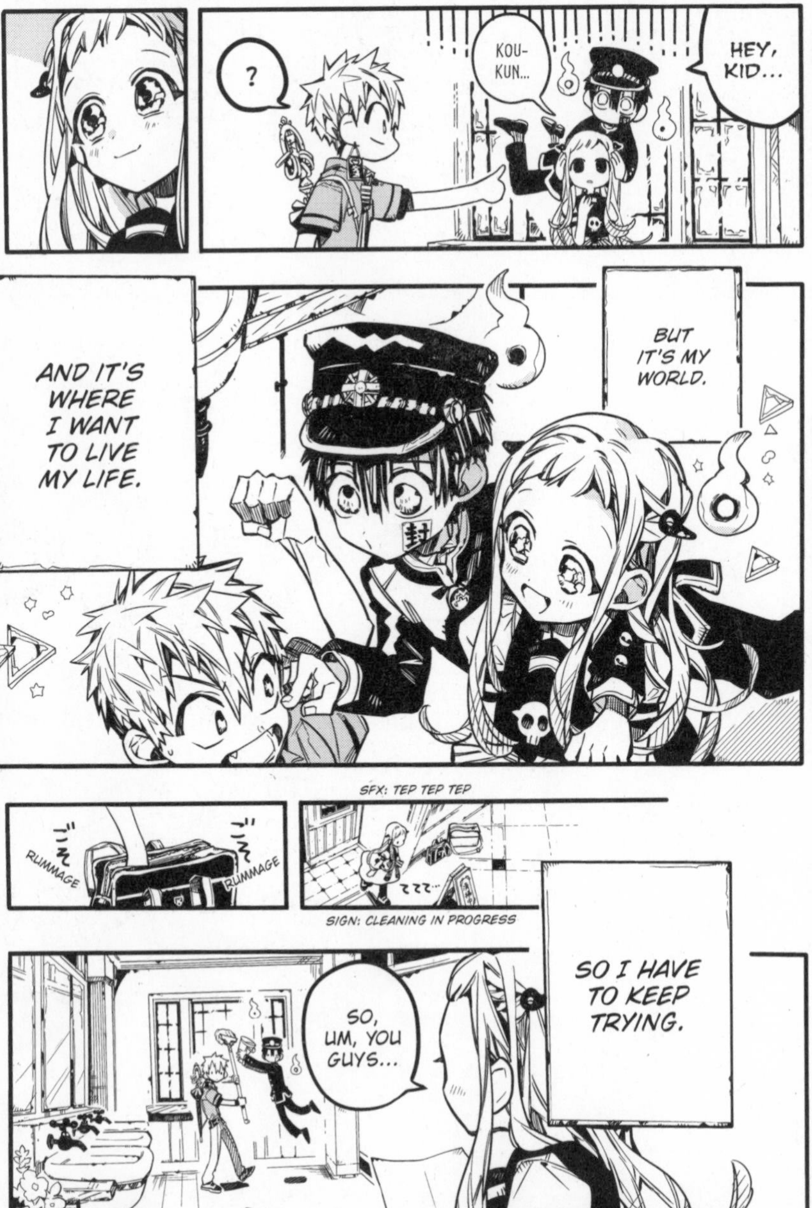
HEY, KID...
KOU-KUN...
?
BUT IT'S MY WORLD.
AND IT'S WHERE I WANT TO LIVE MY LIFE.
SFX: TEP TEP TEP
zzz...
SIGN: CLEANING IN PROGRESS
RUMMAGE
RUMMAGE
SO I HAVE TO KEEP TRYING.
SO, UM, YOU GUYS...

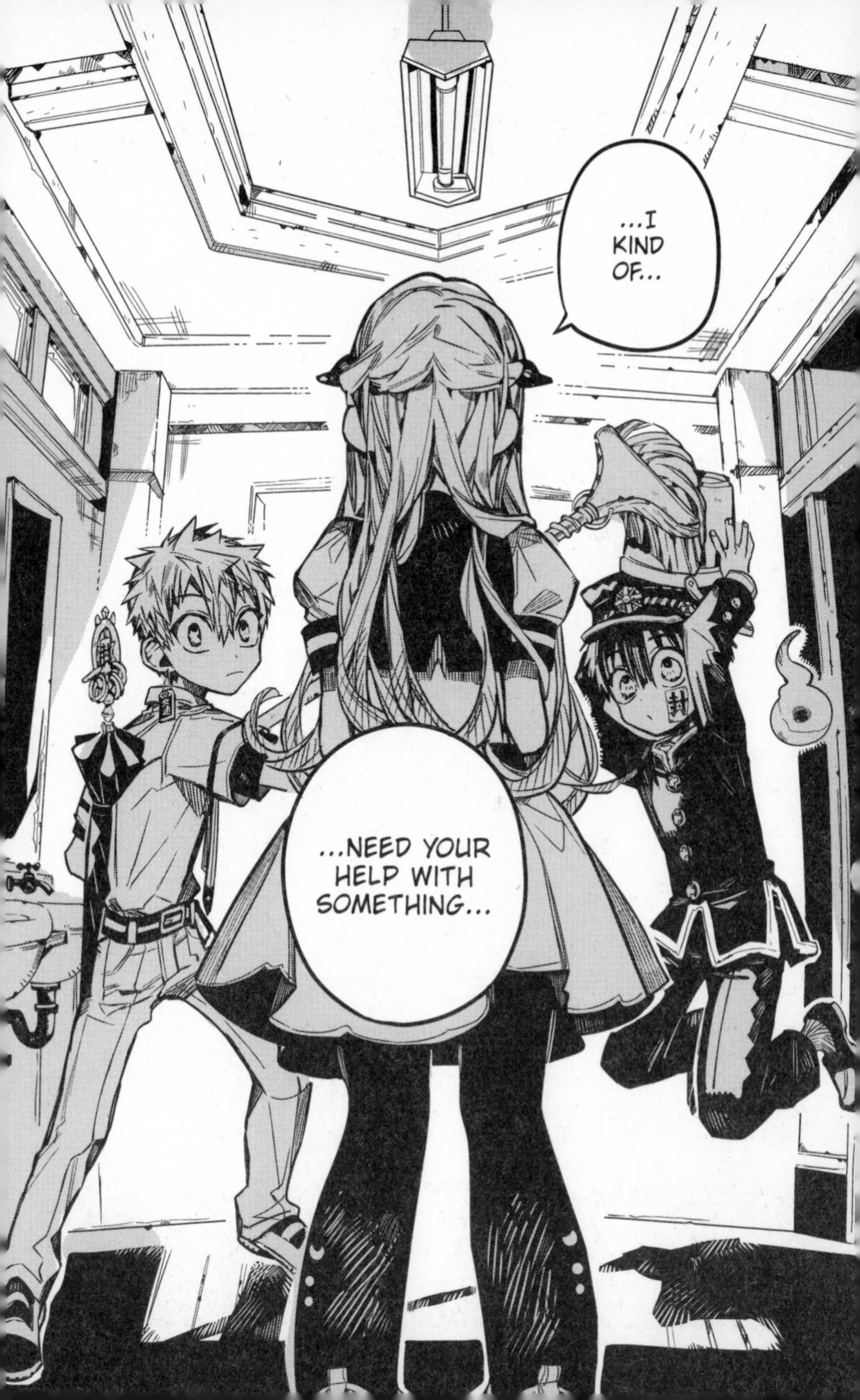
...I KIND OF...
...NEED YOUR HELP WITH SOMETHING...

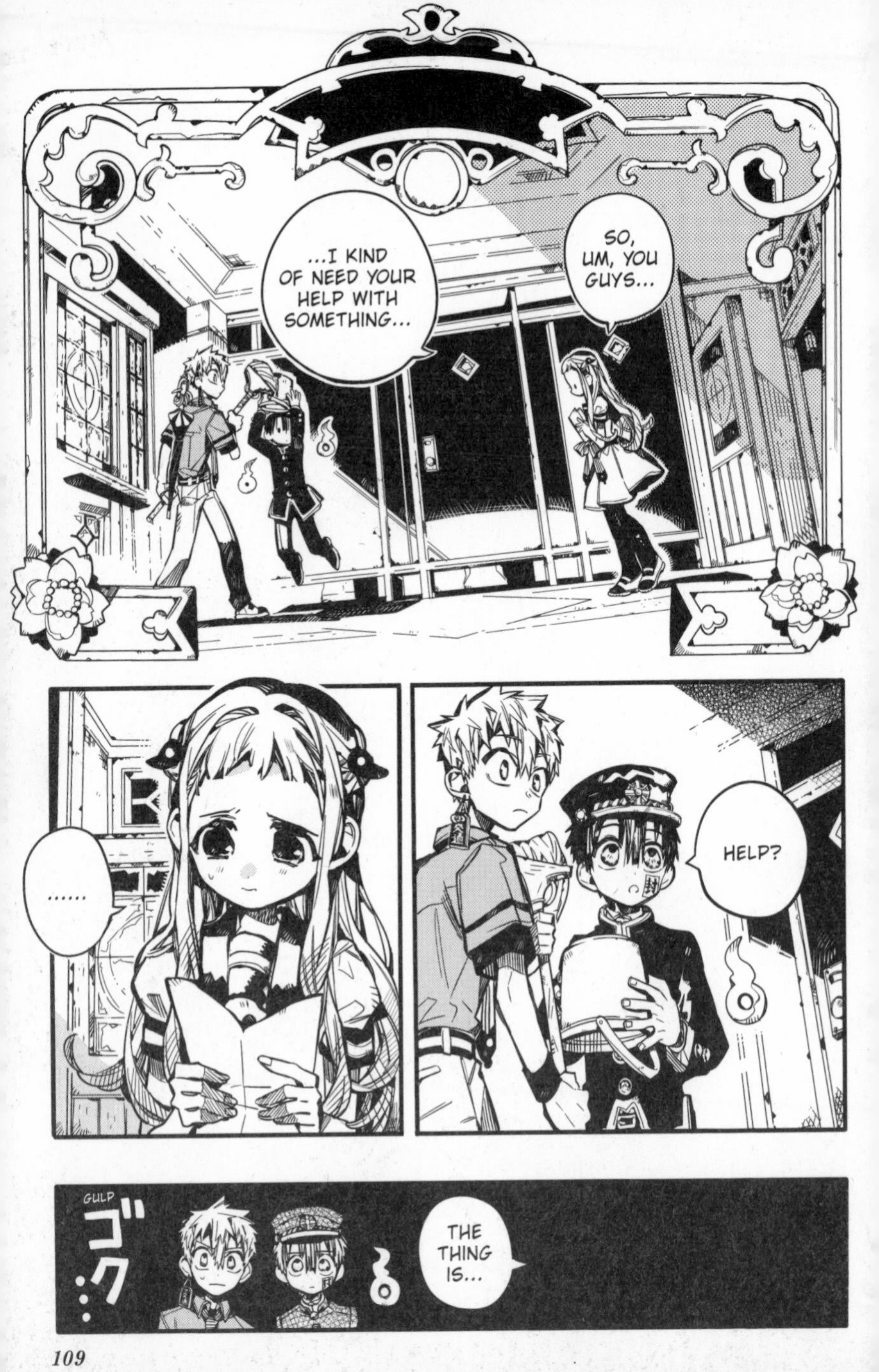
SO, UM, YOU GUYS...
...I KIND OF NEED YOUR HELP WITH SOMETHING...
HELP?
......
THE THING IS...
GULP
ゴク

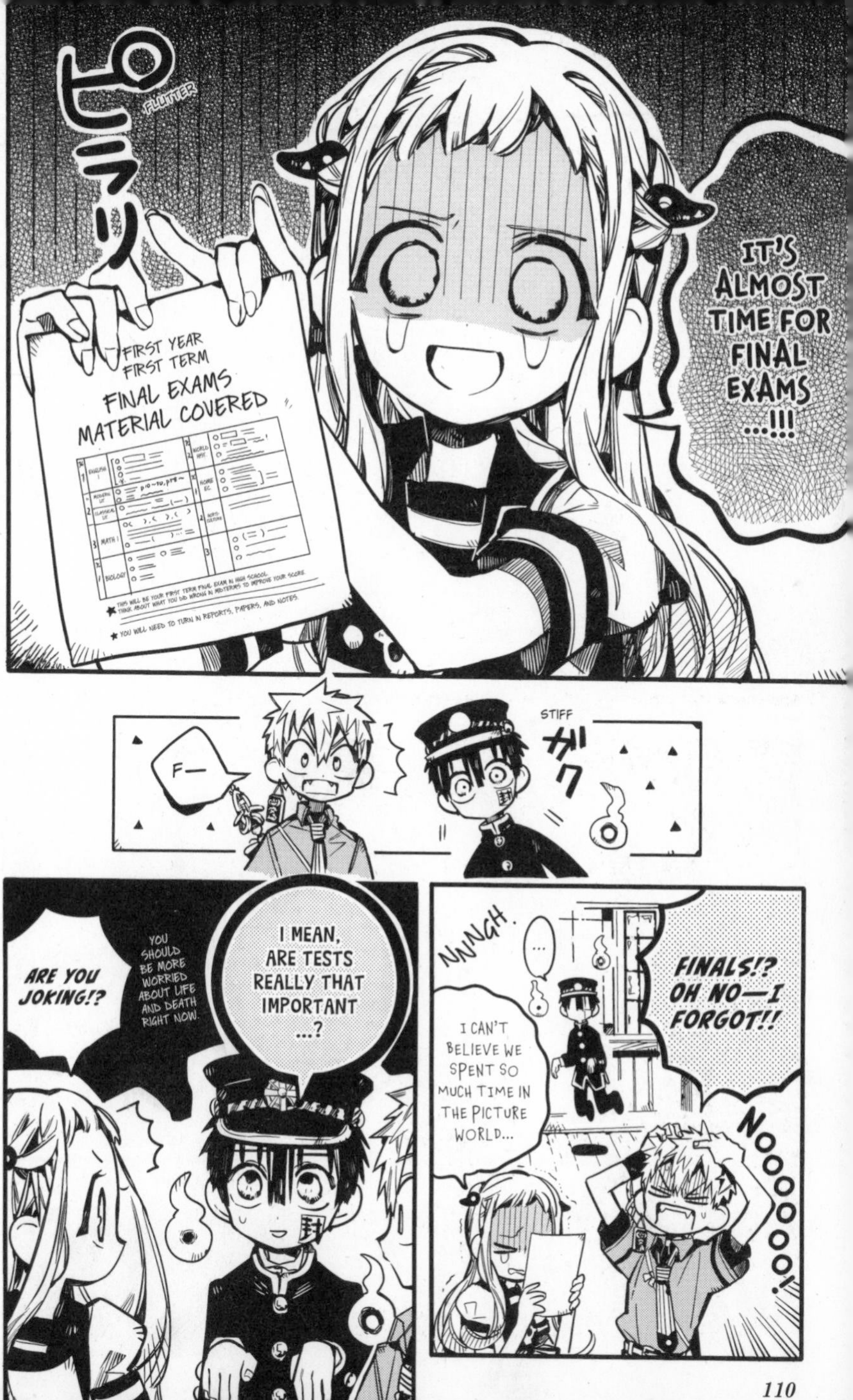
FLUTTER
FIRST YEAR FIRST TERM
FINAL EXAMS MATERIAL COVERED
ENGLISH I
MODERN LIT
CLASSICAL LIT
MATH I
BIOLOGY
WORLD HIST.
HOME EC.
THIS WILL BE YOUR FIRST TERM FINAL EXAM IN HIGH SCHOOL. THINK ABOUT WHAT YOU DID WRONG IN MIDTERMS TO IMPROVE YOUR SCORE.
YOU WILL NEED TO TURN IN REPORTS, PAPERS, AND NOTES.
IT'S ALMOST TIME FOR FINAL EXAMS ...!!!
STIFF
F—
FINALS!? OH NO—I FORGOT!!
NOOOOOOO!
NNNGH.
...
I CAN'T BELIEVE WE SPENT SO MUCH TIME IN THE PICTURE WORLD...
I MEAN, ARE TESTS REALLY THAT IMPORTANT ...?
YOU SHOULD BE MORE WORRIED ABOUT LIFE AND DEATH RIGHT NOW.
ARE YOU JOKING!?

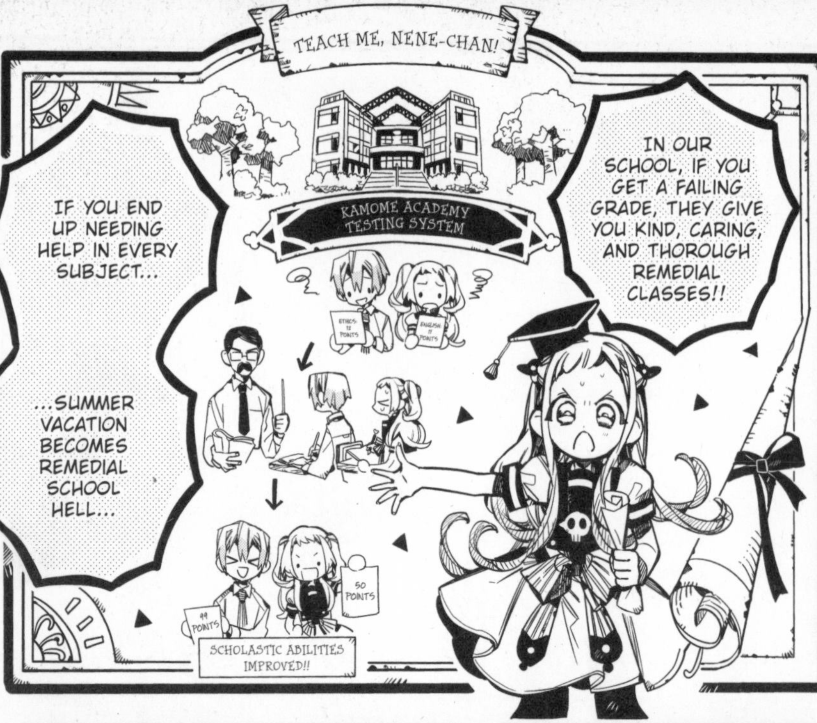
TEACH ME, NENE-CHAN!
IN OUR SCHOOL, IF YOU GET A FAILING GRADE, THEY GIVE YOU KIND, CARING, AND THOROUGH REMEDIAL CLASSES!!
KAMOME ACADEMY TESTING SYSTEM
ENGLISH 11 POINTS
ETHICS: 12 POINTS
50 POINTS
99 POINTS
SCHOLASTIC ABILITIES IMPROVED!!
IF YOU END UP NEEDING HELP IN EVERY SUBJECT...
...SUMMER VACATION BECOMES REMEDIAL SCHOOL HELL...

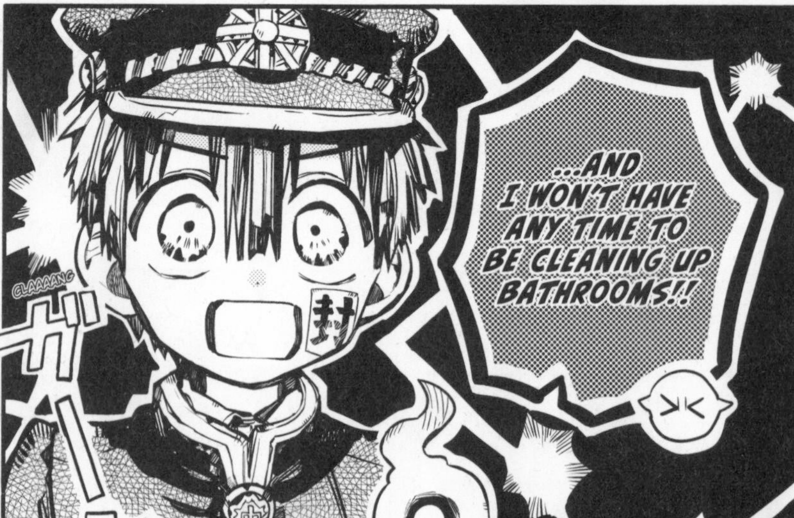
...AND I WON'T HAVE ANY TIME TO BE CLEANING UP BATHROOMS!!
CLAAAANG

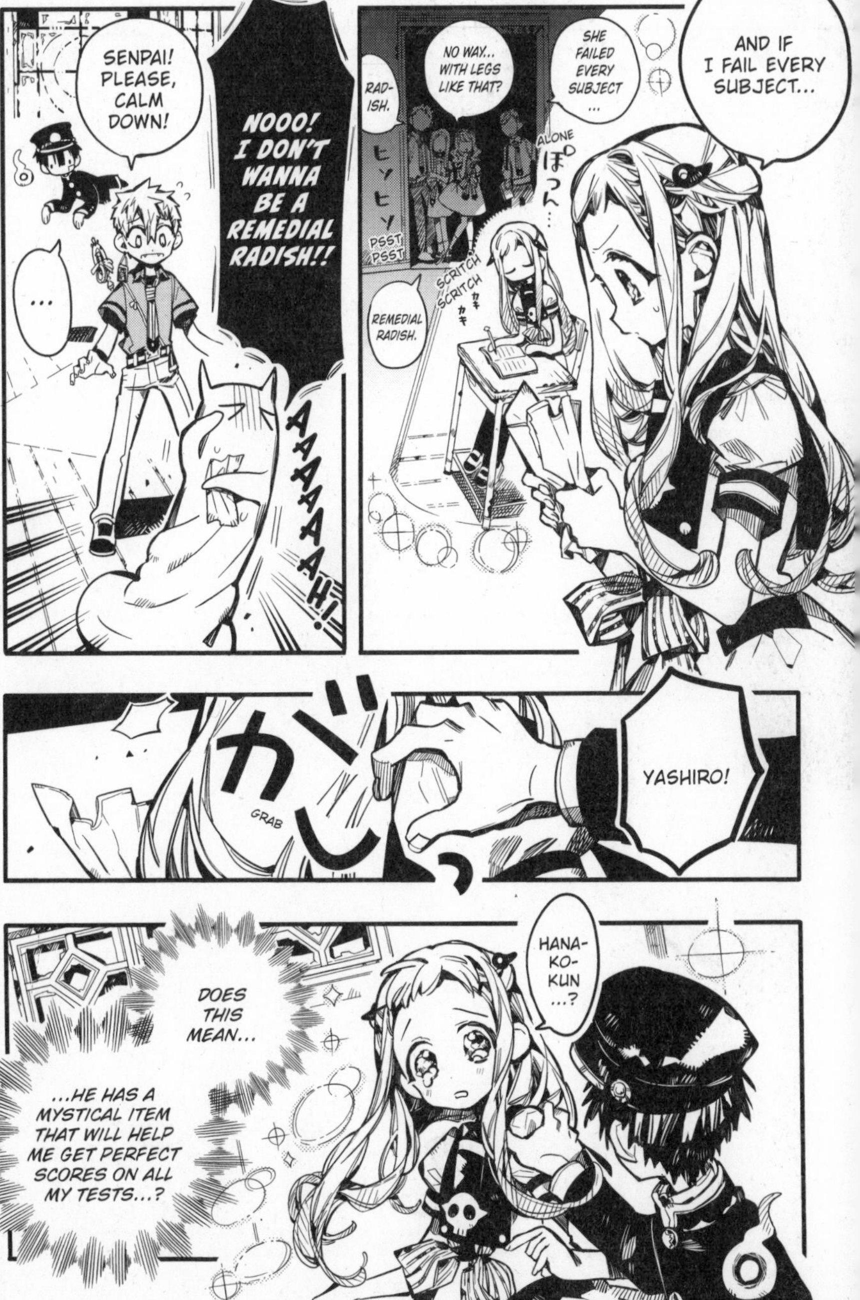
AND IF I FAIL EVERY SUBJECT...
SHE FAILED EVERY SUBJECT...
NO WAY... WITH LEGS LIKE THAT?
RADISH.
ALONE
ぽつん…
ヒソヒソ
PSST PSST
SCRITCH SCRITCH
カキカキ
REMEDIAL RADISH.
NOOO! I DON'T WANNA BE A REMEDIAL RADISH!!
AAAAAAAH!
SENPAI! PLEASE, CALM DOWN!
...
YASHIRO!
ガシっ
GRAB
HANAKO-KUN...?
DOES THIS MEAN...
...HE HAS A MYSTICAL ITEM THAT WILL HELP ME GET PERFECT SCORES ON ALL MY TESTS...?

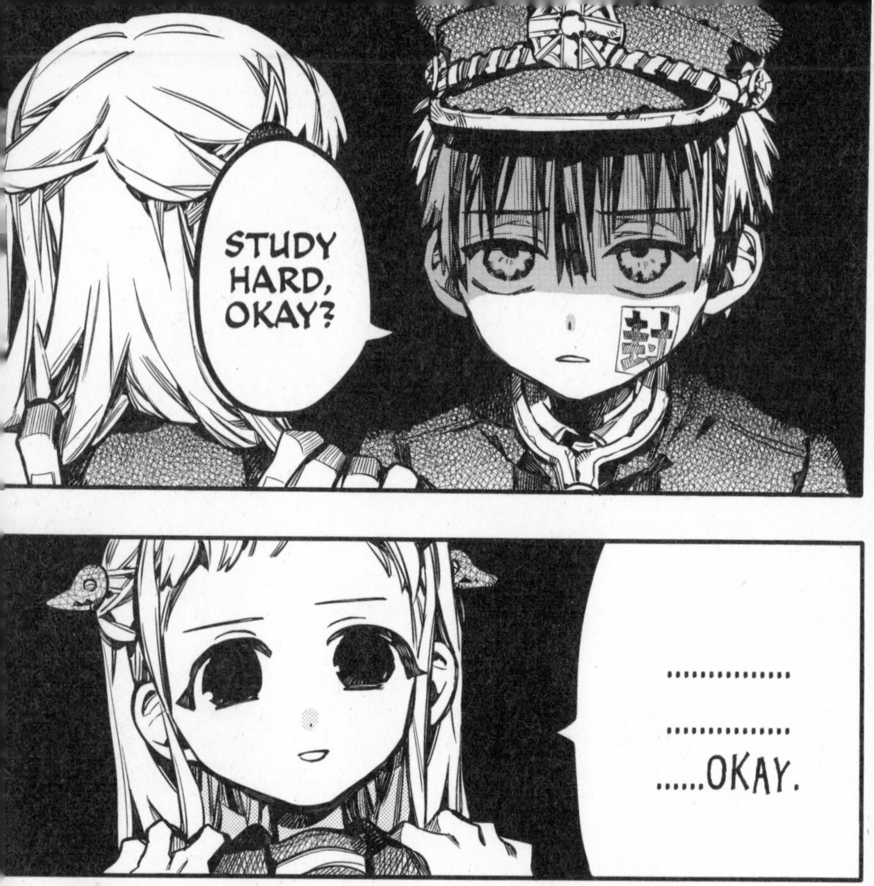
STUDY HARD, OKAY?
....
....
......OKAY.

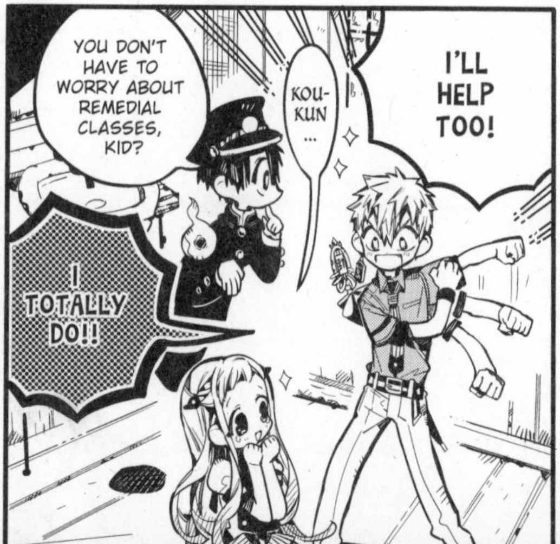
I'LL HELP TOO!
KOU-KUN...
YOU DON'T HAVE TO WORRY ABOUT REMEDIAL CLASSES, KID?
I TOTALLY DO!!

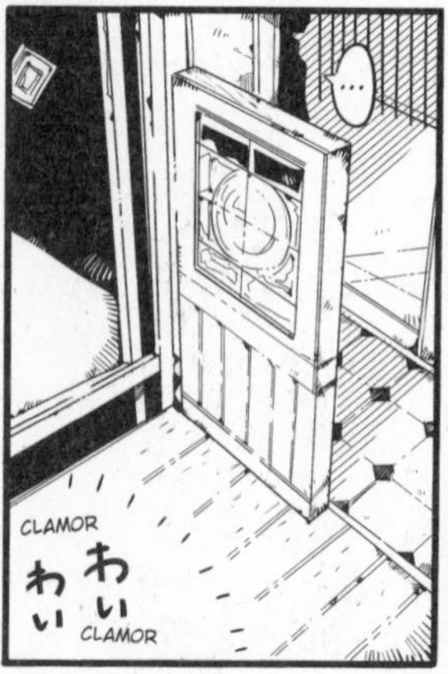
...
CLAMOR
わい
わい
CLAMOR

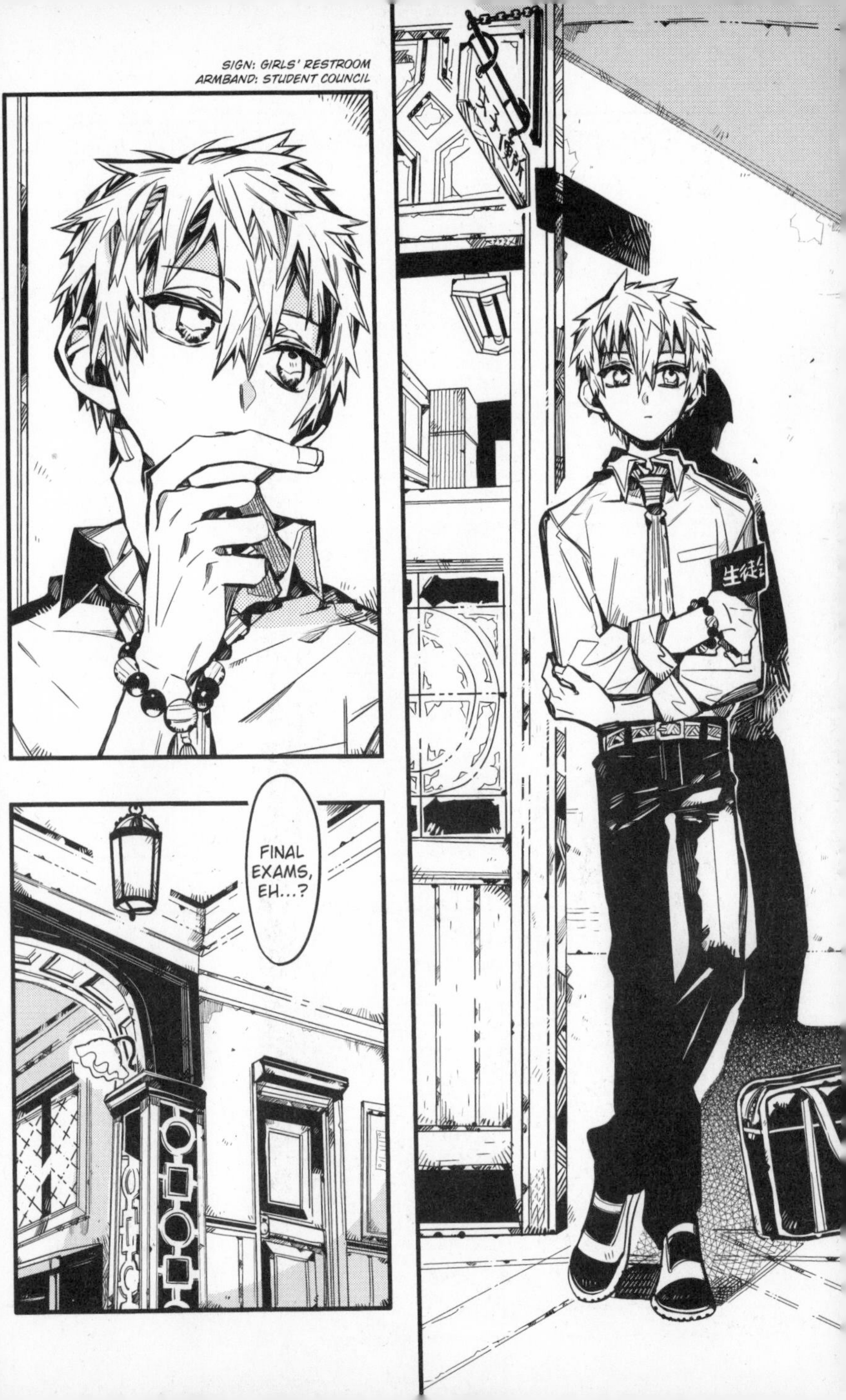
SIGN: GIRLS' RESTROOM
ARMBAND: STUDENT COUNCIL
FINAL EXAMS, EH...?

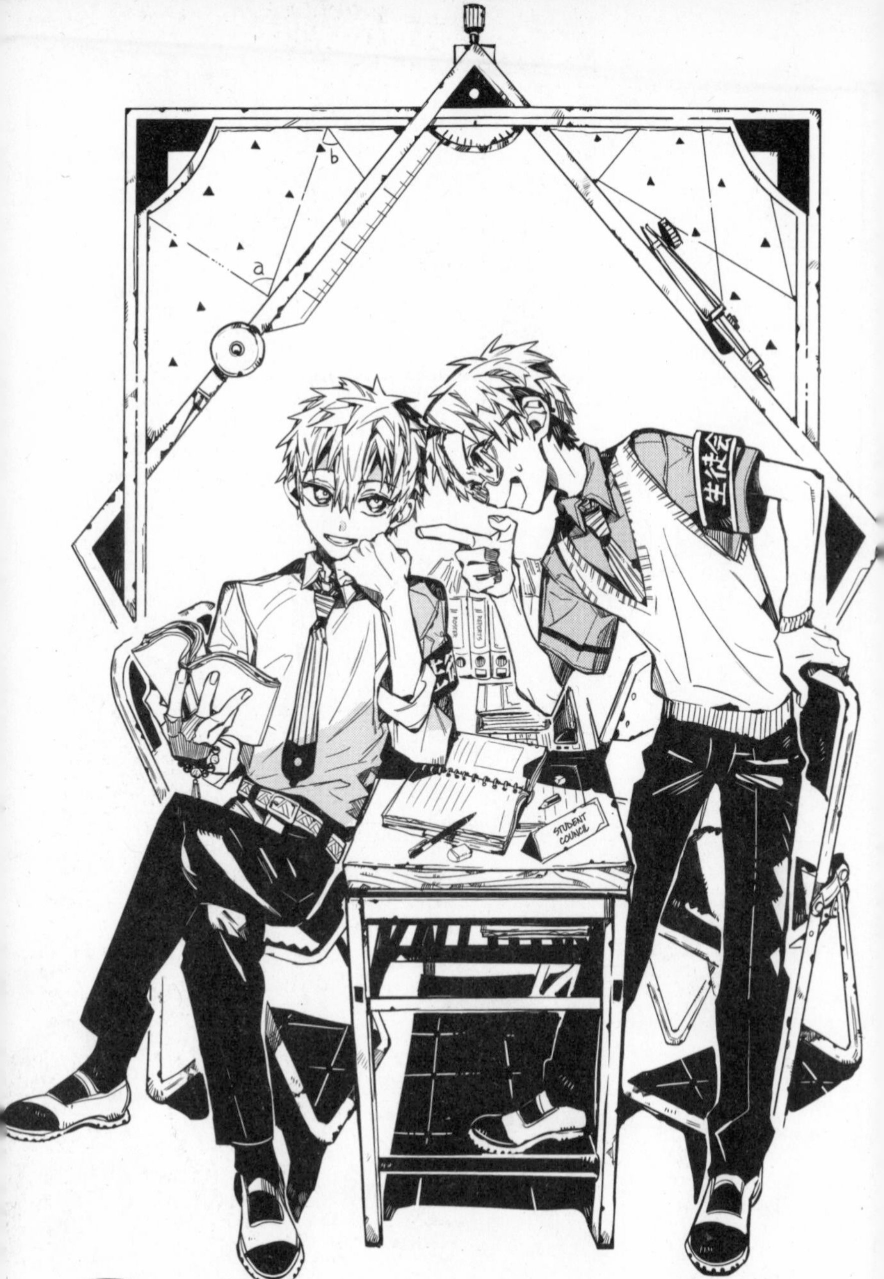
a
b
STUDENT COUNCIL

SPOOK 59

FINAL EXAMS

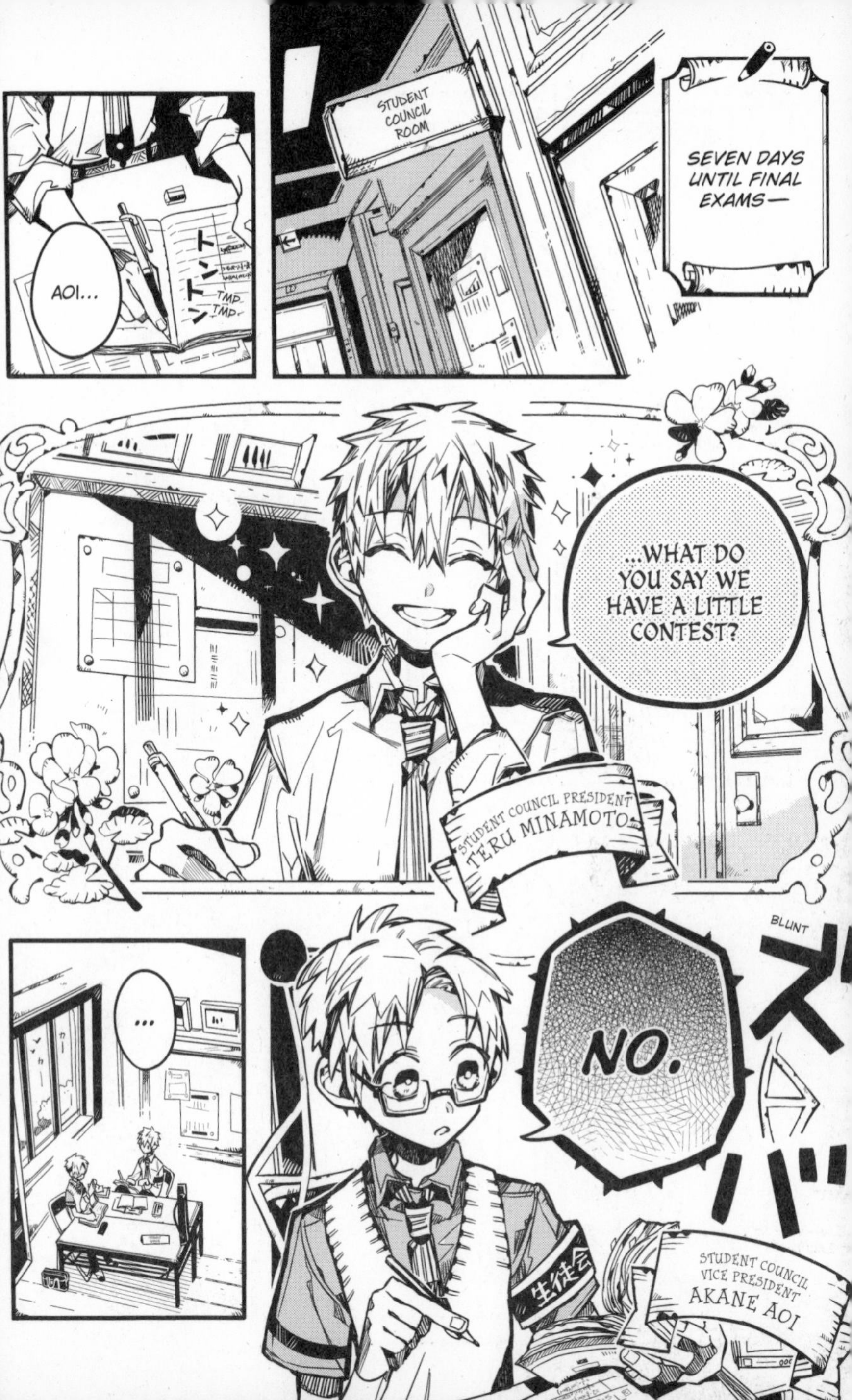
SEVEN DAYS UNTIL FINAL EXAMS—
STUDENT COUNCIL ROOM
AOI...
TMP TMP
...WHAT DO YOU SAY WE HAVE A LITTLE CONTEST?
STUDENT COUNCIL PRESIDENT TERU MINAMOTO
BLUNT
NO.
STUDENT COUNCIL VICE PRESIDENT AKANE AOI
生徒会
...

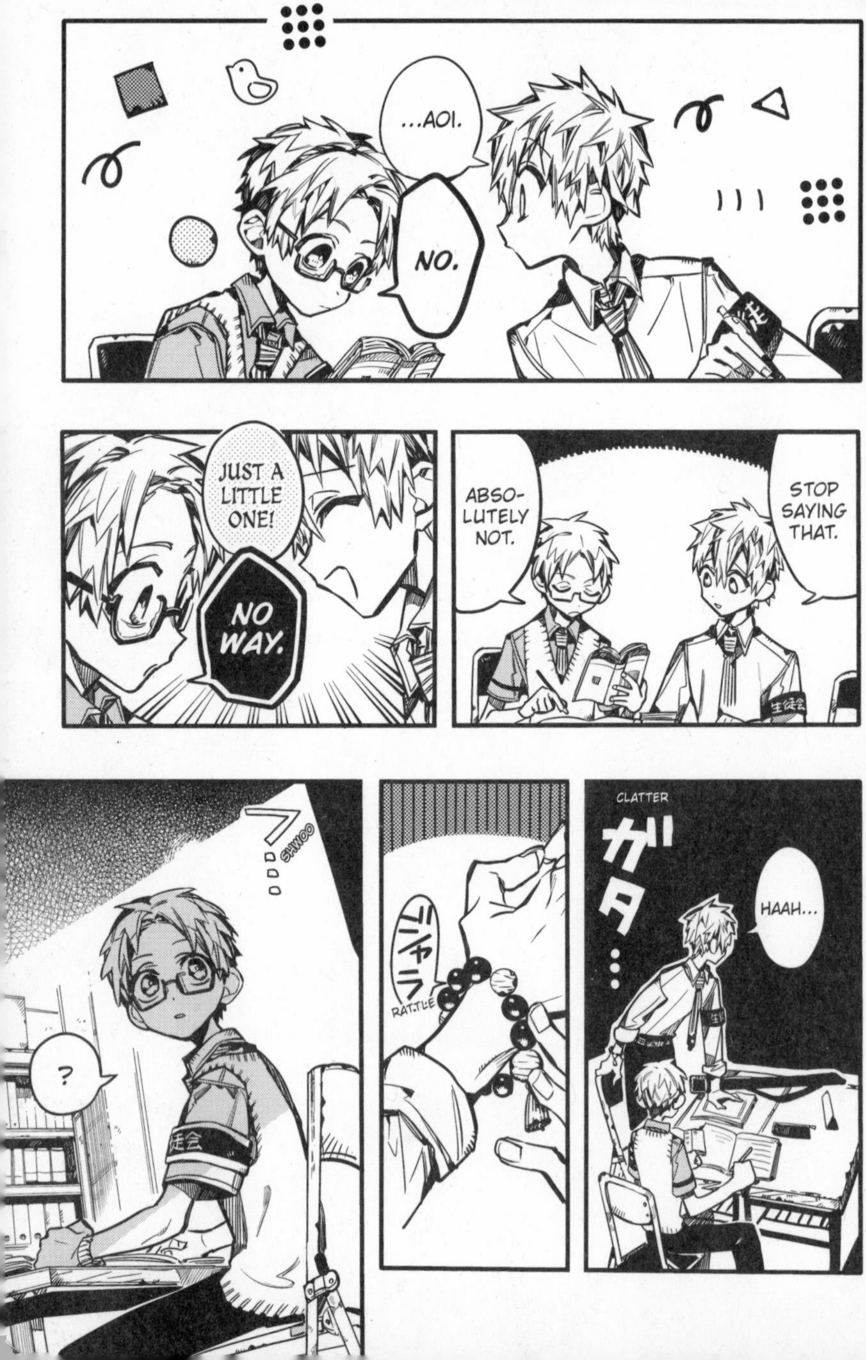
...AOI.
NO.
STOP SAYING THAT.
ABSO-LUTELY NOT.
JUST A LITTLE ONE!
NO WAY.
CLATTER
ガタ…
HAAH...
ジャラ
RATTLE
フ…
SHWOO
?

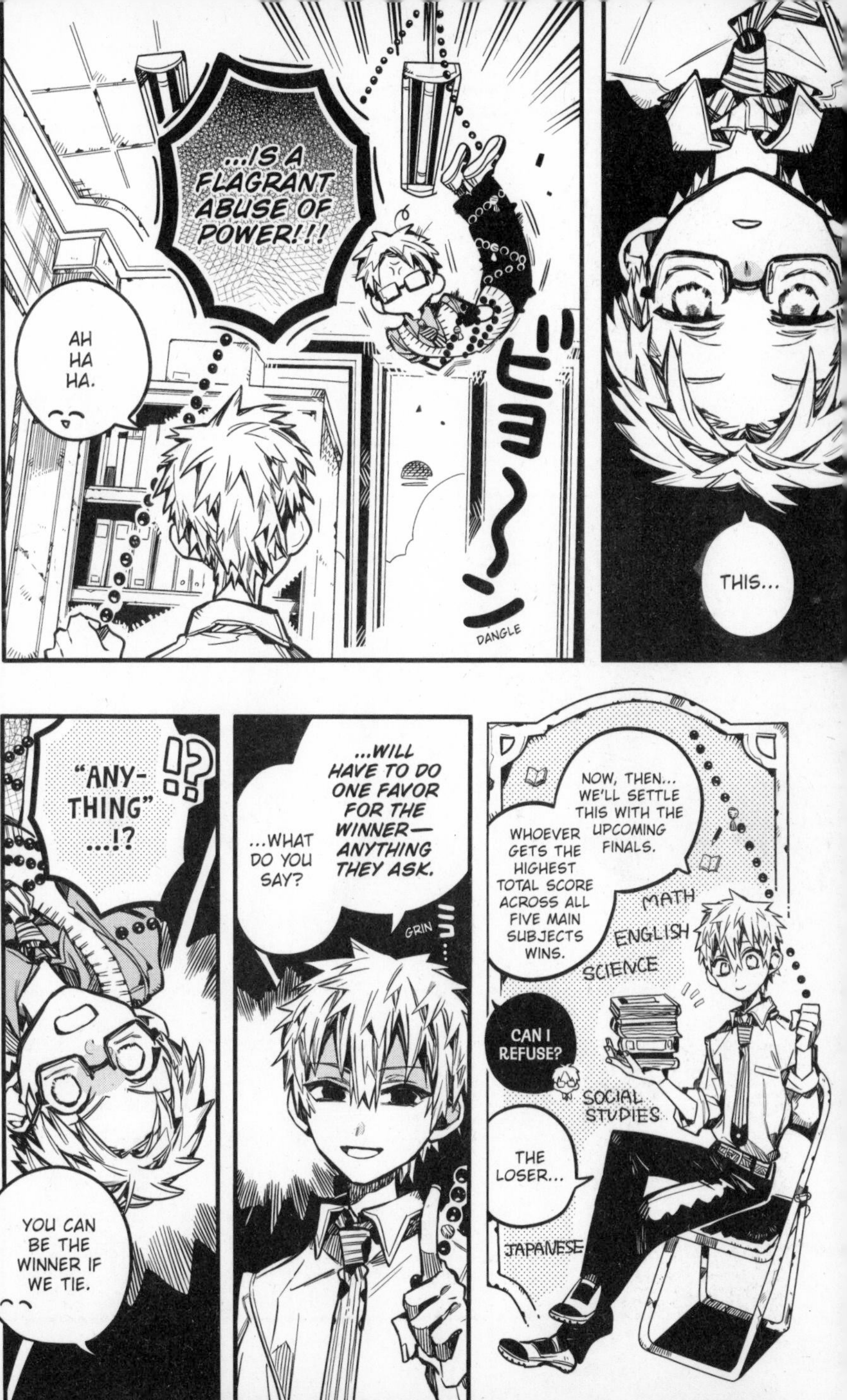
THIS...
...IS A FLAGRANT ABUSE OF POWER!!!
AH HA HA.
DANGLE
NOW, THEN... WE'LL SETTLE THIS WITH THE UPCOMING FINALS.
WHOEVER GETS THE HIGHEST TOTAL SCORE ACROSS ALL FIVE MAIN SUBJECTS WINS.
MATH
ENGLISH
SCIENCE
CAN I REFUSE?
SOCIAL STUDIES
THE LOSER...
JAPANESE
...WILL HAVE TO DO ONE FAVOR FOR THE WINNER—ANYTHING THEY ASK.
...WHAT DO YOU SAY?
GRIN
!?
"ANY-THING" ...!?
YOU CAN BE THE WINNER IF WE TIE.

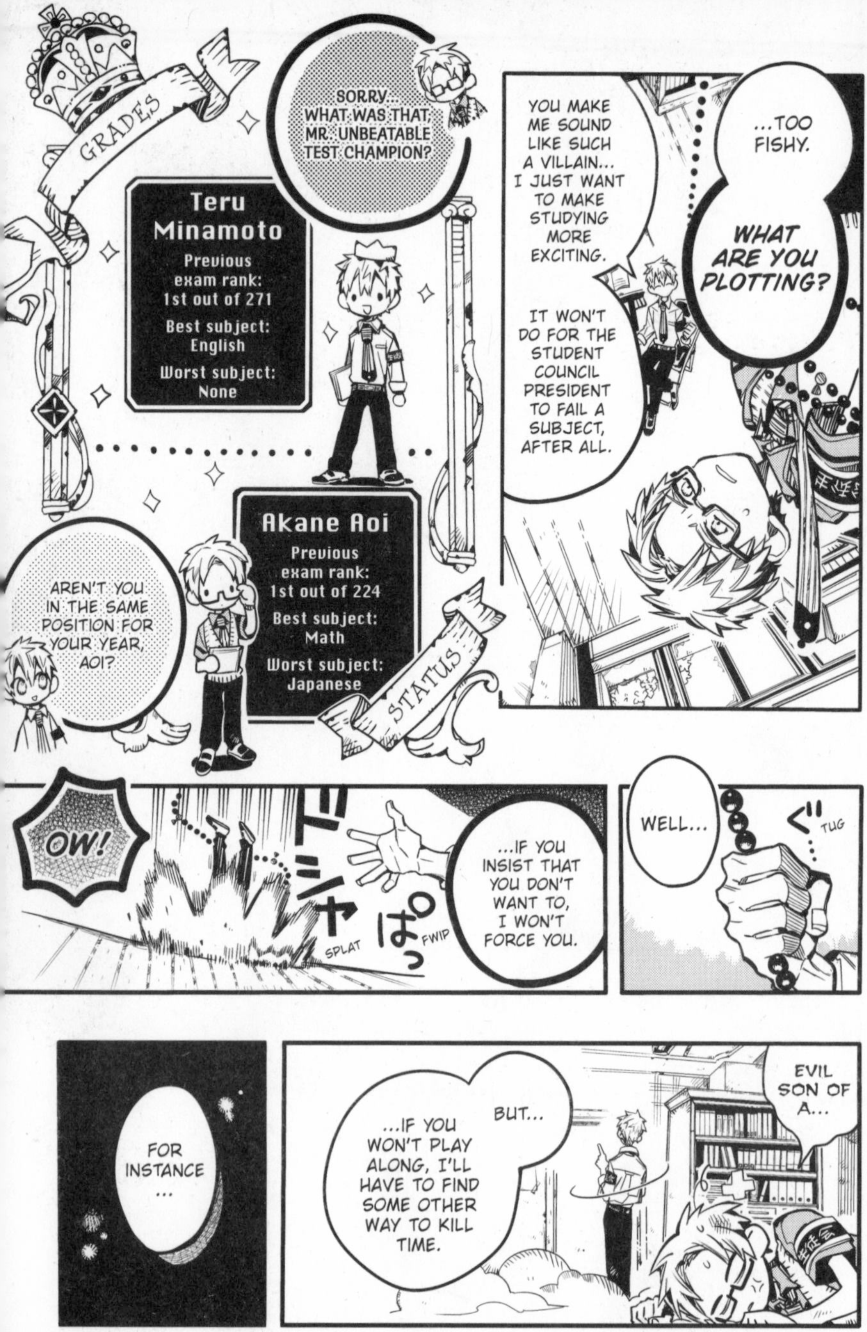
...TOO FISHY.
WHAT ARE YOU PLOTTING?
YOU MAKE ME SOUND LIKE SUCH A VILLAIN... I JUST WANT TO MAKE STUDYING MORE EXCITING.
IT WON'T DO FOR THE STUDENT COUNCIL PRESIDENT TO FAIL A SUBJECT, AFTER ALL.
SORRY... WHAT WAS THAT, MR. UNBEATABLE TEST CHAMPION?
GRADES
Teru Minamoto
Previous exam rank: 1st out of 271
Best subject: English
Worst subject: None
Akane Aoi
Previous exam rank: 1st out of 224
Best subject: Math
Worst subject: Japanese
STATUS
AREN'T YOU IN THE SAME POSITION FOR YOUR YEAR, AOI?
WELL...
TUG
...IF YOU INSIST THAT YOU DON'T WANT TO, I WON'T FORCE YOU.
FWIP
SPLAT
OW!
EVIL SON OF A...
BUT...
...IF YOU WON'T PLAY ALONG, I'LL HAVE TO FIND SOME OTHER WAY TO KILL TIME.
FOR INSTANCE...

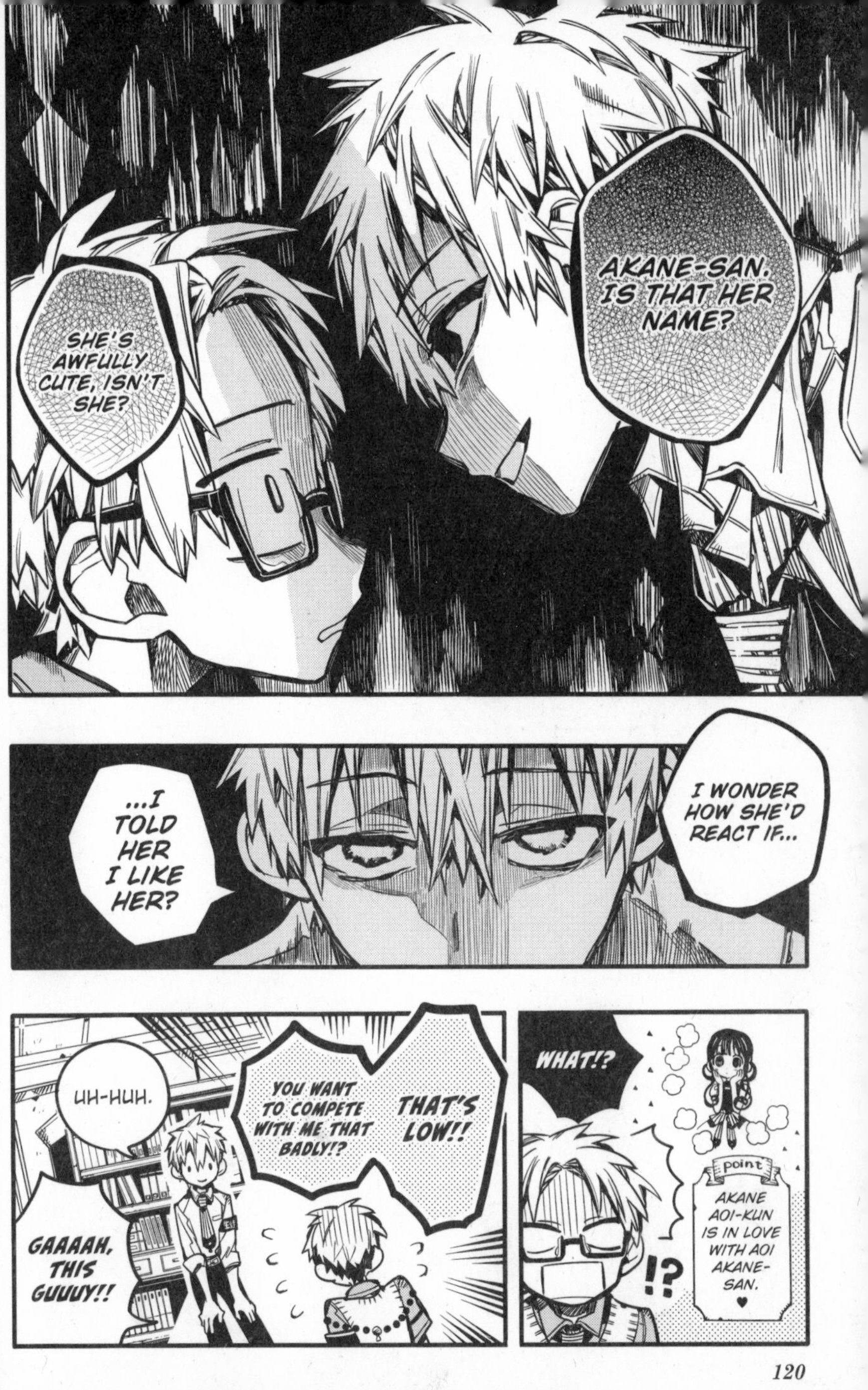

AKANE-SAN. IS THAT HER NAME?
SHE'S AWFULLY CUTE, ISN'T SHE?
I WONDER HOW SHE'D REACT IF...
...I TOLD HER I LIKE HER?
WHAT!?
point
AKANE AOI-KUN IS IN LOVE WITH AOI AKANE-SAN. ♥
!?
THAT'S LOW!!
YOU WANT TO COMPETE WITH ME THAT BADLY!?
UH-HUH.
GAAAAH, THIS GUUUY!!

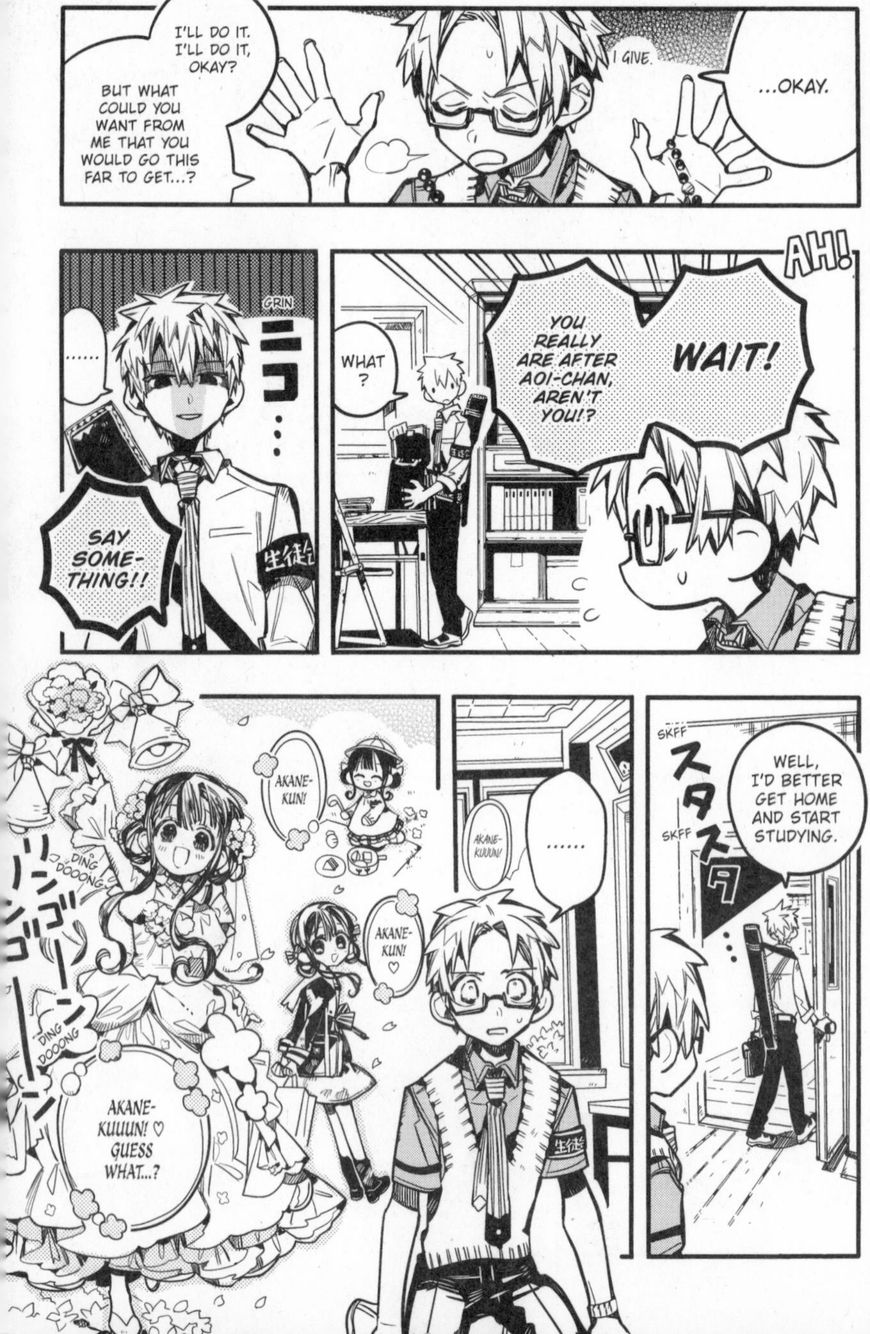
...OKAY.
I GIVE.
I'LL DO IT. I'LL DO IT, OKAY?
BUT WHAT COULD YOU WANT FROM ME THAT YOU WOULD GO THIS FAR TO GET...?
AH!
WAIT!
YOU REALLY ARE AFTER AOI-CHAN, AREN'T YOU!?
WHAT?
GRIN
......
SAY SOME-THING!!
SKFF
SKFF
WELL, I'D BETTER GET HOME AND START STUDYING.
......
AKANE-KUUUN!
AKANE-KUN!
AKANE-KUN! ♡
DING DOOONG
DING DOOONG
AKANE-KUUUN! ♡ GUESS WHAT...?

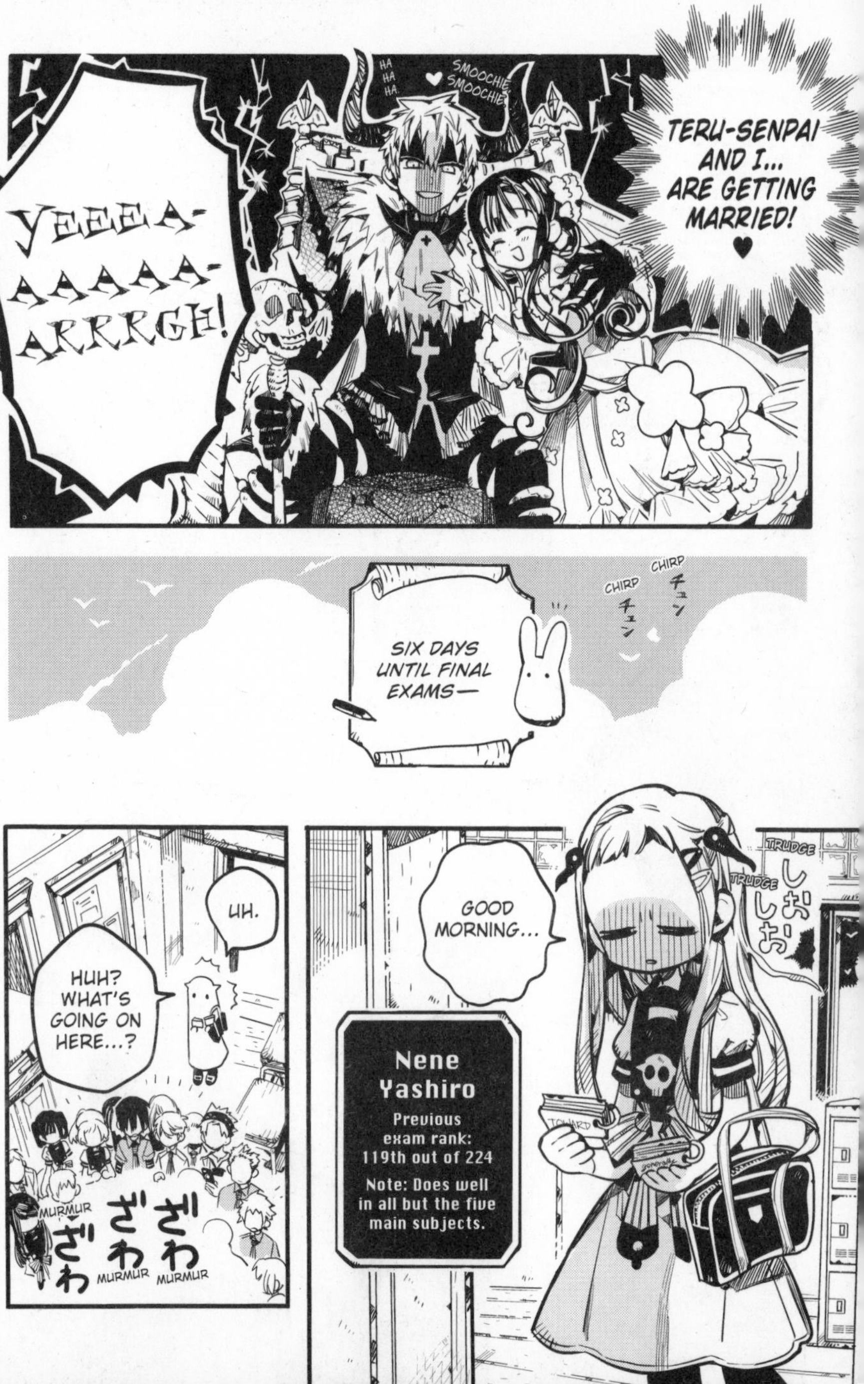
TERU-SENPAI AND I... ARE GETTING MARRIED! ♥
HA HA HA.
SMOOCHIE SMOOCHIE
YEEEA-AAAAA-ARRRGH!
CHIRP チュン
CHIRP チュン
SIX DAYS UNTIL FINAL EXAMS—
TRUDGE しお
TRUDGE しお
GOOD MORNING...
Nene Yashiro
Previous exam rank: 119th out of 224
Note: Does well in all but the five main subjects.
UH.
HUH? WHAT'S GOING ON HERE...?
MURMUR ざわ
MURMUR ざわ
MURMUR ざわ

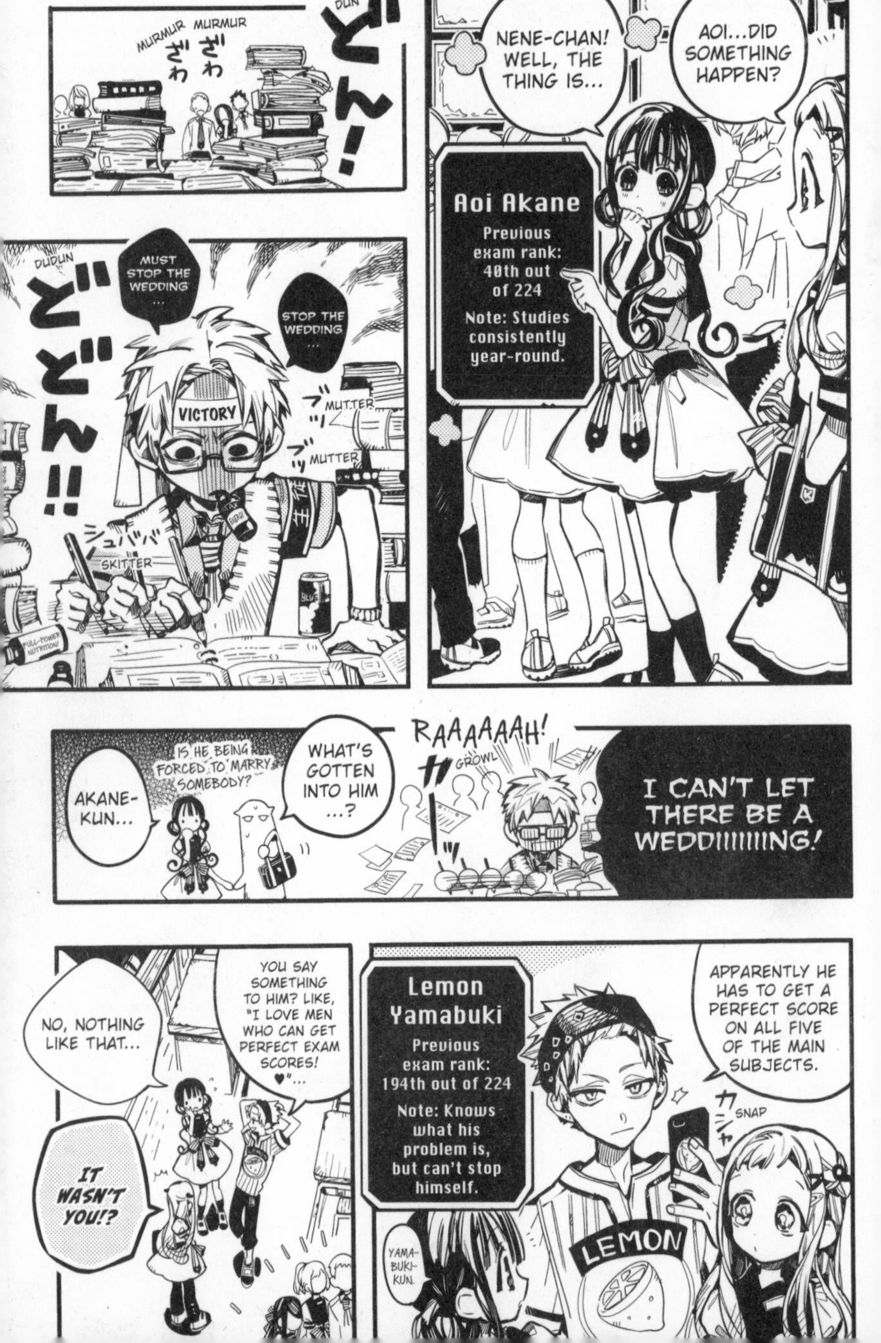
AOI...DID SOMETHING HAPPEN?
NENE-CHAN! WELL, THE THING IS...
Aoi Akane
Previous exam rank: 40th out of 224
Note: Studies consistently year-round.
DUN
どん!
MURMUR MURMUR
ざわざわ
DUDUN
どどどん!!
STOP THE WEDDING...
MUST STOP THE WEDDING...
MUTTER
ブツ
MUTTER
ブツ
VICTORY
SKITTER
シュバババ
FULL-POWER NUTRITION!
I CAN'T LET THERE BE A WEDDIIIIIIIING!
RAAAAAAH!
GROWL
ガッ
WHAT'S GOTTEN INTO HIM ...?
IS HE BEING FORCED TO MARRY SOMEBODY?
AKANE-KUN...
APPARENTLY HE HAS TO GET A PERFECT SCORE ON ALL FIVE OF THE MAIN SUBJECTS.
SNAP
カシャ
Lemon Yamabuki
Previous exam rank: 194th out of 224
Note: Knows what his problem is, but can't stop himself.
LEMON
YAMABUKI-KUN.
YOU SAY SOMETHING TO HIM? LIKE, "I LOVE MEN WHO CAN GET PERFECT EXAM SCORES! ♥"...
NO, NOTHING LIKE THAT...
IT WASN'T YOU!?

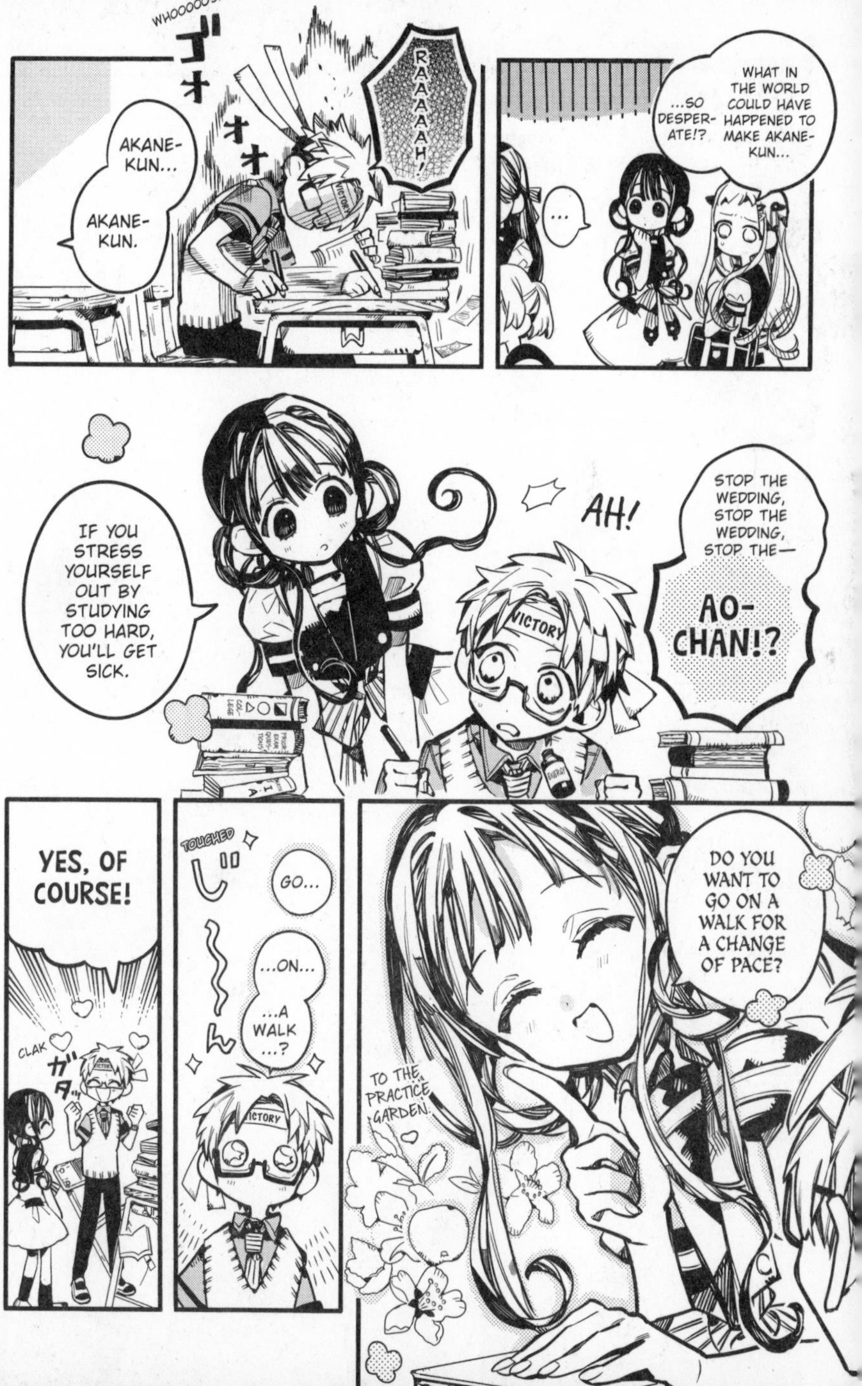
WHAT IN THE WORLD COULD HAVE HAPPENED TO MAKE AKANE-KUN...
...SO DESPERATE!?
...
WHOOOOOSH
ゴオオオ
RAAAAAAH!
AKANE-KUN...
AKANE-KUN.
STOP THE WEDDING, STOP THE WEDDING, STOP THE—
AO-CHAN!?
AH!
IF YOU STRESS YOURSELF OUT BY STUDYING TOO HARD, YOU'LL GET SICK.
DO YOU WANT TO GO ON A WALK FOR A CHANGE OF PACE?
TO THE PRACTICE GARDEN
TOUCHED
し〜ん
GO...
...ON...
...A WALK...?
YES, OF COURSE!
CLAK
ガタッ

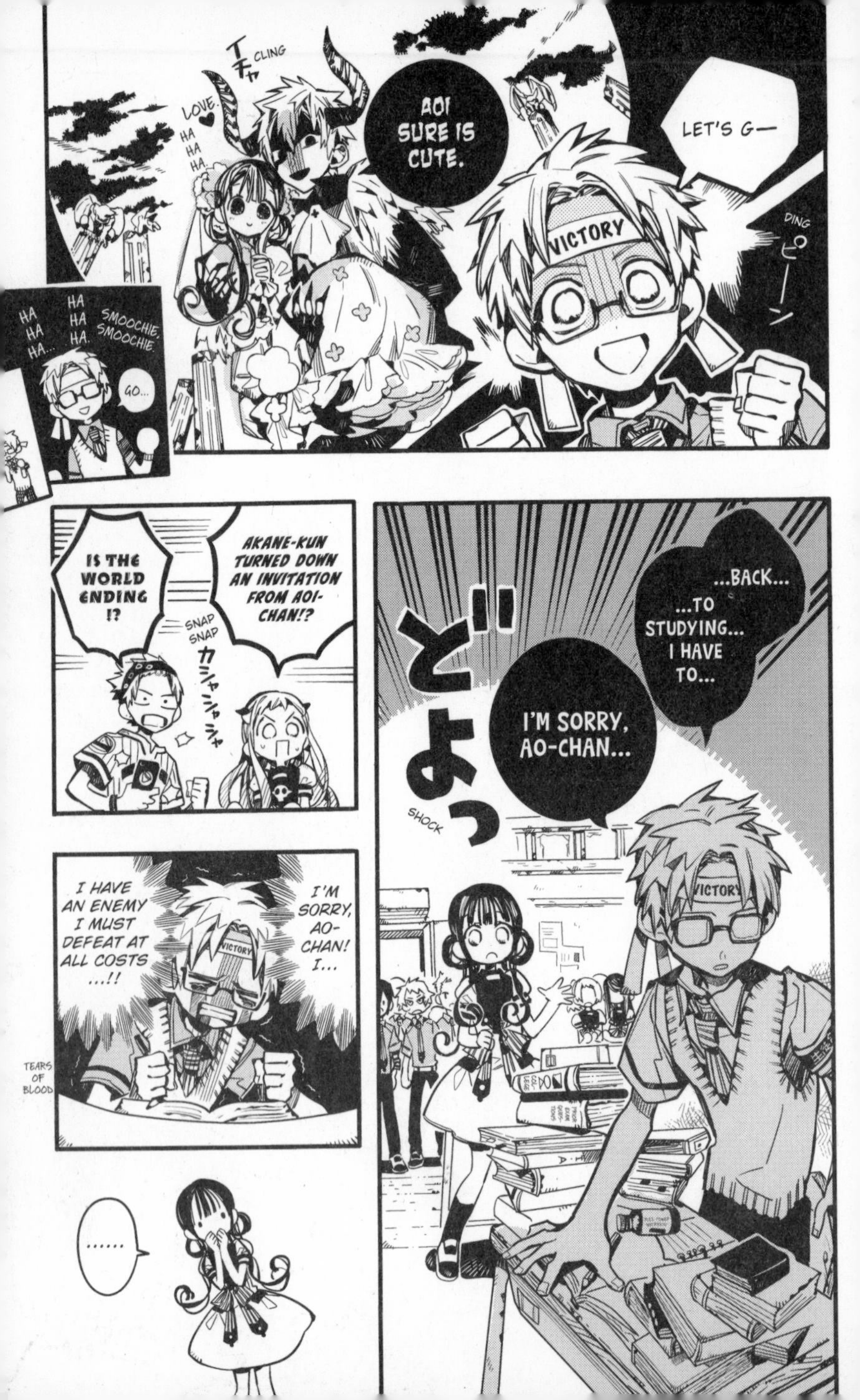
LET'S G—
DING
VICTORY
AOI SURE IS CUTE.
CLING
LOVE. ♥
HA HA HA.
HA HA HA...
HA HA HA.
SMOOCHIE, SMOOCHIE.
GO...
...BACK... ...TO STUDYING... I HAVE TO...
I'M SORRY, AO-CHAN...
SHOCK
VICTORY
AKANE-KUN TURNED DOWN AN INVITATION FROM AOI-CHAN!?
IS THE WORLD ENDING!?
SNAP SNAP
I'M SORRY, AO-CHAN! I...
I HAVE AN ENEMY I MUST DEFEAT AT ALL COSTS...!!
VICTORY
TEARS OF BLOOD
......

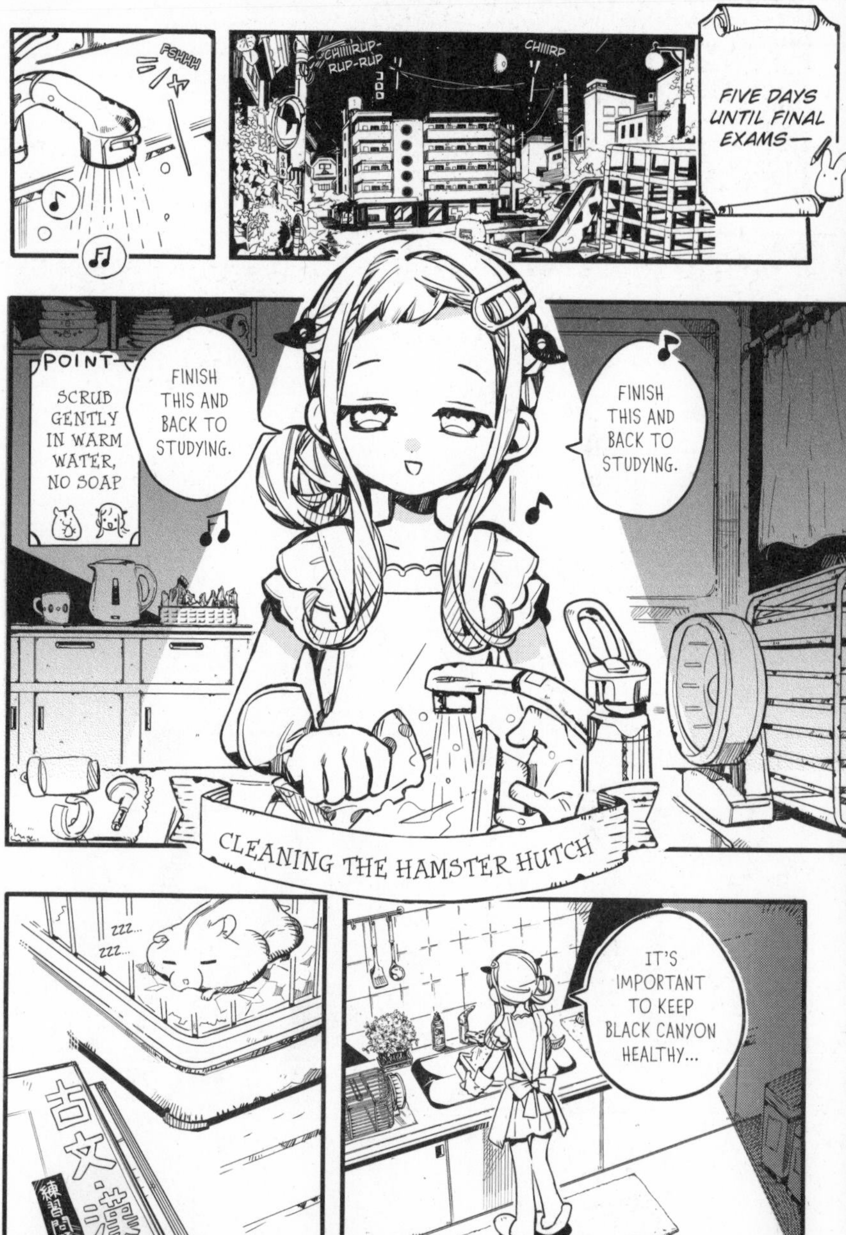
FIVE DAYS UNTIL FINAL EXAMS—
CHIIIRP
CHIIIRUP-RUP-RUP
FSHHH
FINISH THIS AND BACK TO STUDYING.
FINISH THIS AND BACK TO STUDYING.
POINT
SCRUB GENTLY IN WARM WATER, NO SOAP
CLEANING THE HAMSTER HUTCH
IT'S IMPORTANT TO KEEP BLACK CANYON HEALTHY...
zzz... zzz...
古文・漢文
練習問題集

BOOK: CLASSICAL & CHINESE LITERATURE PRACTICE PROBLEMS

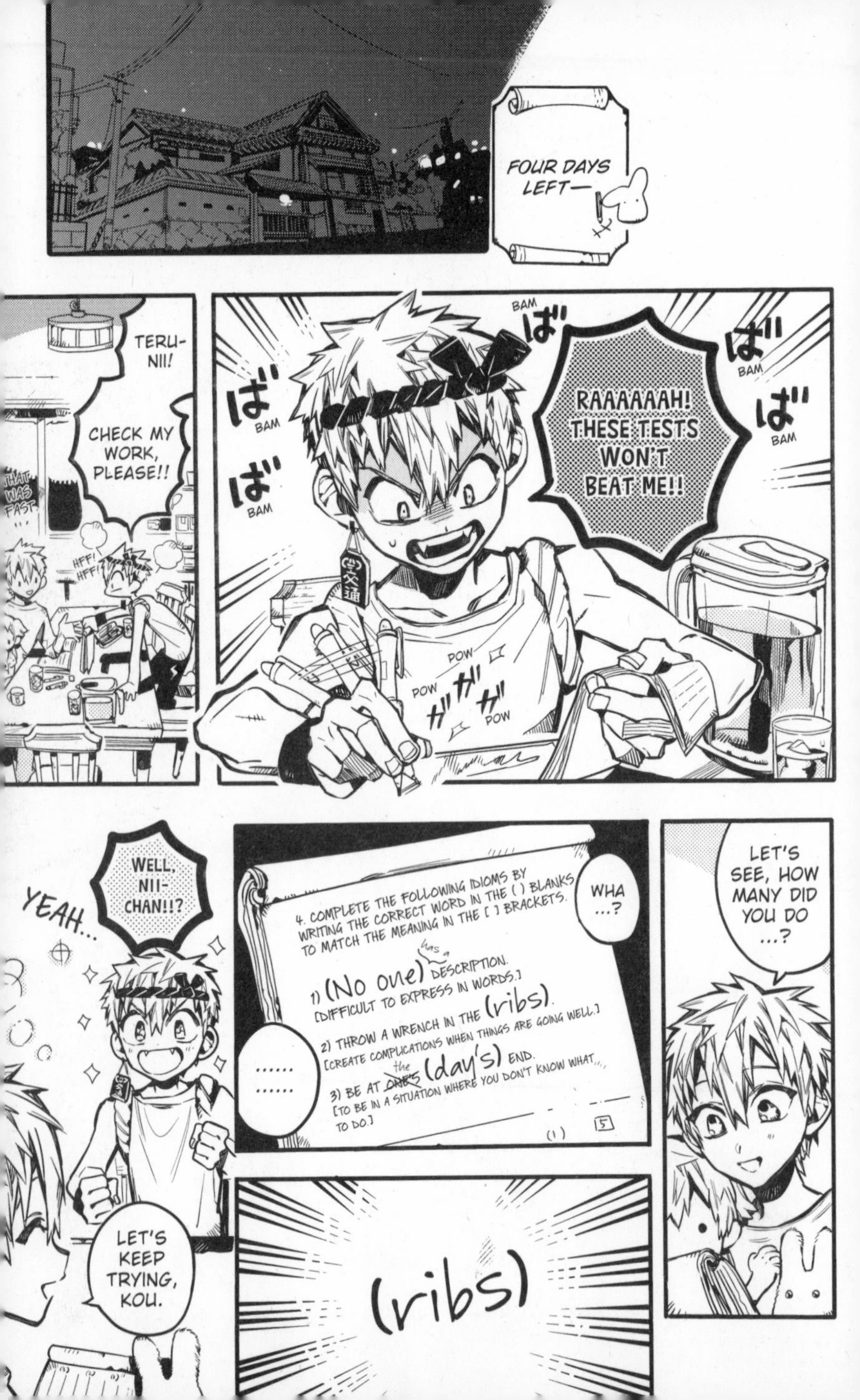
FOUR DAYS LEFT—
ば BAM
ば BAM
ば BAM
RAAAAAAH! THESE TESTS WON'T BEAT ME!!
ば BAM
ば BAM
POW
POW
ガガガ
POW
TERU-NII!
CHECK MY WORK, PLEASE!!
THAT WAS FAST...
HFF! HFF!
LET'S SEE, HOW MANY DID YOU DO...?
WHA...?
4. COMPLETE THE FOLLOWING IDIOMS BY WRITING THE CORRECT WORD IN THE ( ) BLANKS TO MATCH THE MEANING IN THE [ ] BRACKETS.
1) (No one) has a DESCRIPTION. [DIFFICULT TO EXPRESS IN WORDS.]
2) THROW A WRENCH IN THE (ribs). [CREATE COMPLICATIONS WHEN THINGS ARE GOING WELL.]
3) BE AT ~~ONE'S~~ the (day's) END. [TO BE IN A SITUATION WHERE YOU DON'T KNOW WHAT TO DO.]
(1) 5
....
(ribs)
WELL, NII-CHAN!!?
YEAH...
LET'S KEEP TRYING, KOU.

SIGN: SCIENCE PREP ROOM 2

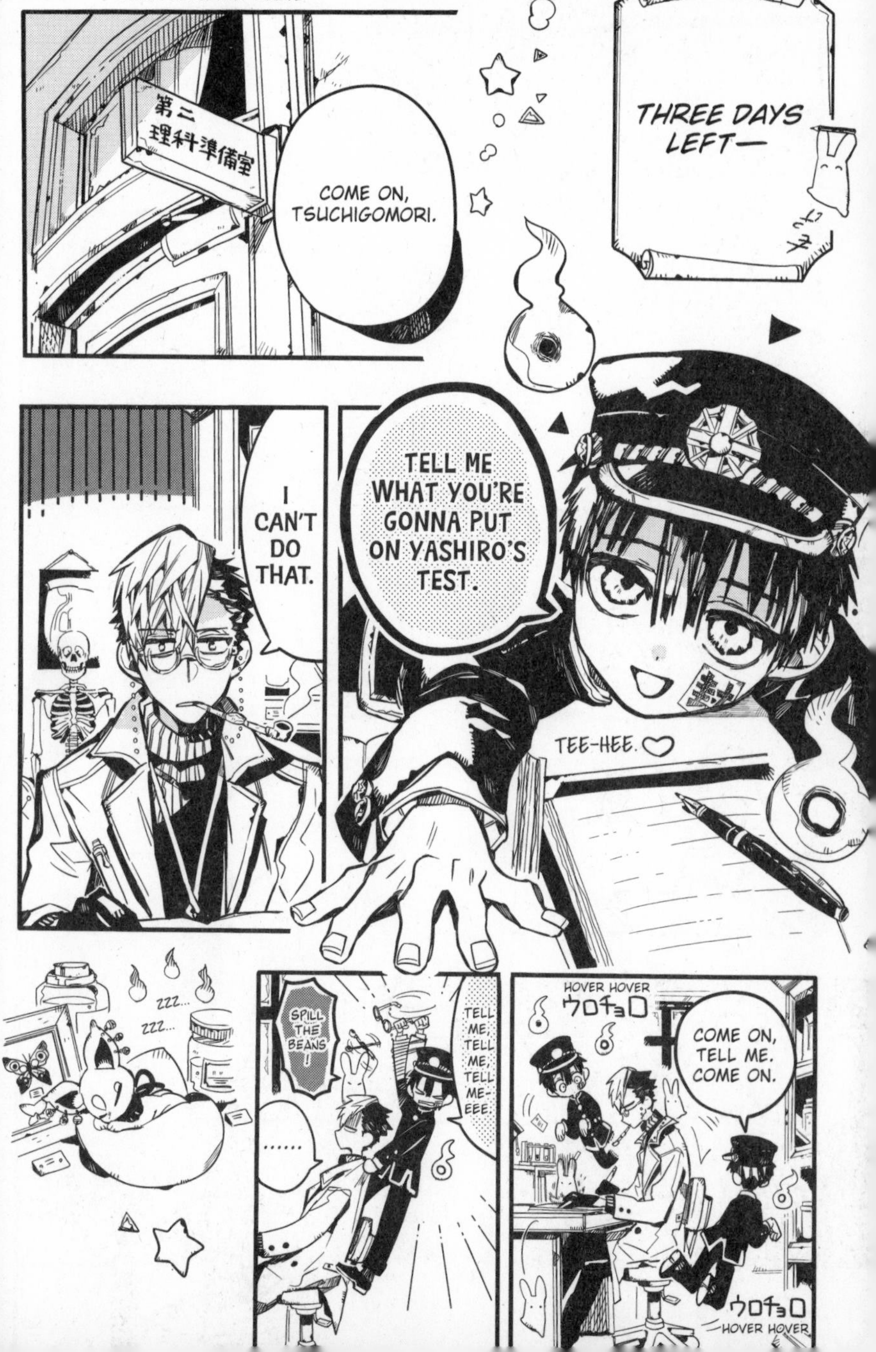
THREE DAYS LEFT—
第二理科準備室
COME ON, TSUCHIGOMORI.
TELL ME WHAT YOU'RE GONNA PUT ON YASHIRO'S TEST.
TEE-HEE.
I CAN'T DO THAT.
HOVER HOVER
ウロチョロ
COME ON, TELL ME. COME ON.
ウロチョロ
HOVER HOVER
TELL ME, TELL ME, TELL ME, TELL ME-EEE.
SPILL THE BEANS!
......
ZZZ...
ZZZ...

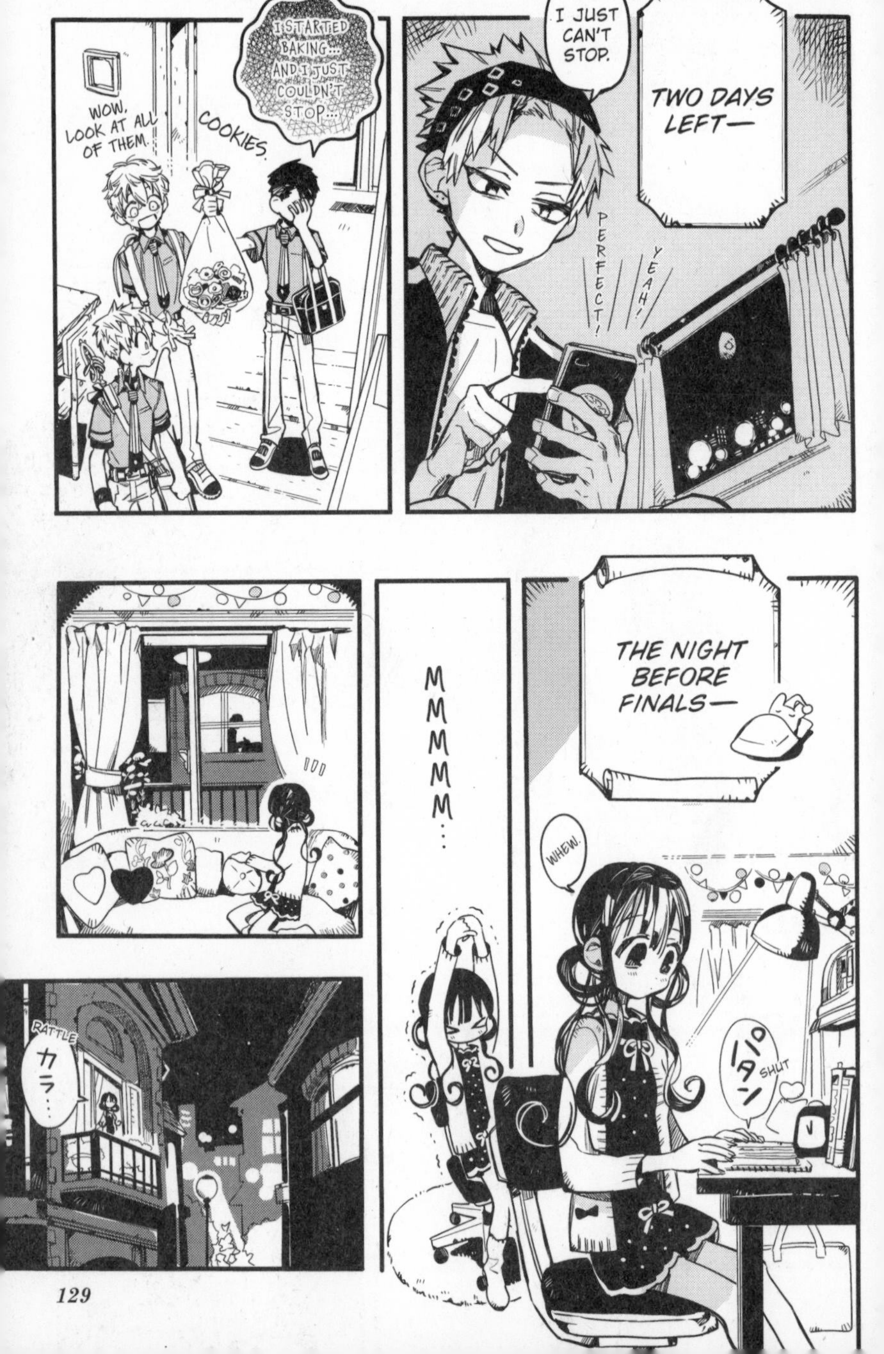
TWO DAYS LEFT—
I JUST CAN'T STOP.
PERFECT!
YEAH!
I STARTED BAKING... AND I JUST COULDN'T STOP...
COOKIES.
WOW, LOOK AT ALL OF THEM.
THE NIGHT BEFORE FINALS—
WHEW.
パタン
SHUT
MMMMM...
RATTLE
カラ...

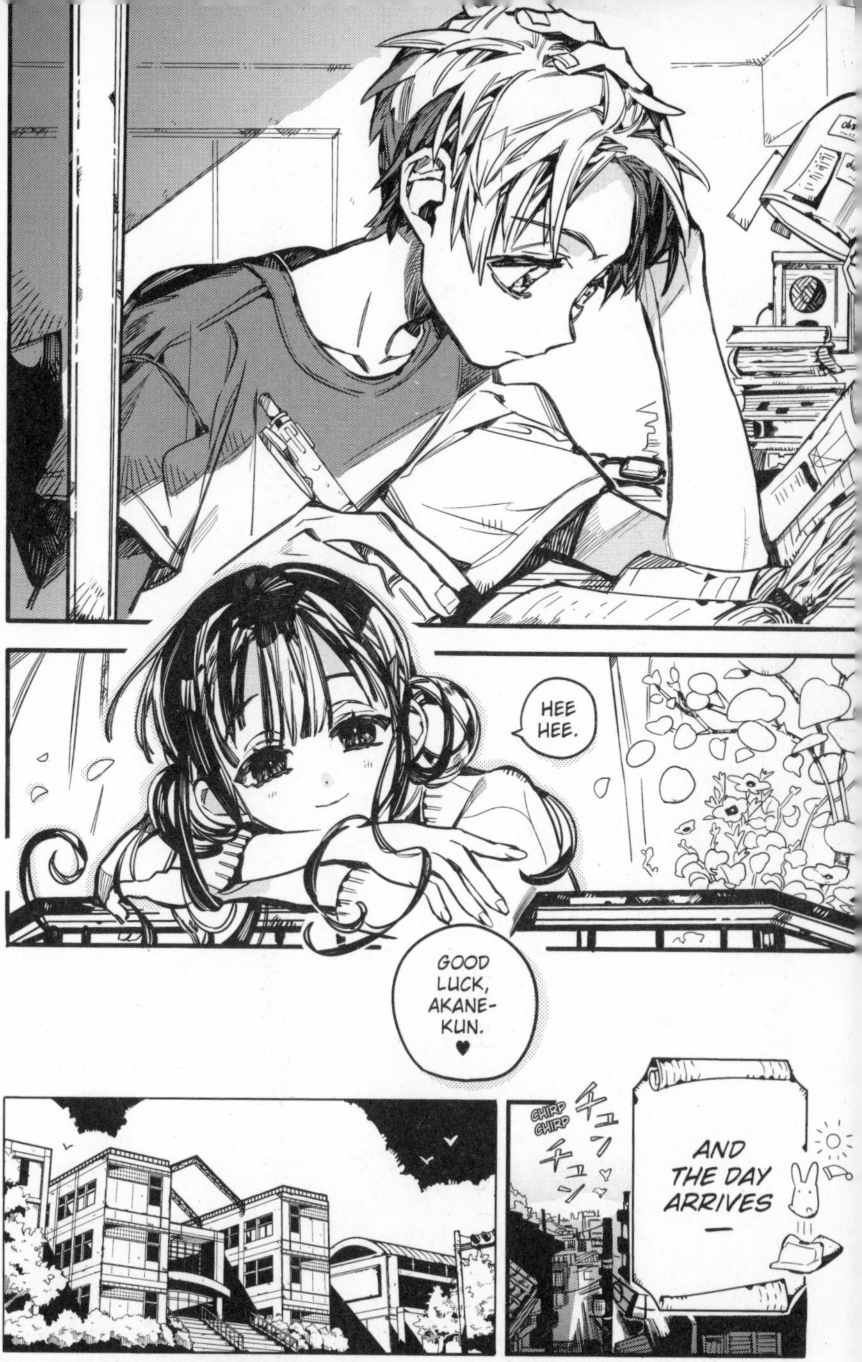
HEE HEE.
GOOD LUCK, AKANE-KUN. ♥
CHIRP CHIRP
チュンチュン
AND THE DAY ARRIVES —

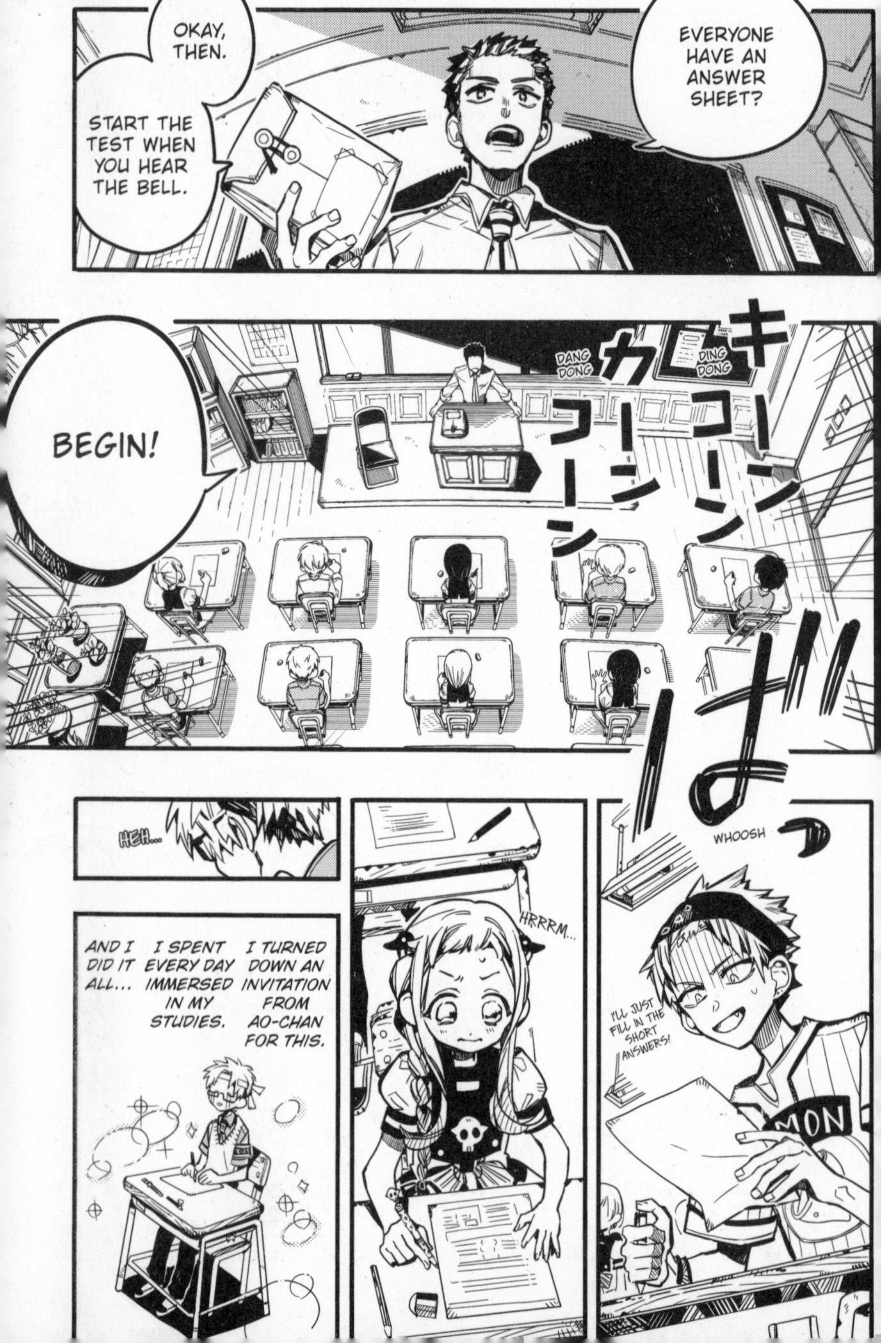
EVERYONE HAVE AN ANSWER SHEET?
OKAY, THEN.
START THE TEST WHEN YOU HEAR THE BELL.
DING DONG
DANG DONG
BEGIN!
WHOOSH
I'LL JUST FILL IN THE SHORT ANSWERS!
HRRRM...
HEH...
I TURNED DOWN AN INVITATION FROM AO-CHAN FOR THIS.
I SPENT EVERY DAY IMMERSED IN MY STUDIES.
AND I DID IT ALL...
MON

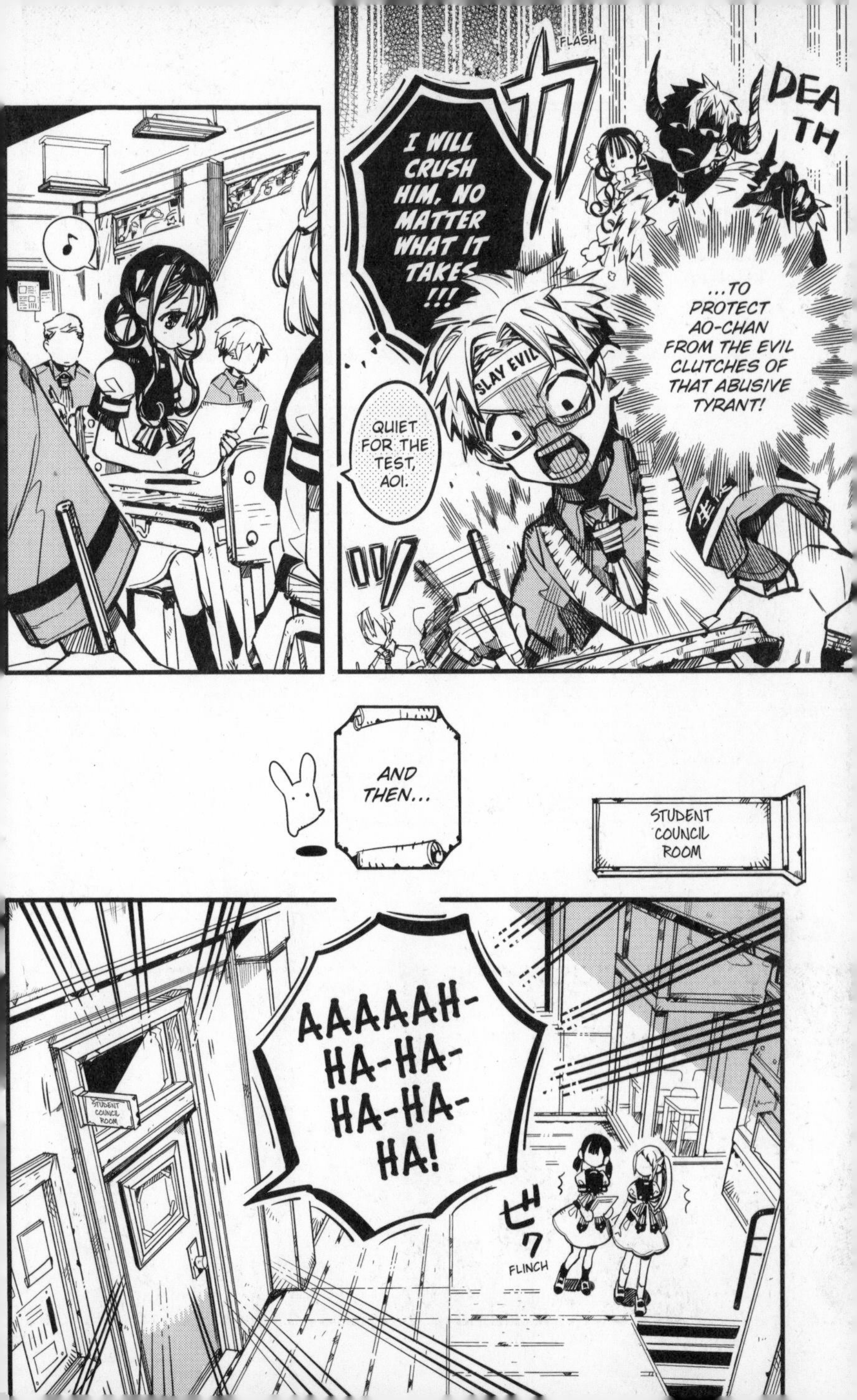
DEATH
FLASH
I WILL CRUSH HIM, NO MATTER WHAT IT TAKES!!!
...TO PROTECT AO-CHAN FROM THE EVIL CLUTCHES OF THAT ABUSIVE TYRANT!
SLAY EVIL
QUIET FOR THE TEST, AOI.
♪
STUDENT COUNCIL ROOM
AND THEN...
AAAAAH-HA-HA-HA-HA-HA!
FLINCH
STUDENT COUNCIL ROOM

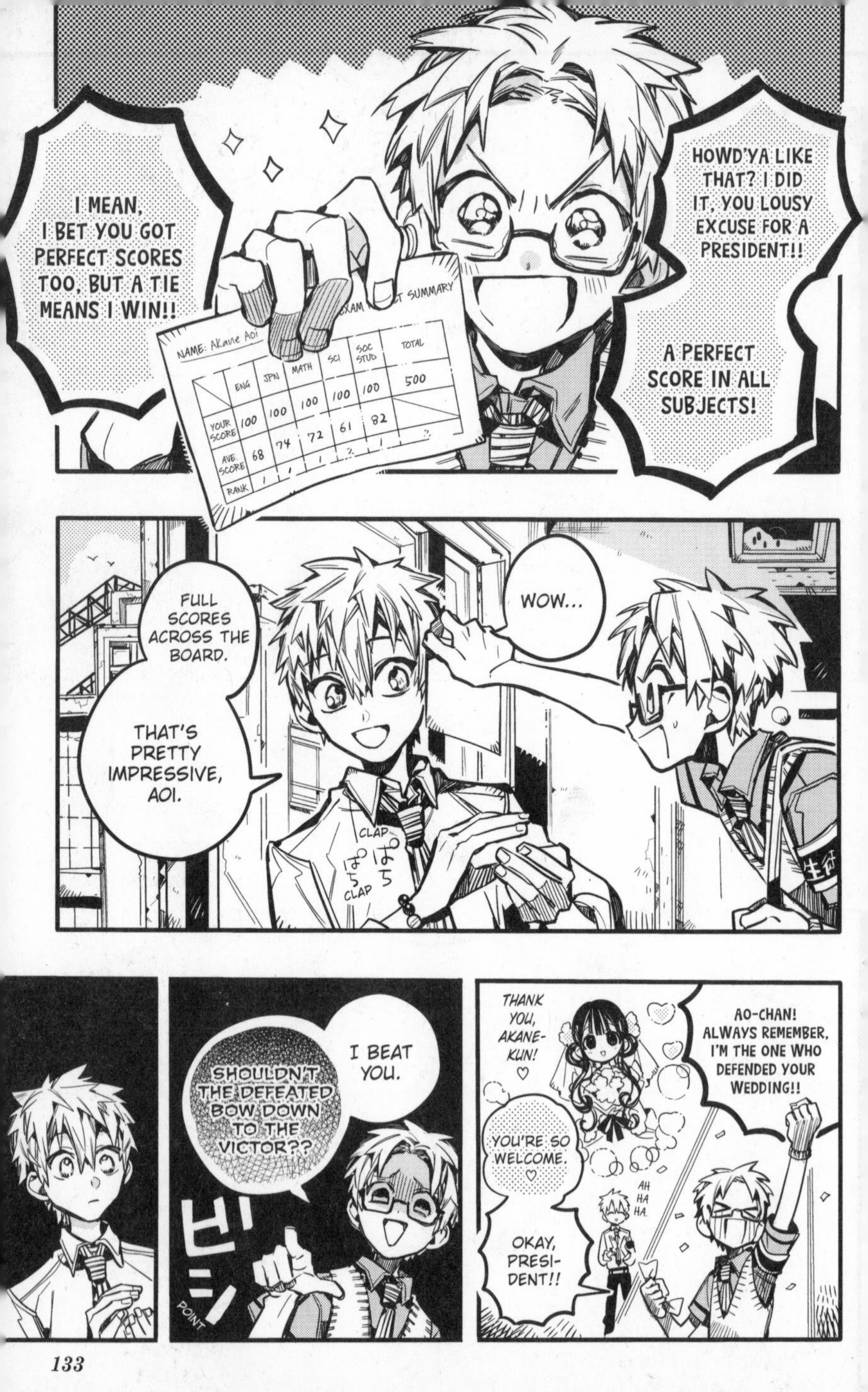

HOWD'YA LIKE THAT? I DID IT, YOU LOUSY EXCUSE FOR A PRESIDENT!!
A PERFECT SCORE IN ALL SUBJECTS!
I MEAN, I BET YOU GOT PERFECT SCORES TOO, BUT A TIE MEANS I WIN!!
NAME: Akane Aoi
ENG JPN MATH SCI SOC STUD TOTAL
YOUR SCORE 100 100 100 100 100 500
AVE. SCORE 68 74 72 61 82
RANK
WOW...
FULL SCORES ACROSS THE BOARD.
THAT'S PRETTY IMPRESSIVE, AOI.
ぱち ぱち
CLAP CLAP
I BEAT YOU.
SHOULDN'T THE DEFEATED BOW DOWN TO THE VICTOR??
ビシ
POINT
AO-CHAN! ALWAYS REMEMBER, I'M THE ONE WHO DEFENDED YOUR WEDDING!!
THANK YOU, AKANE-KUN! ♡
YOU'RE SO WELCOME. ♡
AH HA HA.
OKAY, PRESIDENT!!

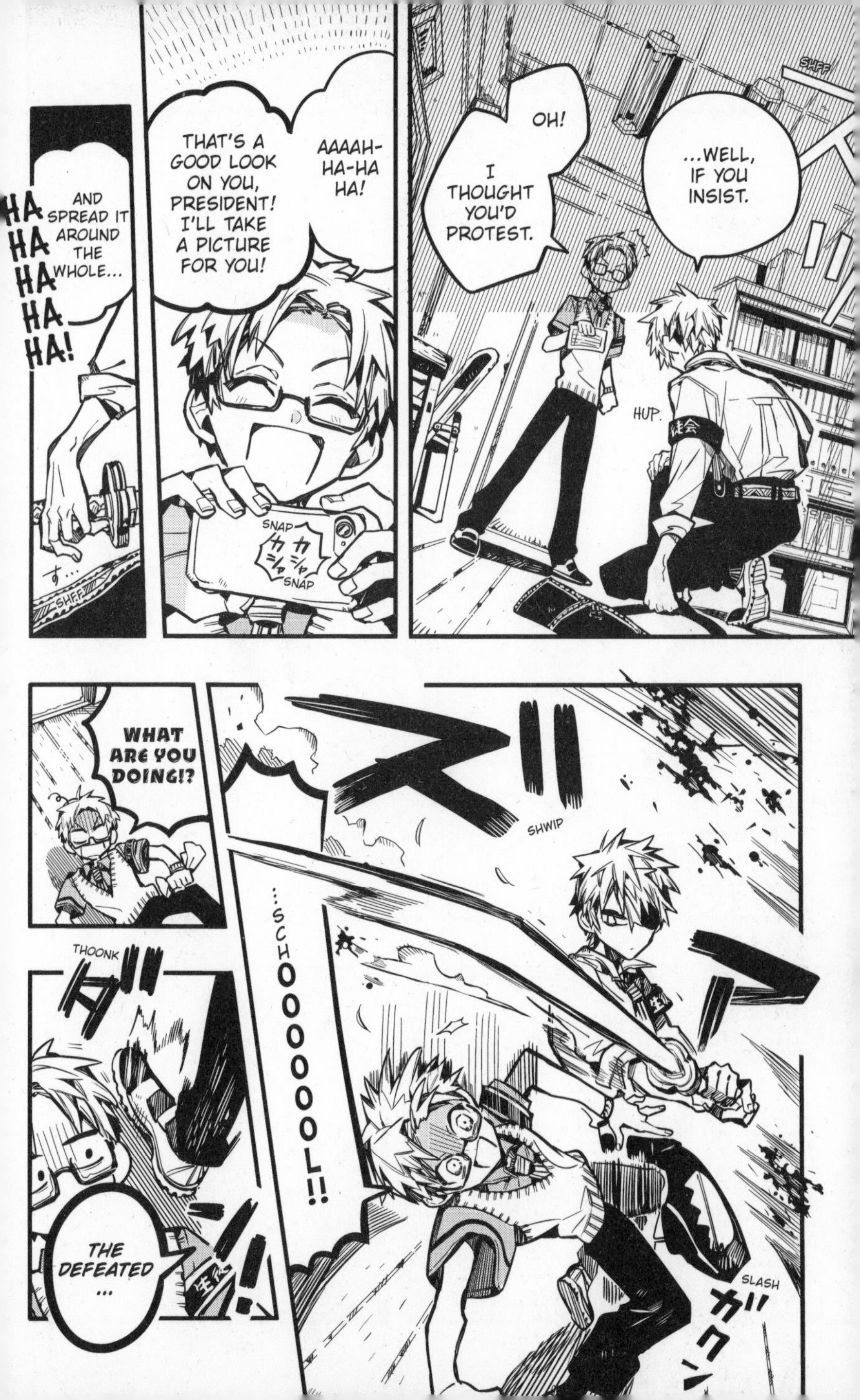
SHFF
...WELL, IF YOU INSIST.
OH!
I THOUGHT YOU'D PROTEST.
HUP.
AAAAH-HA-HA HA!
THAT'S A GOOD LOOK ON YOU, PRESIDENT! I'LL TAKE A PICTURE FOR YOU!
SNAP
SNAP
AND SPREAD IT AROUND THE WHOLE...
HA HA HA HA HA!
SHFF
SHWIP
...SCHOOOOOOL!!
SLASH
WHAT ARE YOU DOING!?
THOONK
THE DEFEATED...

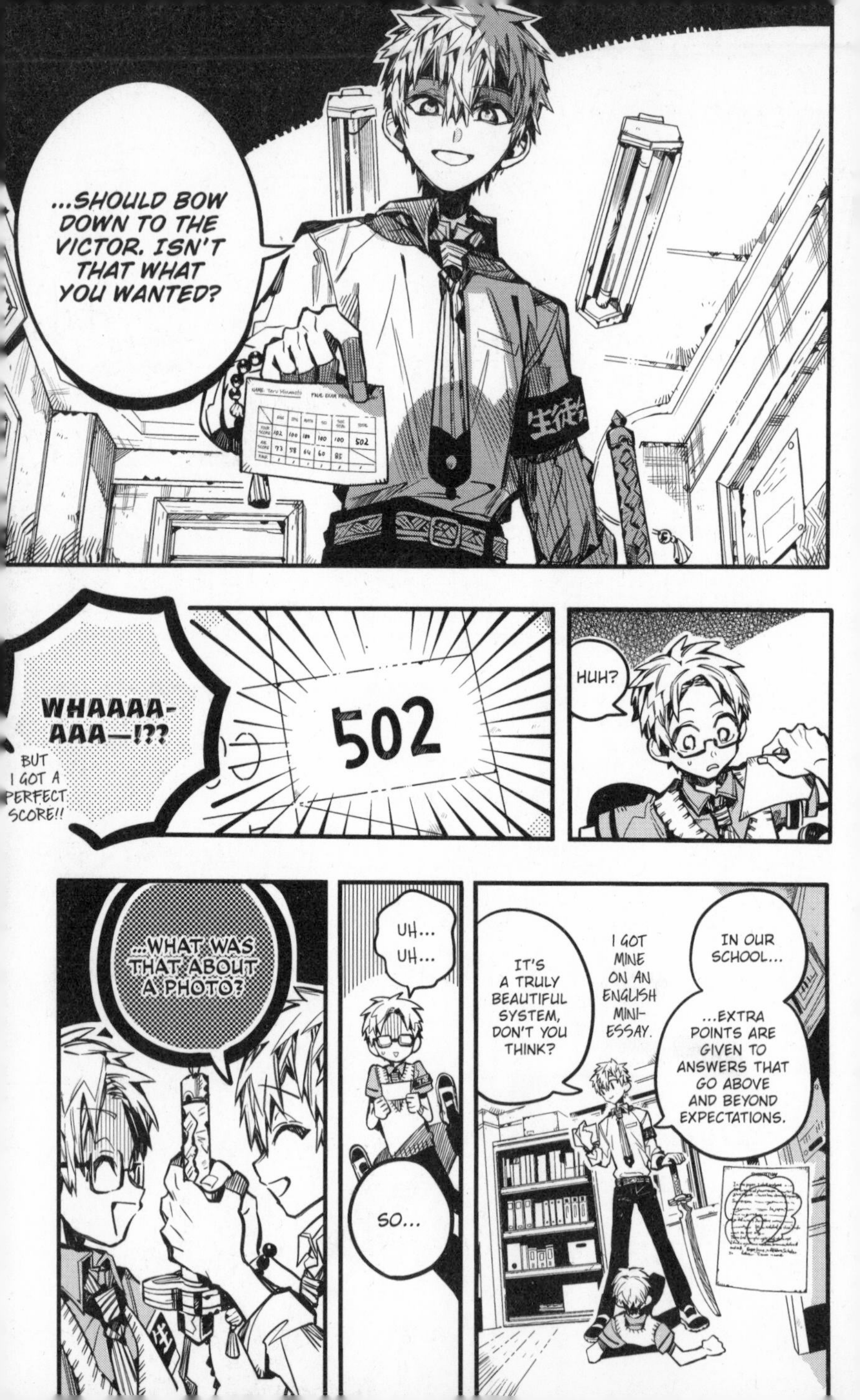
...SHOULD BOW DOWN TO THE VICTOR. ISN'T THAT WHAT YOU WANTED?
HUH?
502
WHAAAA-AAA—!??
BUT I GOT A PERFECT SCORE!!
IN OUR SCHOOL...
...EXTRA POINTS ARE GIVEN TO ANSWERS THAT GO ABOVE AND BEYOND EXPECTATIONS.
I GOT MINE ON AN ENGLISH MINI-ESSAY.
IT'S A TRULY BEAUTIFUL SYSTEM, DON'T YOU THINK?
UH... UH...
SO...
...WHAT WAS THAT ABOUT A PHOTO?

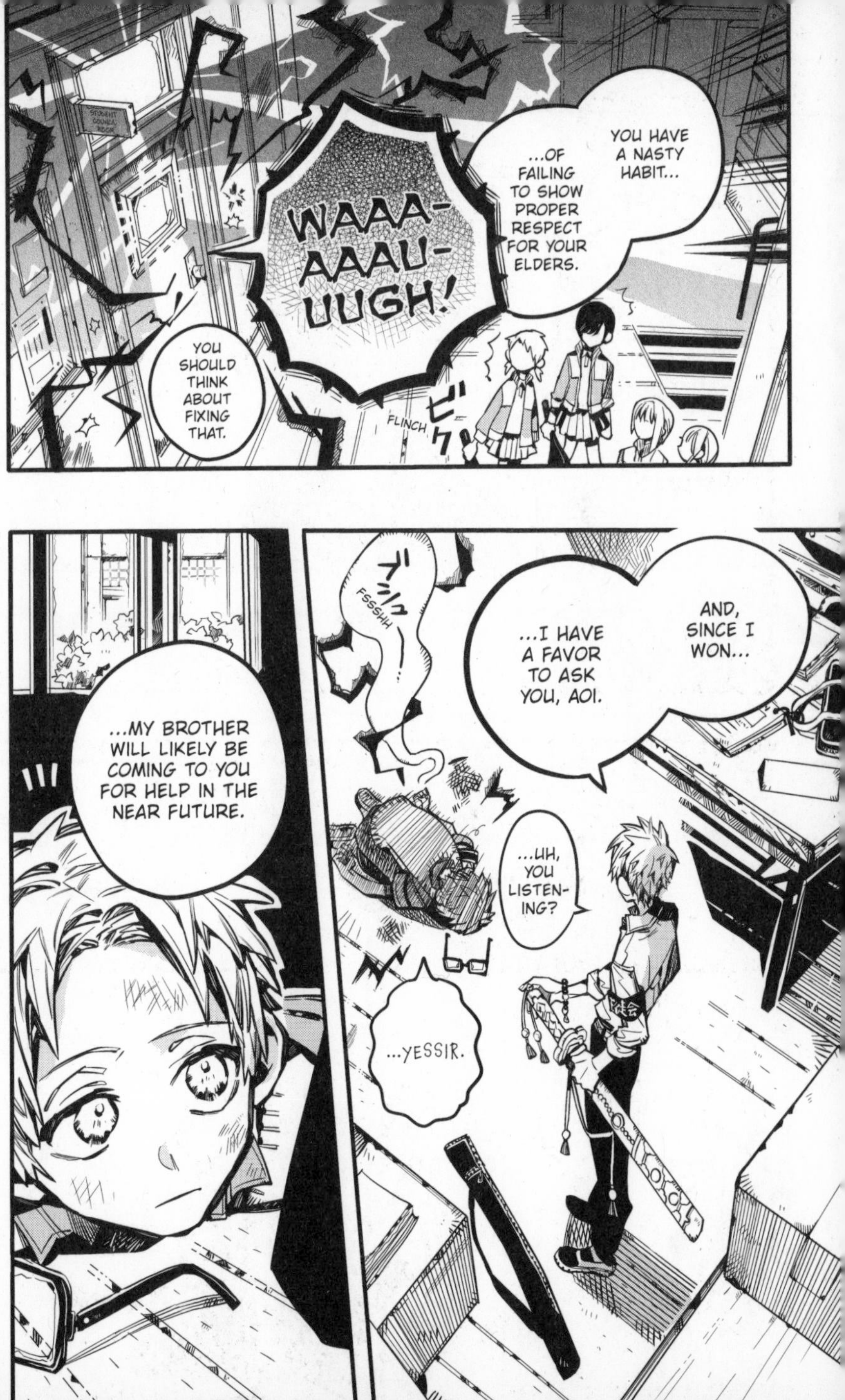
YOU HAVE A NASTY HABIT...
...OF FAILING TO SHOW PROPER RESPECT FOR YOUR ELDERS.
WAAAA-AAAU-UUGH!
FLINCH
YOU SHOULD THINK ABOUT FIXING THAT.
FSSSHH
AND, SINCE I WON...
...I HAVE A FAVOR TO ASK YOU, AOI.
...UH, YOU LISTEN-ING?
...YESSIR.
...MY BROTHER WILL LIKELY BE COMING TO YOU FOR HELP IN THE NEAR FUTURE.

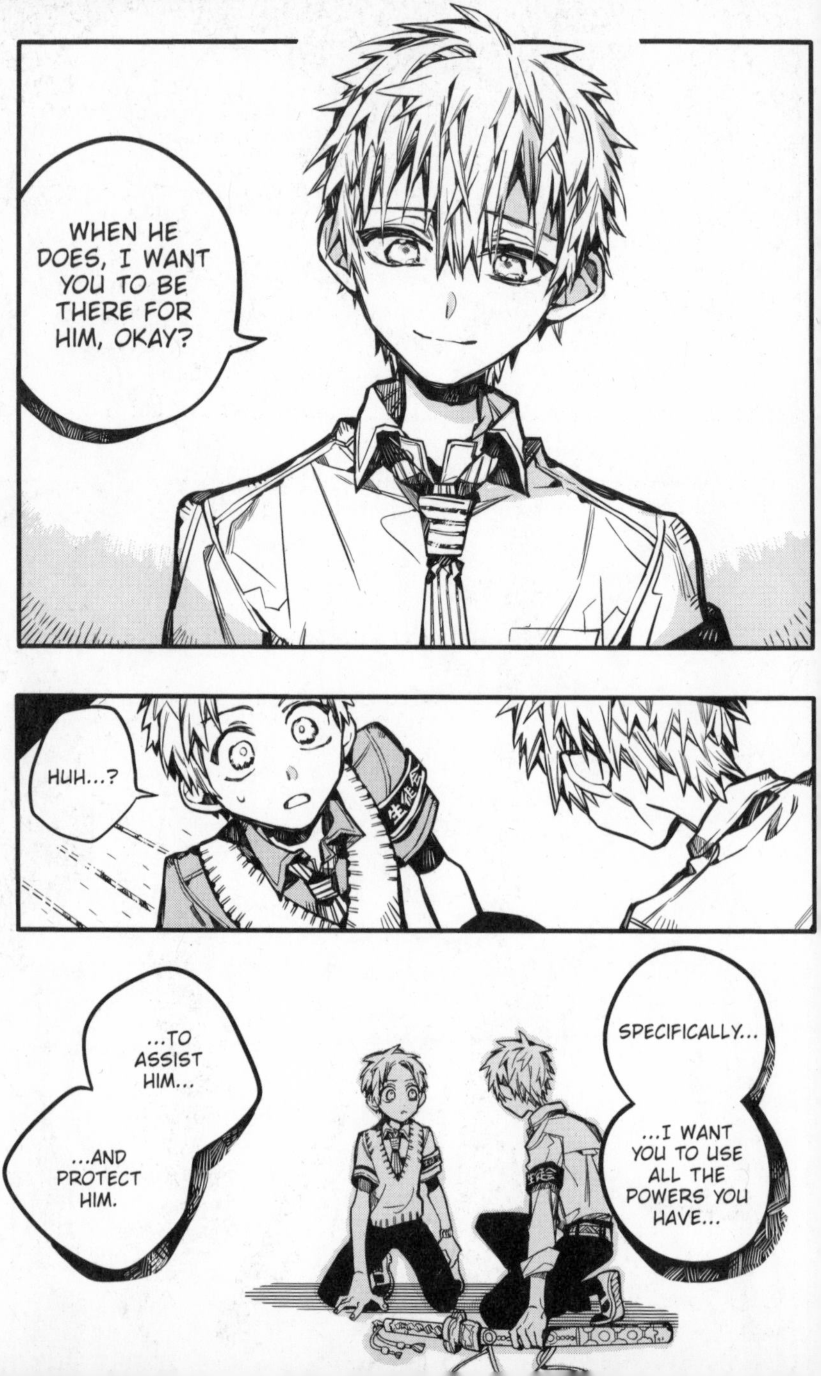
WHEN HE DOES, I WANT YOU TO BE THERE FOR HIM, OKAY?
HUH...?
SPECIFICALLY...
...I WANT YOU TO USE ALL THE POWERS YOU HAVE...
...TO ASSIST HIM...
...AND PROTECT HIM.

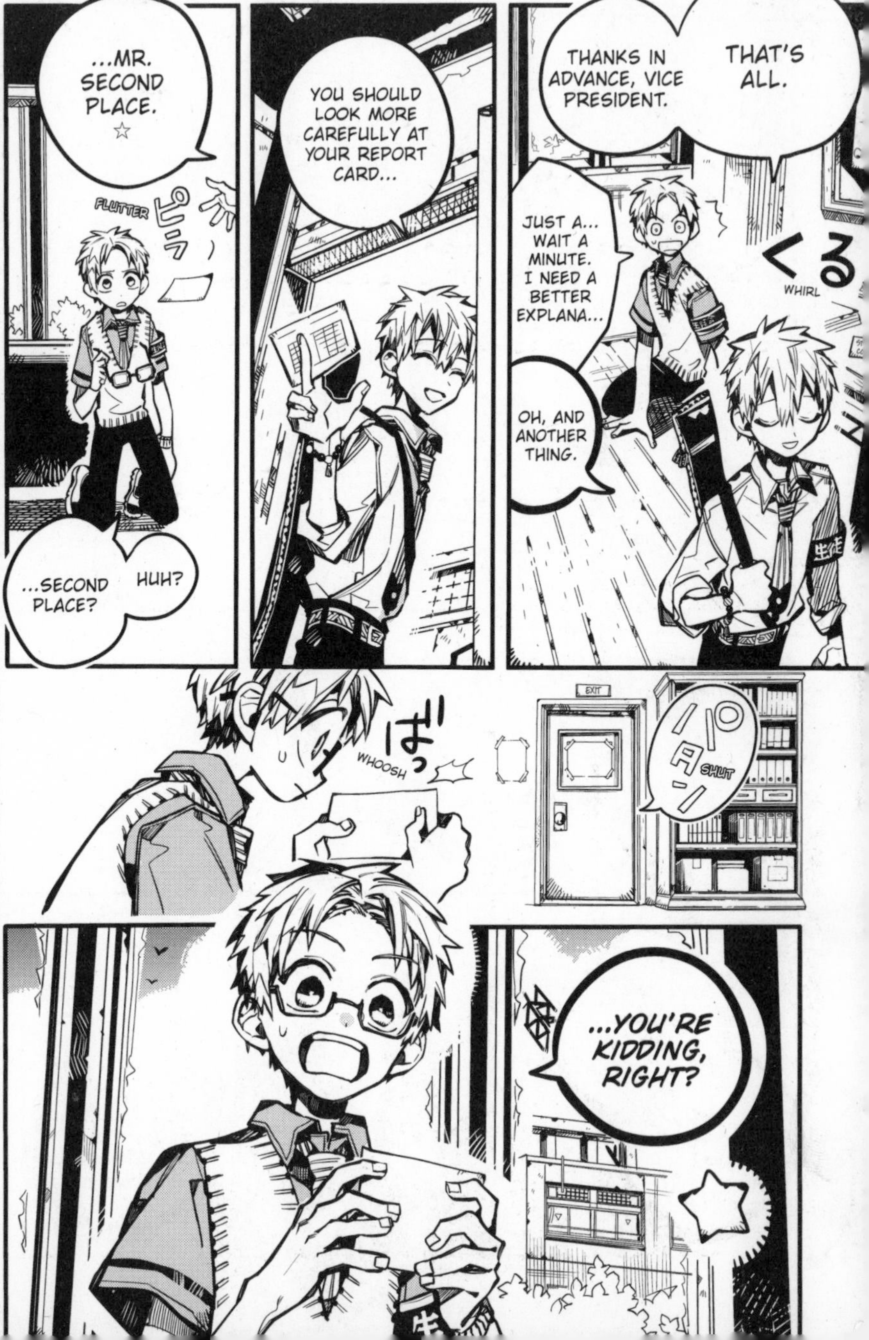
THAT'S ALL.
THANKS IN ADVANCE, VICE PRESIDENT.
くる
WHIRL
JUST A... WAIT A MINUTE. I NEED A BETTER EXPLANA...
OH, AND ANOTHER THING.
YOU SHOULD LOOK MORE CAREFULLY AT YOUR REPORT CARD...
...MR. SECOND PLACE. ☆
ピラ
FLUTTER
HUH?
...SECOND PLACE?
EXIT
パタン
SHUT
ばっ
WHOOSH
...YOU'RE KIDDING, RIGHT?

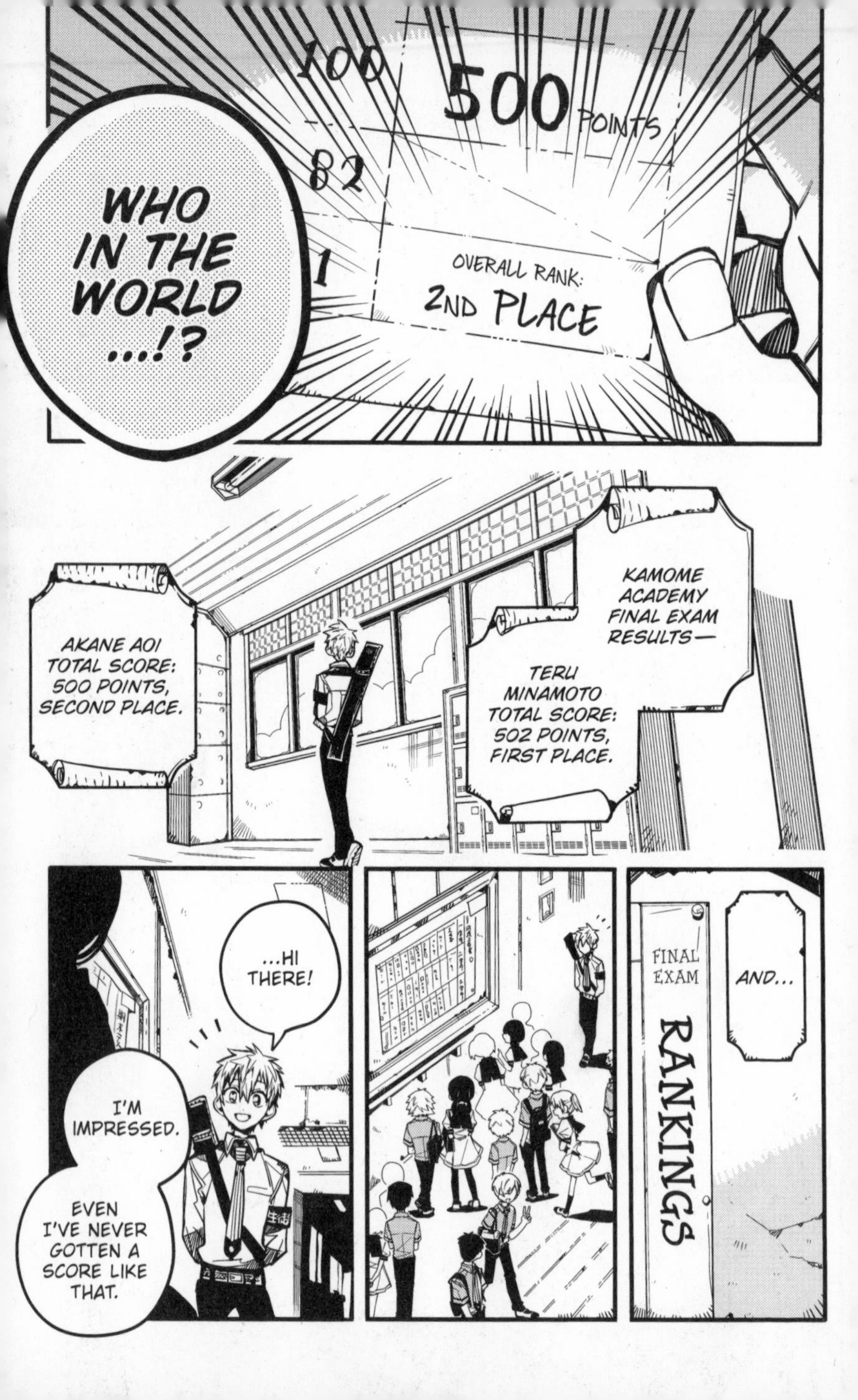
500 POINTS
100
82
OVERALL RANK: 2ND PLACE
1
WHO IN THE WORLD ...!?
KAMOME ACADEMY FINAL EXAM RESULTS—
TERU MINAMOTO TOTAL SCORE: 502 POINTS, FIRST PLACE.
AKANE AOI TOTAL SCORE: 500 POINTS, SECOND PLACE.
AND...
FINAL EXAM
RANKINGS
...HI THERE!
I'M IMPRESSED.
EVEN I'VE NEVER GOTTEN A SCORE LIKE THAT.

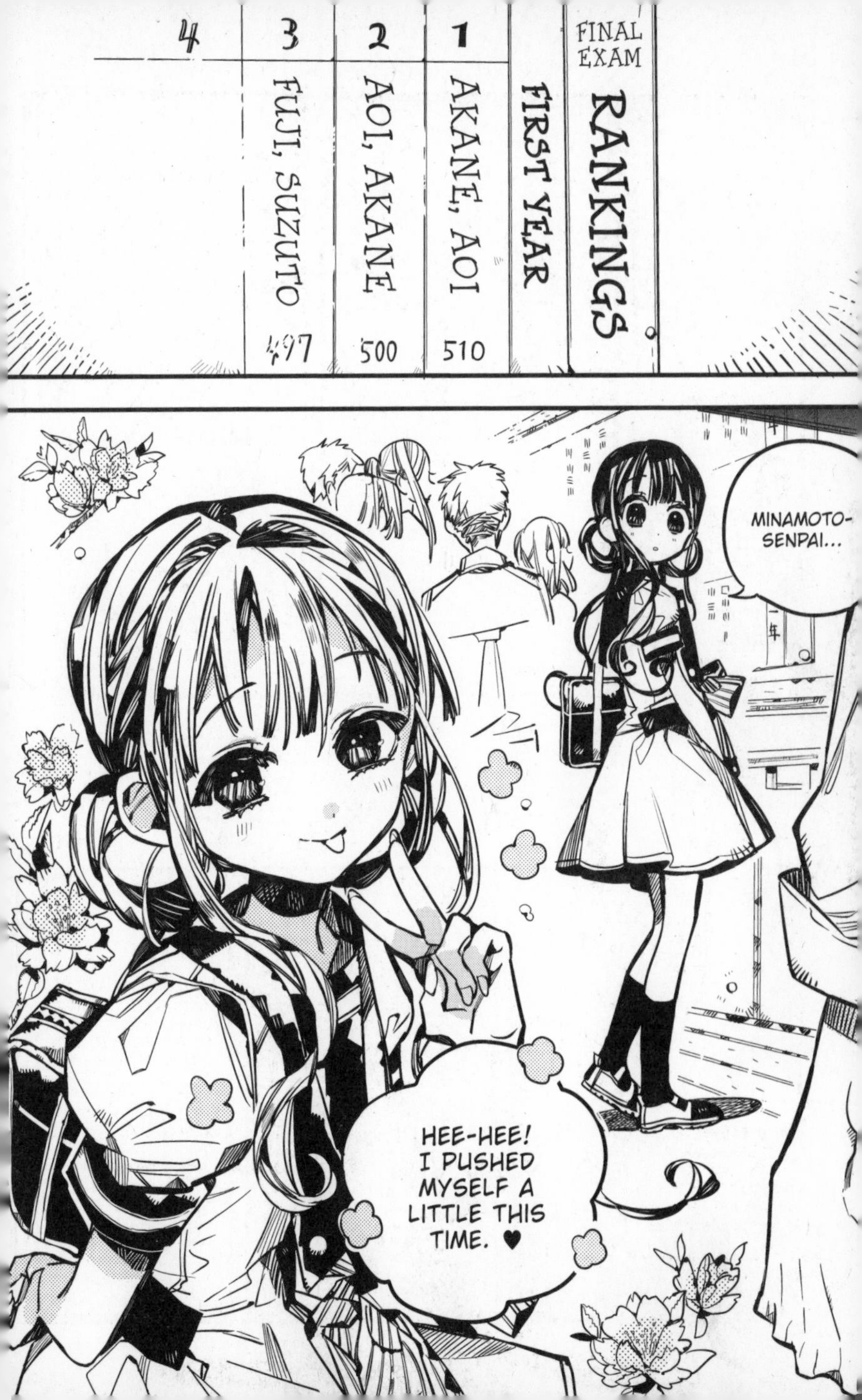
FINAL EXAM
RANKINGS
FIRST YEAR
1 AKANE, AOI 510
2 AOI, AKANE 500
3 FUJI, SUZUTO 497
4
MINAMOTO-SENPAI...
HEE-HEE! I PUSHED MYSELF A LITTLE THIS TIME. ♥

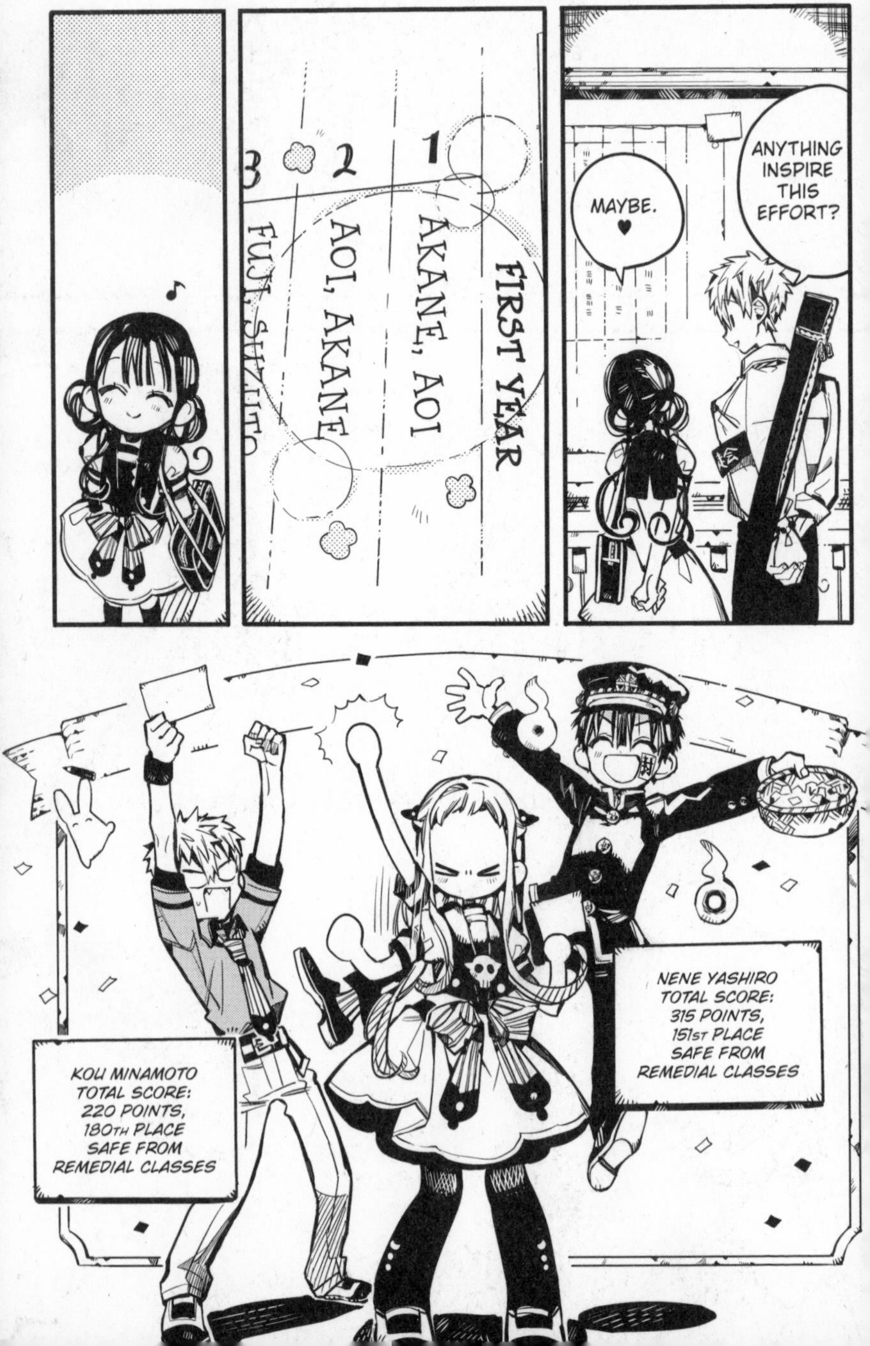

ANYTHING INSPIRE THIS EFFORT?
MAYBE. ♥
FIRST YEAR
1 AKANE, AOI
2 AOI, AKANE
3 FUJI, SUZUTO
NENE YASHIRO TOTAL SCORE: 315 POINTS, 151ST PLACE SAFE FROM REMEDIAL CLASSES
KOU MINAMOTO TOTAL SCORE: 220 POINTS, 180TH PLACE SAFE FROM REMEDIAL CLASSES

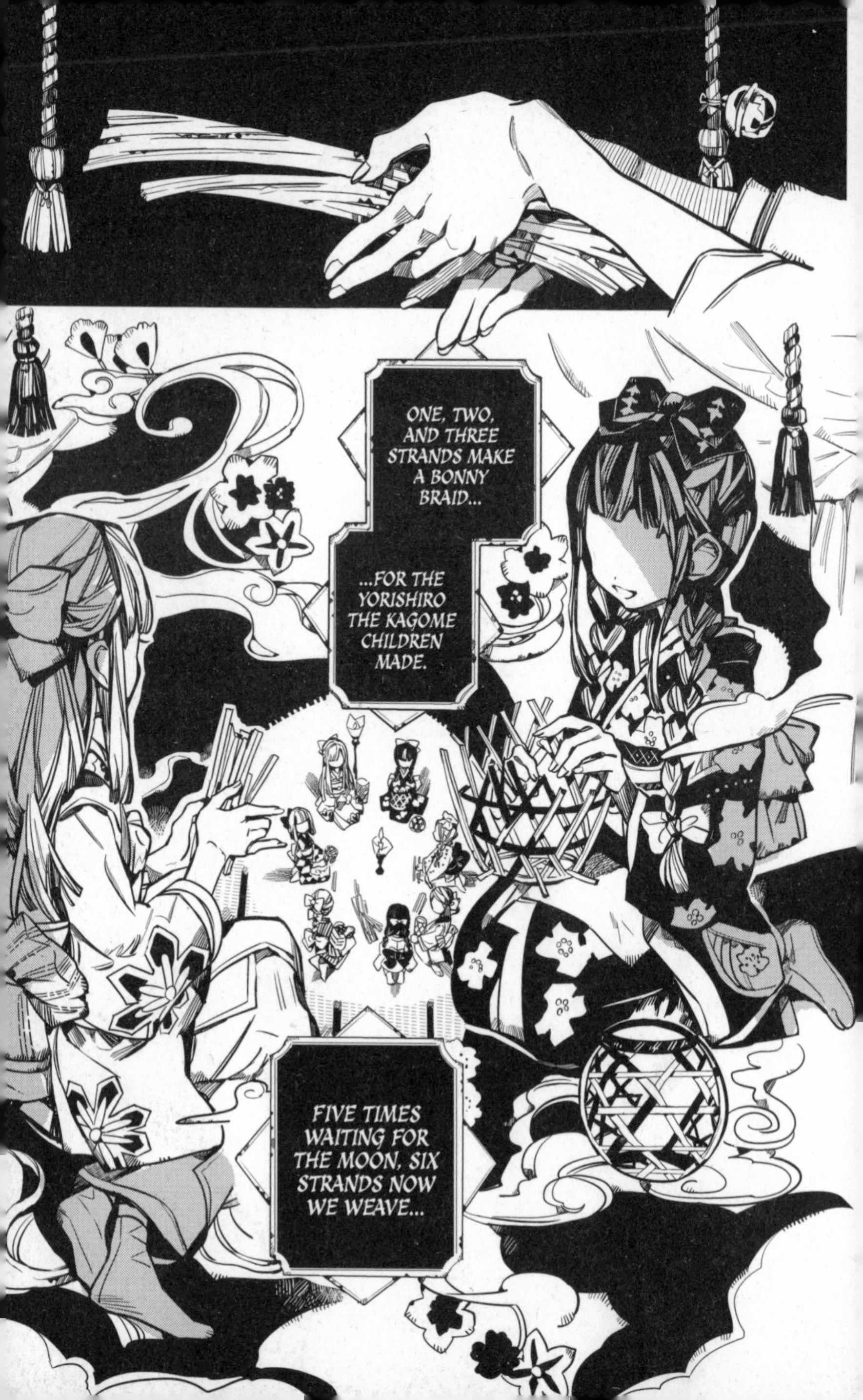
ONE, TWO, AND THREE STRANDS MAKE A BONNY BRAID...
...FOR THE YORISHIRO THE KAGOME CHILDREN MADE.
FIVE TIMES WAITING FOR THE MOON, SIX STRANDS NOW WE WEAVE...

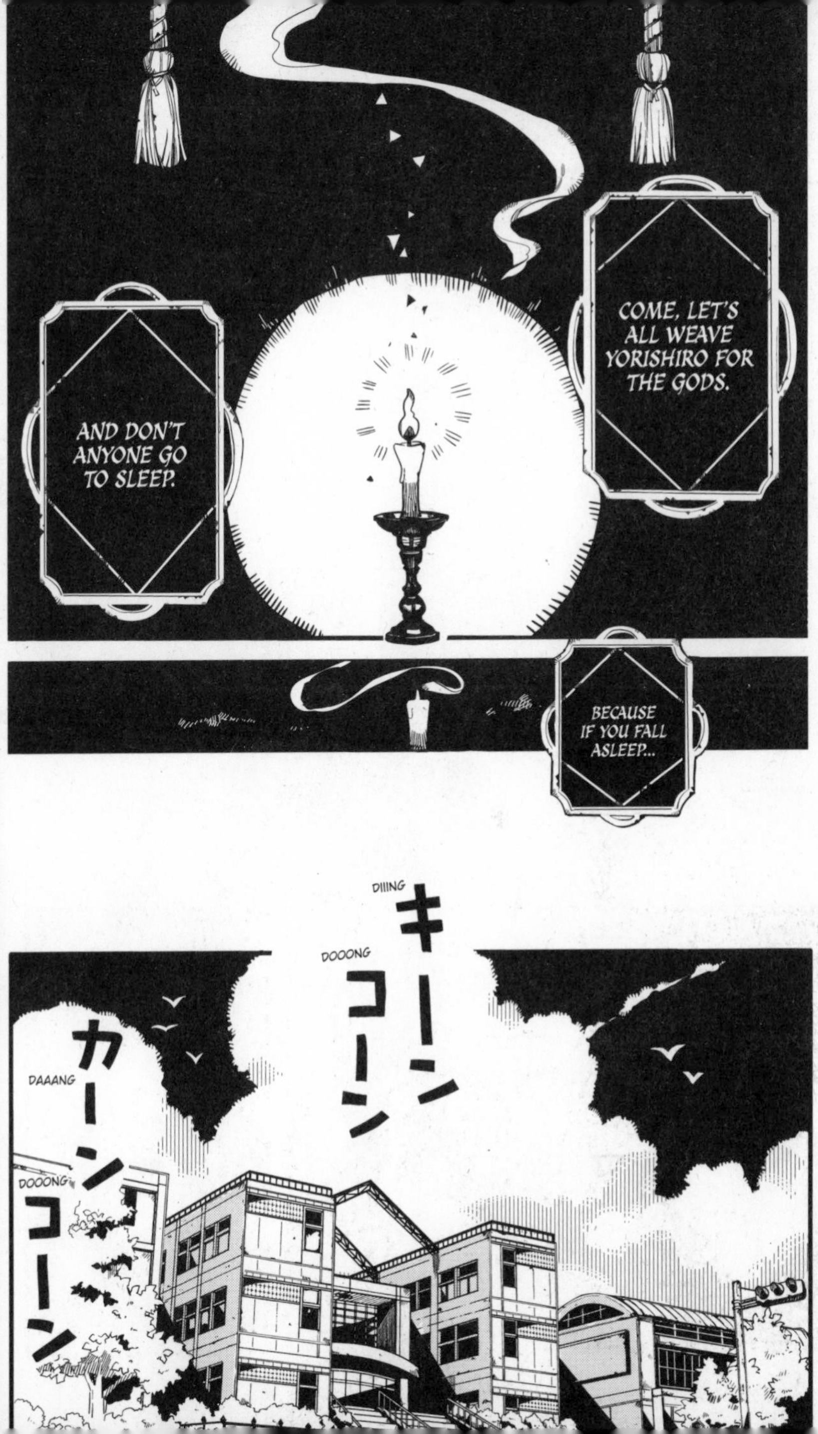
COME, LET'S ALL WEAVE YORISHIRO FOR THE GODS.
AND DON'T ANYONE GO TO SLEEP.
BECAUSE IF YOU FALL ASLEEP...
DIIING
キーン
DOOONG
コーン
DAAANG
カーン
DOOONG
コーン

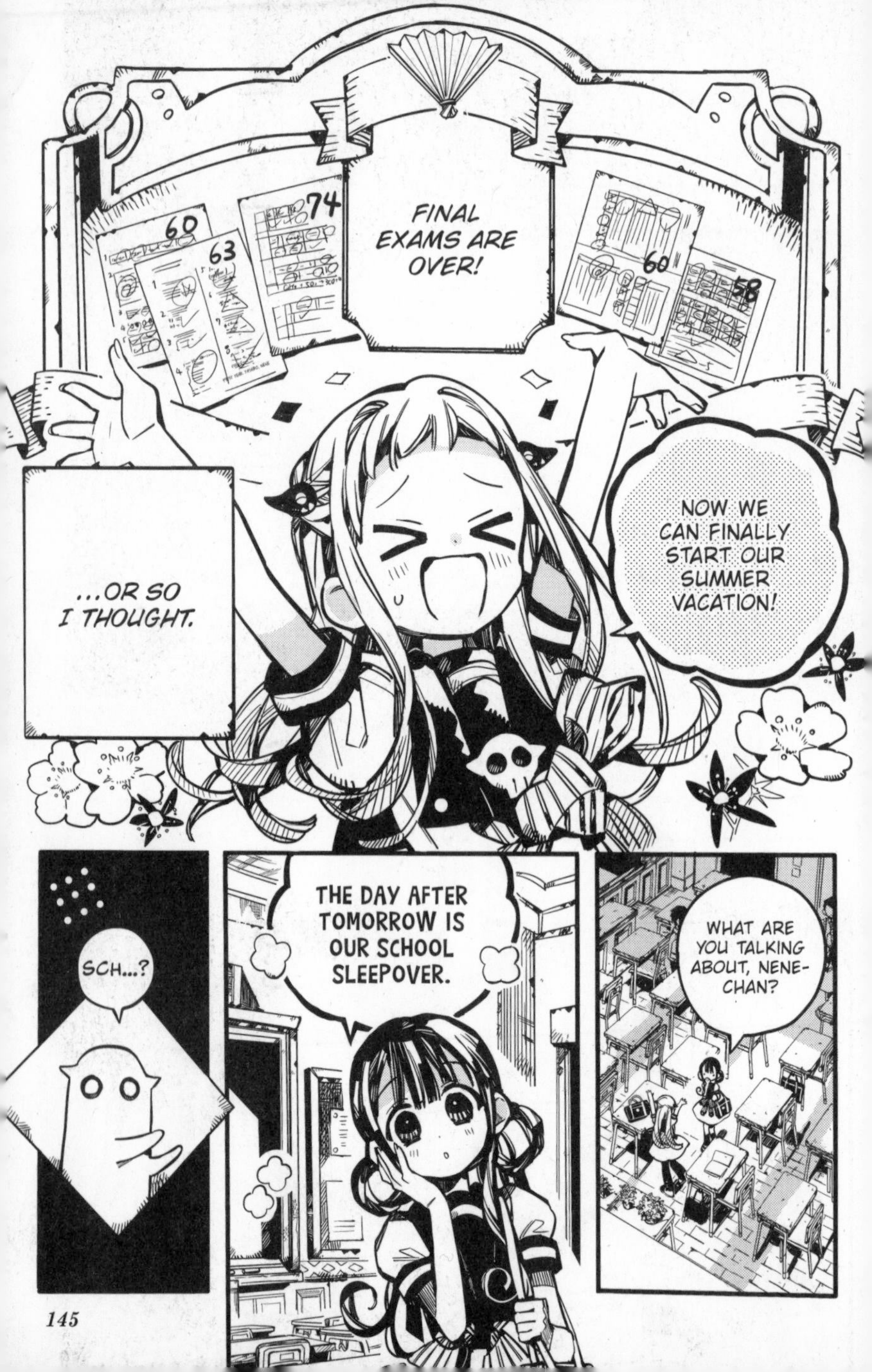
FINAL EXAMS ARE OVER!
NOW WE CAN FINALLY START OUR SUMMER VACATION!
...OR SO I THOUGHT.
WHAT ARE YOU TALKING ABOUT, NENE-CHAN?
THE DAY AFTER TOMORROW IS OUR SCHOOL SLEEPOVER.
SCH...?

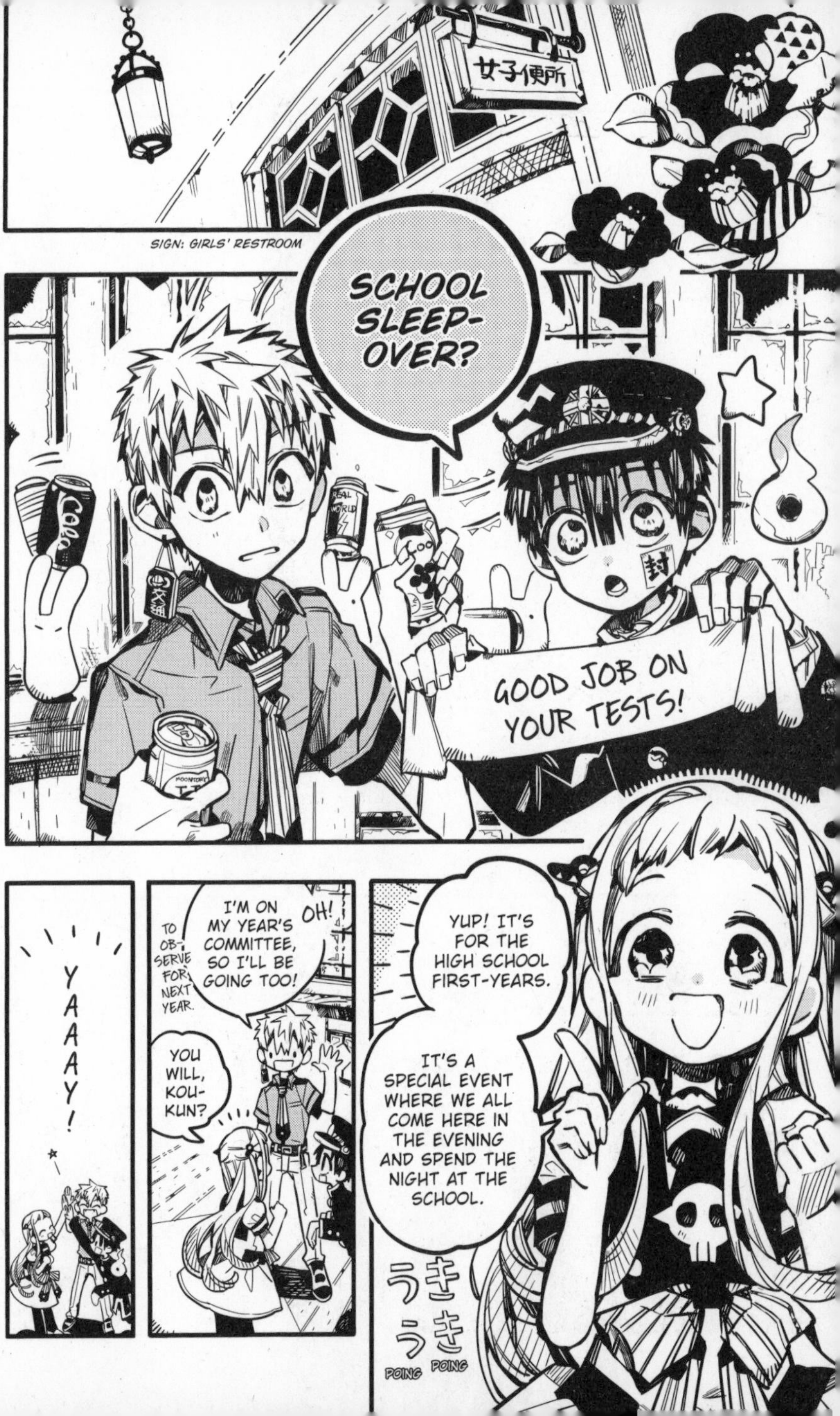
女子便所
SIGN: GIRLS' RESTROOM
SCHOOL SLEEP-OVER?
GOOD JOB ON YOUR TESTS!
YUP! IT'S FOR THE HIGH SCHOOL FIRST-YEARS.
IT'S A SPECIAL EVENT WHERE WE ALL COME HERE IN THE EVENING AND SPEND THE NIGHT AT THE SCHOOL.
うき うき
POING POING
OH!
I'M ON MY YEAR'S COMMITTEE, SO I'LL BE GOING TOO!
TO OBSERVE FOR NEXT YEAR.
YOU WILL, KOU-KUN?
YAAAAY!

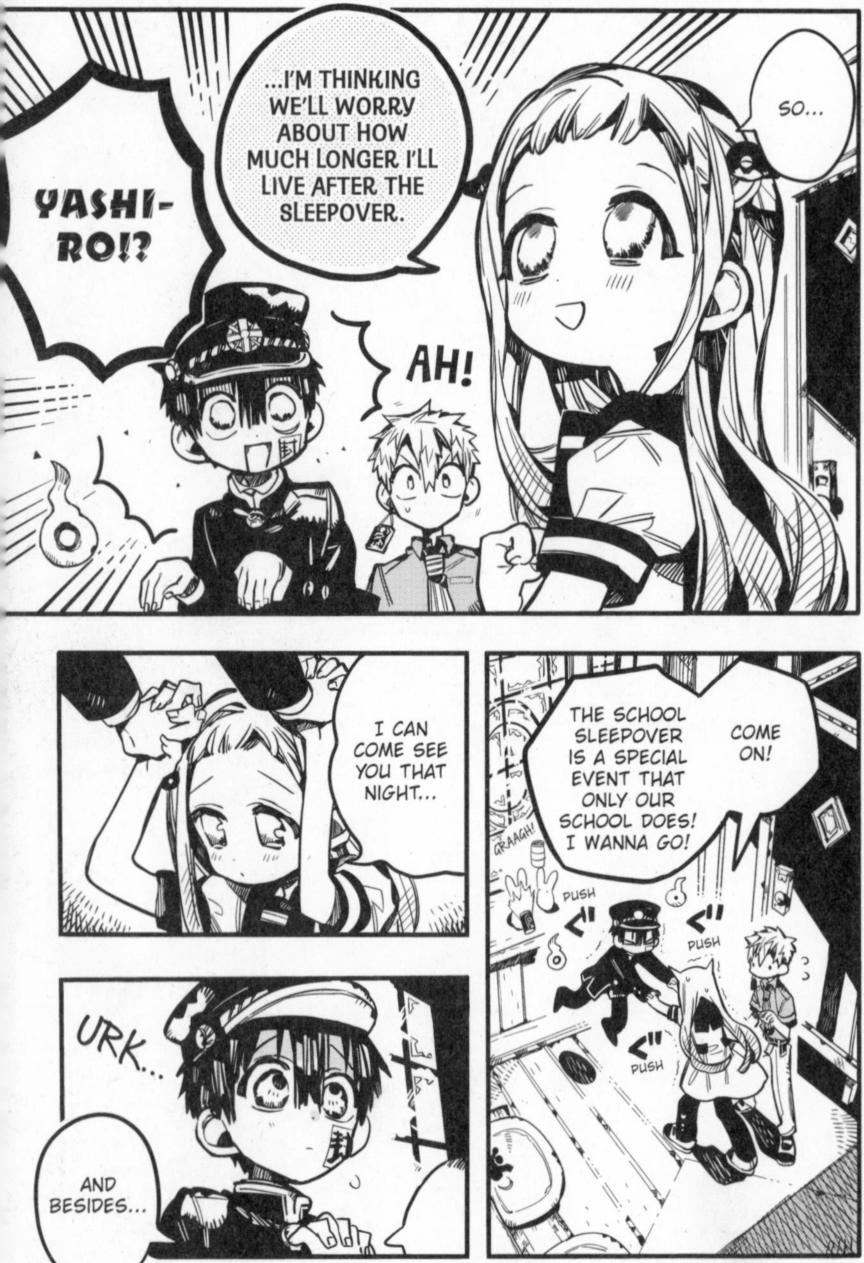
SO...
...I'M THINKING WE'LL WORRY ABOUT HOW MUCH LONGER I'LL LIVE AFTER THE SLEEPOVER.
AH!
YASHI-RO!?
COME ON!
THE SCHOOL SLEEPOVER IS A SPECIAL EVENT THAT ONLY OUR SCHOOL DOES! I WANNA GO!
GRAAGH!
PUSH
PUSH
PUSH
I CAN COME SEE YOU THAT NIGHT...
URK...
AND BESIDES...

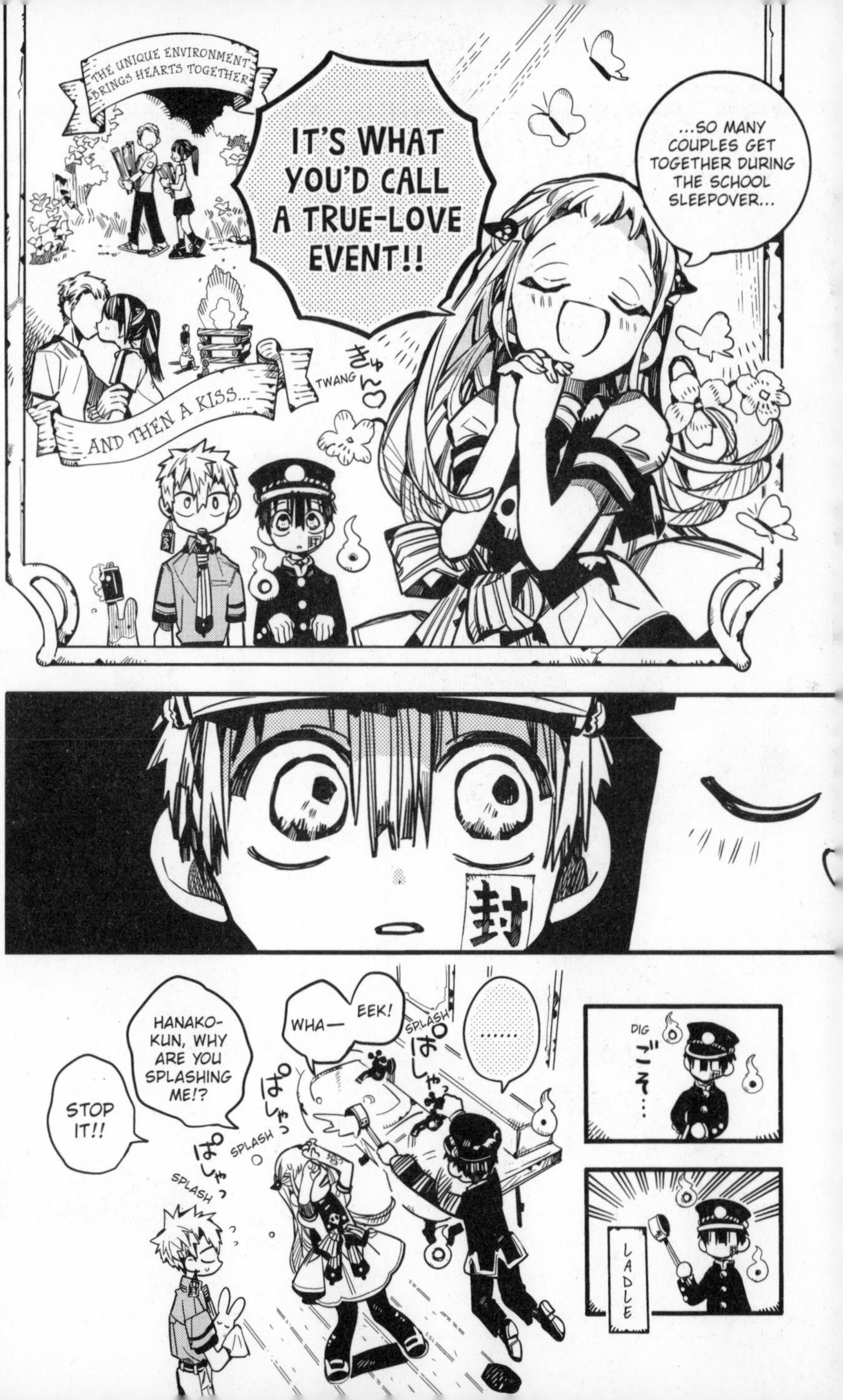
...SO MANY COUPLES GET TOGETHER DURING THE SCHOOL SLEEPOVER...
IT'S WHAT YOU'D CALL A TRUE-LOVE EVENT!!
THE UNIQUE ENVIRONMENT BRINGS HEARTS TOGETHER
きゅん
TWANG
AND THEN A KISS...
ごそ…
DIG
LADLE
......
EEK!
WHA—
ぱしゃっ
SPLASH
ぱしゃっ
HANAKO-KUN, WHY ARE YOU SPLASHING ME!?
STOP IT!!
ぱしゃっ
SPLASH
ぱしゃっ
SPLASH

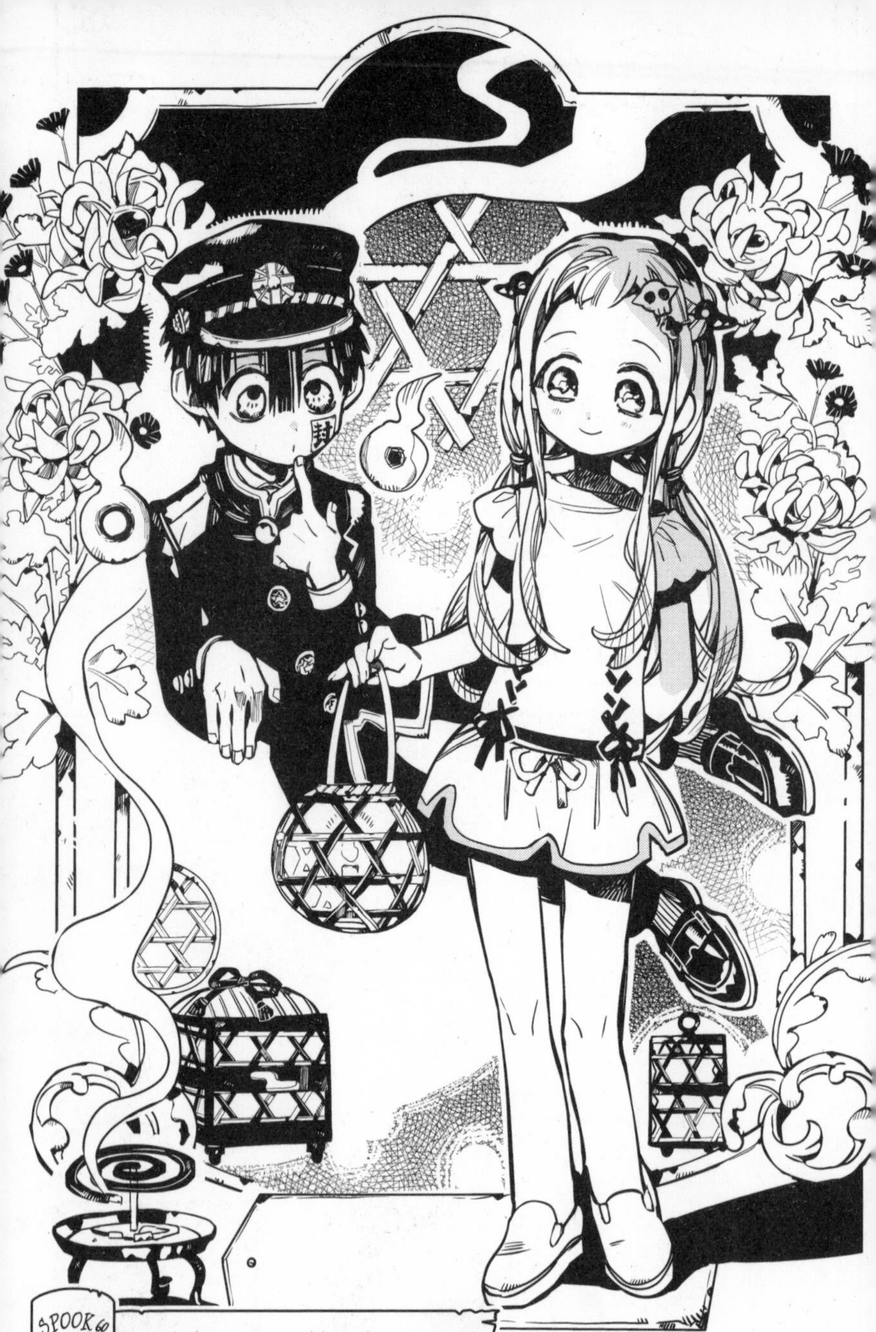
封

SPOOK 60

THE SCHOOL SLEEPOVER (PART 1)

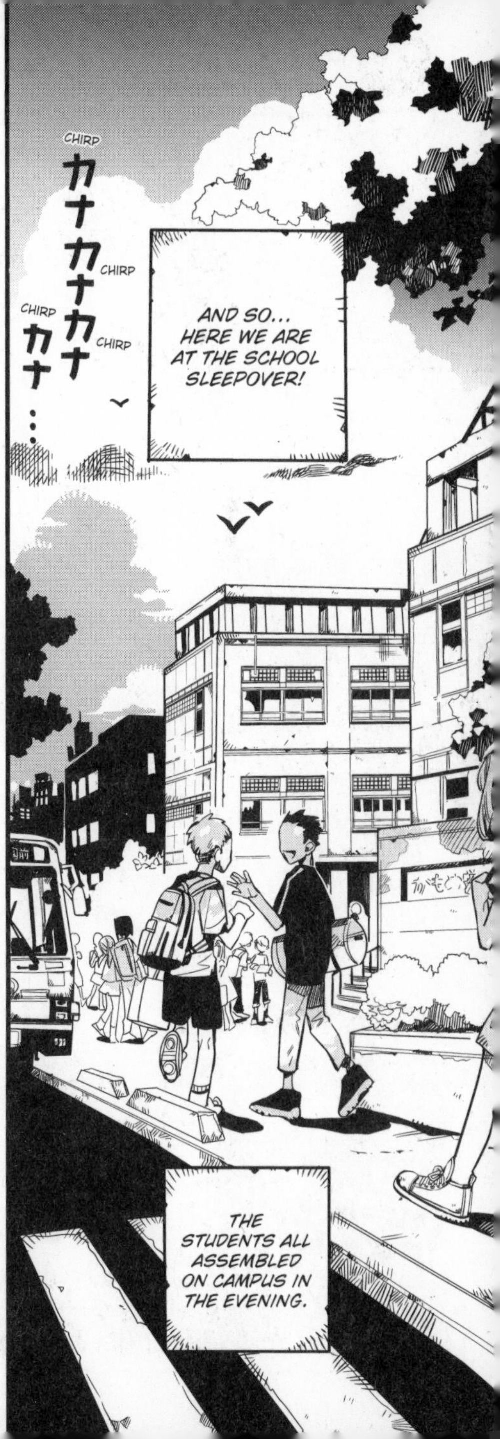
AND SO... HERE WE ARE AT THE SCHOOL SLEEPOVER!
CHIRP
カナカナカナ
CHIRP
CHIRP
カナ…
CHIRP
THE STUDENTS ALL ASSEMBLED ON CAMPUS IN THE EVENING.
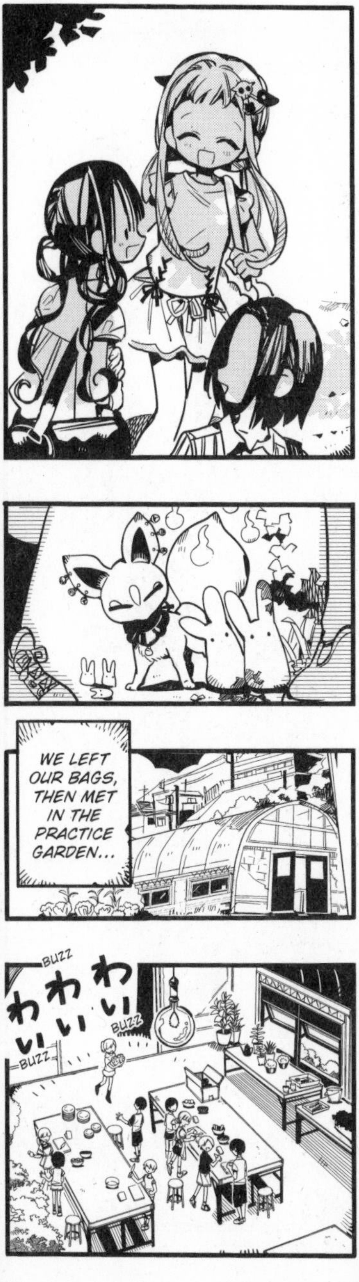
WE LEFT OUR BAGS, THEN MET IN THE PRACTICE GARDEN...
わい
BUZZ
わい
BUZZ
わい
BUZZ

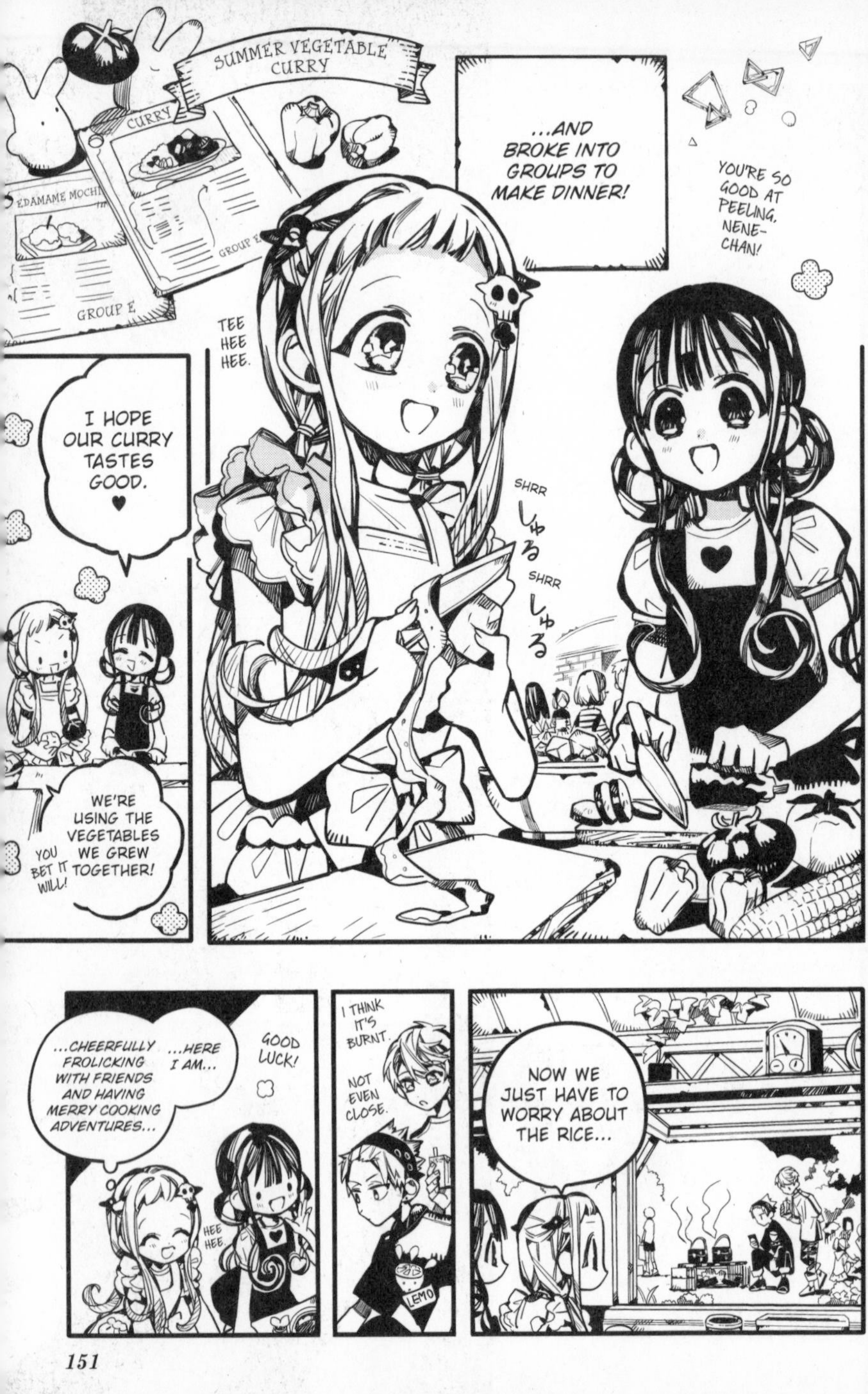
SUMMER VEGETABLE CURRY
CURRY
EDAMAME MOCHI
GROUP E
GROUP E
...AND BROKE INTO GROUPS TO MAKE DINNER!
YOU'RE SO GOOD AT PEELING, NENE-CHAN!
TEE HEE HEE.
SHRR しゅる
SHRR しゅる
I HOPE OUR CURRY TASTES GOOD. ♥
WE'RE USING THE VEGETABLES WE GREW TOGETHER!
YOU BET IT WILL!
NOW WE JUST HAVE TO WORRY ABOUT THE RICE...
I THINK IT'S BURNT.
NOT EVEN CLOSE.
LEMO
GOOD LUCK!
...HERE I AM...
...CHEERFULLY FROLICKING WITH FRIENDS AND HAVING MERRY COOKING ADVENTURES...
HEE HEE.

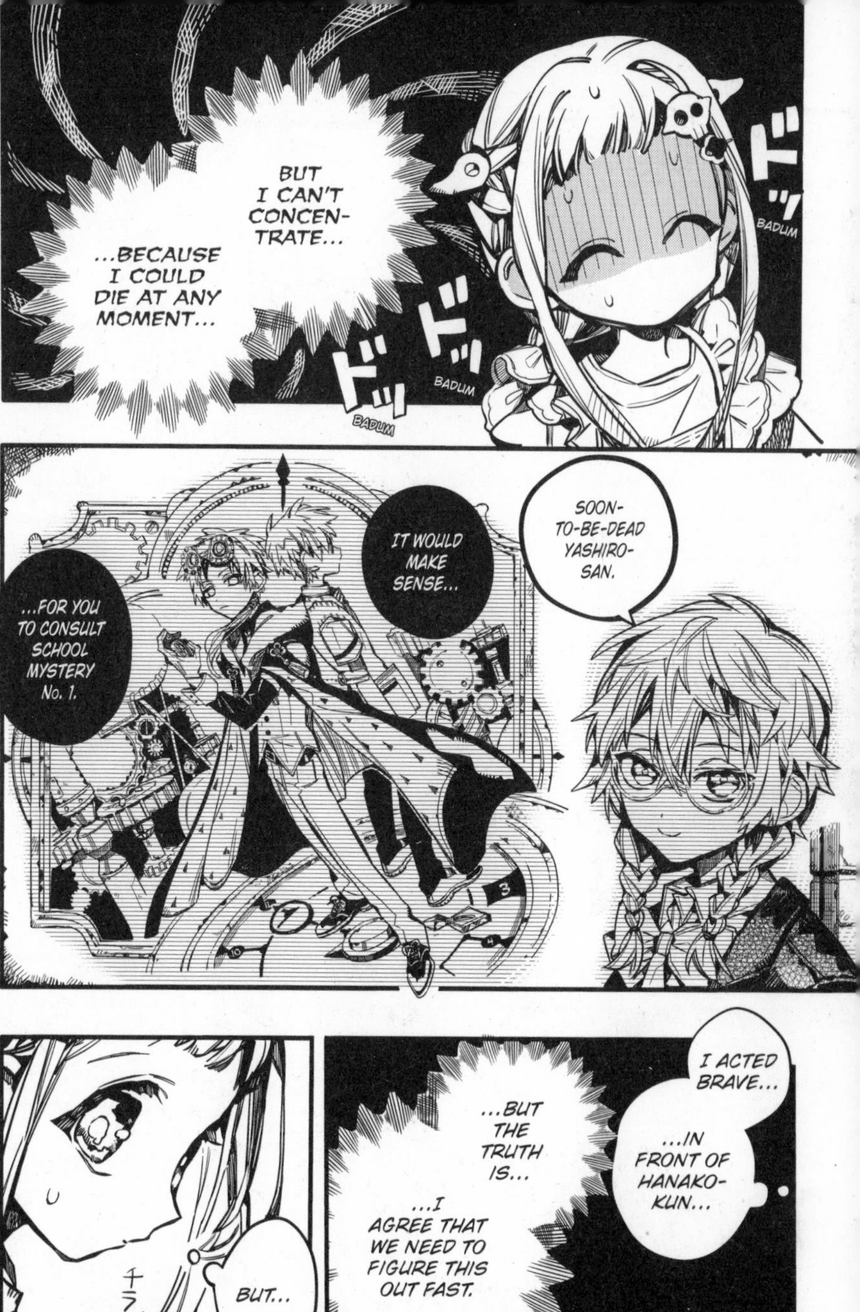
ドッ
BADUM
BUT I CAN'T CONCENTRATE...
...BECAUSE I COULD DIE AT ANY MOMENT...
ドッ
BADUM
ドッ
BADUM
SOON-TO-BE-DEAD YASHIRO-SAN.
IT WOULD MAKE SENSE...
...FOR YOU TO CONSULT SCHOOL MYSTERY No. 1.
I ACTED BRAVE...
...IN FRONT OF HANAKO-KUN...
...BUT THE TRUTH IS...
...I AGREE THAT WE NEED TO FIGURE THIS OUT FAST.
BUT...
チラ
GLANCE

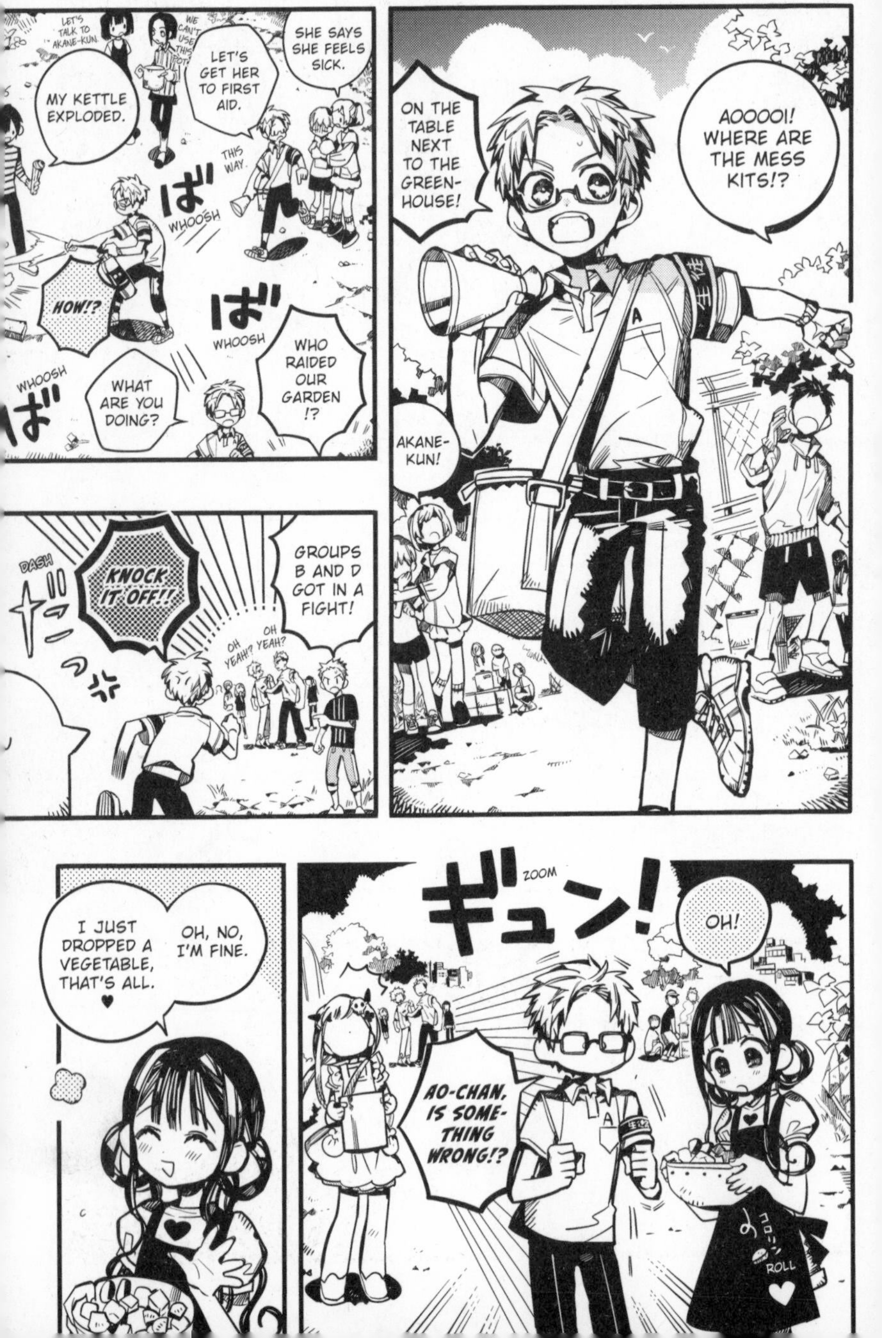
AOOOOI! WHERE ARE THE MESS KITS!?
ON THE TABLE NEXT TO THE GREEN-HOUSE!
AKANE-KUN!
SHE SAYS SHE FEELS SICK.
LET'S GET HER TO FIRST AID.
WE CAN'T USE THIS POT!
LET'S TALK TO AKANE-KUN.
MY KETTLE EXPLODED.
THIS WAY.
ば
WHOOSH
ば
WHOOSH
WHO RAIDED OUR GARDEN!?
HOW!?
ば
WHOOSH
WHAT ARE YOU DOING?
GROUPS B AND D GOT IN A FIGHT!
OH YEAH!?
OH YEAH!?
KNOCK IT OFF!!
DASH
ギュン!
ZOOM
OH!
AO-CHAN, IS SOME-THING WRONG!?
ROLL
OH, NO, I'M FINE.
I JUST DROPPED A VEGETABLE, THAT'S ALL. ♥

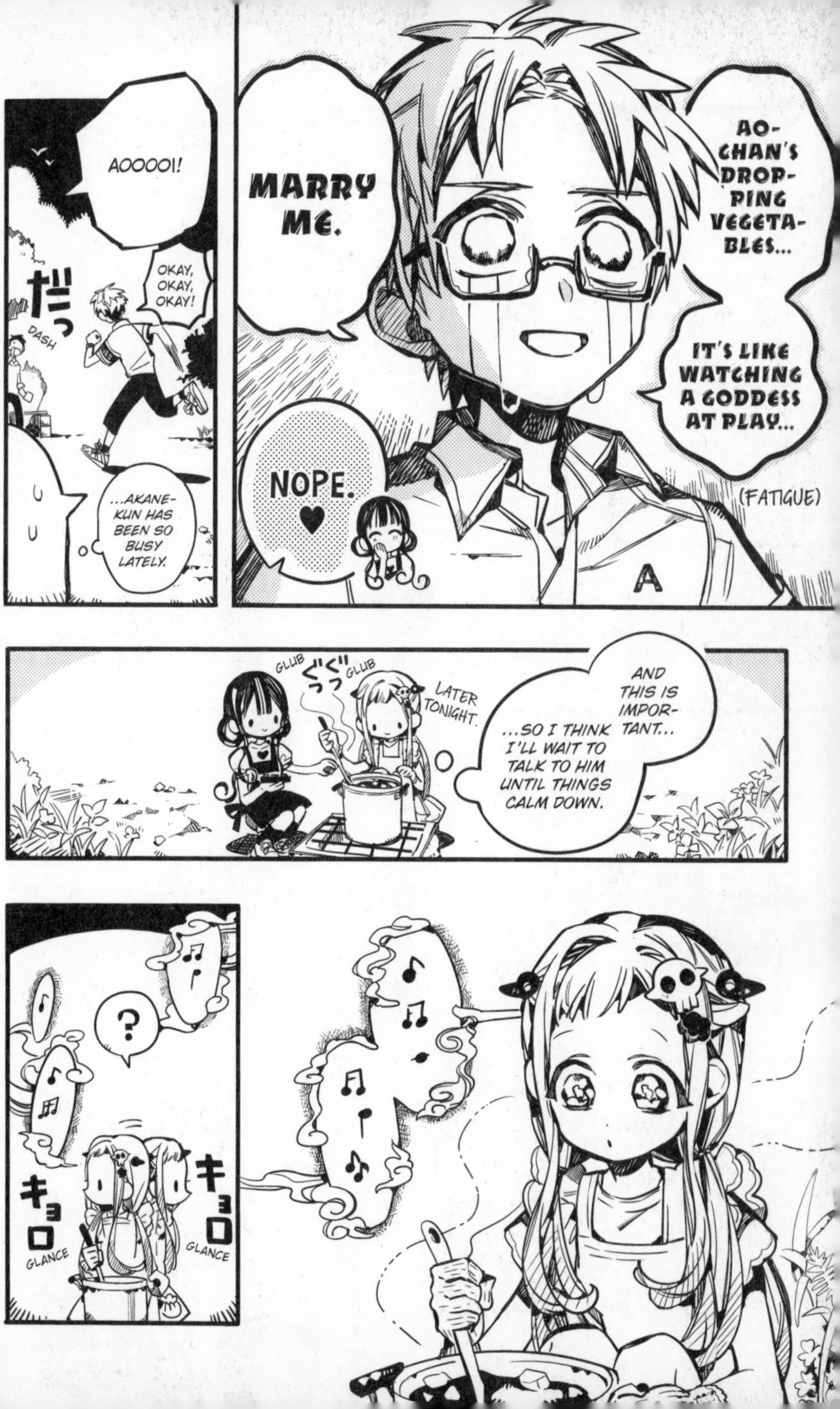
AO-CHAN'S DROPPING VEGETABLES...
IT'S LIKE WATCHING A GODDESS AT PLAY...
(FATIGUE)
MARRY ME.
NOPE. ♥
A
AOOOOI!
OKAY, OKAY, OKAY!
だっ
DASH
...AKANE-KUN HAS BEEN SO BUSY LATELY.
LATER TONIGHT.
ぐつぐつ
GLUB GLUB
AND THIS IS IMPORTANT...
...SO I THINK I'LL WAIT TO TALK TO HIM UNTIL THINGS CALM DOWN.
?
キョロ
GLANCE
キョロ
GLANCE

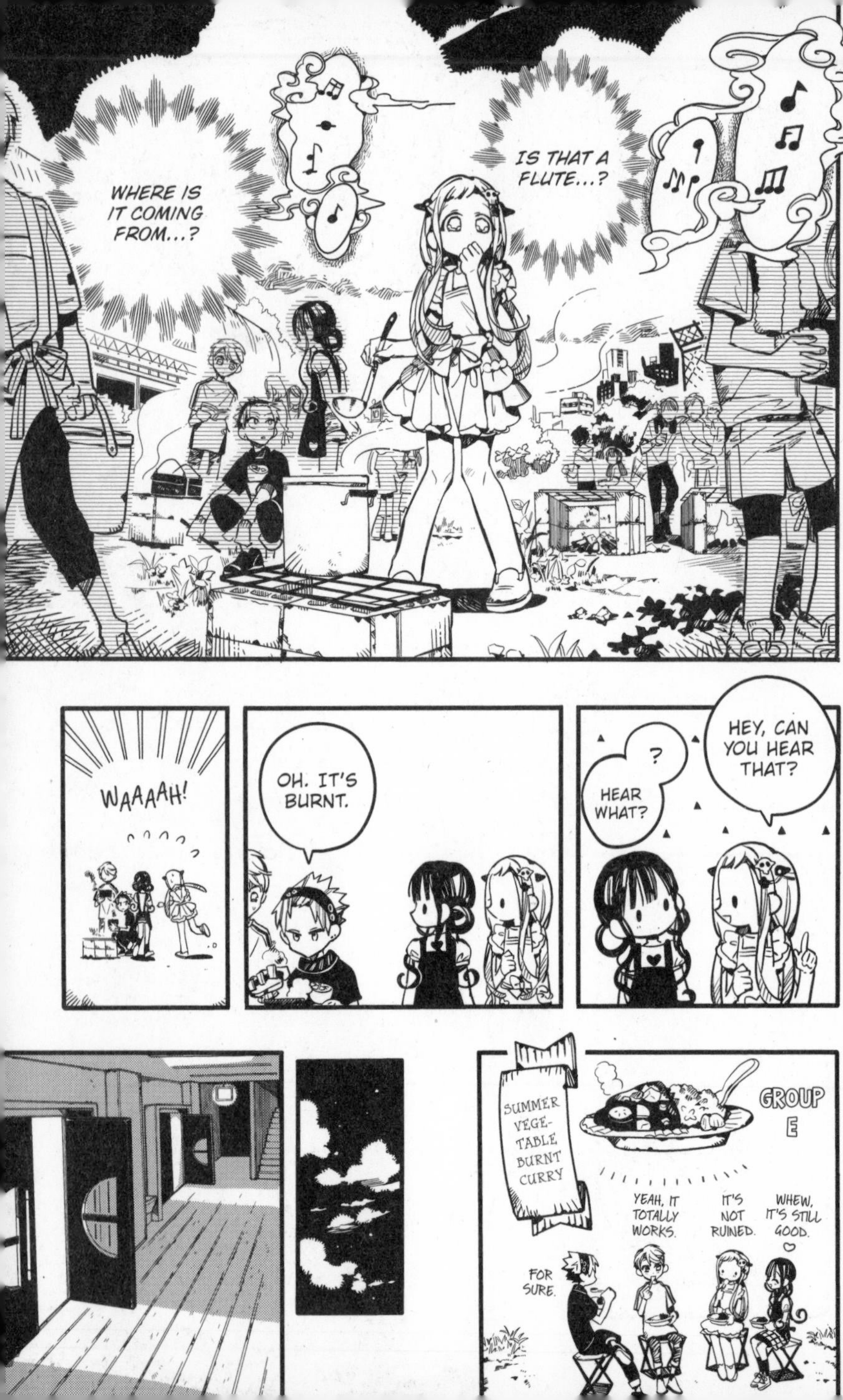
IS THAT A FLUTE...?
WHERE IS IT COMING FROM...?
HEY, CAN YOU HEAR THAT?
?
HEAR WHAT?
OH. IT'S BURNT.
WAAAAH!
SUMMER VEGE-TABLE BURNT CURRY
GROUP E
WHEW, IT'S STILL GOOD.
IT'S NOT RUINED.
YEAH, IT TOTALLY WORKS.
FOR SURE.

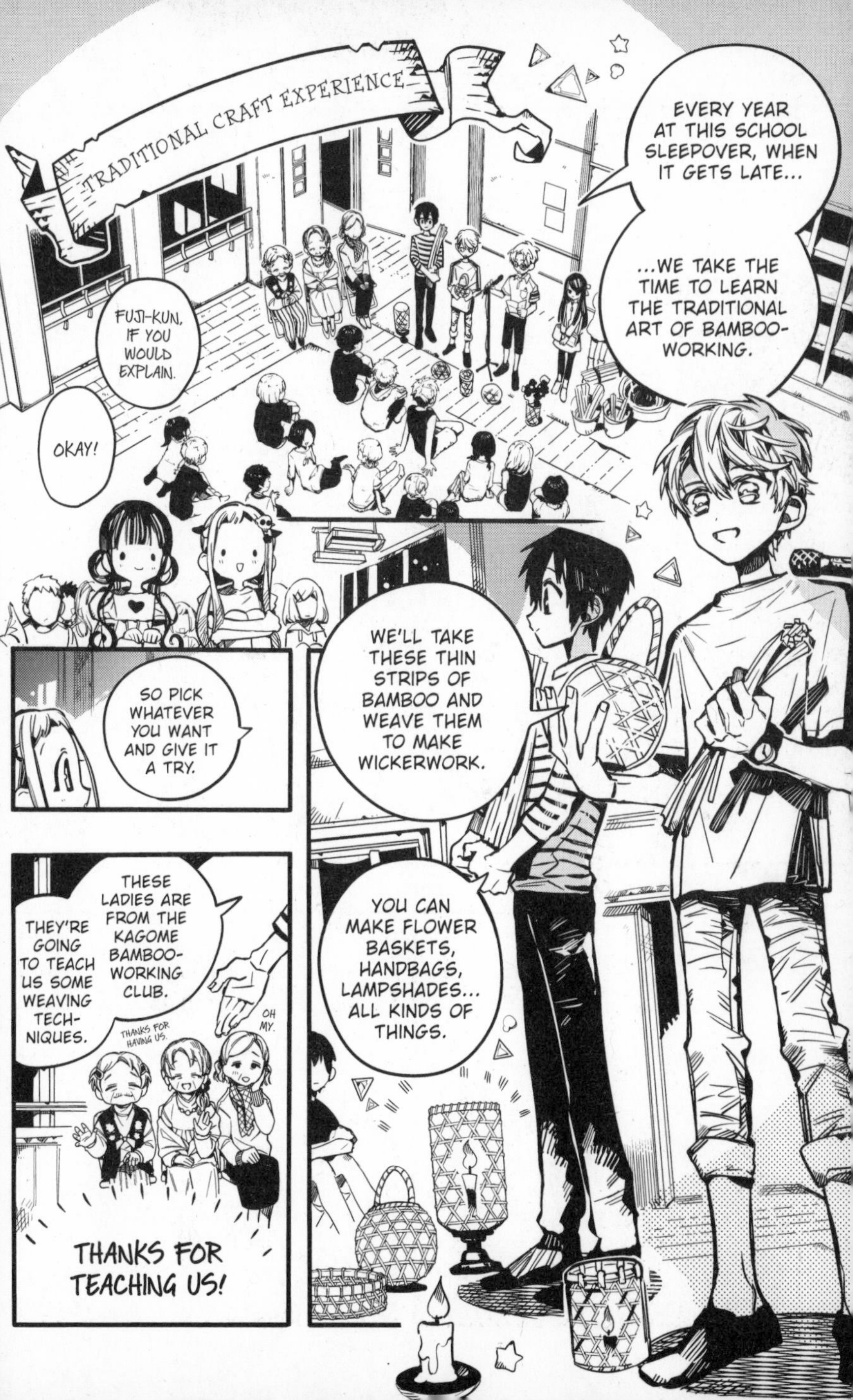
TRADITIONAL CRAFT EXPERIENCE
EVERY YEAR AT THIS SCHOOL SLEEPOVER, WHEN IT GETS LATE...
...WE TAKE THE TIME TO LEARN THE TRADITIONAL ART OF BAMBOO-WORKING.
FUJI-KUN, IF YOU WOULD EXPLAIN.
OKAY!
WE'LL TAKE THESE THIN STRIPS OF BAMBOO AND WEAVE THEM TO MAKE WICKERWORK.
YOU CAN MAKE FLOWER BASKETS, HANDBAGS, LAMPSHADES... ALL KINDS OF THINGS.
SO PICK WHATEVER YOU WANT AND GIVE IT A TRY.
THESE LADIES ARE FROM THE KAGOME BAMBOO-WORKING CLUB.
THEY'RE GOING TO TEACH US SOME WEAVING TECH-NIQUES.
OH MY.
THANKS FOR HAVING US.
THANKS FOR TEACHING US!

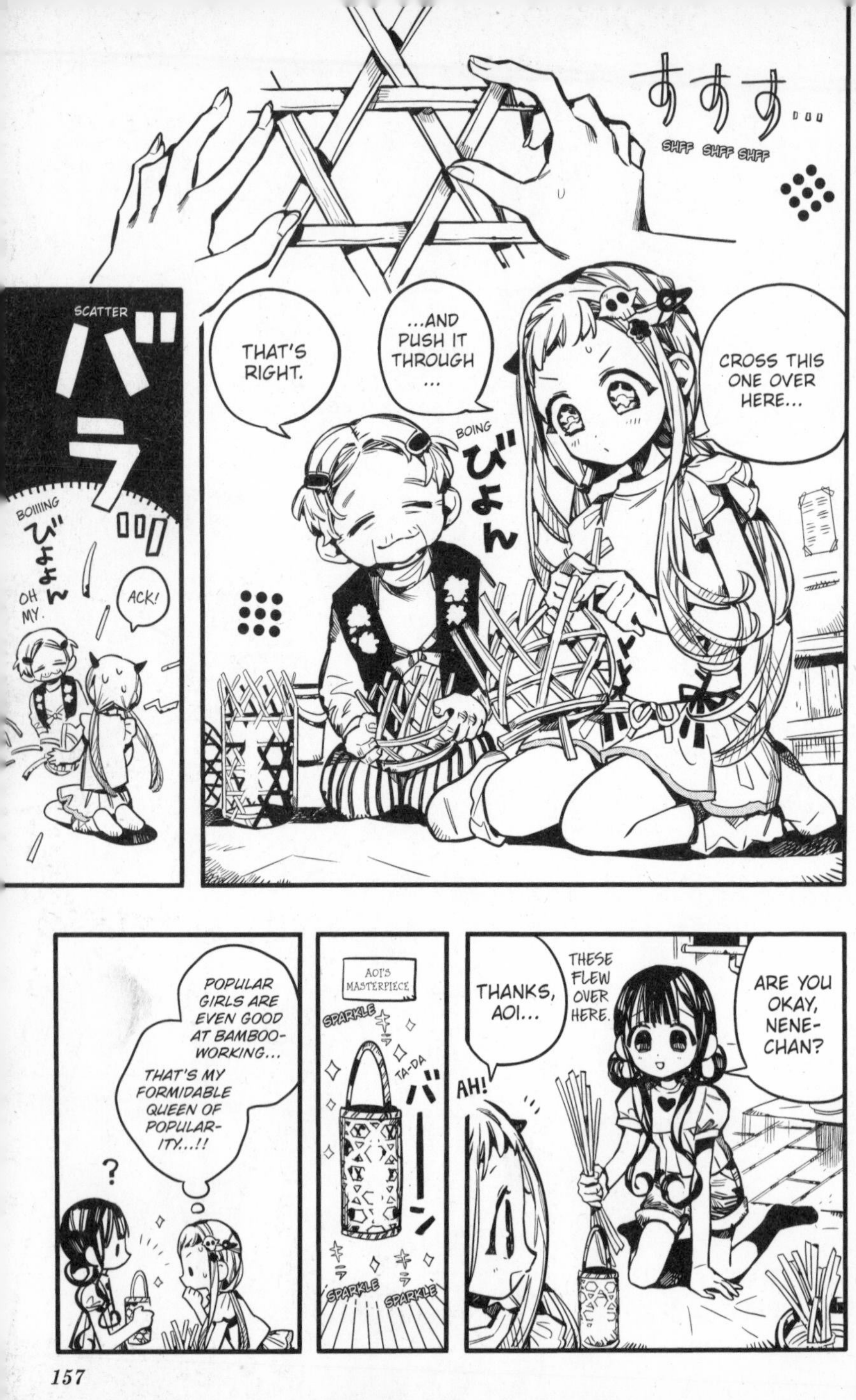
すすす…
SHFF SHFF SHFF
CROSS THIS ONE OVER HERE...
...AND PUSH IT THROUGH...
BOING
びよん
THAT'S RIGHT.
SCATTER
バラ
BOIIIING
びよよん
ACK!
OH MY.
ARE YOU OKAY, NENE-CHAN?
THESE FLEW OVER HERE.
THANKS, AOI...
AH!
AOI'S MASTERPIECE
SPARKLE
キラ
TA-DA
バーン
キラ
SPARKLE
キラ
SPARKLE
POPULAR GIRLS ARE EVEN GOOD AT BAMBOO-WORKING... THAT'S MY FORMIDABLE QUEEN OF POPULARITY...!!
?

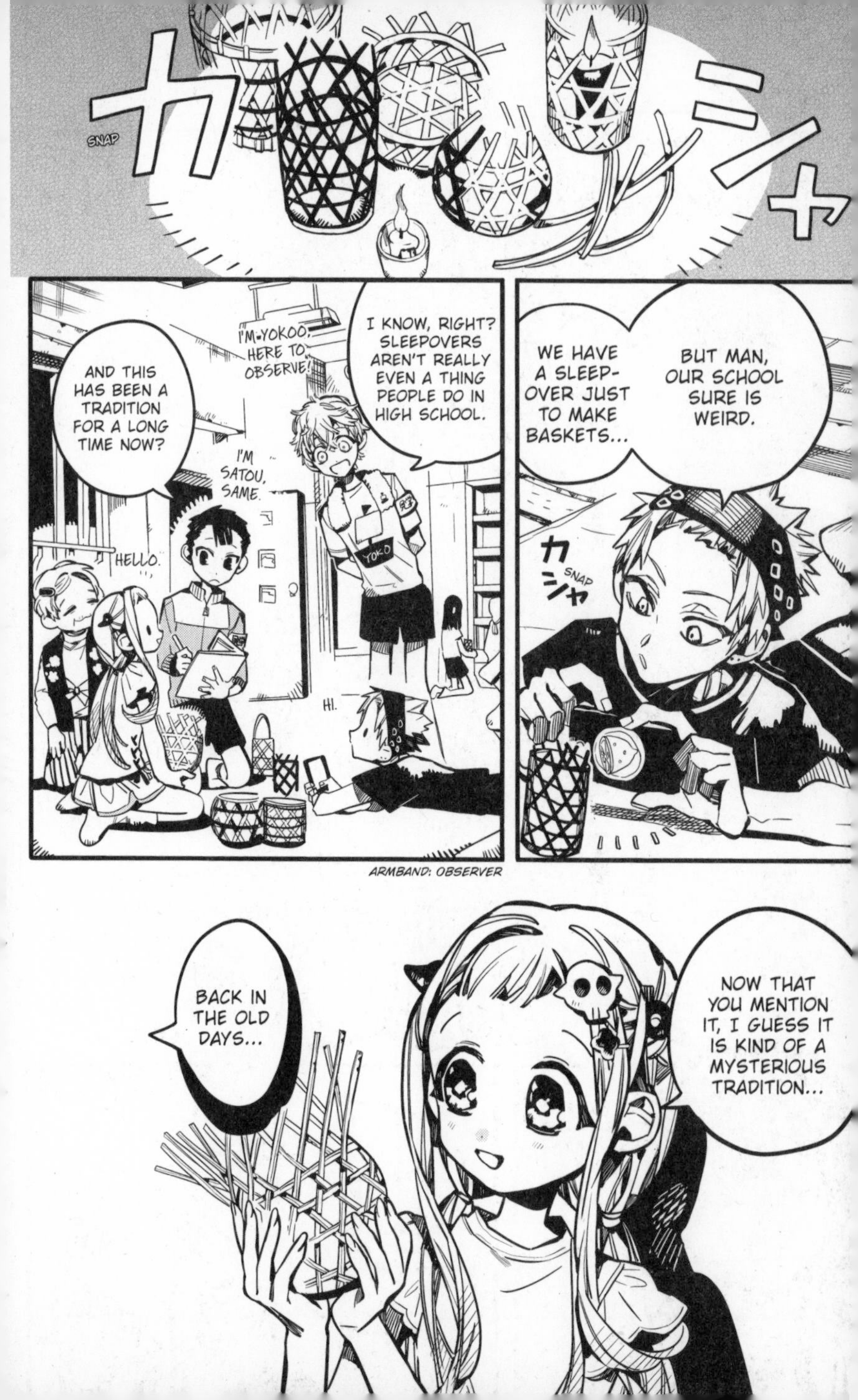

カシャ
SNAP
BUT MAN, OUR SCHOOL SURE IS WEIRD.
WE HAVE A SLEEPOVER JUST TO MAKE BASKETS...
カシャ
SNAP
I KNOW, RIGHT? SLEEPOVERS AREN'T REALLY EVEN A THING PEOPLE DO IN HIGH SCHOOL.
I'M YOKOO. HERE TO OBSERVE!
AND THIS HAS BEEN A TRADITION FOR A LONG TIME NOW?
I'M SATOU, SAME.
HELLO.
YOKO
HI.
ARMBAND: OBSERVER
NOW THAT YOU MENTION IT, I GUESS IT IS KIND OF A MYSTERIOUS TRADITION...
BACK IN THE OLD DAYS...

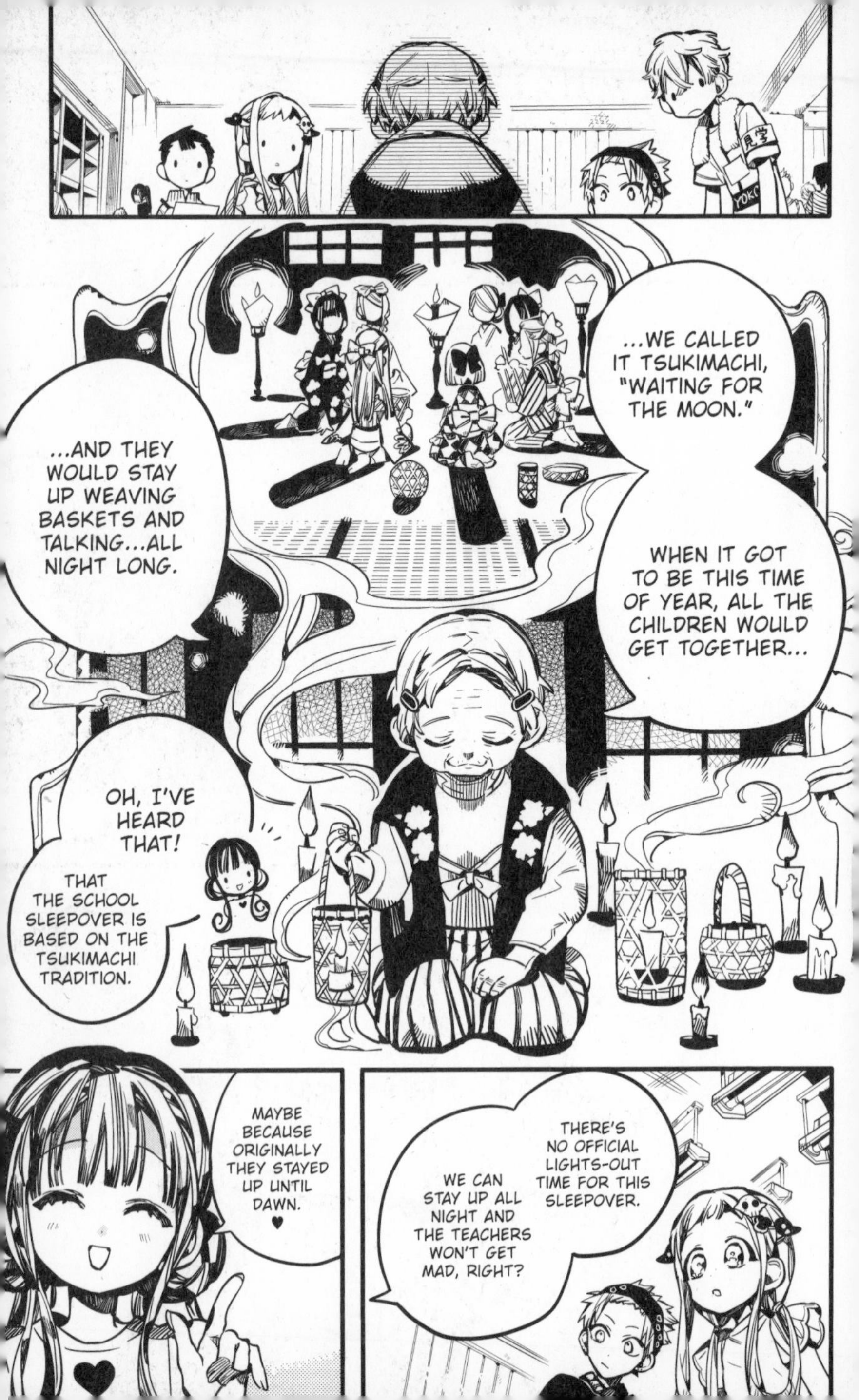
WHEN IT GOT TO BE THIS TIME OF YEAR, ALL THE CHILDREN WOULD GET TOGETHER...
...AND THEY WOULD STAY UP WEAVING BASKETS AND TALKING...ALL NIGHT LONG.
...WE CALLED IT TSUKIMACHI, "WAITING FOR THE MOON."
OH, I'VE HEARD THAT!
THAT THE SCHOOL SLEEPOVER IS BASED ON THE TSUKIMACHI TRADITION.
THERE'S NO OFFICIAL LIGHTS-OUT TIME FOR THIS SLEEPOVER.
WE CAN STAY UP ALL NIGHT AND THE TEACHERS WON'T GET MAD, RIGHT?
MAYBE BECAUSE ORIGINALLY THEY STAYED UP UNTIL DAWN. ♥

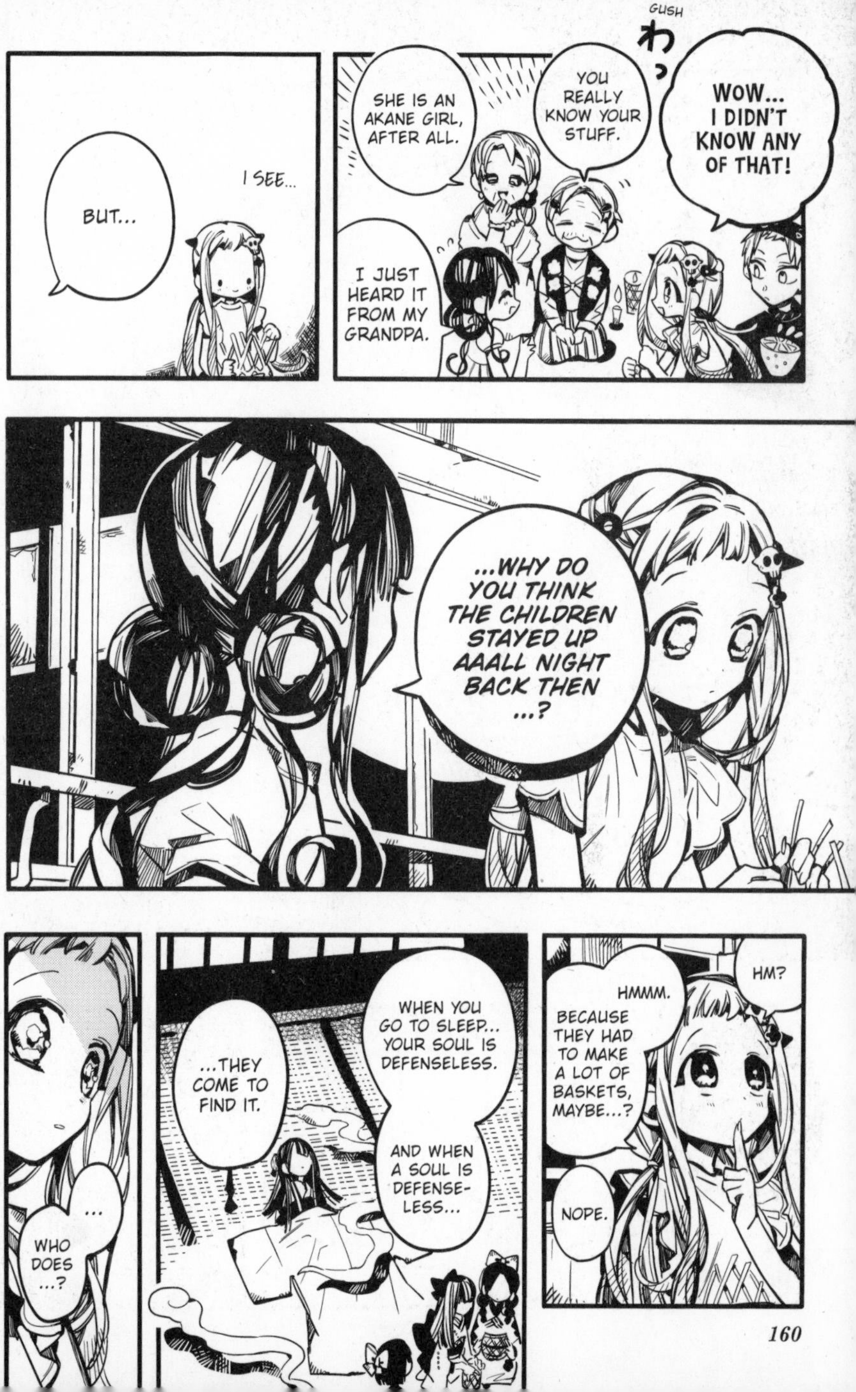
GUSH
わっ
WOW... I DIDN'T KNOW ANY OF THAT!
YOU REALLY KNOW YOUR STUFF.
SHE IS AN AKANE GIRL, AFTER ALL.
I JUST HEARD IT FROM MY GRANDPA.
I SEE...
BUT...
...WHY DO YOU THINK THE CHILDREN STAYED UP AAALL NIGHT BACK THEN ...?
HM?
HMMM.
BECAUSE THEY HAD TO MAKE A LOT OF BASKETS, MAYBE...?
NOPE.
WHEN YOU GO TO SLEEP... YOUR SOUL IS DEFENSELESS.
AND WHEN A SOUL IS DEFENSE-LESS...
...THEY COME TO FIND IT.
...
WHO DOES ...?

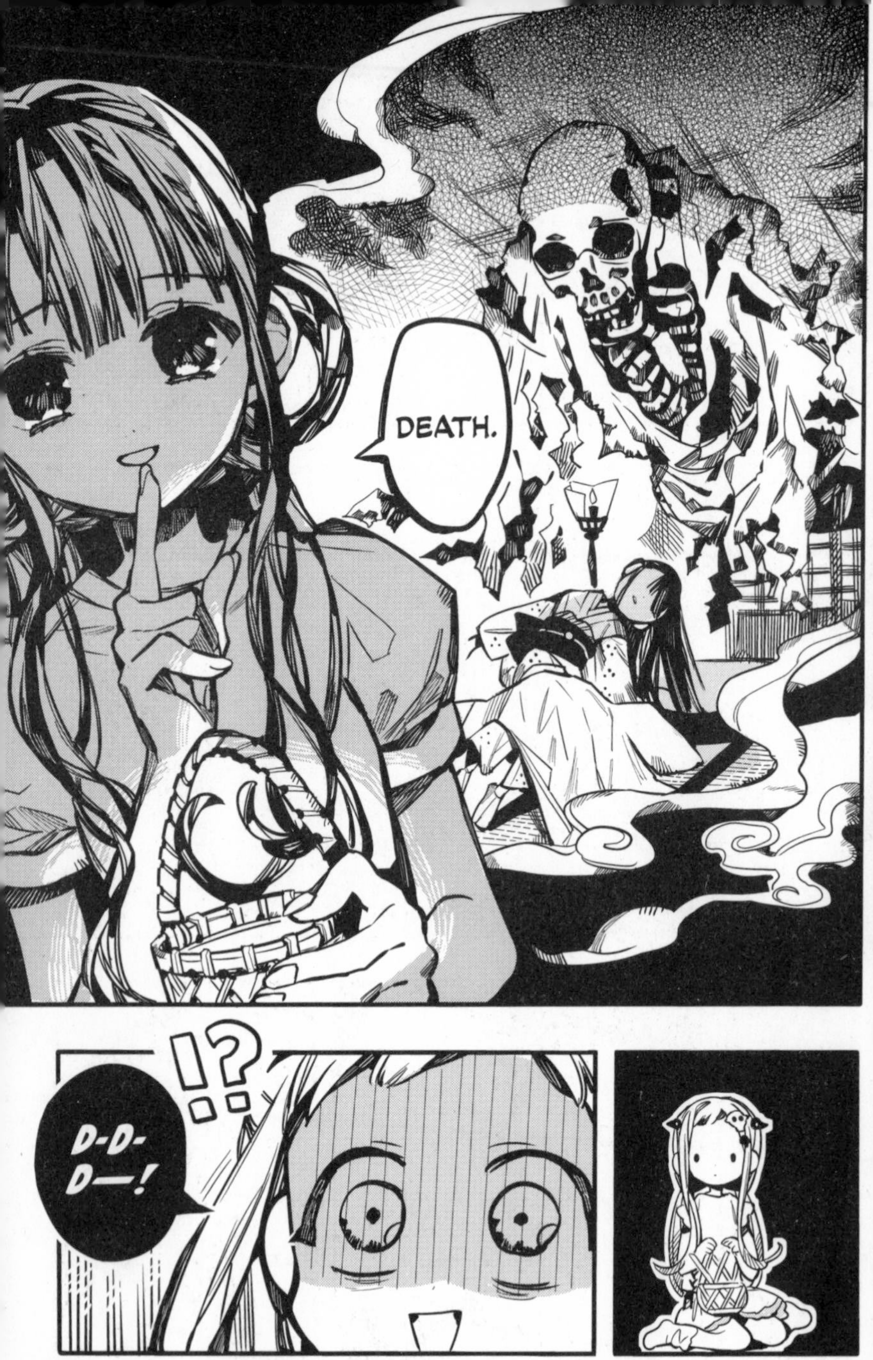
DEATH.
!?
D-D-D—!

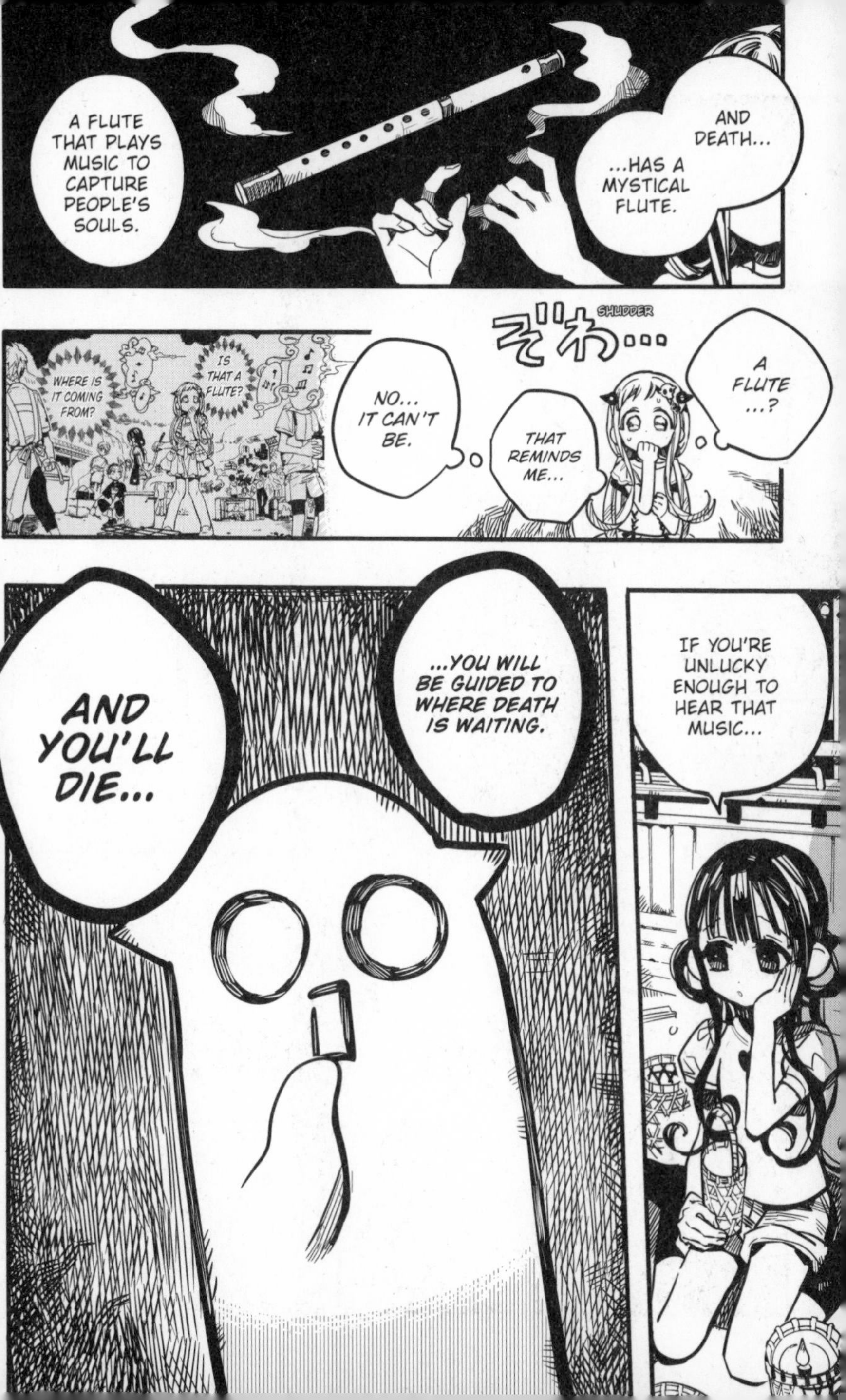
AND DEATH...
...HAS A MYSTICAL FLUTE.
A FLUTE THAT PLAYS MUSIC TO CAPTURE PEOPLE'S SOULS.
ざわ...
SHUDDER
A FLUTE ...?
THAT REMINDS ME...
NO... IT CAN'T BE.
IS THAT A FLUTE?
WHERE IS IT COMING FROM?
IF YOU'RE UNLUCKY ENOUGH TO HEAR THAT MUSIC...
...YOU WILL BE GUIDED TO WHERE DEATH IS WAITING.
AND YOU'LL DIE...

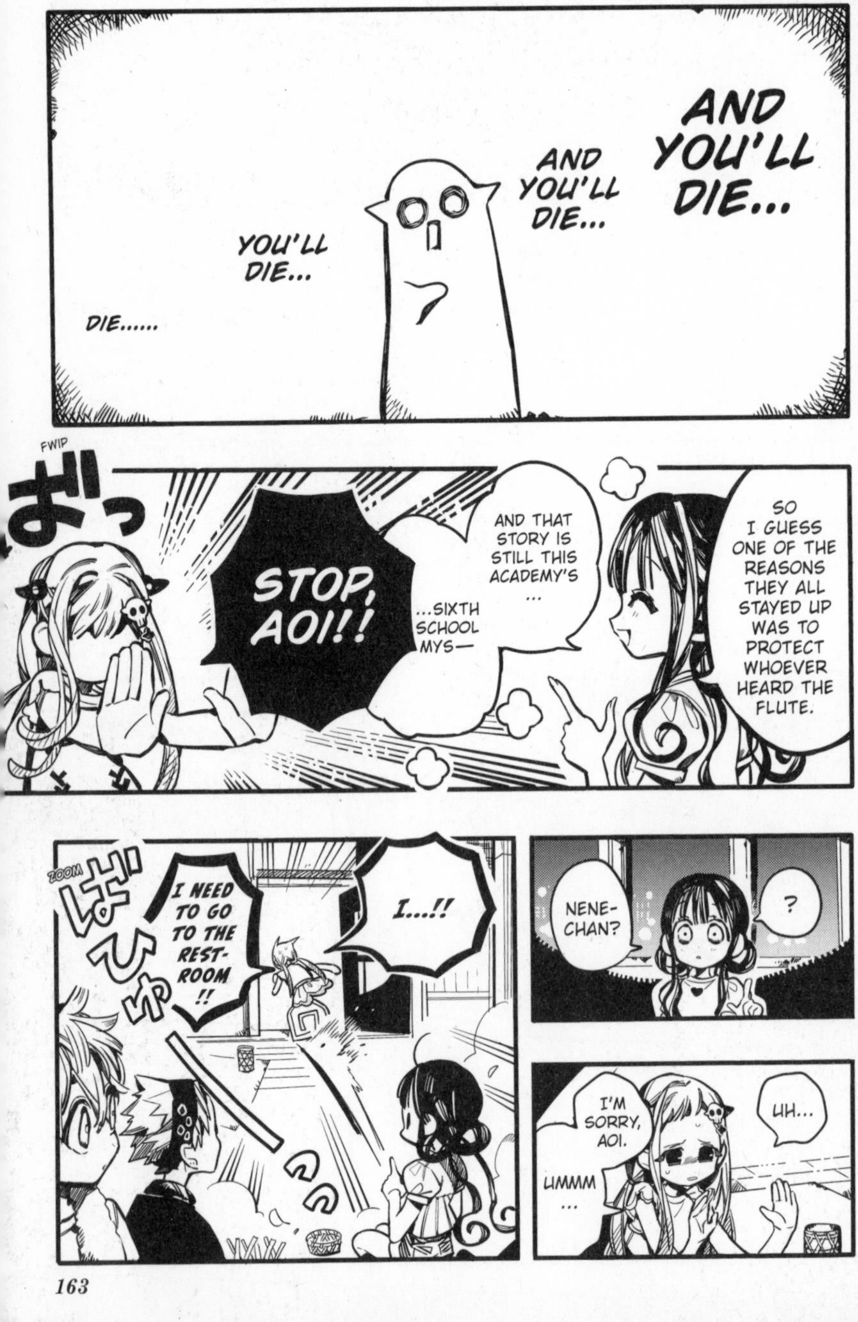
AND YOU'LL DIE...
AND YOU'LL DIE...
YOU'LL DIE...
DIE......
SO I GUESS ONE OF THE REASONS THEY ALL STAYED UP WAS TO PROTECT WHOEVER HEARD THE FLUTE.
AND THAT STORY IS STILL THIS ACADEMY'S ...
...SIXTH SCHOOL MYS—
STOP, AOI!!
FWIP
?
NENE-CHAN?
UH...
I'M SORRY, AOI.
UMMM ...
I...!!
I NEED TO GO TO THE REST-ROOM!!
ZOOM

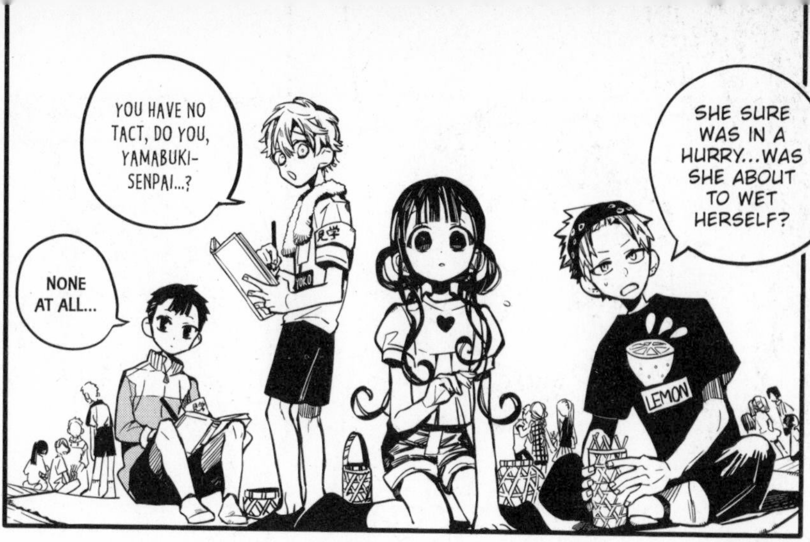
SHE SURE WAS IN A HURRY...WAS SHE ABOUT TO WET HERSELF?
YOU HAVE NO TACT, DO YOU, YAMABUKI-SENPAI...?
NONE AT ALL...
LEMON

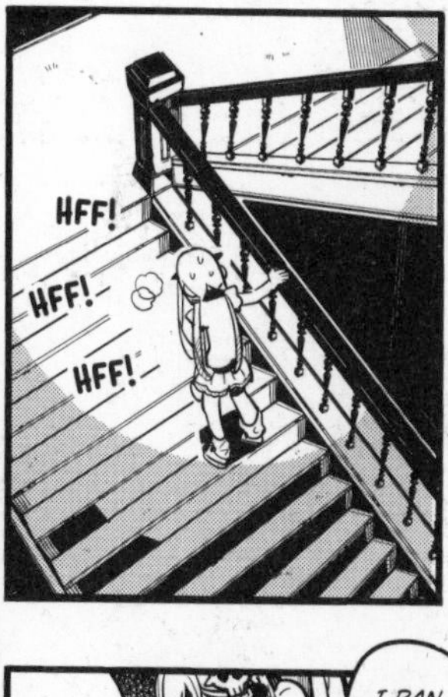
HFF!
HFF!
HFF!

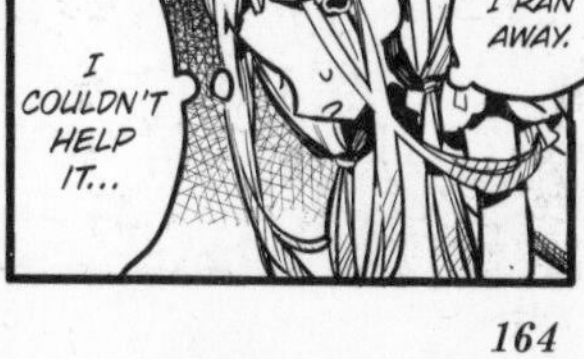
I RAN AWAY.
I COULDN'T HELP IT...

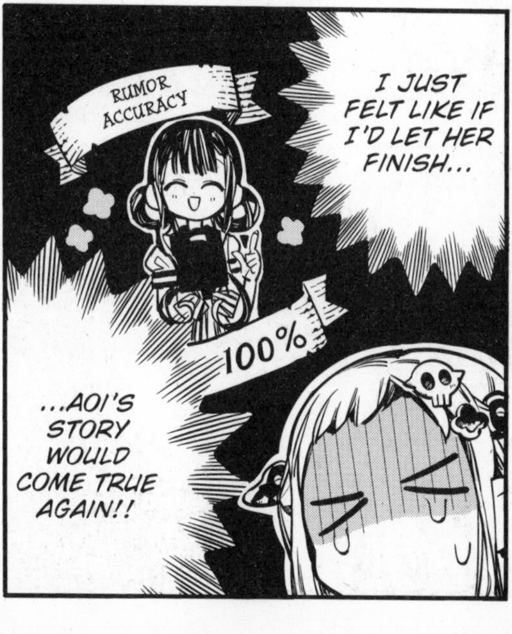
I JUST FELT LIKE IF I'D LET HER FINISH...
RUMOR ACCURACY
100%
...AOI'S STORY WOULD COME TRUE AGAIN!!

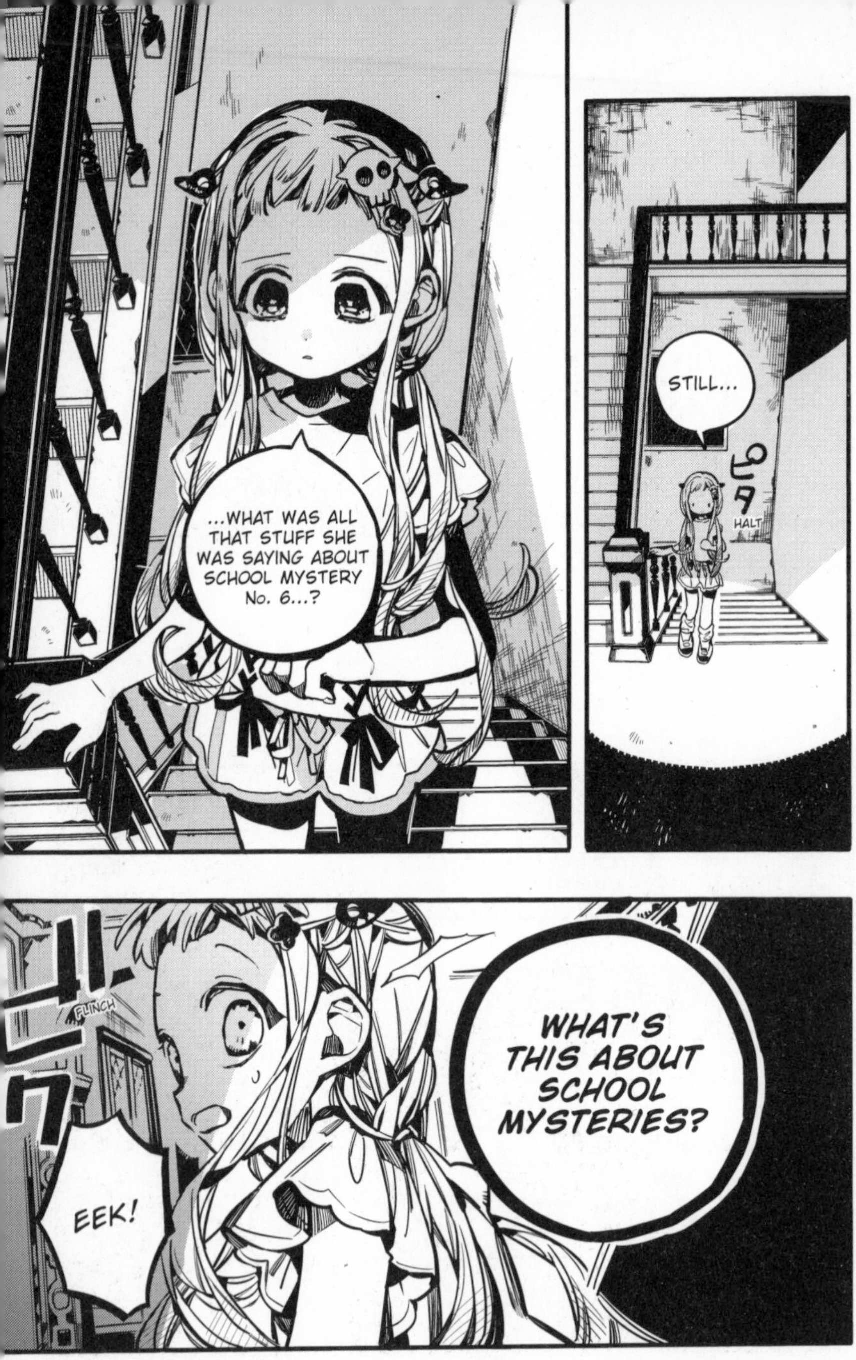
STILL...
ピタ
HALT
...WHAT WAS ALL THAT STUFF SHE WAS SAYING ABOUT SCHOOL MYSTERY No. 6...?
WHAT'S THIS ABOUT SCHOOL MYSTERIES?
FLINCH
EEK!

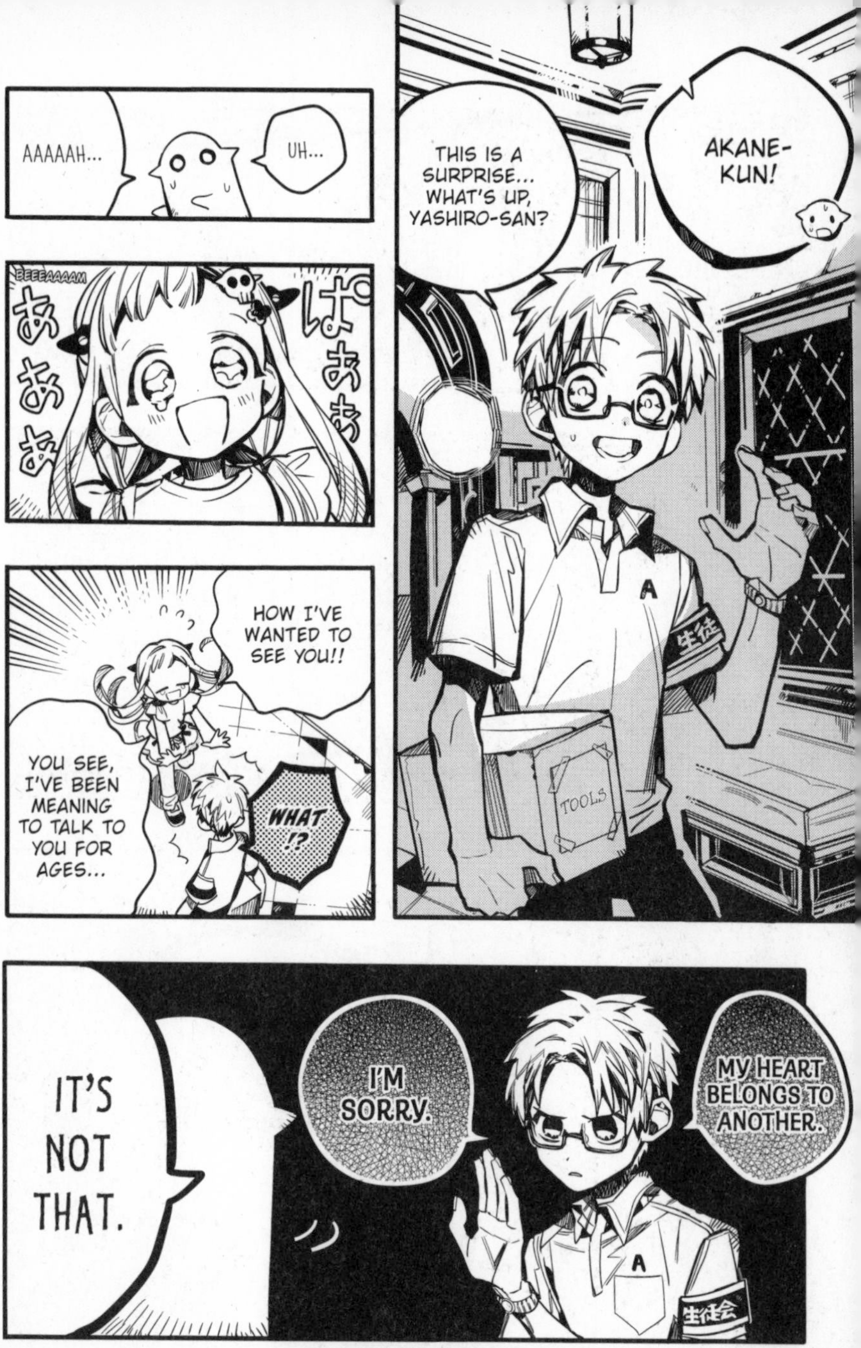
AKANE-KUN!
THIS IS A SURPRISE... WHAT'S UP, YASHIRO-SAN?
UH...
AAAAAH...
BEEEAAAAM
ぱあああ
ああああ
HOW I'VE WANTED TO SEE YOU!!
WHAT!?
YOU SEE, I'VE BEEN MEANING TO TALK TO YOU FOR AGES...
MY HEART BELONGS TO ANOTHER.
I'M SORRY.
IT'S NOT THAT.

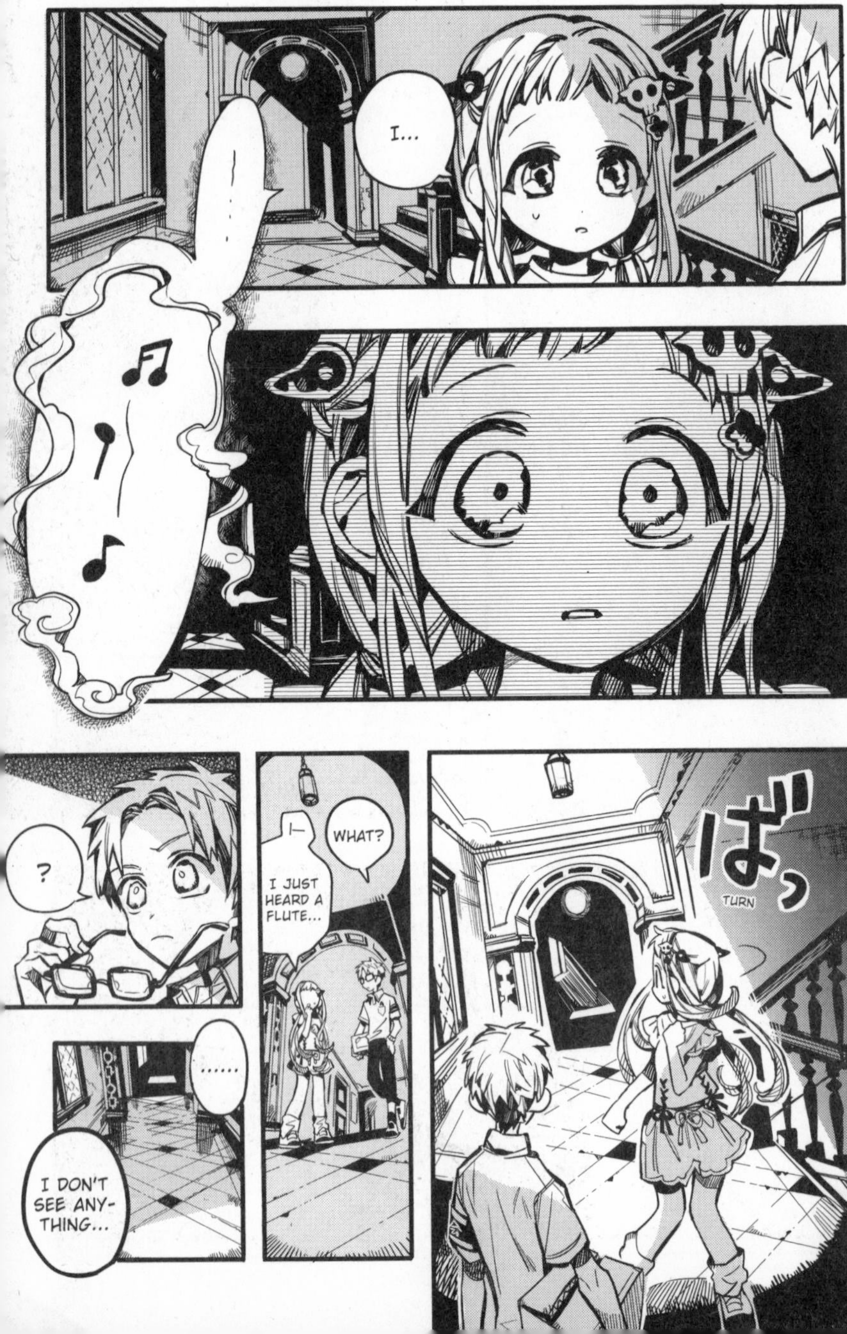
I...
ばっ
TURN
WHAT?
I—
I JUST HEARD A FLUTE...
?
......
I DON'T SEE ANYTHING...

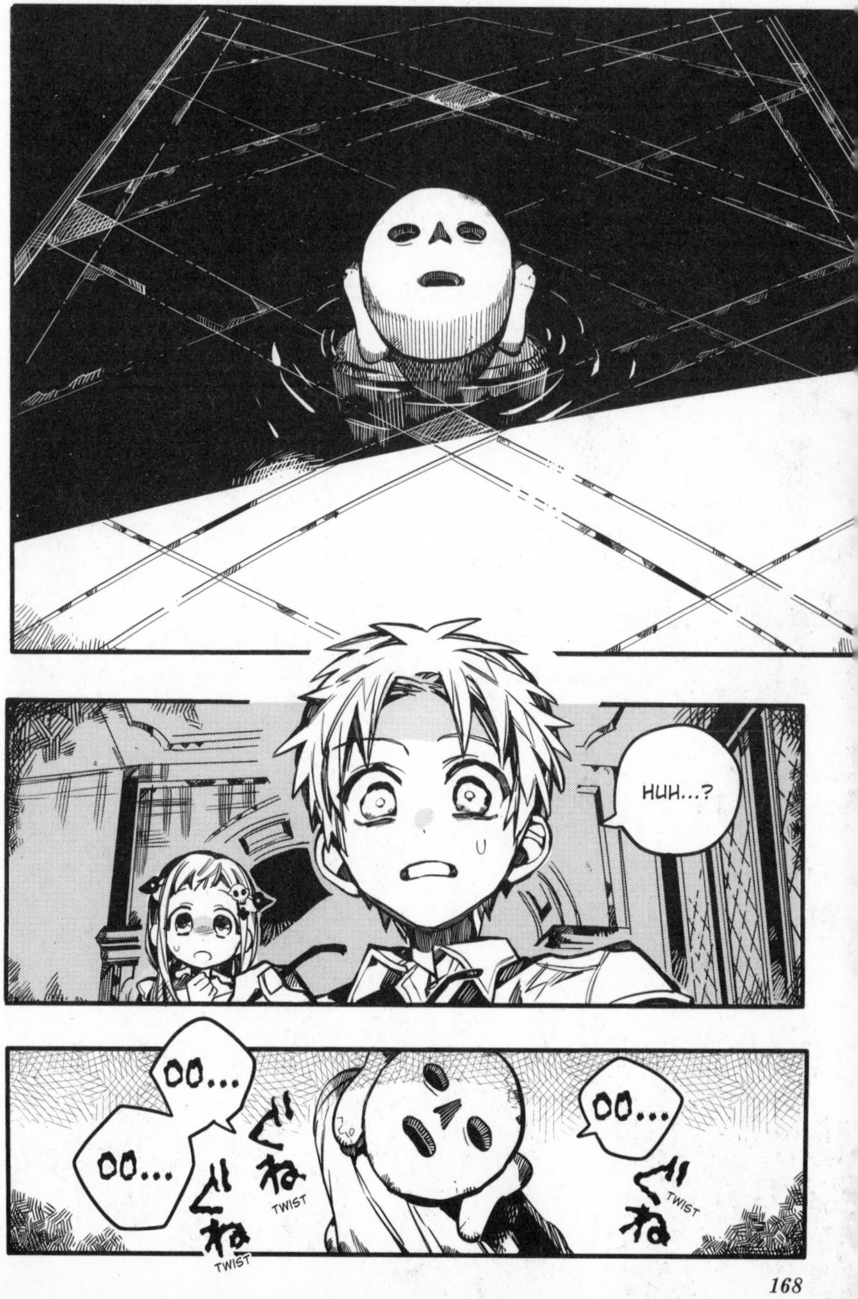
HUH...?
OO...
ぐね TWIST
ぐね TWIST
OO...
OO...
ぐね TWIST

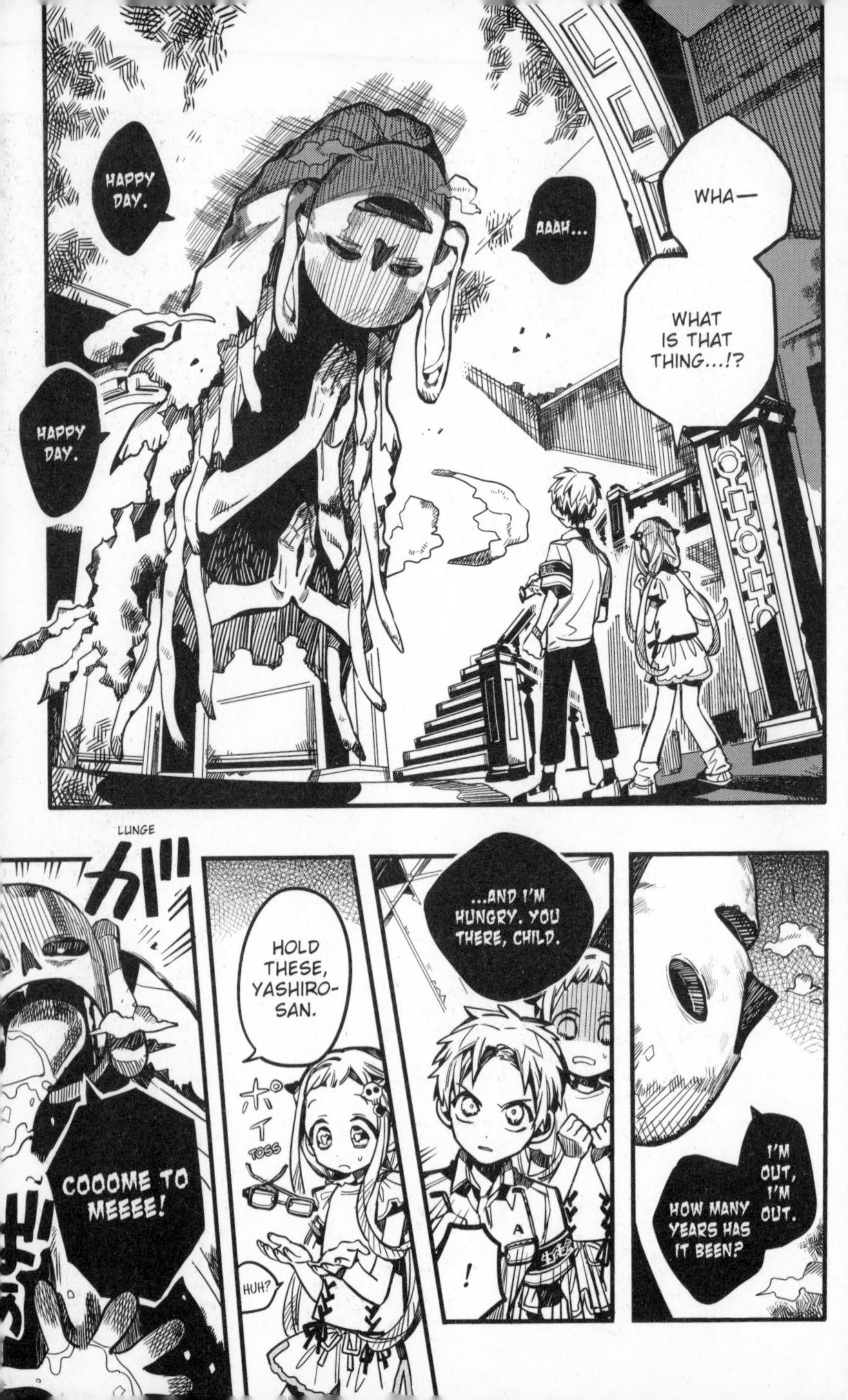
WHA—
WHAT IS THAT THING...!?
AAAH...
HAPPY DAY.
HAPPY DAY.
I'M OUT, I'M OUT.
HOW MANY YEARS HAS IT BEEN?
...AND I'M HUNGRY. YOU THERE, CHILD.
!
HOLD THESE, YASHIRO-SAN.
ポイ
TOSS
HUH?
ガバ
LUNGE
COOOME TO MEEEE!

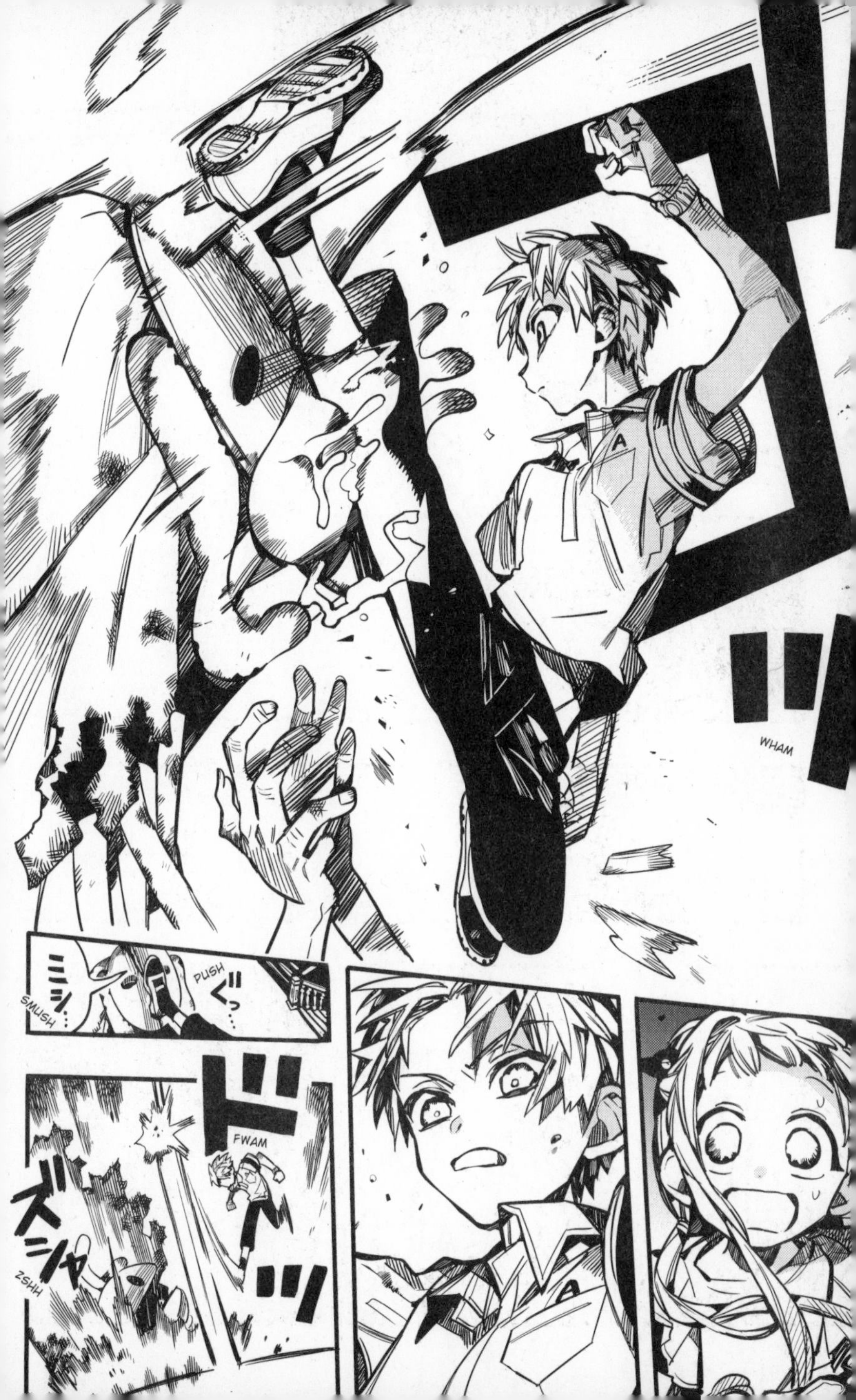

WHAM
ぐっ…
PUSH
ミシ…
SMUSH
ドッ
FWAM
ズシャーッ
ZSHH

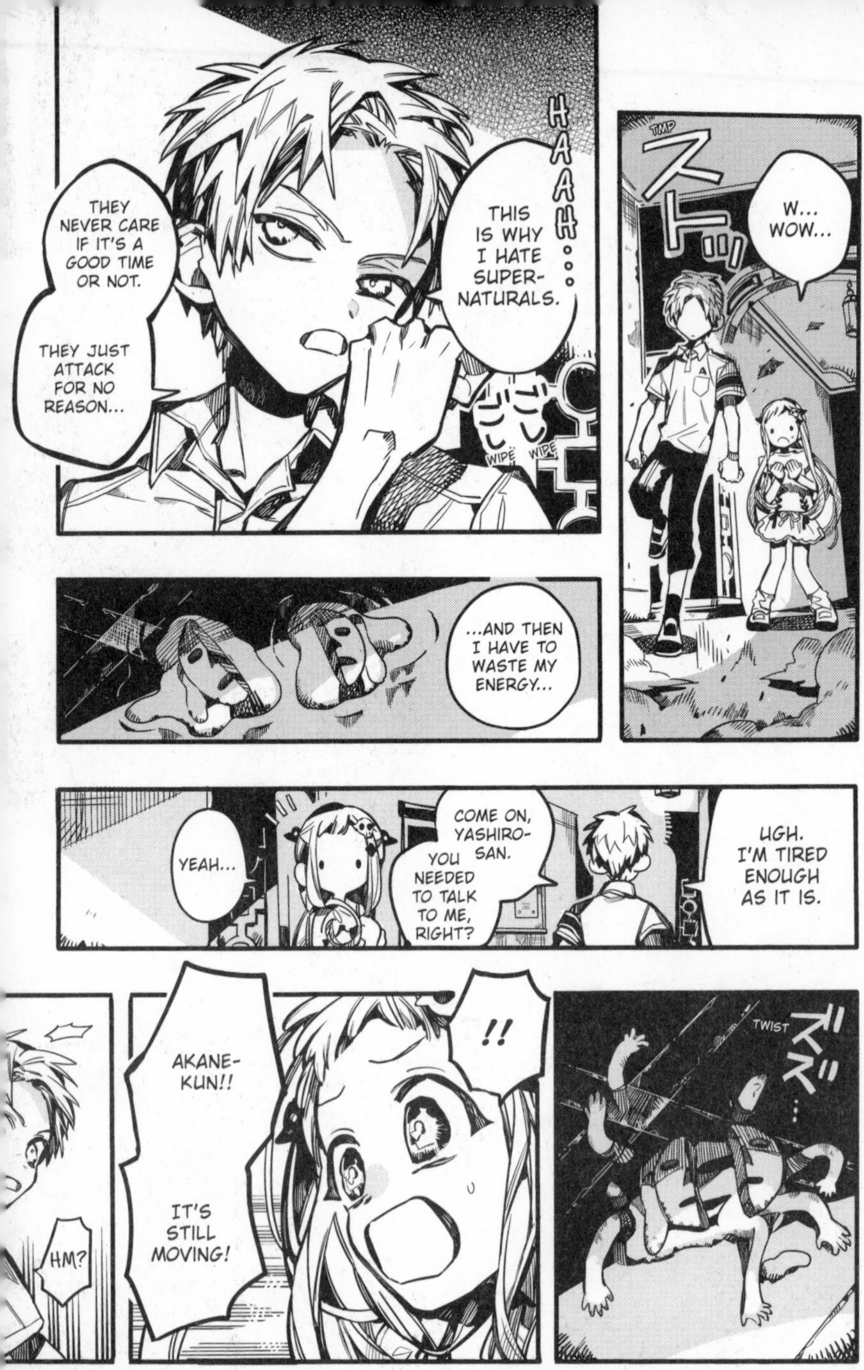
TMP
W... WOW...
HAAAH...
THIS IS WHY I HATE SUPER-NATURALS.
WIPE WIPE
THEY NEVER CARE IF IT'S A GOOD TIME OR NOT.
THEY JUST ATTACK FOR NO REASON...
...AND THEN I HAVE TO WASTE MY ENERGY...
UGH. I'M TIRED ENOUGH AS IT IS.
COME ON, YASHIRO-SAN.
YOU NEEDED TO TALK TO ME, RIGHT?
YEAH...
TWIST
!!
AKANE-KUN!!
IT'S STILL MOVING!
HM?

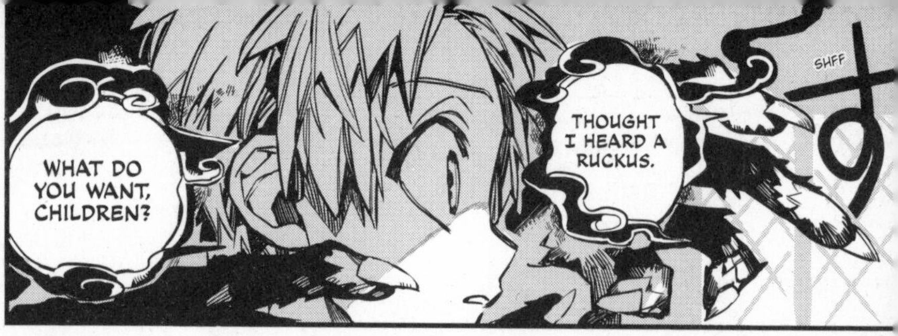
SHFF
THOUGHT I HEARD A RUCKUS.
WHAT DO YOU WANT, CHILDREN?
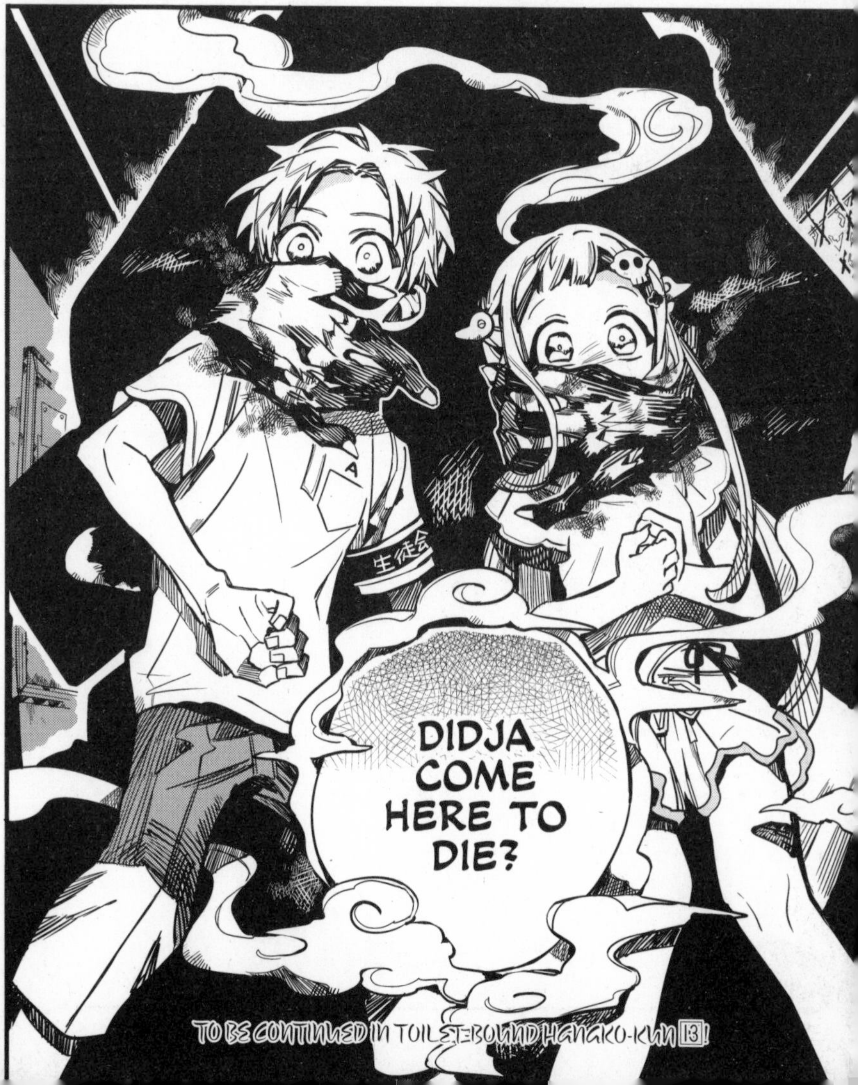
生徒会
DIDJA COME HERE TO DIE?
TO BE CONTINUED IN TOILET-BOUND HANAKO-KUN 13!

TRANSLATION NOTES

Common Honorifics

no honorific: Indicates familiarity or closeness; if used without permission or reason, addressing someone in this manner would constitute an insult.

-san: The Japanese equivalent of Mr./Mrs./Miss. If a situation calls for politeness, this is the fail-safe honorific.

-sama: Conveys great respect; may also indicate that the social status of the speaker is lower than that of the addressee.

-kun: Used most often when referring to boys, this indicates affection or familiarity. Occasionally used by older men among their peers, but it may also be used by anyone referring to a person of lower standing.

-chan: An affectionate honorific indicating familiarity used mostly in reference to girls; also used in reference to cute persons or animals of either gender.

-senpai: A suffix used to address upperclassmen or more experienced coworkers.

-sensei: A respectful term for teachers, artists, or high-level professionals.

Page 44

The word Shijima-san uses for "shrine" is *yashiro*, a homophone of Nene's family name. (The kanji for Nene's given name mean "great size," which is probably another crack at her ankles.)

Page 127

The first and third original Japanese idioms both parallel the literal and metaphorical meanings of the English translations quite closely, as do the words Kou clumsily tries to complete them with, but the second isn't as one-to-one. The original is *mizu o sasu*, or "pour water over," meaning to butt in to or sabotage someone's relationship, and the example sentence had left the word for "water" blank. However, the words for "pour" and "poke" are also homophones, and the example sentence doesn't provide the kanji to specify which verb is used, so Kou interpreted it as "poke in the ribs."

Page 143

"Kagome children" refers to the children's rhyme and game "Kagome, Kagome," where one person stands blindfolded in the center while everyone else circles around them singing the associated rhyme. When they get to the end, the person who's "it" (known as the *oni*, or "ogre") has to guess who is standing behind them. Kagome is also an alternative pronunciation of Kamome, the name of their school.

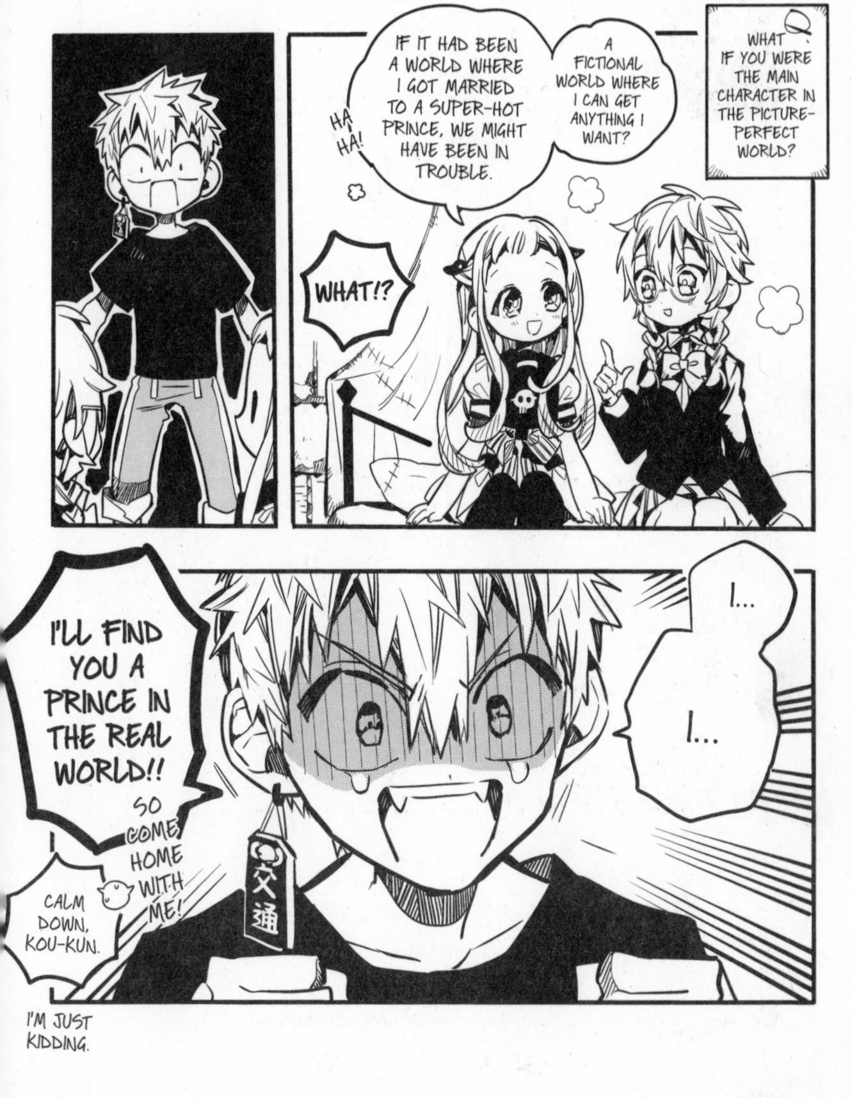
Q
WHAT IF YOU WERE THE MAIN CHARACTER IN THE PICTURE-PERFECT WORLD?
A FICTIONAL WORLD WHERE I CAN GET ANYTHING I WANT?
IF IT HAD BEEN A WORLD WHERE I GOT MARRIED TO A SUPER-HOT PRINCE, WE MIGHT HAVE BEEN IN TROUBLE.
HA HA!
WHAT!?
I...
I...
I'LL FIND YOU A PRINCE IN THE REAL WORLD!!
SO COME HOME WITH ME!
CALM DOWN, KOU-KUN.
I'M JUST KIDDING.

PICTURE-PERFECT EPILOGUE

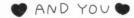

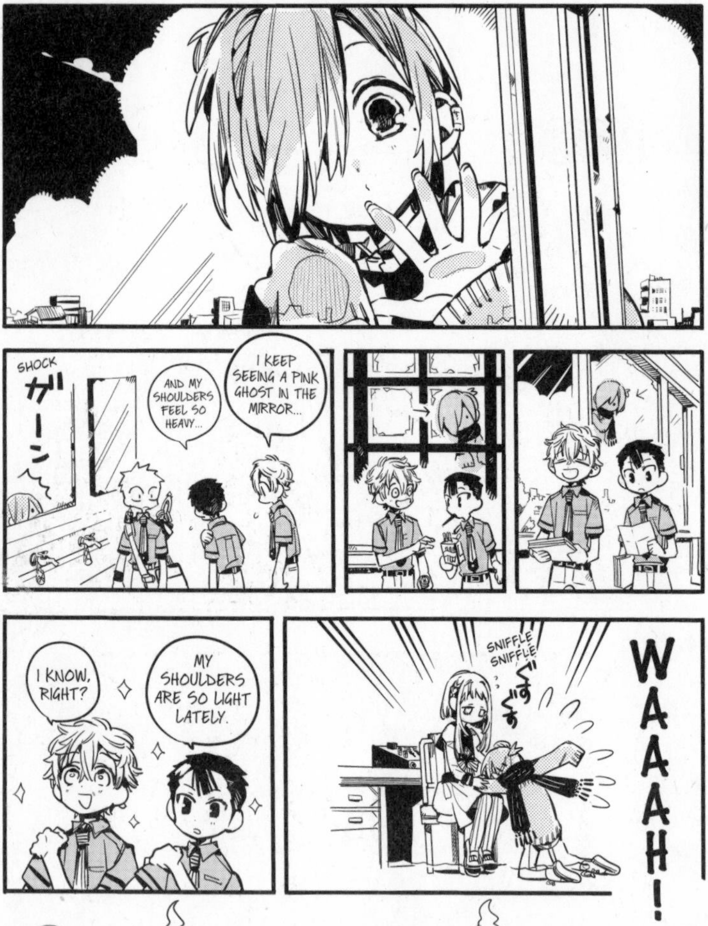
I KEEP SEEING A PINK GHOST IN THE MIRROR...
AND MY SHOULDERS FEEL SO HEAVY...
SHOCK
ガーン
WAAAH!
SNIFFLE SNIFFLE
ぐすぐす
MY SHOULDERS ARE SO LIGHT LATELY.
I KNOW, RIGHT?

SPECIAL THANKS

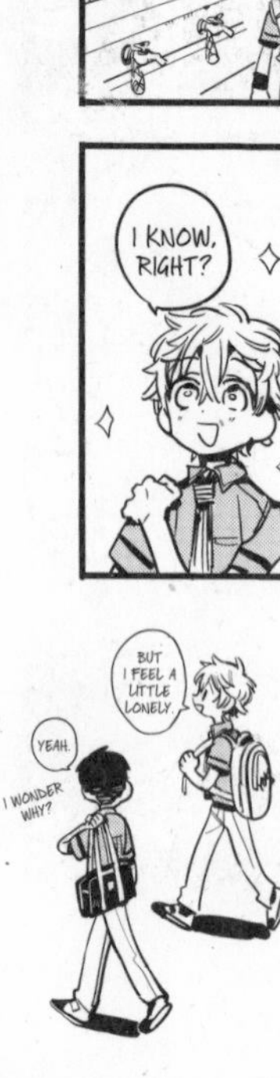
BUT I FEEL A LITTLE LONELY.
YEAH.
I WONDER WHY?

EKE-CHAN OMAYU-TAN YUUJI-CHAN
RUI-CHAN REYU-CHAN KURUMI-CHAN
MY EDITOR COVER DESIGN
IMANITY NAKAMURA-SAMA
AND YOU

PREVIEW

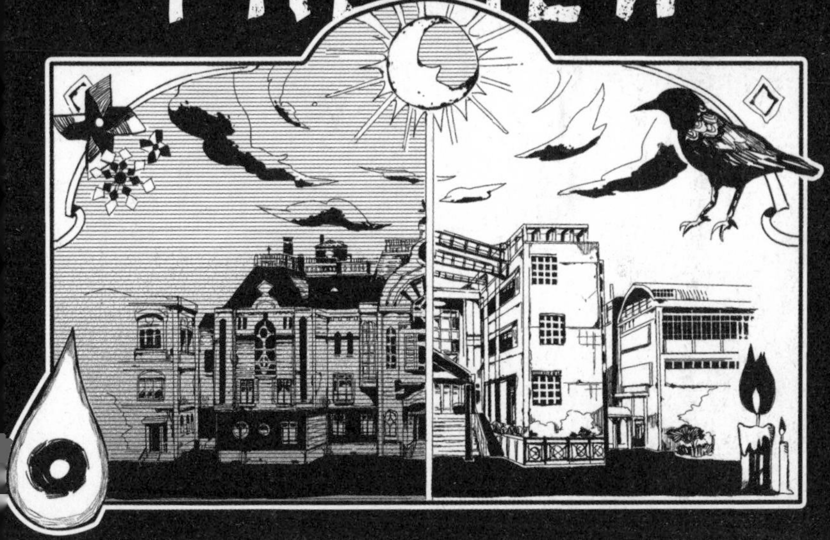

ONE: THE CLOCK KEEPERS
TWO: THE MISAKI STAIRS
THREE: THE HELL OF MIRRORS
FOUR: ART ROOM SHIJIMA-SAN
FIVE: THE FOUR P.M. BOOKSTACKS
SIX:
SEVEN: HANAKO-SAN OF THE TOILET

SCHOOL MYSTERY

NUMBER 6

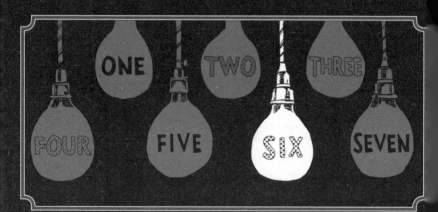

ONE TWO THREE

FOUR FIVE SIX SEVEN

MAKES ITS MOVE.

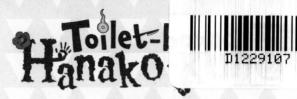

AidaIro

Translation: Alethea Nibley and Athena Nibley
Lettering: Kimberly Pham

JIBAKU SHONEN HANAKO-KUN Volume 12 ©2019 AidaIro / SQUARE ENIX CO., LTD.
First published in Japan in 2019 by SQUARE ENIX CO., LTD. English translation rights arranged with SQUARE ENIX CO., LTD. and Yen Press, LLC through Tuttle-Mori Agency, Inc.

English translation © 2021 by SQUARE ENIX CO., LTD.

Yen Press
150 West 30th Street, 19th Floor
New York, NY 10001

Visit us at yenpress.com • facebook.com/yenpress • twitter.com/yenpress • yenpress.tumblr.com • instagram.com/yenpress

First Yen Press Print Edition: November 2021
Originally published as an ebook in April 2020 by Yen Press.

Yen Press is an imprint of Yen Press, LLC.
The Yen Press name and logo are trademarks of Yen Press, LLC.

The publisher is not responsible for websites (or their content) that are not owned by the publisher.

Library of Congress Control Number: 2019953610

ISBN: 978-1-9753-1687-7 (paperback)

10 9 8 7 6 5 4 3 2 1

TPA

Printed in South Korea

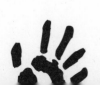